42

BALANCING
ACTS

CONTEMPORARY STORIES

BALANCING
ACTS

BY RUSSIAN WOMEN

EDITED BY HELENA GOSCILO

INDIANA UNIVERSITY PRESS
Bloomington and Indianapolis

Publication of this anthology is by agreement with the Copyright Agency of the USSR. Permission to include "Peters" by Tatiana Tolstaia was given by Tolstaia's American publisher, Alfred A. Knopf.

© 1989 by Indiana University Press

Manufactured in the United States of America

Library of Congress Cataloging-in-Publication Data

Balancing acts.

Bibliography: p.
Includes index.
1. Short stories, Russian—Translations into English. 2. Short stories, English—Translations from Russian. I. Goscilo, Helena
PG3286.B25   1989   891.73'01'089287   88-45390
ISBN 0-253-31134-9
ISBN 0-253-20500-X (pbk.)
1   2   3   4   5   93   92   91   90   89

To Brittain,
for twelve incomparable years

"er ist mir ewig,
er ist mir immer,
Erb' und Eigen,
ein' und all' "

C O N T E N T S

PREFACE

Contemporary feminism has revolutionized educated readers' concepts of literature through its (re)discovery of neglected women writers and its revisionist, gender-focused readings of what have conventionally been deemed mainstream texts. The reverberations of that revolution, however, have yet to reach Russian literature and its critics. Although the last decade has witnessed the emergence of English, American, French, German, Scandinavian, and Japanese women's prose—through belated original publications, republications, or new translations—nothing comparable has occurred in the field of Slavic letters. Slavists, in fact, remain largely ignorant of or indifferent to both feminist criticism and fiction authored by Russian and other Slavic women. Hence this anthology, born in part from a desire to stimulate awareness and appreciation of a rich but unexplored area in contemporary Soviet culture that merits attention and invites analysis: modern Russian women's self-perceptions cast in literary form.

No selective principle for texts in an anthology of contemporary fiction by Russian women could satisfy all its readers. Indeed, some will decry the inclusion of writers who strike the editor as essential and the exclusion of others whom I never contemplated as serious possibilities. In all likelihood certain readers will impugn the validity or usefulness of an enterprise that implicitly classifies creativity according to gender as well as chronology, while another faction will deplore the editor's refusal to align herself with radical feminism by speaking in the occasionally forked and frequently hackneyed tongue that purports to recast "herstory"—in a more "hertrionic" key. Scylla and Charybdis, however, are old and dear friends: wedged between them, I elected to tread the path of subjectivity tempered by circumspection. After perusing countless journals and volumes for stories published over the last two decades that are representative of their authors' fiction in general, I chose the nineteen narratives contained herein for their typicality, unorthodoxy, originality, and/or superior artistic quality. Both the apparent and the real contradictoriness of the criteria result automatically from the dual goal shaping the collection—to give a substantial enough sampling of each writer to establish a sense of major tendencies, without, however, sacrificing diversity.

Admirers of Baranskaia's "A Week Like Any Other" (Nedelia kak nedelia) will encounter an unexpectedly different perspective in "The Kiss," a story much less susceptible to a feminist reading and selected partly to dispel simplistic assumptions about Baranskaia's feminism on the basis of a single text. Like the majority of selections included here, "The Kiss" centers on a female protagonist with a prestigious profession that seems to vouchsafe scant personal fulfillment. In that respect Ganina's heroine in "Stage Actress" offers an apparently diametrical contrast, even if the subtext occasionally implies otherwise. The conflict or distance between professional development or ambition, on the one hand, and private joys, on the other, that dominates recent Russian women's fiction likewise surfaces in Uvarova's "Love" and the works by Kazakova, Mass, Shcherbakova, Tokareva, Varlamova, and Velembovskaia. Within that context, the two selections by Mass form a diptych, since the woman in "A Business Trip Home" forfeits maternal rewards to further her career, whereas her counterpart in the literarily inferior narrative "The Road to Aktanysh" discovers the primacy of motherhood in the course of a geological expedition. Professional but above all familial problems also beleaguer Katerli's male protagonists, through whose eyes Katerli, like Kozhevnikova in "Home," filters events. The synthesis of so-called quintessentially feminine concerns with an anomalously masculine perspective made the inclusion of these narratives in the anthology irresistible. Uvarova's "Be Still, Torments of Passion" deviates from the familiar paradigm precisely because it lacks any dilemma or difficulty that the extraordinarily self-sufficient heroine cannot solve; voluntarily terminating a troublesome liaison, she moves from one professional triumph to another, experiencing no regrets and finding unclouded happiness not in a man, but in work and steadfast female companionship. Such a sunny fate independent of males cannot even be conceived by Petrushevskaia's protagonists, who belong to a drastically different segment of Russian womanhood. Calculating yet tractable victims of men as well as of their own temperaments, they function on a disquietingly desperate level of human intercourse that Petrushevskaia communicates starkly through the compulsive monologues constituting her narratives.

Whereas most authors represented in the anthology operate within an instantly recognizable frame of reference that tradition has labeled women's province, Makarova and especially Tolstaia fall outside of the identifiable current. Makarova shifts the field of discussion through her choice of protagonist and setting, building her narrative around an adolescent and placing the story's action in Odessa. As women's fiction in Russia generally favors an urban locale, and primarily Moscow, I decided to include Varlamova's drama on the collective farm, Velembovskaia's tale about a postwoman in a nondescript little town, and Mass's "Road to Aktanysh" partly for the sake of their uncharacteristic settings and the consequent atypicalities. Originally the anthology represented Tolstaia more generously than the other writers; the sheer excellence of her imaginative, complex, and luxurious prose more than justifies such largesse and makes clear why some consider Tolstaia the most gifted young author to emerge in the decade of glasnost. Owing to unexpected snags in copyright negotiations, however, only one of the three pieces slated earlier for the volume has been retained.

Had space permitted, the collection would have contained samples of I. Grekova's and T. Nabatnikova's prose. Since a number of Grekova's narratives have already been translated into English, and several Nabatnikova stories will appear in a forthcoming issue of *Russian Literature Triquarterly* (Ardis), their omission from this volume does not strike me as crucial.

As a rule in the Soviet Union stories are published first in a literary journal and only later are reprinted in a collection, often with alterations. In those cases where more than one edition of a story exists, wherever possible I have translated the original, journal version. Details pertaining to publication can be found in the Addendum.

Transliteration by and large follows the Library of Congress system throughout. Minor modifications occur wherever necessary to avoid awkward vowel combinations and to enable a reader unfamiliar with Russian to approximate correct Russian pronunciation of names and places. Sections providing information that would be of interest only to a specialist retain the standard Library of Congress transliteration.

In assembling this volume, I have incurred numerous debts of an intangible nature, relying on the cooperation, generosity, and expertise of the following Slavists, to whom I extend heartfelt thanks: all the translators, and especially John Fred Beebe, Joseph Kiegel, Jerzy Kolodziej, and Mary Fleming Zirin, for their patience and skill; Nancy Condee, a stylish cicerone in the labyrinths of contemporary Russian culture, and Vladimir Padunov, a cool-headed but warm-hearted critic, for their readiness to share what others hoard; Mark Altshuller, David Lowe, and Aleksandr Osipovich for clarification of murky patches; Ronald Meyer for useful texts and tips; Brittain Smith and Bozenna Goscilo for reprising their signature role of ideal reader; and Janet Rabinowitch of Indiana University Press for her professionalism and determination. In addition, my gratitude goes to Janet S. Bean, for typing parts of the manuscript; the Russian and East European Studies program at the University of Pittsburgh, and particularly my rival in Polish push-ups, Robert Donnorummo, for the grant that financed Janet's assistance; and the Summer Research Laboratory and Slavic and East European Library of the University of Illinois at Urbana-Champaign, where I conducted most of the preliminary research for the volume, with the aid of a "Travel to Collections" grant from the National Endowment to the Humanities.

Helena Goscilo

INTRODUCTION

> Everyday life, the world of women,
> shines through only in the gaps between
> the descriptions of battle.
>
> Christa Wolf
>
> The happiest women, like the
> happiest nations, have no history.
>
> George Eliot

"What does 'women's literature' mean? You can have a women's sauna, but literature?" Attributed to Lidia Korneevna Chukovskaia, doyenne of post-Stalinist liberalism and author of *The Deserted House* (Opustelyi dom, 1965), this provocative rhetorical question summarizes a familiar attitude: that of intellectuals so entrenched in traditional modes of thinking as to discount some of the most stimulating literary criticism and theory published in the last two decades that has both occasioned and issued from dramatic social realignments. Chukovskaia's query receives a neutral answer from Ruth Zernova in her volume of *Women's Stories* (Zhenskie rasskazy, 1981), where she somewhat tautologically and guardedly characterizes women's literature as "a literature created by women about women." To elaborate on her minimal formulation, Zernova cites the appreciably more controversial definition implied in Boris M. Eikhenbaum's pronouncement of the 1940s: "It is given to woman to preserve and transmit memory, to effect the link between generations."[1] Some feminists would surely balk at the seemingly stereotyped, passive role of secretary cum mother that Eikhenbaum assigns women authors. History, however, appears to have authenticated his opinion. Several of the most impressive publications by Russian women over the last twenty-odd years belong to the genre of memoir: Evgenia Ginzburg's *Journey into the Whirlwind* (Krutoi marshrut, 1967) and *Within the Whirlwind* (Krutoi marshrut II, 1979), Nadezhda Mandelshtam's *Hope against Hope* (Vospominaniia, 1970) and *Hope Abandoned* (Vtoraia kniga, 1972), Maria Ioffe's *One Night: A Story about Truth* (Odna noch': Povest' o pravde, 1978),[2] Natalia Ilina's *Fates* (Sud'by, 1980), and Lidia Chukovskaia's own *Process of Expulsion* (Protsess iskliucheniia, 1979). Yet one could argue that although memoirs provide the most obvious and unmediated venue for preserving memory, they hardly exhaust the formal possibilities; all genres, after all, have the potential for fulfilling that function, as Anna Akhmatova's magnificent *Requiem* (Rekviem, 1940) attests. Moreover, in Russia, male authors such as Aleksandr Solzhenitsyn, Lev Kopelev, Andrei Amalrik, and Valentin Kataev have likewise lent their talent to the potentially hazardous task of keeping the past alive in the present, which suggests that the impulse to safeguard cultural continuity through memory is not a gender-specific prerogative.

We need to look elsewhere to elucidate women's literature as a phenomenon and to validate its status as a viable corpus for critical inquiry. The concept of women's literature derives both its meaning and its legitimacy as a discrete category directly from history's assumptive polarization of gender, whereby woman is conceived, in Simone de Beauvoir's term, as the Other. It is the feminist revisionary imperative necessitated by women's ubiquitous cultural alienation, their social marginality and exclusion from "the great parade of culture,"[3] that confers significance and validity upon women's literature as an independent object of study. For, *pace* Eikhenbaum, it is given women not merely to preserve memory, but also to create the works of art that constitute their nation's culture. Women's contributions to any phenomenon of that stature and scope, however, still await discovery and recognition. Until we incorporate gender into our model of history,[4] until women's writings become integrated into the mainstream, thereby redefining the enshrined canons of achievement,[5] readers cannot have a complete and balanced sense of a country's literary heritage.[6]

Active participation in forging their national cultural heritage was inconceivable for women in pre-Soviet Russia. Control over all artistic forms of expression directed at a public resided in the hands of men; while the poetry and prose of gifted, resourceful individuals such as Karolina

Pavlova, Evdokia Rostopchina, and Nadezhda Durova saw publication, such isolated "successes" invariably fell outside the mainstream that rested on hypothetical foundations to form what is called the Russian literary tradition. As Judith Gardiner, among others, has observed, "Precisely because novelists can make their own worlds to fit their own values, the novel provides a privileged arena for moral analysis. Women writers, in particular, wield fiction to analyze what society means for women."[7] Women in nineteenth-century Russia, however, favored genres other than the novel;[8] large-scale fiction, as the ideal vehicle for "mainstream thought," remained a male medium. Even the works deploring sexual inequality and advocating women's emancipation that exerted the strongest influence were authored by men: in fiction, V. Odoevskii's "Princess Mimi" (Kniazhna Mimi, 1834), A. Druzhinin's *Polinka Saks* (1846), A. Herzen's *Who Is to Blame?* (Kto vinovat?, 1846), and N. Chernyshevskii's *What Is to Be Done?* (Chto delat'?, 1863); in journalism, D. Pisarev's and M. Mikhailov's articles.[9] These indictments from within the patriarchal system overshadowed women's efforts to document their own experiences, to speak in their own voice, such as N. Durova's *The Cavalry Maiden: It Happened in Russia* (Zapiski kavalerist-devitsy, 1836), K. Pavlova's *Double Life* (Dvoinaia zhizn', 1848), E. Rostopchina's "Duel" (Poedinok, 1838) and *A Happy Woman* (Schastlivaia zhenshchina, 1852), E. Gan's "Society's Judgment" (Sud sveta, 1840) and *Liubonka* (1842), E. Zhukova's "Self-Sacrifice" (Samopozhertvovanie, 1840) and "An Error" (Oshibka, 1841), E. Tur's *The Niece* (Plemiannitsa, 1851), *Three Stages of Life* (Tri pory zhizni, 1854), and many others.[10] As self-appointed and self-ratifying spokesmen for the woman's cause, male proponents of reform arrogated the right to situate those reforms in a hierarchy of priorities. Consequently, the dilemma of women's marginality, which entered Russian literature in the 1830s as a theme reflecting a vital social concern, trailed far behind other, presumably more urgent and less "parochial" issues throughout the nineteenth century and well into the twentieth.

While women's writings during the Decadent and Symbolist movements at the turn of the century (1890s–1910s) gained a firmer foothold in the cultural sphere, the ubiquity of the Feminine Ideal (inherited from Romanticism's literary icons) and the immemorial Madonna/Whore dichotomy stigmatizing female sexuality in the male poetry and prose of these movements indicate that received notions of womanhood thrived as vigorously as ever. Publishers, editors, and critics remained predominantly male. Just as Durova in the 1810s had appropriated the *nom de guerre* of Aleksandrov to join the army, so now Zinaida Hippius, Poliksena Soloviova, and Nadezhda Lohkvitaskaia found it professionally expedient to mask their feminine identity: the first two through the use of male endings in verbs (which in the past tense in Russian unavoidably disclose the sex of the subject), and both Soloviova (Allegro) and Lokhvitskaia (Teffi) through the adoption of pseudonymous surnames that did not automatically betray their gender.[11] Although the cult of individualism and the readiness to experiment that distinguished Modernist art permitted women greater access to the ranks of the literati, neither the literary establishment nor the public reared on the same troglodytic premises as that constabulary of culture accorded women's writing a reception comparable to men's. During this era, woman's chief asset "as empirical being" continued to be her "supposed inspirational powers,"[12] as amply illustrated in the oeuvre of A. Blok, A. Belyi, and other, lesser luminaries within the movement.

The widely publicized though largely nominal rights guaranteed women by the Soviet Constitution after the October Revolution of 1917 might mislead one to assume that their sociopolitical standing and opportunities for artistic involvement have improved dramatically. In reality, however, the single verifiable gain for Soviet women from these much-vaunted rights has proved to be increased obligations camouflaged as expanded benefits. As the recent émigré feminist Tatiana Mamonova has complained, "Ideally, a [Russian] woman is expected to have children, to be an outstanding worker, take responsibility for the home, and, despite everything, still be beautiful."[13] Russian women are overburdened because now, as before, economic needs rather than a quixotic sense of justice have motivated the state's implementation of a sustained affirmative-action policy.[14] Indeed, the government that officially boasts of having conferred equality upon women repeatedly exposes its androcentric bias. Only a few years after the country's formal adoption of socialist values, Leon Trotsky in his abusive *Literature and Revolution* (Literatura i revoliutsiia, 1924) voiced the waspish complaint that "one reads with dismay most of the [recent] poetic collections, *especially those of the women.* Here, indeed, one cannot take a step without God. The lyric circle of Akhmatova, Tsvetaeva, Radlova, *and other real and near-poetesses,* is very small"[15] (emphasis mine, HG). Misogyny reared an even uglier head twenty-two years later when, in denouncing Anna Akhmatova on the occasion of her expulsion from the Union of Writers, Stalin's commissar for cultural affairs Andrei Zhdanov borrowed vocabulary applied by B. Eikhenbaum to Akhmatova's heroines to label (and libel) one of Russia's most inspired poets a "nun" and a "fornicatrix," the two apparently meriting the same opprobrium.[16] Whatever the ideological casualties of the Revolution, the Madonna/Whore paradigm, regrettably, had survived intact. By telling contrast, the real or imagined sexual habits of Mikhail Zoshchenko, whom the union harangued and expelled at the same time, received no mention.

Literature and literary production in contemporary Russia suffer from the same gender imbalance one detects in other professions. Literary organizations, publishing houses, and editorial boards, just like the decision-making organs within the government, invariably relegate the women admitted into their midst to subordinate status, while appointing men to positions of power. None of the standard literary journals such as *New World* (Novyi mir), *Aurora* (Avrora), *October* (Oktiabr'), the *Star* (Zvezda), the *Banner* (Znamia), or *Our Contemporary* (Nash sovremennik), which publish fiction by both sexes, has ever had a woman as chief editor, and only a negligible percentage of women gain membership to the editorial boards of these journals, e.g., Rimma Kazakova and M. Ozerova at *Youth* (Iunost'), and Iu. Drunina and V. Trubina at the *Banner*.[17] In 1976, female authors accounted for only 1,097 of the Union of Writers' total membership of 7,833.[18] At the union's Eighth Congress in 1986, approximately a dozen women were elected to executive posts, as opposed to over 360 men—a gender-based inequity that Maia Ganina deplored in her uncompromising speech at the congress.

Defenders of Soviets' purportedly enlightened, equal-handed treatment of the sexes often adduce women's magazines, e.g., *Soviet Woman* (Sovetskaia zhenshchina) and *Working Woman* (Rabotnitsa), as evidence of official egalitarianism in gender issues. Russians have no comparable male-oriented magazines, goes the argument. That shallow reasoning, however, fails to discern that the very existence of a separate woman's press in the USSR betrays women's status as an ideological "minority" to be accorded "special interest" consideration, although they far outnumber men in the country's population. Of the 5,967 regularly published journals, 39 are specifically aimed at women. Whereas these publications, which are part of the ideological structure promoting the image of woman as the tirelessly smiling superachiever, address themselves explicitly to women, *all* other journals implicitly presuppose a predominantly male readership. "Clearly, in terms of magazine publication, there is the world, and there is the women's world."[19] Furthermore, mass-circulation women's magazines in general are rightly regarded as deleterious to the emancipation of women insofar as their resolutely uncontroversial content and orientation reinforce the traditional range of activities and interests typically attributed to women. During a series of interviews conducted in anticipatory celebration of International Women's Day—March 8, observed with ostentatious ritual each year—Galina Semionova, the editor-in-chief of *Working Woman*, listed "sympathy, compassion, and cooperation" as the most crucial qualities in a woman. On the same occasion Lilia Nikolaevna, the head of the rehabilitation department at the Miasnikov Institute of Cardiology, opined that "a woman should primarily love, care and cherish her own family."[20] Ironically enough, the *Calendar for Women* (Kalendar' dlia zhenshchin), which intersperses recipes, sewing patterns, beauty tips, and advice on rearing and educating children with poems, political tidbits, and edifying mini-essays on sundry topics, has a male chief editor. Most of the less prestigious positions on the staff are filled by women. That discrepancy proliferates in virtually all professions open to women: men ascend to the uppermost levels of the hierarchy, while women remain overconcentrated in subordinate, lower-paying slots. When spokesmen for the Soviet government boast of their liberal hiring policies, they cite only women's access to specialized fields without revealing their standing within the personnel structure. Omissions such as these foster a false impression of sexual equality that bears little relationship to the facts.[21]

In a recent interview, Elena Ventsel, the eighty-year-old respected Doctor of Sciences and specialist in applied mathematics who has earned an international reputation as prosaist under the pseudonym of I. Grekova, volunteered the following about her experiences as a professional woman:

> Everyone knows how difficult, exhausting and nerve-racking the never-ending surmounting of daily problems is for a woman. Despite women's equal rights with men in our country, her fate is still a hard one. On top of such "male" responsibilities as job and social activity, she has to cope with heaps of nagging trifles. Our service industry, the development of which is deemed very important in our country, is still unable to take the brunt of woman's chores off her shoulders. Exhausted by the burden of multiple loads she has to carry, woman sees her life turn into a succession of forlorn attempts to "embrace the boundless"[22] and combine the incompatible. I'm afraid I don't quite believe the poster image of woman who just doesn't have any problems: she is a front-rank worker, an active public figure, an excellent mother and a superb housewife who keeps her house in spick-and-span order and raises wonderful children. . . . She has leisure for reading and going to theatres, concert halls and exhibitions. . . . Such women may well exist but I've somehow failed to come across any of them. . . . In my experience, a working woman always has to sacrifice something: it is either work or home (with me it was my home that suffered). As a woman and up to my ears in the daily toils and problems of my gender, I naturally write quite a lot about women's life and fate. . . .[23]

Galina Volchek, the principal director of the Contemporary (Sovremennik) Theater, likewise lamented her hectic routine, while unwittingly revealing her tacit acceptance of prescribed gender roles in the remarks, "Thank God my son has married well, and my daughter-in-law helps with everyday chores. . . . I sometimes stop and look at myself with horror. The only naive feminine feature I have retained is an interest in clothes."[24] Whatever professional affirmation Volchek has received from the theatrical world, where she wields considerable power, evidently has not encouraged her to challenge the automatic assumption that absorption with fashion is an inherently female trait, just as a readiness to help out with housework is exclusively a woman's duty.[25] That retrograde viewpoint recently received endorsement from no less a personage than First Secretary Mikhail

Gorbachev in his highly publicized *profession de foi* published as *Perestroika* last year. While exhorting his audience to participate actively in the "new thinking" officially inaugurated by his ostensibly "revolutionary" campaign of *perestroika*, Gorbachev voiced his intention to enable Russian women "to return to their purely womanly mission." That mission entails "housework, the upbringing of children and the creation of a good family atmosphere." These, Gorbachev contends, have suffered on account of the Soviets' "sincere and politically justified desire to make [sic] women equal with men in everything."[26] Such sentiments bode a bleak future for Soviet women, who in any event have never enjoyed job opportunities equal to men's.

Across the board, women of all ages, spanning the entire spectrum of education, and holding the most diverse jobs, adamantly insist that women must retain their "femininity." The implication behind that widespread anxiety springs from a commonplace conviction. The linchpin of conventional feminine ideology has traditionally been self-sacrifice, "a virtue directly antagonistic to the masculine ideology of self-interest and self-advancement"[27] so essential for upward mobility in one's career. A woman aggressively pursuing a successful career perforce runs the risk of embracing "male ideology," thereby presumably jeopardizing her so-called femininity. Assailable syllogisms of this type underlie countless exchanges reported on the pages of the Soviet press. And these concerns, which exemplify women's internalization of their culture's stereotypes, resonate throughout current women's literature in the Soviet Union.

Although sweeping generalizations about that literature necessarily lead to reductive conclusions and ignore crucial aspects of individual authors, certain preoccupations, themes, and stylistic traits nevertheless link a number of women authors of Russian fiction today. The fiction of their nineteenth-century predecessors (whose narrowness of thematic range mirrored the circumscribed experiences of the women themselves) dwelled monotonously on the marital prospects or disillusionments of the idealistic and refined young heroine who transparently projected her author. That prose articulated above all an impotent, ambivalent resentment and frustration. Recent women's prose, by contrast, reflects the expansion of horizons stemming from real-life transformations in woman's estate. Virtually all modern Russian female protagonists, like their Soviet real-life counterparts, fulfill familial, social, and professional roles. This multiplicity of identities, in fact, breeds many of the problems that have solidified into the genre's topoi. Women of all ages, social backgrounds, occupations, and temperaments have replaced the homogenized decorative dreamer who populated Russian Romantic fiction. That thwarted virginal ideal has ceded to vigorous grandmothers (Baranskaia's "The Kiss," Katerli's "The Farewell Light"), lonely widows (Velembovskaia's "Through

Hard Times"), middle-aged divorcées (Ganina's "Stage Actress," Tokareva's "Between Heaven and Earth"), self-reliant unwed mothers (Varlamova's "A Threesome," Tokareva's "Nothing Special," Petrushevskaia's "The Violin"), adulterous wives (Uvarova's "Love," Tokareva's "Between Heaven and Earth"), single and married career women (Kazakova's "The Experiment," Mass's "A Business Trip Home," Shcherbakova's "The Wall"), and naive adolescents (Makarova's "Herbs from Odessa").

The overwhelming majority of these protagonists represent the urban intelligentsia, although several come from the village or small town and have limited education (e.g., Varlamova's and Velembovskaia's stories). Although love continues to be a pivotal force in their lives (e.g., Baranskaia's "The Kiss," Uvarova's "Love," Kazakova's "The Experiment," Tokareva's "Nothing Special"),[28] few if any of these women harbor fantasies about unique, eternal love with the tellingly italicized *him*, as Romantic fashion and idealist philosophy dictated in the preceding century. A down-to-earth realism that occasionally teeters on cynicism prevents contemporary heroines from idealizing their situation, their self-image, and their men. Typically, these heroines marry and have children, or bear children outside of marriage without necessarily carrying the stigma that in earlier times attached to unwed motherhood; they often divorce and have affairs (not always in that order), and possibly remarry. Though not devoid of the romantic yearnings that the 1830s apotheosized, they know sexual desire and surrender to it, just as they succumb to pragmatism, vulgarity, alcohol, and greed. In keeping with this spirit of deglamorization, their authors do not shrink from portraying women who age and fear aging, and whose main attributes do not inhere in ethereal beauty (e.g., Velembovskaia's "Through Hard Times," most of Ganina's fiction). Furthermore, the recent female protagonist falls prey to maladies other than fatal despondency (terminal heartbreak having been Romanticism's favorite affliction and cause of heroines' death). In several of their works, Ganina, Varlamova, and Grekova, for instance, deal with heart disease, breast cancer, and other "unappealing" sicknesses that demystify and demythologize a woman's body. Yet that body, even in the most enlightened texts, does not escape the strictures and structures of the Sacred Purpose that tradition has legislated for it: Motherhood.

Where motherhood is concerned, the values embedded or vociferously advocated in recent women's prose converge directly with official Soviet policy, as well as with the Marianism that has exerted such a powerful but simplifying influence on the Western mentality.[29] In a country such as Russia, where the government offers material rewards for prodigious feats of procreation to encourage an expanding work force, maternity represents unmediated participation in the highly valorized mission of building the nation's future. According to state ideology and popular belief, through exercising her childbearing capabilities, a woman not only realizes her "natural (biological) function," but simultaneously forges links with the mythical socialist future, a future which Soviets invariably posit in the optimistic belief that whatever lies ahead by definition *must* be better than the dismal present. Maternity as investment and act of faith thus possesses a biological, social, and political dimension in the Soviet Union; a woman's reluctance to have children because of professional considerations is tantamount to civic apostasy and an "unnatural" repudiation of life's teleological plan. Such a premise, which Grekova's fiction iterates with obstinate regularity (e.g., "One Summer in the City" [Letom v gorode], *The Ship of Widows* [Vdovii parokhod], *The Hotel Manager* [Khoziaika gostinitsy]), informs the story by Mass entitled "The Road to Aktanysh" and, in a more complex fashion, Shcherbakova's "The Wall." The "maternity complex" has the tenacious hold of a boa constrictor on women's thinking, prompting categorical assertions that reinforce patriarchal dogma even by self-proclaimed feminists such as Natasha Maltsev: "The greatest good that nature has intended for woman is for her to fulfill her purpose as a mother."[30] It is difficult to grasp the distinction, if any exists, between such pronouncements and "the coercive glorification of motherhood" by the traditional doctrine that prescribes a monolithic sexology on the assumption of an innate precultural femininity.[31] As Elizabeth Berg has astutely observed, "it is the double move of reifying a diversity of traits into a determination as masculine or feminine, and then essentializing that determination, that holds one in the hierarchy of the sexes."[32] By absolutizing maternity, both Soviet ideology and the majority of Russian Women perpetuate the binary opposition of male versus female that ultimately oppresses *both* sexes.

This radically moralized concept of motherhood, which casts the figure of the mother as a self-abnegating arch-nurturer,[33] became indelibly imprinted on the Russian consciousness after the Second World War, when the colossal mortality rate that decimated the male population forced many widows to shoulder the responsibilities normally shared by both parents. Since then women have not managed to shake off that burden, which, moreover, has had far-ranging consequences, inasmuch as it spawned a national habit that continues to fuel heated debates today: men in modern Russian society dissociate themselves entirely from domestic tasks, especially housework and parenting. The predictable result is that "family" has become synonymous with womanhood, while fathers are notorious for their literal or metaphorical absence. Katerli's story "Between Spring and Summer" boldly confronts the phenomenon, which some commentators have mislabeled the "feminization of Russian society," through the interior monologue of its male protagonist Vasia:

Equal rights. Of course. But equality had turned out to mean that a man was no longer the master of his home, but that he was the least important person in it. What had happened to men? And where had these women come from who ran everything, whether at home or on the job? And suddenly Vasia understood what had happened. War had happened. Not once, but three times. And remember, all three right in a row. And what was the result? The men had been killed off, and the women were left with the kids. Who was the head of the house? The strongest? The smartest? Who was the protector? Who knew how to do everything? The mother. Okay, now the daughter grows up and gets married. How will she handle everything in her own family? Naturally, like her mother, since she hasn't known anything else. Not that she would have to nag or yell at her husband. She would just treat him the way a mother treats her child, teaching him, making him do things her way, wiping his nose. And he'd like it just fine. At first. Poor fellow. It was what he expected, was used to. His father had been killed, his mother had raised him, and the first thing he looked for in a wife was a mammy, to fuss over him, cater to him, baby him. . . .
. . . There it was: the war. So many years later, its influence could still be felt! The war, the war. That was the whole problem. . . . And it wasn't equal rights. Quite the contrary. Equal rights were good—our big achievement. But raising kids without fathers—a disaster.

In this respect, among others, Katerli's story "Between Spring and Summer" runs counter to gender clichés, whereas Shcherbakova's "The Wall" partly reinforces them. Countless narratives portray solitary women rearing children amidst emotional uncertainties, financial hardships, and social pressures. Whatever aid or support they receive usually comes from other women, whether they be mothers, daughters, friends, colleagues, or neighbors. By and large women rely on themselves or other members of their own sex for devising solutions to everyday problems. Perhaps for that reason female authors often situate their narratives in a hospital ward, a metaphorical microcosm of an ailing, segregated society in which women, its quintessential victims, join forces to struggle, however unavailingly, against colossal incompetence, shoddiness, general indifference to their plight, and a dreary sense of isolation (e.g., Petrushevskaia's "The Violin," Tokareva's "Nothing Special," Iulia Voznesenskaia's *Women's Decameron* [Damskii Dekameron, 1986],[34] Varlamova's *A Counterfeit Life* [Mnimaia zhizn', 1978], and Uvarova's *Of This World* [Ot mira sego, 1987]. Such a setting, of course, also provides the appropriate environment for exchanges of confidences and discussions of abortion and illegitimacy, which play a sizable role in the thematics of many Russian women's prose, e.g., Ganina, Grekova.

Another legacy from the wartime era that figures prominently in women's fiction is the prevalence of the double-shift syndrome—women's responsibilities on the two conflicting fronts of home and job—to which Grekova referred in her interview and which Baranskaia brought to the awareness of a broad public through her novella *A Week Like Any Other* (Nedelia kak nedelia). Given the unquestioning acceptance by both sexes that child care, housekeeping, and shopping belong exclusively to women's domain, Russian working women with career aspiration ineluctably sacrifice family for profession, or vice versa.[35] "A Business Trip Home" makes no reference to paternal obligations, but explicitly treats the emotional reparation exacted for "maternal neglect" (i.e., opting for the career): guilt and identity crisis. By contrast, Shcherbakova orchestrates several different perspectives on the question, ultimately challenging the either/or formulation itself. Fully acknowledging the problem, Uvarova in "Be Still, Torments of Passion" brings an original slant to it by conferring on her heroine an emblematic, canonically male prerogative: the loving "wife/housekeeper" figure whose doting ministrations free the husband (here, the mistress) from household cares, enabling the breadwinner to concentrate single-mindedly on a profession uncontaminated by associations with domesticity—in this case, acting. Uvarova's story offers a rare literary instance of voluntary, fulfilling "female bonding," independent of males. Its portrayal of a talented woman whose primary loyalty is to her calling has much in common with Ganina's depiction of her comparably strong-willed protagonist. In both instances the aesthetic, multifaceted nature of the protagonists' profession safeguards against a trivialization of their complete immersion in their field. Had both been employed as manicurists or waitresses, the narrative would have degenerated into unwitting comedy or farce. In any event, such images of self-assured, decisive career women do not frequently populate Russian women's literature; when they do occur, they are apt to pattern themselves on prefabricated male paradigms.

Women's participation in both domestic and professional life (medicine, construction, science, education, engineering, sanitation, art, etc.) makes it possible for writers who depict their experiences to range over a wide terrain of social issues while simultaneously detailing specific aspects of everyday life. Women's fiction achieves the "solidity of specification" that Henry James singled out as the supreme virtue of the novel mainly through circumstantiating the realia of which Soviet women have an especially intimate knowledge in the sphere of consumer goods, living quarters (and particularly the nightmare of communal apartments), educational institutions, child-care centers, medical services, and the like. These areas collectively constitute the practical side of day-to-day life— what Russians call *byt*. Recent women's writing in Russia has come in for considerable supercilious criticism because of what some commentators view as its unwarranted preoccupation with *byt*. As Grekova accurately recalls: "I . . . [have been] often criticized for my excessive attention to the daily routine ('pedestrian description of everyday trifles')."[36] The very applicability of the term *byt* to literature, however, has been rejected by Iurii Trifonov, whose novels share many traits with women's fiction and, like the latter, have elicited deprecating remarks about the author's attachment to *byt*. Trifonov remonstrates:

> There is perhaps no word in the Russian language more enigmatic, multidimensional, and incomprehensible. What on earth is *byt?* Does it really mean humdrum existence, domestic daily life, fussing around the stove, in stores and at laundries. The dry cleaners, hairdressers. . . . Yes, that's called *byt*. But family life is also *byt*. Relations between husband and wife, parents and children, distant and close relatives—these are too. And births, and the death of old men, and sickness and weddings are also *byt*. And mutual relations between friends, co-workers, love, arguments, jealousy, envy—that's all *byt* too. But that, after all, is what life consists of![37]

Trifonov proceeds to argue that since the family is a universally recognized unit of society, fiction's portrayal of a given person's death or a couple's love may be construed synecdochically to embrace society at large (p. 104). With the frame of reference extended in this way, recent Russian women's literature may be said to diagnose the ills of the modern urban intelligentsia.

Many of the social failings to which contemporary male literature gives prominence likewise emerge in women's fiction, but rarely hold center stage: alcoholism ("The Wall," "Be Still, Torments of Passion," Tatiana Nabatnikova's "Speak, Maria" [Govori, Mariia, 1987], Ganina's *Hear Your Hour Strike* [Uslysh' svoi chas]); infidelity and a soaring divorce rate (Nabatnikova's *Every Hunter* [Kazhdyi okhotnik, 1987]); materialism and careerism ("The Wall," "The Farewell Light," Nadezhda Kozhevnikova's "Vera Perova" and "The Second Plan" [Vtoroi plan], Katerli's *Polina*, 1984); widespread corruption, inefficiency, and bureaucracy ("Nothing Special," "Stage Actress"); generational conflict; and middle-age crises (a hallmark of Trifonov's prose) that manifest themselves in disillusionment, a sense of aimlessness, and atrophy of the spirit. In moral issues women's literature regularly emphasizes integrity and active commitment to humanitarian principles.

In the final analysis, recent women's fiction paints a bleak picture of Russian society, exposes the disintegration of family ties,[38] and communicates all too vividly the debasing indignities with which Russian women contend daily. Perhaps the single strongest impression conveyed by this fiction is that of an overall lack; of an imprecisely grasped loss or simply an absence of stable, secure identity; of experiences to be surmounted rather than recaptured. Writers of the older generation, such as Grekova, Velembovskaia, Uvarova, and Baranskaia, and those who like Katerli, Shcherbakova, and Ganina lived through World War II as children, cannot jettison the mental habits and emotional trappings of those harrowing

years. In some significant and final way, that period shaped their perceptions and values, as Ganina's "Stage Actress," novels, and other narratives
recognize. Whatever the havoc and devastation wrought by World War
II, the German invasion nevertheless forced the Russian population to
prove its mettle, uniting the country in a communal spirit of resistance
and patriotic fervor. When recalling that era, writers such as Uvarova,
Baranskaia, and Ganina lament the erosion of high-principled stoicism,
resilience, and camaraderie into the coarse practicality and self-indulgent
opportunism that motivate the contemporary urbanite. According to Uvarova's "Editorial Assignment" (Redaktsionnoe zadanie, 1987) and Ganina's "Stage Actress" (which necessarily romanticize the war experience
out of habit as well as to buttress their argument), the last thirty years
have witnessed a precipitous moral decline among the intelligentsia. By
contrast, Shcherbakova conceives of the clash between humanistic and
utilitarian ethics ahistorically, imputing causes to individual personality
rather than historical determinism. Yet for her also the war years serve
as a barometer for morality, as the most reliable test of humanity. Even
the younger writers born after the war, such as Makarova, Kozhevnikova,
Nabatnikova, and Tatiana Tolstaia, have a marked penchant for retrospection, often seeking explanations or vindication for the present in the
past.[39]

Whereas women's fiction coheres into a corpus when examined the-
matically, one would be hard pressed to discern a parallel unity on the
stylistic level.[40] Certain common features, nevertheless, do obtain. By far
the most popular prose genre among female authors is the small form,
i.e., the short story or novella *(povest')*; and the relatively few forays into
large-scale narratives have not proved overly impressive. In that respect,
the modern era continues the nineteenth-century tendency in Russian
letters of women's literary creativity finding expression in forms other
than the male-dominated novelistic genre. Voznesenskaia's *Women's Decameron,* the longest fictional work by a woman published in recent years,
significantly, is not a novel but a compendium of oral tales, each rarely
exceeding four pages in length.[41]

In addition to brevity, most women's prose, unsurprisingly, favors a
female point of view, usually transmitted through first-person narration
or narrated monologue *(style indirect libre/ erlebte Rede)*. Both modes rely
heavily on emotionally colored narrated interior monologue which implicitly enjoins readers to distance themselves from male attitudes both
by spotlighting concrete instances of men's insensitivity (Mass's "Road to
Aktanysh," Kazakova's "The Experiment," Velembovskaia's "Through
Hard Times," Tokareva's "Between Heaven and Earth") and by extrap-
olating from isolated acts or statements universal categories of "male
complexes," as Ganina does in "Stage Actress," Varlamova in "A Three-

some," Voznesenskaia in *Women's Decameron*, and especially Katerli in *Polina*. ("Could it be that all men have such self-esteem? Like the head baboon?" "Everyone knows what a weak race men are.") This tone of critical but confiding intimacy draws the reader into the narrator's female orbit. An antithetical technique of external presentation is often applied to male characters, as a result of which the implied irrelevance or absence of inner motivation in men transforms them into remote objects inhabiting the heavily problematized background against which women view themselves. Whenever a male character is filtered through intensely feminized eyes, the gender-specific perspective encourages the reader's complicit alienation from the distanced "object." Even Katerli, who has frankly admitted her preference for male narrators on the unexpected grounds that "they know women better, just as women know men better,"[42] invariably has women appropriate the narrating function at some juncture to "tell their story" directly in their own voice. One of Katerli's favorite strategies, in fact, is the bifurcated narrative, whereby the storyline proceeds along two distinct but internally related narrative tracks that alternate and occasionally intersect, with a track assigned to each gender. This dialogic device of symbiotic correctives operates most rewardingly in stories that seek to expose the flawed awareness of protagonists/narrators *(Polina,* "Between Spring and Summer"). The revelation of their blindness to their own shortcomings and others' strengths, and their attendant misinterpretation of situations undermine their technical function as reliable guides of readers' responses, thereby augmenting the tension in, and complexity of, a text.[43]

That complexity, regrettably, is not a constant feature of current women's fiction. Like Soviet literature in general, women's fiction at its weakest slides into monotony, verges on journalese, and acquires a generic flavor. If, as Matthew Arnold equipped, journalism is literature in a hurry, then women's fiction in Russia, like the men's, sometimes suffers from excessive speed. Various Soviet commentators have deservedly criticized Uvarova, Grekova, and Ganina for flaccid formulations, lack of narrative drive, and an insipid descriptiveness that occasionally makes for interchangeability, for anonymity. Their best narratives overcome these weaknesses, but their less successful efforts do not. Part of the problem surely lies in the authors' tendency to eschew stylistic experimentation. Although their retrospective mode often displaces chronology (hence the infrequency of what feminists identify as a quintessentially masculine linear structure), the majority of female authors basically adhere to narrative principles that one associates primarily with nineteenth-century realism. The flattening effect of such conservatism produces texts that sometimes lack a personal stylistic imprint.

As with every rule, of course, exceptions can be found. Among the older and middle-aged generations, Baranskaia's irony and Tokareva's sardonic wit respectively infuse verve into their prose. Katerli's elliptical manner and love of fantasy, to which she gave free rein in her early collection *The Window* (Okno), set her apart from her technically less adventuresome colleagues, and closer to the younger generation. And of that generation, Makarova reveals her receptivity to modernist stylistic influences through her subversively colorful language and the irregular, jagged pacing of her narrative, which presupposes the reader's readiness to supply all the connections that Makarova calculatedly omits. Above all it is Tatiana Tolstaia whose prose bears a unique, unmistakable signature and could never be misattributed to any other writer. Tolstaia's mastery of postmodernist techniques creates a fictional world that explodes all expectations bred by a reader's steady contact with typical Soviet prose. With a panache and sureness of touch that instantly engage the reader, Tolstaia manipulates multiple perspectives, blends allegory and myth with grotesque realism, spins packed sentences over entire paragraphs that stretch to half a page, freights her rhythmic, ornamental prose with epic recherché metaphors, anaphoric constructions, and musical assonance, and shifts without warning from poignancy to absurd humor. Her irrepressible enthusiasm for overthrowing cultural clichés finds a splendid outlet in at least two stories that satirize gender assumptions: "The Poet and the Muse" (Poet i muza) and "The Mammoth Hunt" (Okhota na mamonta).[44] Tolstaia's freshness of vision and vigorous independence of recognized "schools of thought," her endlessly rich imagination, and the vibrancy of her lush, poetic language give one reason to wax optimistic about the possibilities of new and productive directions for Russian women's fiction.

Right now that fiction is vulnerable to the same charges that one can level against stories and novellas authored by any Soviet writer: above all, it is uneven in quality. Though bold in its selection of topics, it is formally timid and somewhat old-fashioned. Though invaluable as a source of information about the society it portrays, it does not always vault free of its national origins to transcend them. It seems to play provincial cousin to the rest of Europe in intellectual and aesthetic sophistication. At the same time, however, it has an emotional intensity, an integrity, and a commitment to moral issues that help one forget its stylistic limitations. Perhaps the increased cultural interaction with the West augured, however cautiously, by glasnost will defang the ideological threat that Soviets unrelentingly associate with modern art and will breathe a healthy iconoclasm into contemporary Soviet fiction. Until that happier time, Tolstaia gives every indication of continuing to reign unchallenged as the most original talent to grace the current literary scene in Russia.

BALANCING
ACTS

THE KISS

NATALIA BARANSKAIA

Translated by

WANDA SORGENTE

THEIR UNTHINKABLE KISS LASTED THE WHOLE WAY down from the eleventh floor.

He unlocked his arms and let her go only when the elevator stopped and reluctantly opened its doors.

Perhaps she should have said something, or at least should have exclaimed, "Well, well!" or "You're crazy!" but her breathing hadn't steadied yet, and so she let it pass. He, too, kept silent.

Nadezhda Mikhailovna went on ahead calmly and unhurriedly, only her shapely back betraying her sense of alienation. Viktor caught up with her, stopped her, and lit up a cigarette. A chilling raw wind was blowing, melting the thin smatter of snowflakes. She examined his face in the brief flickers of light from the flame. He was good-looking, with strong features and a firm mouth. She looked at the flame in his cupped palms and thought how good it was to abandon oneself into such strong, firm, and reliable hands.

It was good, but not for her. With a sigh, she turned and continued walking toward the bus. She felt like being alone.

Nothing, in fact, had happened. They had attended a family celebration at some friends' of theirs. They'd met there two or three times before. Viktor was an older friend of the young people, and she was a younger acquaintance of the parents. However, no one ever took her for over thirty-five. She was still an attractive woman, elegant and lively. And today, she knew, she looked especially attractive.

When the guests began to disperse and Nadezhda Mikhailovna got up to leave too, Viktor said: "Wait, I'm putting your favorite record on." She stayed, without even asking him what record he was holding. True, she was very fond of Grieg, but Viktor had no way of knowing that. Was it sheer coincidence? Or fate? While listening to "Solvejg's Song," Nadezhda Mikhailovna no longer felt as dispirited as usual, and she even chuckled to herself: "And here I've picked up a young guy!" She was terribly happy, and there was something a little shameless about her happiness.

And here he was walking beside her, and she had no idea what to do with him.

At that moment, however, there was a flash of green light and a screech of brakes as Viktor flagged down a taxi. He asked where he should take her, and as soon as the taxi moved off he put his arm around her shoulders, trying to draw her closer to him. She refused to yield, but her heart stopped, then instantly began to pound as it had in the elevator. But he firmly took her by the arm and moved his knees closer to her legs. She drew away. "The incident"—that's how she regarded the kiss in the elevator—was beginning to turn into a banal adventure. He was driving her across Moscow, from the southwest side all the way to the northeast, at one o'clock in the morning. Nadezhda Mikhailovna was skeptical about men's chivalrous impulses. If his motives were self-seeking, then they were pointless: her personal account in the love department had been closed for over a year.

She freed herself from his grasp and opened her purse as if to get her handkerchief or wallet (certainly not her glasses). Viktor asked if he could smoke, then pulled out his cigarettes. The taxi raced along the paved nocturnal expanse. The silence was growing tense.

"You're a philologist, but what is it exactly that you do? What's your position?" asked Viktor.

"A philologist, but more precisely a linguist. I'm working on a dictionary of synonyms." Thankful for the conversation, Nadezhda Mikhailovna answered readily.

"Synonyms. . . . Different sound, same general sense?"

"What does 'same general sense' mean? The identical meaning or one close to it."

"Details. Not essential for an artist. I'm sure not too many philologists know the difference between tempera and sanguine."

The conversation certainly wasn't getting off the ground. The tension was still there.

"Ah, 'sanguine'? Indeed. . . . Well, then, take 'homonyms.' Well?" She tried to enliven the forced conversation. It was useless.

"Homonyms? Sýnonyms-synónyms, hómonyms-homónyms . . . ," Viktor kept repeating aimlessly.

2

At that moment the driver unexpectedly joined the conversation.

"Hey, anonyms—those people are no fools. Everybody wants to add his two cents' worth. . . ."

They all laughed. Moscow cabbies are notorious for their wit!

The taxi stopped. Viktor got out, helped Nadezhda Mikhailovna out, and slammed the door shut.

"Thank you, you're very kind."

That sounded colder than she'd intended.

But it didn't even occur to Viktor to prolong their goodbyes. He kissed her hand, then got in next to the driver and left.

"Well and good," said Nadezhda Mikhailovna on the way upstairs. "Good, good, even very good," she hummed as she locked the door to her one-room apartment. Here in her nice, cozy home, "the incident" should be quickly forgotten.

However, instead of hurrying to bed, Nadezhda Mikhailovna sat down in front of the mirror and began studying her face. She was tired. Her slight flush had faded, and her wrinkles had become more pronounced. A plain woman in her forties. You could see that clearly in the mirror. . . . She took off her beads and her rings, threw off her dress, and went into the bathroom.

As soon as she lay down and blissfully stretched out on her back, she felt the dry, firm lips that had been pressed to her mouth. . . . She turned onto her side, hoping to fall asleep as fast as possible. But her memories took her back, year by year, to her first love and their separation by war, through the joys and sorrows of family life, with its discord and divorce, followed by single motherhood and work, work, work—her burden and her joy. And somewhat apart from her work and her daughter, there were delusive infatuations, love that wasn't love, jealousy, partings. . . . And finally—solid equilibrium.

Yet not so solid, it appears.

Nadezhda Mikhailovna took a sleeping pill and angrily moved the hand on her alarm clock. "Go to sleep, grandma!" she said spitefully. Her daughter had given birth to a little girl half a year ago.

Nadezhda Mikhailovna had a hard time getting up and was sluggish and dissatisfied with herself all day long. And what was strange about it was that she felt that she'd been dumped! Wasn't that nonsense, a real absurdity?

She tried to submerge herself in synonyms, then switched over to maternal sentiments, wondering how Natulia[1] was doing in her dismal Chertanov. . . . But it didn't help. The synonyms multiplied reluctantly. And her daughter wasn't alone—she had her husband. Whereas Nadezhda Mikhailovna, who was a senior scholar at the Institute of the USSR Academy of Sciences, the occupant of a one-room apartment, and an attractive woman—she'd been dropped, abandoned, cast off. Or, to use that horrible colloquial expression, she'd been dumped.

Viktor phoned that evening. He must have gotten the number from information. "I need to see you without fail," he said.

"Need to?" She meant to sound mocking, but came across as pleased.

"All right, I don't need to, but I'd like, really like, to see you. Do let me come. Now."

"What do you mean, 'now'?" she was taken aback. "That's impossible."

"Tomorrow, then. When do you get back from work? All right, I'll be there at eight."

The date was arranged before she had a chance to agree. But wasn't that what she wanted? All right, enough complications. Everything's simple and fine. Small joys? If there aren't any big ones, small ones will do. . . .

Nadezhda Mikhailovna cleaned the apartment, then took a bath, applied a yeast facial mask, and went to bed earlier than usual. Even before she had time to think about what she was going to wear in the evening, she'd fallen asleep.

She arose refreshed and walked a part of the way with pleasure. All day long she heard Solvejg's words ringing in her head: "And you'll return to me, my heart tells me, my heart tells me. . . ."[2] She tried to stifle this singing with self-mockery, though, for that was really going too far.

Nadezhda Mikhailovna decided to leave work an hour early in order to prepare for the evening. She still had to do some shopping for supper. She already had her coat on when the phone rang.

Natasha wanted her to come and visit. It would be great if she could spend the night. Seriozha would be late again. The baby was crying a lot—it was probably her teeth. The wind was so strong it was blowing right through the windows. It was cold and very bleak. They were just returning from a walk. And if it wasn't a bother, would Mom please buy some fruit? There was none there. And one more favor—would she get some two-kopek pieces for the phone?

Nadezhda Mikhailovna pictured her tall, slender daughter in the phone booth, a baby carriage standing nearby with its top raised. Straight strands of blonde hair escaped from under her blue mohair hat, and the tip of her long, chiseled nose was red. She always froze quickly outdoors.

She disliked disappointing her daughter, but Nadezhda Mikhailovna firmly declared that she couldn't make it.

While doing the evening's shopping, she bought some apples and grapes for Natasha as well. At home she put away the fruit and appetizers in the refrigerator, placed the wine out on the balcony, and lay down on her back for ten minutes, her eyes closed. Then she dressed and went to the kitchen to get everything ready for supper.

She sliced the bread, opened some cans, and covered the table with a bright striped tablecloth. On it she set some yellow ceramic plates and dark-blue cups, then added a sprig of ivy in a tall glass. She admired the table, which looked like spring. Oh, yes, she'd forgotten the goblets! And just as she was placing the smoky Czech glass goblets on the table, the alarming thought occurred to her that she knew nothing, absolutely nothing, about her guest: his tastes, habits, and views. Nothing. Maybe today she'll feel good with him, but what about tomorrow? What if, after spending the night with her, he suddenly says that he intends to move in? Or the other way round: he'll disappear one morning and never come back. But before leaving her, he'll become inattentive and forgetful, while she'll be suspicious and jealous. He's young and handsome. Her fear of old age will grow tenfold. She'll start counting her wrinkles, dying her hair, and running to facial salons. She'll lose her independence; she'll lose that carefree ease that you see in people who work well and relax well. . . . My God, she doesn't even know his last name, doesn't know if he's married! On the other hand, what business is that of hers? She's not planning to marry him, after all.

All these considerations didn't prevent Nadezhda Mikhailovna from carefully and deliberately getting ready to receive her guest. She took her apron off, rubbed some lotion into her hands, and went over to the large mirror to fix her hair and put on her rings and earrings. She called that "the final touch."

From the transparent remoteness of the mirror emerged an anxious elderly woman. Moving her face closer to the glass, she saw the hectic flush on her cheekbones and her frightened eyes. In that moment of confusion, she wondered: "Should I take some Valium?" No, she didn't need any. There was no point in all this.

Twelve minutes remained till the appointed time. Quickly, decisively, Nadezhda Mikhailovna got ready, and half an hour later she was sitting in the subway with a heavy shopping bag. Besides the apples and grapes, it contained cheese, ham, cake, and chocolate. The only thing she hadn't taken was the wine. Somehow she'd have to explain the wine to Natasha, but she couldn't explain a thing.

PETERS

TATIANA TOLSTAIA

Translated by

MARY FLEMING ZIRIN

FROM CHILDHOOD PETERS HAD FLAT FEET AND A BROAD, womanish belly. His late grandmother, who loved him just the way he was, taught him good manners: to chew, chew, chew every bite, to tuck his napkin into his collar, to hold his tongue when his elders were talking. So Grandmother's friends always took a liking to him. When she brought him along on visits, they never thought twice about letting him handle a valuable little picture book—he wouldn't rip it—and at meals he never picked the fringe off the tablecloth or scattered pastry crumbs: he was a paragon of a boy. They liked the way he came in, gravely straightening his little velvet jacket, adjusting his bow or lacy tie, like a turkey cock's wattle and no less yellowed than Grandmother's cheeks; he scraped his little fat foot and introduced himself to the old women: "Peters, ma'am." He was aware that this amused and touched them.

"Ah, Petrushka, dear child! What is it you call him, Peter?"

"Yes. . . . Well. . . . It's just that we're teaching him German now," said Grandmother nonchalantly. And, reflected in dingy mirrors, Peters walked sedately down the corridor, past old trunks, past old odors, into rooms where rag dolls sat in the corners and, on the table under a green lampshade, green cheese slumbered and homemade pastry breathed vanilla. While the hostess was laying out little silver spoons eaten away on one side, Peters wandered around the room, looking at the dolls on the chest of drawers, the portrait of a stern, offended old man, and the patterns on the wallpaper, or he went over to the window and looked out through a thicket of aloes at the sunny frost where gray pigeons flew about and rosy children sledded down slicked hills. He was not allowed to play outdoors.

And that silly nickname—Peters—stuck to him for life.

Peters's Mama—Grandmother's daughter—ran away to warmer lands with a scoundrel; Papa spent his time with women of low morals and took no interest in his son. Listening to the grownups' talk, Peters pictured the scoundrel as a Negro under a banana palm and Papa's women as sky-blue and airy, light as spring clouds, but, well brought up by Grandmother, he held his tongue. Besides Grandmother, he had a grandfather; at first he lay quietly in an armchair in the corner, watching Peters in silence with bright glassy eyes. Then they laid him on the dining-room table, kept him there for two days, and took him away somewhere. That day they ate rice porridge.

Grandmother promised Peters that if he was a good boy he would have a wonderful life when he grew up. Peters held his tongue. At night he took his plush rabbit to bed and told him all about his future life— how he would play outdoors whenever he wanted and make friends with all the children; how Mama and the scoundrel would come to visit him and bring him sweet fruits; how Papa's light women would fly him through the air wide awake just like in a dream. The rabbit believed him.

Grandmother taught him German as best she could. They played the ancient game of Black Peter, drawing picture cards from each other and pairing them off: gander and goose, rooster and hen, dogs with haughty muzzles. Only the tomcat, Black Peter, was left with no mate; he was always alone—somber, ruffled—and whoever held Black Peter at the end of the game lost and was left sitting as the fool.

There were also colored postcards labeled "Wiesbaden" or "Karls-ruhe" and transparent penholders without nibs but with tiny windows. When you looked in the window, you could see something far off, small, on horseback. He and Grandmother also sang "O Tannenbaum, O Tannenbaum!" All this was the German language.

When Peters turned six, Grandmother took him to a New Year's party. The children there had been certified free of contagion. Peters walked through the snow as fast as he could. Grandmother could hardly keep up with him. A white scarf was pulled tight around his throat, and his eyes shone in the dark like a tomcat's. He was hurrying to make friends. The beautiful life was about to begin. The large, hot apartment smelled of pine needles; toys and stars sparkled; strange mothers ran around with tarts and pretzels; agile children squealed and dashed about. Peters stood in the center of the room and waited for them to start making friends. "Come chase us, Fatty!" they shouted. Peters ran somewhere at random and stopped. They swooped on him; he fell down and bounced up again like a weighted doll. Hard adult hands moved him over to the wall, where he stood until teatime.

At tea all the children except Peters were naughty. He ate everything on his plate, wiped his mouth, and waited for something to happen, but all that happened was that one little girl, black as a beetle, asked him if he had warts and showed him hers.

Peters took an instant fancy to the little girl with warts and began following at her heels. He invited her to sit on the sofa for a while and keep the others away. But since he couldn't either wiggle his ears or roll his tongue into a little tube as she proposed, she quickly became bored with him and abandoned him. Then he suddenly wanted to spin around on one spot and shout out loud, and he spun around and shouted, and at that point his grandmother dragged him home through the dark-blue snowdrifts, saying indignantly that she wouldn't have known him, he had gotten all sweaty, and they would never visit the children again. And in fact they never did.

Until he was fifteen, Peters went for walks arm in arm with Grandmother. At first she supported him, then it was the other way around. At home they played dominoes and laid out games of patience. Peters did fretwork. He was a mediocre student. Before Grandmother died, she got Peters accepted in an institute for librarians. Her last bequest to him was to be careful of his throat and wash his hands meticulously.

The day they buried her, the ice broke up on the Neva.

In the library where Peters worked, there were no attractive women, and Peters liked them attractive. But what did he have to offer if he were to meet women like that? A pink belly and tiny eyes? If only he could shine in conversation; if only, for instance, he knew German properly, but no, "Karlsruhe" was about all that had stuck in his mind from childhood. But he pictured it this way: here he is, starting a romance with a sumptuous woman. While she's doing this or that, he is reading Schiller[1] out loud to her. In the original. Or Hölderlin.[2] She doesn't understand a word of it, of course, and can't understand, but that doesn't matter: what matters is the way he reads—in an inspired, modulated voice. . . . He brings the book up close to his nearsighted eyes. . . . No, he will be fitted with contact lenses, of course. Although people say they rub. So here he is reading. "Put down the book," she says. And there are kisses and tears and dawn, dawn[3]. . . . But the lenses are rubbing. He's blinking and squinting and poking his fingers in his eyes. . . . She waits and waits and says, "Well, take those little glass things out, for hea-ven's sake!" She gets up and slams the door.

No. It's better this way. A sweet, quiet blonde. She nestles her little head against his shoulder. He is reading Hölderlin out loud. Or maybe Schiller. Dark oak groves. Undines. He reads and reads; his tongue gets parched. She yawns and says, "For hea-ven's sake, how much of that boring stuff can you listen to?"

No, that won't do either.

How about without German? Without German, it might go this way: an amazing woman—like a leopard. And he himself like a tiger. Ostrich feathers of some kind, a lithe silhouette on the sofa. . . . (He should get it reupholstered.) The silhouette, that should do it. Falling sofa pillows. And dawn, dawn. . . . Perhaps I'll even marry her. Well? Peters looked at his reflection in the mirror—thick nose, eyes agitated by passion. Well, what did he see? Something a bit polar-bearish; women should like that and be agreeably scared. Peters blew on himself in the mirror to cool off.

But neither acquaintances nor adulteries got off the ground.

Peters tried going to dances. He stomped to the beat, breathing heavily and treading on the girls' feet. He went up to a laughing, chattering group and, clasping his hands behind his back and tilting his head, listened to their conversation. It was nightfall. August blew a cool breeze out of the coarse bushes and sowed the red dust of the last sunbeams over the black foliage and paths of the park; lights went on in the wine and ice-cream stalls and kiosks. Peters passed them sternly, holding tight to his wallet, and then, overwhelmed by sudden hunger pangs, bought half a dozen pastries, went off to a secluded spot, and in almost complete darkness ate them hastily off a shiny little metallic plate. When he emerged from the gloom, blinking, licking his mouth, with white cream on his chin, he screwed up his resolve and went over and introduced himself—breaking in at random, too scared to see what was going on, scraping his flat foot. The women shied away, and the men came close to hitting him but, after a closer look, thought better of it.

Nobody wanted to play with him.

At home Peters made himself an egg flip, washed and wiped the glass, and, after setting his slippers neatly on the night rug, got into bed, stretched out his arms on top of the blanket, and lay motionless, staring at the dusky, pulsating ceiling until sleep came for him.

Sleep came and invited him into its trap doors and corridors, fixed meetings on secret staircases, locked the doors and reconstructed familiar buildings, scaring him with storerooms, women, plague sores, and black tambourines; it led him rapidly down dark passages and pushed him into a stifling room where, at a table, shaggy and grinning, kneading his fingers, sat a connoisseur of many evil things.

Peters struggled in his sheets, begged for forgiveness, and, forgiven this time, plunged into the depths again until morning, tangled in the reflections of the crooked mirrors of a magic theater.

Peters was excited when a new woman, dark and fragrant, wearing a cranberry-red dress, reported for work at the library. He shuffled over to the barber, had his colorless hair cut short, and, for some reason or other, swept his room an extra time and switched the positions of the chest of drawers and the armchair. It was not that he was counting on Faina's coming to see him right away, but Peters wanted to be prepared for anything.

At work they were celebrating New Year's. Peters bustled about, cutting out paper snowflakes the size of saucers and pasting them to the library windows, hanging pink tinsel and getting tangled in the metallic rain and tangled in his dreams and desires. The little Christmas tree lamps were reflected in his agitated eyes; there was a smell of fir and horseradish, and grains of snow drifted in the open air vent. He reflected: if she has, let's say, a suitor—he will go over to him, quietly take his hand, and, in a man-to-man, friendly way, ask him: "Give up Faina, let me have her. What does it matter to you? You'll find somebody else, you know how. But I don't, my mama ran away with a scoundrel, Grandmother devoured my grandfather with rice porridge, devoured my childhood, my one and only childhood, and little girls with warts don't want to sit on the sofa with me. So give me something, at least, eh?"

Burning candles stood suffused down to the breast in transparent, apple-hued light, like a promise of benevolence and peace; the pink-and-yellow flame shook its head, champagne fizzed, Faina sang to a guitar, and the portrait of Dostoevskii on the wall looked the other way. Afterwards they told fortunes by opening Pushkin at random. Peters landed on "Admire, Adele, my reedpipe's knell."[4] They laughed at him, asking him to introduce them to Adele, and then, noisily self-absorbed, forgot all about him. He sat quietly in the corner, crunching his cake and considering how he was going to take Faina home. The party started to break up; he rushed after her into the coatroom and held her fur coat in his outstretched hands; he watched her changing her shoes, thrusting her foot in its colored stocking into a cozy little fur boot, muffling herself in a white shawl, and shrugging her purse onto her shoulder—it all excited him. The door slammed, and the last he saw of her was the wave of her mitten as she jumped onto the trolley bus and disappeared into the white snowstorm. But even that was like a promise.

Festive bells pealed in his ears, and his eyes were opened to the heretofore unseen. All roads led to Faina; all winds trumpeted her glory, shouted out her dark name, rushed over steep slate roofs, over towers and spires, coiled into plaits of snow and threw themselves at her feet, and the entire city, all the islands—the waters and embankments, statues and gardens, bridges and grilles, wrought-iron roses and horses—all twined into a hoop, weaving a famous winter wreath for his beloved.

He never got a chance to be alone with her; he tried to catch her on the street, but she always swept past him like the wind, like a ball, like a snowball thrown by an agile hand. And her friend who dropped into the library in the evenings was horrible, impossible, like a toothache: an impertinent journalist, always in squeaky leather, long-legged, long-haired, full of international anecdotes. The journalist wrote brief notes for a newspaper full of fibs, saying that "it is always particularly crowded near the stands with books on sugarbeet raising" and, as he put it, "visitors call librarian Faina A. their pilot through the ocean of books." Faina laughed, happy to see her name in the paper; Peters suffered in silence. And he went on trying to work up the nerve at last to grab her arm, take her home with him, and, after a spell of passion, work out their future life together.

Late that winter on a damp, consumptive evening, Peters was drying his hands in the men's room under the hot air jet of the automatic dryer and eavesdropping as Faina talked on the telephone out in the corridor. The dryer shuddered and fell silent, and in the ensuing hush the beloved voice laughed distinctly, "No-o, there are only women in our collective. Who? Him? He's not a man, but a dishrag. Some sort of glandular washout."

"Admire, Adele, my reedpipe's knell." . . . Peters's insides felt as if he'd been run over by a streetcar. He looked around at the wretched yellowed tile, the old mirror swollen from within by silver blisters, the faucet dripping rust—life had chosen correctly the place for this last humiliation. He wound his scarf meticulously around his throat to keep from catching a chill in the tonsils, made his way home, fumbled into his slippers, went over to the window he intended to fall from, and pulled at the casement. The window was well taped for the winter; he had pasted it shut himself, and it was a shame to waste his labor. Then he turned on the oven, put his head on the drip pan with the cold breadcrumbs, and lay there. Would anyone eat rice porridge in his memory? After a while Peters remembered that the gas had been off since morning; there had been a breakdown on the line. He flew into a rage, dialed the controller's office with trembling fingers, and began shouting dreadfully and incoherently about the outrageous failures in municipal facilities. He sat down in his grandfather's armchair and stayed there until morning.

In the morning outside the window, large, slow snowflakes were falling. Peters looked at the snow, the hushed sky, the new drifts, and quietly rejoiced that his youth was over and done with.

But a new spring came through the communicating courtyards; the snows disappeared, the earth breathed a sweet rot, blue ripples ran across the puddles, and the wild Leningrad cherries once again showered blossoms on matchbook sailboats and newspaper ships—what does it matter whether a new voyage begins in the gutter or at sea, when spring is calling and the same wind blows everywhere? The new galoshes Peters bought himself were wonderful: they were lined inside with fuchsia-blossom pulp, their taut rubber shone like varnish and promised to mark his earthly journeys with waffled ovals wherever he might turn his steps in search of happiness. At a leisurely pace, hands clasped behind his back, he strolled along the stone streets, glancing deep into yellow gateways, sniffing the air of canals and rivers, and the evening women, the Saturday women, watched him with a long gaze that held nothing promising, thinking: this one's an invalid of some kind, we don't need him.

He didn't need them either, however, but he was overwhelmed by the sight of scandalously young little Valentina—she was buying spring postcards on the sunlit embankment, and the lucky wind swooped in gusts, shaping and changing and reshaping her close-cropped black hair. Peters followed in Valentina's tracks, careful not to get too close, trembling in fear of a rebuff. Athletic youths ran up to the lovely girl and scooped her up with laughter. She frolicked off after them, and Peters saw them buying and presenting purple violets to the frisky girl; he heard them calling her name—it tore loose and flew away on the wind—and the laughing group disappeared around a corner, and Peters was left with nothing—stout, white, with nobody to love him. Well, and what could he say to her anyway—to a young girl like that, a girl with violets? Approach her on his padded feet and reach out his padded palm, "Peters, ma'am." ("What a strange name. . . . "It's what my grandmother. . . . "Why did your grandmother? . . . " "Sort of German. . . . " "Do you know German? . . . " "No, but Grandmother. . . . ")

Oh, if only he had learned German while he had the chance! Oh, then, undoubtedly. . . . Oh, then, of course. . . . Such a difficult language; it hisses, sputters, and wriggles in the mouth, O Tannenbaum, probably nobody even knows it. . . . Peters would go ahead and learn it and impress the lovely girl. . . .

Watching out for policemen, he pasted notices to poles: "I wish to know German." They hung there all summer long, fading and wriggling their pseudopodia. Peters made frequent visits to his poles, retouching letters washed out by the rains and repairing torn-off corners; late in the fall they rang him up, and it was like a miracle: out of the human sea, two people rose to the surface and responded to his quiet, feeble, slanting, violet-on-white appeal. Hey, you called? Yes, I did, I called. Peters rejected the assertive, bass-voiced man who once again dissolved into nonexistence, but he quizzed the twittering lady, Elizaveta Frantsevna from Vasilevskii Island, in detail: how to get there, and where, and how much, and whether she had a dog, since he was afraid of dogs.

They talked it over. Elizaveta Frantsevna was expecting him that evening, and Peters went to the corner he had chosen to keep watch on

Valentina—he had trailed her; he knew she would go past as always, swinging her sports bag, at twenty to four, and flit into a large red building where she capered on a trampoline among others just as quick and young as she. She would go past without suspecting that Peters even existed, that he planned a great exploit, that life was beautiful. He had decided that the best thing would be to buy a bouquet, a large, yellow bouquet, and offer it to Valentina on the familiar corner in silence, just like that, in silence, but with a bow. "What's this? O-oh!"—in that spirit.

The wind was blowing in gusts, and it was pouring when he came out onto the embankment. Behind the shroud of rain, the indistinct red barrier of the sodden fortress lay in a blur; its pewter spire raised a blurred exclamatory finger. It had rained all night, and up there above, they had stored up reservoirs of water like prudent housekeepers. When the Swedes left these shores, they forgot to take their sky with them, and they must be gloating now on their clean little peninsula—they have a clear, sky-blue frost, black firs, and white rabbits, and Peters was left coughing here among the granite and the mildew.

Every fall Peters took pleasure in hating his native city, and it returned the compliment: it spat icy streams from thundering roofs, flooded his eyes with an opaque dark torrent, slipped particularly wet and deep puddles under his feet, and lashed his nearsighted face with slaps of rain. The slimy buildings, stumbling up against Peters, deliberately covered themselves with delicate bead-white fungi, mossy poisonous velveteen, and the wind, flying in from bandit-ridden highways, tangled in his drenched legs, weaving deadly tubercular figure-eights.

He stood at his post with the bouquet, but October kept falling from the skies; his galoshes were like bathtubs, and the newspaper wrapped three times around the expensive yellow flowers slipped off in shreds, and the time came and went, and Valentina didn't come and wouldn't come, but still he stood there, chilled to his underclothes, to the white hairless body dotted with tender red moles.

It struck four. Peters shoved his bouquet into the trash can. What was there to wait for? He had already realized that studying German was silly and too late; that the lovely Valentina, reared among athletic, springy youths, would just smile and step over him, stout and thick in the waist; that ardent passions and light steps, quick dances and capers on the trampoline, dewy April violets casually bought, the sunny wind off the grey waters of the Neva, laughter, and youth were not for him in this existence; that all his strivings were in vain; that he should have married his own grandmother while he had the chance and moldered quietly in a warm room to the tick of the clock, eating a sugar bun and setting his old plush bunny beside the plate—to comfort and amuse him.

He was suddenly hungry, and he wandered into the welcoming light of a snack bar, bought some soup, and settled down next to two pretty girls who were eating onion tarts and blowing cloudy film off pink cocoa grown cold.

The girls were chattering, about love, of course, and Peters heard the story of a certain Irochka who had gone about for a long time with a fellow student from fraternal Yemen, or maybe it was Kuwait, in hopes of his marrying her. Irochka had heard that over there, on the sandy steppes of Arab lands, oil was as common as berries, and every respectable fellow was a millionaire and flew his own airplane with a gold toilet seat. It was the gold toilet seat that drove Irochka mad. She had grown up in the Iaroslav district, where the conveniences were three walls without a fourth and a view over the pea-green fields—straight out of a painting by Repin.[5] But the Arab was not itching for marriage, and when Irochka put the question pointblank, he expressed himself in no uncertain terms: "Arre you ghiddin'? Nod a dzhance!" and so on and chucked her out with all her wretched belongings. The girls didn't notice Peters, and he listened and pitied the unknown Irochka and imagined first the pea-green open spaces of Iaroslav, edged on the horizon with dark wolf forests thawing in blissful quiet under the sky-blue luster of the northern sun, and then the dry morose whistle of millions of grains of sand, the taut pressure of the desert hurricane, a brownish orb glowing through the driving gloom, and lost white palaces covered with a deadly dust or enchanted by long-dead sorcerers.

The girls went on to the story of the complicated relations between Olia and Valerian and Aniuta's shameless behavior, and Peters drank his bouillon and, all ears, entered like an invisible spirit into the strangers' story. He became intimately involved in others' secrets; he stood just outside the door with bated breath; he sensed, smelled, and touched it all as if in a magic movie; glimpses of faces, tears in distressed eyes, flashes of smiles, sun in someone's hair shooting pink and green sparks, dust in sunbeams, and the heat of the warmed parquet floor creaking beside him in this foreign, happy, lively life were all unbearably accessible—he had only to stretch out his hand.

"We've finished, let's go!" one of the pretty girls ordered the other, and, unfurling their transparent umbrellas like signs of another, higher existence, they swam out into the rain and ascended into the heavens, into the transcendental azure beyond the range of human eyes.

Peters selected a rough cardboardlike bit of napkin from a plastic glass and wiped his mouth. Life had roared past, flowed around him, and sped off just as a driving current flows around a heavy pile of rocks.

The cleaning woman passed like a simoom across the tables, waved her rag in Peters's face, snatched up twenty plates in a single agile motion, and dissolved in the pastry-filled air.

"But it's not my fault," said Peters to somebody. "None of it's my fault at all. I want to be a part of it, too. But they won't let me. Nobody wants to play with me. Why? But I'll exert myself, I'll win yet!"

He went out—into the icy spray and the freezing, lashing water. I'll pervail. I'll provail. I'll prevail. I'll clench my teeth and break through. And I'll learn, I'll learn that damned language. Over there, on Vasilevskii Island, in the dampest of Leningrad damp spots, Elizaveta Frantsevna is waiting, swimming like a seal or an undine, muttering faintly in a gloomy Teutonic dialect. She would arrive, and they would begin to mutter together. O Tannenbaum! O, I repeat, Tannenbaum! What comes after that? I'll find out when I get there

Well, farewell then to Valentina and her swift sisters; there's only an old German woman ahead—too late to back out now. . . . Peters pictured his journey, his looping tracks through the soggy city, with failure dogging him and sniffing at the waffled imprint of his soles, and the old woman at journey's end; to put fate off the track, Peters hailed a taxi and swam off through the rain—steam rose from his legs, the driver was morose, and he immediately wanted to get out again. Taka-taka-taka-taka—money was clicking away bit by bit.

"Stop here."

A doorkeeper stood guard over the entrance to a den of vice—the door led to a half-basement, and behind the door music rumbled hollowly and lamps shone in the windows like long tubes of poisonous syrup. In front of the door were youths with teeth chattering in the eddies of rain—all candidates for Valentina's hand—farewell, Valentina. The place was filled, but the doorkeeper, deceived by Peters's solid appearance, let him in; Peters passed by him, and two of the others sneaked in at his side. It was a great place. With dignity Peters took off his hat and raincoat; with a glance he promised tips. He took a step into the blaring hall and trumpeted his arrival by blowing his nose in his handkerchief. A great place! He picked out the pinkest cocktail and a pagoda pastry, drank, nibbled, drank another, and began to relax. A great, great place. A butterfly of a girl sprang up, appearing under his elbow from out of the air somewhere, from the colored cigarette smoke; a red dress, a green one—the lights were blinking—blossomed on her like an orchid, her lashes blinked like wings, bracelets jingled on her thin little paws, and she was devoted to Peters body and soul. He waved for more of the pink nectar, afraid to say anything, to scare off the little girl, the marvelous peri, the airborne blossom, and they sat in silence as amazed at one another as a goat and an angel would be if they were to meet.

He waved his hand again—and they even brought them some meat.

"Ahem," said Peters, praying to the heavens not to recall their envoy immediately. "I had a plush rabbit when I was a child, you see—a real friend—and what didn't I promise him! And now I'm on my way to a German lesson, ahem."

"I like plush rabbits, they're awfully funny," the peri remarked coldly.

Peters marveled at such angelic stupidity—a rabbit couldn't be funny; it was either a friend or a nonentity, a little sack filled with sawdust.

"We also played cards, and I always ended up with the tomcat," Peters recalled.

"A tomcat's awfully funny, too," repeated the girl through her teeth like a well-learned lesson, while her eyes roved around the hall.

"Not at all. Why would it be?" objected Peters hotly. "And that's not the point at all! That's not what I mean; I'm talking about life, and how it always teases us, showing us and then taking away, showing and taking. You know, it's like a shop window, all shiny and locked up tight, and you can't get anything out of it. And the question is: why?"

"You're awfully funny, too," persisted the indifferent girl, who wasn't listening. "You dropped something on the floor."

When he managed at last to crawl out from under the table, the angel had already flown, taking Peters's wallet and money with her. Naturally. Well, what of it? How could it be otherwise? Peters sat over the leftovers as motionless as a suitcase. He sobered up, picturing how he was going to explain, beg—the grinning contempt of the cloakroom attendant as Peters fished damp rubles from the swampy pockets of his raincoat and shook out the small change that had slipped like minnows into the lining. . . . The music machines were stamping; drums were beating to herald the onset of someone's passion. The cocktail vaporized out his ears. Coocoo! That's the way.

What are you anyway, life? A mute shadow-puppet show, a chain of dreams, a swindler's shop? Or the gift of unrequited love—is that all that's in store for me? And happiness? What kind of happiness is that? Ungrateful man, you're alive and you weep, you love, strive, and fail, isn't that enough for you? So? Not enough!? Oh, so that's how it is? But there's nothing else.

"I've been waiting," shouted Elizaveta Frantsevna, a quick, frizzled woman, throwing back hooks and bolts and admitting the plundered Peters, dark, dangerous, up to his neck in trouble, up to the last tight button. "Come on in! We'll get started right away. Take a seat on my sofa. Lotto first, and then a cup of tea. All right? Quick now, take a card. Who has the billy goat? I do. Who has the guinea hen?"

I'll kill her now, Peters decided. Elizaveta Frantsevna, look away. I'm going to kill you now. You and my late grandmother and the little girl with warts and Valentina and the false angel and all the rest of them— all those who promised and deceived, enticed and abandoned; I am going to kill you on behalf of all the obese and asthmatic, the tongue-tied and slow-witted; on behalf of everyone locked in a dark storeroom, everyone left at home on holidays. Prepare yourself, Elizaveta Frantsevna, now I'm going to smother you with that embroidered pillow right over there. And nobody will ever know.

"Frantsevna-a!" A fist thumped at the door. "Give me three rubles and I'll scrub the corridor for you!"

The fit passed. Peters put down the pillow. He was suddenly sleepy. The old woman rustled money; Peters lowered his eyes to the "Domestic Animals" card.

"A penny for your thoughts? Who has the tomcat?"

"I do," said Peters. "Who else?" He edged his way out, crumpling the cardboard cat in his fist. To hell with life. To sleep, sleep, go to sleep and never wake up.

Spring came and spring went, and came again and spread sky-blue flowers over the meadows and waved her hand and called through his sleep: "Peters! Peters!" but he was sleeping too soundly to hear any of it.

Summer rustled and roamed at will through the gardens—she sat on a bench, swished her bare feet in the dust, and called Peters out into the heated streets, onto the warm pavement; she whispered and twinkled in the splash of lindens, in the shiver of poplars; she called, got no answer, and went away, trailing her skirts, toward the bright line of the horizon.

Life stood on tiptoes and peeped in the window in amazement: Why was Peters sleeping, why didn't he come out to play her cruel games with her?

But Peters slept and slept and lived through his sleep: wiping his mouth neatly, he ate his vegetables and drank his milk, shaved his dingy face—around his pursed mouth and under his sleeping eyes—and one day inadvertently, in passing, he married a cold, firm woman with big feet and a hollow name. The woman had a stern view of the human race; she knew that they were all rogues and you couldn't trust anyone; her purse smelled of stale bread.

She took Peters everywhere with her, clutching his arm as tightly as his grandmother once had. On Sunday they went to the zoological museum, into the hollow, polite halls—to look at woolly mice grown cold, and white whalebones. On weekdays they went shopping; they bought dead yellow vermicelli and senile brown soap, and watched lean, heavy meat, as dense as anguish, as endless and sticky as the sands of the Arabian desert, pouring out the narrow orifice of a funnel.

"Tell me," the woman would ask sternly, "those chickens, are they frozen? Give me that one, over there." And "that one" lay down in the musty bag, and the sleeping Peters carried home the cold young cockerel who had known neither love nor freedom—nor the greensward nor the merry round eye of a lover. And at home, under the attentive gaze of the firm woman, Peters himself had to split open the frozen creature's breast with knife and axe and tear out the slippery brown heart, the scarlet roses of the lungs, and the sky-blue stem of the windpipe in order to wipe out forever the memory of one who was born and hoped, stirred his young wings, and dreamed of a regal green tail, a pearly seed, and a golden dawn flooding the waking world.

Summers and winters skidded and thawed, dissolved and died out; harvests of rainbows hung over distant buildings; avid young snowstorms dashed out of the northern forests and moved time forward, and there came a day when the woman with big feet left Peters, quietly drew the door shut, and went off to buy soap and slowly stir food in another man's saucepans. Then Peters cautiously opened his eyes and woke up.

The clock was ticking, stewed fruit swam in a glass jug, and his slippers had grown cold overnight. Peters felt himself all over and counted his fingers and the hairs on his head. Regret flashed up and flew away. His body still remembered the hinterlands of the years that had flown by, the calendar's viscous sleep, but deep in his emotional pulp something long forgotten, something young and trusting, was already reviving, rising up from its bed on the stove, shaking itself and smiling.

Old Peters pushed at the window frame—the blue glass began to ring, thousands of yellow birds flared up, and the naked golden spring began to shout, laughing, "Chase me! Chase me!" New children with little pails romped in puddles. Desiring nothing, deploring nothing, Peters smiled gratefully at life racing past, indifferent, ungrateful, deceitful, mocking, meaningless, foreign—and beautiful, oh so beautiful.

HERBS FROM ODESSA

ELENA MAKAROVA

Translated by

HELENA GOSCILO

THE GENTLE VOICES OF WOMEN GROWING PLUMP
jingled in the darkness like rattles.

"A room?" The receptionist burst out laughing. Turning to the empty
foyer of the hotel as if there were stalls full of spectators in front of her,
she repeated, "A room. . . . Be satisfied with a bunk!"
"I was sent by Liusia Smertonosnaia. . . ."[1]
"The excursion office!" exclaimed the receptionist in the resounding
voice of a circus manager.
She traced out the number 48 on a card and placed the piece of paper
on the smooth, glassy surface of the counter.
"You should be grateful!" could be heard behind me.

. . . It was a bathhouse from a painting by the Armenian artist Bazh-
beuk Melikian. Darkness, illuminated from within by gold. Inside it ov-
erflowed naked women grown languid from the water and the heated
stones. Water streamed down their chestnut hair like sunflower oil. . . .
Or no. It was a bathhouse where my aunt took me when I was five
years old. The horror of pink nakedness. Pink women sat on long grey
benches, and when my aunt entered naked, she was infused with pink
before my eyes. As I moved along, I covered myself with my free hand,
and the women shouted with raucous laughter. One of them doused me
with warm water from a small washtub. I burst into tears. I sobbed violently, and my aunt, who was dry, led me off into the changing room.

I was cold and ashamed for my aunt's sake that she, who was always smartly dressed and smelled of perfume, had suddenly become shockingly naked and pink.

Or no. It was a boarding school, where everything happened in full view: a bathroom without doors, and a secret diary stolen by the girls and read aloud in class. . . .

"Shut the door! Can't you see we're naked?" said a woman. "Here's your bunk."

The steamy air billowed around the lusterless nightlamp. An old woman stroked her hair with a comb as she speared the number 48 with a dry, crackling sound. The bunk shook and creaked under the shifting bodies.

"Lady, take your passport!" The attendant tossed the passport on the glassy surface of the counter.

Varvara Semionovna Skazka.

The rasp of a chain. Then the door opened only as far as the chain allowed, and a face appeared with deep-set, gimletlike eyes, as if they were hidden in a pit. A mouth covered with husks from sunflower seeds uttered:

"Y-y-yes?"

It was the voice of a child who's barely started to speak.

The door closed and opened again. The old woman-infant gazed as pleadingly as a child, like the neighbor's daughter Zareta, who in the evenings would wait for her dissolute mother. When the latter finally arrived, Zareta wouldn't throw herself at her, but would look at her with a long, happy gaze.

Having gazed her fill, the old woman-infant in a cone-shaped dress (almost like a nun, yet not a nun; the dress grey and patched—you couldn't even call it a dress, but precisely a cone with slits for arms) moved forward.

After turning the key in the door, Skazka entered a big room. Above a tall, snow-white bed hung an antique clock mounted on dark wood. And on the piano with a white cover stood two photographs, of a man and a woman, in cardboard frames, with a statue of Buddha between them.

"These are my f-father and m-mother. They took F-Father during the Ezh-zhov purges,[2] and M-Mother recently d-died in the hospital."

She burst into tears but, regaining control of herself, wiped her eyes with a plump hand.

"Your mother's Varvara Semionovna Skazka?"

"Yes, yes," nodded Skazka. "Are you from Z-Zoinka? D-don't be afraid of me, I'm not all h-here. But I can p-play the p-piano. . . ."

Skazka nimbly unfastened the button of the cover and ran her hand over the shiny surface of the piano.

"Z-Zoinka always used to s-stay with us. Our place is c-clean, and there isn't room in the h-hotel. Do s-sit down, you must be tired from traveling."

Her voice vibrated, faltering on the consonants and resting on the vowels, as if she felt pleasure in pronouncing the drawling sounds.

"Since M-Mama died, I c-cry and sing all the time."

She raised the lid, and, lowering her cone-shaped body into the swivel chair, she touched the keys with both hands.

"L-Lord, keep M-Mama," she sang, and glanced at me as if asking me whether it had come out coherently.

Encouraged by my praise, she sang her song a couple of times more and lowered the lid.

"Are you on v-vacation?" asked Skazka.

She heard out my brief story without blinking. Her light eyes were indeterminate in color, like a newborn's, with transparent lids in the white fluff of her eyelashes. All this colorless lightness was sunk in the darkness of her sockets, which were almost black.

"L-Lord, keep G-Grandf-father," she sang with gentle compassion.

. . . On the kitchen table stood a box from which protruded bunches of colored thread.

"You s-sing, and I'll w-work a bit."

She took a skein of the tangled thread and like a virtuoso pulled out a red thread, then another. She placed them side by side, took a thick sheet of paper out of the table drawer, tore an even strip off, and rolled it into a little tube.

"I bought it at the f-flea market. Pretty th-threads, and only ten kopeks for the l-lot. I have s-sugar and j-jam, too. Mama used to cook it."

The old woman-infant drank tea from a saucer. She rejected the cheese, but took a cookie and beslobbered it like a toothless child.

"Wh-while M-Mama was still alive I was treated to a pastry with r-real cream. W-without eating it, I brought it to M-Mama, but the cream dripped out.

"And M-Mama said I was clumsy. I'm so c-clumsy and ug-gly, no one will m-marry me.

"And I'm th-thirty.

"I b-bought a red d-dress with a white c-collar at the flea market, can I sh-show you?"

She minced into the room, returning quickly with the dress. She held it against her; it was twice the size she needed. She stood rooted to the spot, holding the dress at her throat with one hand, with the other at her barely defined hip.

"I d-don't look old in it, do I?"

"Of course not! It really suits you. You look twenty years old in it."

She blushed to the tips of her protruding ears and gave a giggle. She had only her front teeth, with black gaps yawning along the sides, which made her face seem even thinner.

"I'll t-tell you s-something later,"[3] she whispered, hanging the dress on the back of the chair. "No, I'll rumple it like this," she said and took the dress into the room.

On the back of the sheets of paper on which she'd wound the thread were some portraits. After she came back and sat on the chair, she tore a blank space with eyes and the tips of ears from a sheet of paper and wound the red thread around it.

"It's b-brand new, not at all rotten," she said and added mysteriously, "I'll tell you s-something later."

Every fifteen minutes the clock at the head of the bed chimed a short tune, similar to "L-Lord, keep M-Mama." I got out of bed in the hope of finding something light to read. In the bottom drawer of the oak sideboard lay a cookbook.

Its cover boasted a plump woman from the fifties with padded shoulders. She was smiling as she gazed at a frying pan with cutlets. Above the frying pan, in uneven handwriting, was inscribed the word "margarine." Evidently this was the late Varvara Semionovna's reference book.

Almost every page contained marks made in an indelible pencil: "butter" was crossed out, and on top was inscribed "margarine." The amount of sugar was halved everywhere, and instead of "roast" was written "braise." But the chapters entitled "Sauces," "Dressings," and "Vegetable Canning" had been left untouched by the late Varvara Semionovna's hand.

The tranquil smoothness of the pages with red bilberry and cranberry dressing, with sauces and anchovies, plunged me into drowsiness, and only in the morning did I hear above my head, "L-Lord, keep M-Mama."

Liusia Smertonosnaia stood on the street outside the dining hall where they'd arranged to meet and smoked a Prima. Her group was having breakfast inside the massive walls of the dining hall, and Liusia chewed nervously on the tip of her cigarette.

"They're inside eating, while I'm freezing! And the bus is standing idle!"

Liusia's luxuriant hair escaped from beneath her mohair hat. In the hat, with her small figure, she looked just like a little chick.

22

"Every day these nerve-racking situations, every single day!" she complained, shifting from one slender foot to the other. "Give me a light!" Lighting her cigarette from a passerby's, she shook her head and calmed down.

The excursion participants, their stomachs filled, now surrounded Liusia in a circle.

"Hurry up! Hurry up!!" she rushed them. "Who's the leader of your group?"

The group pushed forward a dumpy woman in a heavy black overcoat with a fur collar, and Liusia gave her a rundown of the excursion schedule.

In the cab she ranted against her work, complained that she couldn't stand it at school, the children drove her crazy, and Liusik[4] had to give her some valerian drops. This work wasn't any easier. For eighty-two rubles she was completely worn out.

"And did Aunt Vera graduate from an institute?" I interrupted Liusia.

"The circle of the intelligentsia is shrinking," she replied, indicating with her cigarette to the driver where to stop.

A yellowish-grey dust covered the houses and the asphalt. There was sun and wind, added structures protruding from balconies, staircases connecting the houses, the aroma of roasted seeds alternating with vanilla. . . .

"Liusia!" cried a freckled woman with a thick black braid. "Look at our visitors!"

Wiping her hands on her padded jacket, she covered Liusia with kisses, and looking past me, she dragged Liusia into the elongated house, which resembled a coach.

"Sit on the bench. I'll be right back."

"Aunt Ver, don't fuss," said Liusia, but Aunt Vera had already disappeared.

A black cat was rumbling on the bunk. Something was cooking on the electric stove, filling the platformlike room with a sweet smell.

A tall old man in a padded jacket stole past.

"Aunt Ver, why'd you send him. . . . "

Aunt Vera banged the saucepans without saying a word. The old man returned with a half-liter of vodka.

"Uncle Sasha." Liusia gave him a somewhat different, new smile. "Now, Uncle Sasha. . . . "

"If Uncle Sasha gave his word, that means he gave his word. We've got our eye on a two-room place. But you have to wait."

Liusia nodded quickly and took off her hat.

"You've dyed it different again," said Uncle Sasha and went out.

"Turkey!" Aunt Vera had exchanged her padded jacket for a black wool dress with a mother-of-pearl brooch on her bosom. "None of this 'I don't want any.' Eat and make yourselves at home."

The room was full of rugs and figurines: reindeer and mermaids, Galina Ulanova[5] in a tutu, Oleg Popov,[6] Carmen,[7] and four roosters with crimson combs.

"I just saw out[8] a man from Novosibirsk." Aunt Vera arranged fat pieces of turkey on the plates. "His wife's thirty-five. Cancer. Has the circus left?"

"No. The bear bit Misha the trainer. Today's his first performance since the accident! It'll be sold out!"

"Is he the one?" asked Aunt Vera meaningfully, and Liusia nodded.

"You did a good job of dying your hair. It looks natural." Words had pooled in Uncle Sasha's Adam's apple as in a reservoir, and he had to push them out by force.

"We drink slowly, we live slowly." Aunt Vera raised her glass. "Even children aren't born in a hurry."

"My grandfather has cancer. He doesn't eat anything and has trouble urinating," I said, and accidentally met Liusia's disapproving gaze.

"Let's sit a while and get to know each other." Aunt Vera placed a moist hand on my arm.

"I have to be home in two days," I insisted dully.

After the vodka that had been forcibly poured into me, I'd grown limp and sat quietly. The fat turkey wrapped around my hungry stomach like a vacuum cleaner. The soft rugs absorbed the monotonous conversation interrupted by Liusia's exclamations.

"Sold out!! Sold out!!!"

"It's time!" rang Liusia's voice in my ear, and I came to.

"Tell me all about it and make it simple," said Aunt Vera and climbed up onto the berth.

" . . . I'll cure him," she concluded upon hearing the whole story of Grandfather's illness. For a long time she jotted down figures on a piece of notebook paper, added, multiplied, and divided in a column. "Two hundred," she totaled the conversation. "My price is your price. And so you'll have no doubts, take this book. I'm going to say the names, and you look for them in the book. There'll be no cheating."

. . . The stupefyingly sweet smell of the potion[9] boiling on the electric stove, the Latin names of the herbs that Aunt Vera would repeat and, immediately forgetting them, would ask to have read out syllable by syllable, the rumbling cat, the warm stove, the vodka I'd drunk. . . .

On top of everything, there was Aunt Vera's granddaughter in an embroidered jacket. She clambered up to join Aunt Vera on the berth and, waving her suede boots in the air, she said:

"A woman on our street was getting married. They dressed her up in a wedding outfit, married her off, and said, as usual: 'Exchange rings as a token of conjugal fidelity.' The groom started to put the ring on her finger, and she—dropped dead! They buried her in her bridal veil, in her wedding dress and with the ring. The gravediggers spotted the gold and came at night with spades. They dug up the grave, took off the lid, and—she was alive. She was in a lethargic sleep. One of the gravediggers suffered an instant heart rupture, but the other didn't get scared. He grasped her hand and took her to her parents. When her mother saw her she gave such a yell: "A ghost! Ah! Ah!" Her father merely opened his mouth wide, swayed, and—dropped dead. They took her mother to the psychiatric ward. And the gravedigger said to her, 'If that's the way things stand—I'll marry you. And if you won't, I'll put you back and bury you.' Well, what choice did she have? She married him. While her mother's undergoing treatment, the young couple's living in her house.'"[10]

"What about the first groom?" asked Aunt Vera, stirring the boiling potion.

"Who on earth knows?! He either took to drink or went crazy. Where are you from?" asked the granddaughter, scratching the cat behind the ears, which caused him to rumble even more violently.

"Moscow."

"Send us a velvet-bound photo album. A woman from our block got one in Moscow; it's a pleasure to look at."

The granddaughter jumped down from the bunk with the cat.

"I'll give him some bones so he won't turn into anything," she explained. "Black cats turn into witches at night.'"[11]

Aunt Vera was rereading the notations syllable by syllable, lifting her brown eyes, shot with gold, to me after each word as if checking to see whether she was reading them right.

"It'll be ready the day after tomorrow," she said. "Or there's another possibility: we could use another herb, but you have to go a long way to get it, and it costs a lot. Do you want to get it? No, I'm not insisting. I don't have the time to go get it."

"I want to get it."

"Then it's three hundred."

I wilted.

"My price is your price," said Aunt Vera. "Two hundred fifty."

"I only have two hundred with me, but I'll get it," I said, realizing belatedly that I should have haggled from the beginning.

"What j-joy!"

The old woman-infant was wearing the red dress. It hung like a sack down her back and chest.

"I wore it for you," she explained, poking her finger at the crimson material. "I l-like you so much. . . . You're not nasty, and you don't make fun of me. We have a n-neighbor. I used to visit her to watch t-television, and she used to make fun of me. I didn't n-notice, but M-Mama said: 'Don't go to her, she makes f-fun of you.' And I didn't n-notice that. I want to w-watch t-television so badly, but I haven't been going since Mama told me that. M-Mama kn-knows best. . . ."

I offered her a pastry. She took it carefully, as if asking whether it really was for her.

I nodded. She took it over to the sideboard in her outstretched hand.

"They really fleece you," she sighed upon hearing how much the herbs cost. "When M-Mama died, our neighbors gave me ten rubles, and social services twenty, and my p-pension brought in t-twenty-one rubles. It wasn't even enough for the f-funeral. I really c-cried, and they said: 'We'll bury your mother for n-nothing.'

"Th-they're kind. . . .

"L-Lord, keep M-Mama," sang the old woman-infant, making the sign of the cross at the empty corner of the kitchen. "Before, when I was l-little and h-healthy, an icon used to hang here. But when they t-took Daddy, M-Mama th-threw out the icon. But I keep th-thinking it's still h-hanging there. . . ."

"Do you want to unravel the thread?" she asked, apparently sensing that I was getting ready to leave.

"I'll w-wait for you," said Skazka, opening the door for me. "And then I'll tell you s-something. . . ."

Liusia, accompanied by a white poodle, met me at the main entrance.

"I was just taking Charlik out," said Liusia, and I was sorry that I'd left Skazka.

Keeping Charlik on his leash, Liusia rushed about the Vorontsov Gardens.

"What's happening is awful," she reported when Charlik finally calmed down and raised his leg at a tree trunk. "The circle of the intelligentsia is shrinking."

Running around the apartment, she complained about the handyman; he'd put in a defective tap for the umpteenth time.

"See that Charlik doesn't get out," she ordered, disappearing behind the door. "Have a seat!" Liusia returned with a floor rag. "Because of that creep I'm late for the circus," she said, wiping the tile in the bathroom.

In panties and brassiere she sailed to the other room, and in a second she emerged in a close-fitting brocade dress.

"The style of '69! That's what I've come to!" Liusia was tearing at her hair with a massage brush. "You stay here a while, look through some art books."

"But can't I go to the circus with you?"

"It's sold out today! Sold out!!" shouted Liusia in answer to the impertinent query. "Misha's had an accident! The bear bit him!"

Someone knocked on the latticed window.

"Here she is again!" Liusia raced to the door.

The woman who burst into the apartment looked as if she was Liusia's mother: the same voice with a touch of hoarseness, the same luxuriant hair, and an overall petite appearance, through which one could clearly discern Liusia in her declining years.

Brushing Liusia aside with a shoulder encased in beaver lamb, the woman ran into the room. Liusia followed. Their loud, excited whispering swelled into a shout.

"Take it all! There's nothing to reproach me for! Nothing!! I haven't needed anything from you for a long time!! Not anything!! And especially your gold! Especially that!! Especially that!!!"

Charlik thrust his paw into the opening and slipped into the room.

"Take it!" Liusia dashed into the corridor, shaking a wedding band in the air. "Here! Here!! I can't stand the sight of it!!! Together with your Liusik!!!"

"You should see a shrink! You're crazy!!" The woman knocked the wedding band out of Liusia's hands, and it rolled with a clatter along the corridor. Charlik leaped toward the ring.

"He'll swallow it!!!" Liusia rushed toward Charlik, trying to get it out of the dog's mouth.

"I hope he chokes on it!!!" shouted the woman, slamming the front door with all her strength.

After getting the ring out of Charlik's mouth, Liusia collapsed on the kitchen couch.

"I'm late! Late!! Late!!!" Liusia had hysterics. "And that Liusik. . . ," she sobbed, stressing "that." "All he cares about is his icons. It's sickening enough without them. Ha! That's what having a man in the house means! The tap leaks, the plaster's falling down. And I've got to do everything, everything, everything myself!

"What a bore!

"The circus is the only safety valve in this drab existence.

"The only one!!!

"You should see Misha!

27

"Grace, grace, and more grace!

"And we fools can't wait to get married. . . . We don't look around, expand our minds a bit. . . . And it's all Mother: Liusik loves you, Liusik's cultured, Liusik's this, Liusik's that. . . . Ugh!" Liusia crushed her cigarette with her index finger.

Charlik started to bark.

"And I'm stuck with his Charlik, too! If he'd only walk him once in a while! Here, gorge yourself!" Liusia threw him a sausage. "And you call this life?!

"You only live once, and there's no joy in it at all!

"You can't buy dresses! You pay double for crummy panties!

"Oh, to be an acrobat! Misha thinks I've got all that it takes.

"Playbills everywhere!

"A sell-out!

"Rehearsals all day!

"And how wonderful circus marriages are! You're always together, day and night! But as things are. . . . What do I care about his icons, and what does he care about my tours!

"It's all hopeless.

"And Liusik has a heart condition besides.

"Have a smoke," said Liusia, not having noticed until then that I wasn't smoking. "You've caught me at a bad time.

"Now I want to live just for the circus.

"Misha has charm.

"And Liusik is vapid, dull, with his eternal 'you can't do this, can't do that,' and those icons. . . .

"Oh, how I want to live! To wake up and feel free! Independent!!!"

Liusia glanced at her watch as if to check whether she'd gone over the time limit.

"It's time to go! Maybe I'll make it for the second part!"

I found Skazka reading the same cookbook.

"I wanted to m-make you an omelette and just c-couldn't find where it's d-described how to do it. M-Mama underlined everything f-for me, but I'm so s-stupid. . . ."

The old woman-infant was clearly upset over something. She drawled more than usual, stumbling over each consonant.

She calmed down as we worked on the thread. She untangled it, and tearing off strips of newspaper ahead of time, I wound the thread around them.

"Do you l-love anybody?" asked Skazka. I dropped a finished skein.

"A m-man," said Skazka more precisely, blushing darkly all over.

The thread from the fallen skein got tangled. Noticing that I was struggling with it, Skazka carefully, as she'd done with the pastry with the real cream, took the skein from my hand and in an instant tidied the thread.

The clock in the room chimed out "L-Lord, keep M-Mama." In the ensuing silence the alarm began to ring, and the drops of rain drummed louder on the roof of Skazka's house.

Anxiety flared in the eyes of the old woman-infant. Pressing her nose against the window pane, she seemed to be on the lookout for someone outside.

"I'm in l-love," muttered Skazka.

After a silence she rose, and with the small steps of a Chinaman she minced into the other room. I could hear her singing in a thin voice, "L-Lord, keep M-Mama." She seemed to know nothing besides this phrase.

"I'm ash-shamed," she uttered, gazing at me with her infant's eyes. I sat down at the piano and asked whom she was in love with.

Skazka's plump hands slid along the faded material of her cone-shaped dress.

"With a th-thief," sighed the old woman-infant. "He l-lives here. He calls me D-Dusia.

"He's on t-tour now, in N-Nikolaev. I lined his w-wig for him, and he kissed me on the ch-cheek and s-said: 'D-Dusia, you're the best of women. And if you keep qu-quiet, I'll b-bring you p-presents.'

"He goes on t-tour wearing the wig, and he st-sticks on a beard, a really b-bushy one, b-black.

"'D-Dusia, you keep quiet and d-don't let anyone in at n-night. I'll l-love you for that.'

"P-poor M-Mama! She w-warned me: 'K-keep out of his way, he's n-no good,' but I l-lock my door to him and am in l-love with him anyway."

Clasping her hands at her sunken chest, Skazka prayed to her "M-Mama's" photograph.

"His M-Mama lives here, too. She s-sells seeds. She doesn't l-like me. 'I'll get you taken off the list of tenants,' she says, 'and I'll s-send you to an insane asylum.'

"And he d-defends me. 'Don't you t-touch her, Mother, she's a c-cripple.'

"And she says, 'This cripple w-will get it f-from me.' If it wasn't for him, she'd s-send me to the insane asylum."

I told Skazka that she had no right to send her to an insane asylum, that she was frightening her out of malice.

"She says, 'When I look at your m-mug, I k-keep tossing and t-turning all n-night.' She can't f-fall asleep," explained the old woman-infant.

"She envies you," I said, "because you're so young and nicely shaped."

Skazka got up from the chair and pulled her dress tight over her puny little body, showing how nicely shaped she was.

29

"I sh-should f-fix my h-hair somehow," she said, pulling her comb through her hair.

I tried to give Skazka something resembling a hairstyle. But her hair was unmanageable. Like a coil, it sprang out from beneath the hairpins and hung along her neck like icicles.

"Do you have a ribbon?"

"I d-do, I d-do!" Rummaging in the drawers of the sideboard, Skazka pulled out a narrow pink ribbon, the kind used for tying gifts. "It's M-Mama's."

I tied the ribbon around her head.

"P-pretty!" rejoiced Skazka, touching the ribbon. She was as happy as a first-grader decked out in snowflakes for a New Year's pageant.

We drank tea. She held her pastry with two fingers, evidently remembering the whole time that the cream could run out of it.

"Wh-what j-joy," she kept saying.

We went to bed late. I dreamed that Charlik was suffocating me; Aunt Vera was holding out some herbs to me, and right before my eyes they turned into pillow down. Grandfather called me in a strange voice; the face was Grandfather's, but the voice was someone else's.

I opened my eyes, but the voice didn't disappear. I listened intently. It wasn't one voice, but several. A velvety baritone and a treble kept interrupting each other.

"Sing, Dusia!" demanded the baritone.

"No, dance!" insisted the treble.

"'If I had mountains of gold . . . ,' " the baritone broke into song.

" ' . . . And rivers filled with wine,' " the treble picked up the next phrase.

" 'I'd give it all up for your caresses, and glances, and you alone would be mistress of all,' " they sang in chorus.

Someone turned the key in the lock. I hid behind the sideboard. Fortunately, it was Skazka.

"They're asking f-for you," muttered Skazka bashfully, handing me the panties and brassiere that I'd hung up on the radiator in the bathroom. "They won't t-touch you. . . ."

In the kitchen three men were sitting at the table. Two of them were identical, small, with receding hairlines and sharp little eyes, twins, or perhaps made up to look like each other; Skazka's beloved was an enormous husky fellow with a narrow forehead and a beard.

"*Kinder*, that's too much!" he droned into his beard. "We don't touch children. 'We're happy-go-lucky mates, we're called the Octobrates,' "[12] he sang, and poured out the remaining vodka into the glasses. "Sing, Dusia!"

"No, dance!" said the twins in unison.

"Dance and sing!" decreed the fellow with the narrow forehead. "How does your song go: 'L-Lord, keep M-Mama!' "

One of the twins twanged a guitar string, and the old woman-infant started marking time.

"Why aren't you singing?" the fellow with the narrow forehead banged on the table.

Skazka struck up, "L-Lord, keep M-Mama!", her vapid infant's eyes staring at the empty corner.

Soon they started yawning.

"Dusia I adore, I take her by the tail, and see her to the door," said the fellow with the narrow forehead, and getting up, he chucked Skazka under the chin.

"Finally!" Aunt Vera enfolded me in a warm embrace. "We didn't sleep all night. Why did I let you go?! I had a vision, you know!"

I was stupefied, and suddenly, all at once, I believed in her and her healing herbs.

After she'd heard out my story, Aunt Vera told me to get up onto the bunk where the cat lay.

"Sleep," said Aunt Vera. She covered me with a sheepskin and left.

The cat didn't take its bright yellow eyes off me. "He turns into something else at night. . . ." I covered myself completely, head included. The cat clawed at the skin. Aunt Vera's speckled golden eyes gazed at me. "What kind of devilry is this!" I said out loud, and the cat jumped aside.

I got down off the bed and sat down beside the stove.

"Can't you sleep?" asked Aunt Vera, thrusting her head through the door. Her speckled yellow eyes glittered like a cat's.

To the accompaniment of the cat's rumbling, we packed the herbs in cellophane bags. Aunt Vera recited spells, combining some roots with others and sprinkling herbs on top of them.

"We get letters every day." Aunt Vera took a little case out from under a cushion. "Read any of them."

And it was true. All the letters called Aunt Vera a healer and a savior; there wasn't a single letter that didn't contain thanks.

"The most important part will be ready tomorrow," said Aunt Vera, indicating the bottle with the brown liquid. "It'll turn black by morning. Your grandfather will feel dizzy from it at first, but then he'll get an appetite. The main thing is for him to start eating."

"And what if he doesn't?" I felt some doubt. He'd eaten nothing the last two weeks, nothing.

"He will," said Aunt Vera firmly, "You've simply got to have faith. Without faith it's impossible."

Liusia wasn't home, but Liusik was. He plied me with tea, put woolen socks on my feet, and ordered me to take some aspirin.

Puffing away at a pipe, he kept looking at his watch, from time to time taking medicines.

"I live off chemicals," he kept sighing, meticulously stuffing the cotton into the next vial.

. . . Liusik and I talked about art, and I thought about the fact that, if it came to that, they could set up a fold-out bed in the kitchen.

At midnight Liusia burst into the room in a whirlwind of yellow.

"Did you take Charlik out?" she asked, imprinting a red kiss on Liusik's bald head. "Misha was in fine form! And the bear almost bit him again!" she said, putting the leash on the peacefully dozing Charlik.

The sleepy Charlik barely dragged himself along, stopping at every tree.

"How do you like my husband?" asked Liusia, getting a light for her cigarette from a passerby. "A nincompoop!" Liusia answered for me. "Misha, now!!!"

Because of Misha I couldn't get a word in edgewise about spending the night, let alone about Aunt Vera.

"Come on, Charlik, let's see our guest to the hotel." Liusia turned to the dog, who was sleeping where he stood.

"Can I spend the night at your place?"

"Only if you sleep on the floor," said Liusia, probably hoping that such an option wouldn't appeal to me, but I agreed quickly.

Aunt Vera packed my knapsack herself. She wound rags around the precious bottle of black liquid and placed it in a bag labeled "Foreign Trade Beriozka."[13]

We had a farewell drink. Aunt Vera's freckles were lost in the glow on her cheeks.

"Your cost is my cost," she kept repeating, and Uncle Sasha echoed her.

"You're h-here?" muttered Skazka, as if asking whether I'd come. "They're not here, but they c-could come," she said, her cone-shaped body blocking the way.

I held out a five-ruble note.

"Too m-much, that's too m-much." The old woman-infant refused it, but I dropped the money in the slit of her pocket.

"How k-kind you are! I'll h-hide it. His M-Mama's there," she indicated the kitchen.

With her red dress and the pink ribbon, the old woman-infant recalled a mad angel, if there is such a thing.

"L-Lord, keep G-Grandfather," she sang in farewell.

I triumphantly carried the glass with the infusion into the room, which was permeated with the smell of medicines. From the precious bottle I poured a tablespoon of the viscous black liquid into a wineglass and held it out to Grandfather.

His eyes darkened with pain, Grandfather looked at the faceted wineglass that promised him salvation.

"Lift me up," he ordered, and I pulled him by the arms, helping him sit up.

"God," whispered Grandfather, and frowning, he took the glass from my hands. "I'll do it myself," he said and touched the herbal concoction to his lips. "Poison! It's poison!" he shrieked, and flung the glass away.

He wouldn't touch the herbs again. He was fading quickly and horribly. In moments of lucidity he would look at me with inflamed, guilty eyes:

"Such bitter stuff, Lenka, such bitter stuff; such bitter stuff cannot cure a person."

A BUSINESS TRIP HOME
ANNA MASS

Translated by

JERZY KOLODZIEJ

NO ONE WAS MEETING ME. ALL THE SAME, AS THE TRAIN slowed by the platform, like many others, I looked out the window, peered into the faces swimming by, and thought, "And what if . . . ?" But this was just a game, an echo of times long past, when from out of the sea of unfamiliar faces my mother's face, searching and excited, would unexpectedly come floating into view, and, experiencing a warm jolt in my chest, I would squeeze my way toward the exit, bumping into everyone with my knapsack.

"Mother!"

She would take a few steps toward me and always uttered the same words:

"Well, at last!"

And even though similar words were uttered by hundreds of people on this and a thousand other platforms all over the globe, these words belonged only to me and to my mother because, after all, how good it was to return *at last* to my mother and father, to become simply a daughter and to relax after many months of geological wanderings.

We would take a cab home, where Father would already be standing on the balcony. With a slight wave, he would run inside the apartment to open the door.

And then I would enter the clean apartment, which seemed unusually large after the cramped quarters of tents. In the entryway I would take off my unbelievably dirty knapsack, and throw my arms around my father, then undertake a tour of my domain. I would note little changes: a new blind in the window, an elegant new oilcloth, a new ceramic vase with a bouquet of fresh gladiolas. . . . Mother and Father would follow on my heels and lovingly examine with *my* eyes the apartment decorated especially for my arrival.

It's so wonderful when something is done especially in honor of your arrival.

In the kitchen my favorite dishes awaited me. Mother certainly knew what I liked. There were pirozhki—long ones stuffed with cabbage and round ones with apples, and roast duck and peaches. Mother and Father planned long and carefully for my arrival; possibly, they even hired someone to clean up and to wash the windows. All so that I would feel cozy and right at home. So that I would say: "How nice it is to be home!" And that very evening I would leave them and all this luxury that had taken so long to prepare, to run off to one of my girlfriends. But they understood and weren't offended.

"Tanechka, your bath is ready!" Mother would announce triumphantly, anticipating with me how I would momentarily throw off my torn tennis shoes, pants, shirt, and faded underwear—the geological hide, so alien to her, which after long months had become molded to my body—and how I would put on a housecoat and at last would turn completely into her daughter Tanechka.

Now this hide would be deposited in a formless heap in a white clothes hamper, and I would crawl into a hot bath—the apogee of my dream of returning. How often when I was out there, during an expedition or in a drenched tent, did I imagine this: the white tile, the white enamel of the tub, the bluish water gently rocking from the running flow, the white gas heater with its blue rows of flames. White and blue, cleanliness and delight.

Afterwards we would all sit at the kitchen table. I'd eat the pirozhki, cut off the most appetizing chunks of duck, stuff myself with juice-covered peaches, and talk and talk about something while my mother and father would listen, opening their eyes wide, shaking their heads, making frightened sounds, and asking questions to clarify some points. But I sensed that they were not so much interested in my adventures—after all, everything was in the past, thank God, and I was with them again—as in looking at me, scrutinizing me, reveling in the fact that I was here, by their sides. In my face and in my intonations—through the thin coating of the new— they would search for the former me, the one they were accustomed to, their own. And I'd do just the opposite as I attempted to emphasize how greatly I'd changed and how much I'd experienced. I talked nonsense and exaggerated. But even in this bragging they saw the former me. And as I chattered away and grew full, I read in their faces such openness, such pure love for me, together with my prattle and my gluttony, that the calm thought would suddenly surface through the excitement of the meeting: "This is happiness."

All that was long ago. My Seriozha will soon be twelve. Now as they see me and my husband off for yet another expedition, the old folks worry not so much for my sake as for their own: Can they hold out until we return? Will they manage with Seriozha? Do they have enough strength? And each time I leave, my heart contracts—will they be there when I return?

Recently they've no longer been meeting me as they did before. No, not like that. Mostly it's been with a feeling of relief: Thank God she's back. Take your child; we've managed to cope, and now we want a break from the responsibility. Now you're in charge.

Without any transition I would plunge into the whirlpool of neglected household chores. I would lug suits and heavy overcoats to the cleaners, wash, cook, and clean. In a word, I would dive headfirst into that world which for the majority of women represents the basis of existence.

In this world there was my son, who, of course, was foremost in my thoughts and cares. It was a pleasant shock to see him for the first time after months of separation, to be astounded at how he had grown, and to hear the altered intonations of his speech. But that's the extent of it. I make attempts to enter his world, but I am less and less able to do so with each passing year.

My husband usually arrives after I do, and his arrival means more household chores for me. With February come the financial report and preparations for a new season of field work. Then we wait impatiently for spring.

I love my work. I love the life in the field. Such a life seems more vivid, more intense, and *more real* than life in a large city with its vanity, thoughts of money, illnesses, the daily need to get something, to wait in lines, and to hurry. In the field, however strange it may sound, I feel more of a woman than in the city, where, tired and loaded down with shopping bags, I return home after work. You can't even call that fatigue, but being overwrought. In the field, now, you can feel fatigue, physical exhaustion. That's another thing altogether.

For some reason, in the city you immediately come down with a cold, or you become indisposed, or irritability sets in. Maybe that's a reaction to a change in life. I don't know. In any case, I'm in constant fear that a year or two will pass, and not only will my old folks not be able to take care of Seriozha, but I will have to stay behind to take care of them.

And now—a letter. Usually Mother wrote the letters and Father would add a few lines at the end. That's why, when I saw Father's handwriting on the envelope, I felt a sense of foreboding. My hands shook as I opened the envelope.

But no, there was no major tragedy. The tone was even quite encouraging. Anyway, my parents always spared me. They were reticent about their illnesses because they hesitated to interfere with the normal course of my life.

" . . . Mother gave us quite a scare a while back," wrote Father. "She felt so bad we simply didn't know what to do. Fortunately there was a doctor among the dacha folk, a marvelous woman, Irina Mikhailovna. She said that Mother had probably suffered a strong attack of stenocardia. She ordered her to stay in bed, brought the necessary medicines, and is giving her the shots herself. Mother feels a lot better now, though she still hasn't gotten up. And it's here that a serious problem has come up. It's the middle of August. Seriozha will have to go to school soon, so it's time to think of moving back to the city. To order the moving van, to pack things up, and so forth. I'm not certain that I can manage all this alone. However, there are kind people in the world, and I hope that everything will get taken care of. . . . As for the rest, everything is fine with us. Seriozha has grown up. He's become unsociable and very independent. In general, he's a fine boy, and Grandmother and I can fault him in nothing. . . .

"In other respects, everything's fine and dandy. . . ." Just like in the song, I thought.

It was an early, sunny morning, already stifling in a typically city way and permeated with smells of asphalt, exhaust fumes, and cigarette smoke. I walked out with the crowd toward the square by the station; a line of people with suitcases, bundles, and children stood waiting there for taxis, which for some reason had formed a long line on the other side of the square and were driving up one by one. Between the line of people and the line of taxis, an angry, excited, sweaty man was rushing about, with a red band on the arm of his tight, short jacket. Something seemed to have set him off early on. Yet, in spite of his frenzied running around, the whole business of seating the citizenry in the taxis was not proceeding any faster. The absurdities of city life were beginning, and suddenly I didn't feel like taking a taxi. I wanted to walk, not all the way home—it was a bit far—but just a stop or two, and then get on the trolley.

As far as anyone was concerned, I hadn't arrived yet. It was as if I existed outside of time and space in these minutes, and I wanted to prolong these moments, to turn off the stopwatch of my life for a little while so that I could take a closer look at myself, at today's self; to focus on myself and only then to continue living.

As I walked, I thought about my two dissimilar lives that were proceeding along parallel lines. From time to time I had to throw a little bridge across to enable me to cross over from one life to the other. In fact, at this very moment I was walking on such a bridge and it was swaying. And I had the sensation that two separate people—not doubles, but totally dissimilar individuals—really ought to merge into one.

I noticed that many women were walking around in long denim skirts. When I left to do field work at the beginning of May, there were only a few skirts like that. I thought to myself now that I would look good in such a skirt and that I would sew one for myself. This thought was a step forward on the swaying bridge, because in *that* life such a thought would simply never occur to me. There were few women there, and the concept "it suits me or doesn't suit me" didn't exist. There, only the person as such was important.

I was struck by the abundance of watermelons in latticed boxes still fastened with hanging locks. I thought, wouldn't it be nice to ship at least one such box there. What a grand occasion that would be for us. And this thought about melons *there* was like a step backward on the precarious bridge.

And so I walked, performing my balancing act outside of time and space. And in this, too, there was yet another of my lives; my very own, unlike anyone else's.

After walking about three stops, I boarded the trolley. The change in my hands felt somehow strange—for several months I hadn't held money at all—and now these two two-kopek pieces seemed a funny convention. Nevertheless, I dropped them into the cashbox and tore off a ticket. And just in time. A ticket inspector was on duty in the trolley. It was a woman, no longer young, with a tired morning face and an unkind, suspicious expression. Her suspiciousness was rewarded with success: she uncovered someone without a ticket. It's possible that he wasn't an evil-intentioned ticketless passenger, this bald citizen in a nice zippered white shirt, wearing glasses and carrying a briefcase. It's also possible that he didn't tear off a ticket from absent-mindedness, or that he lost it, but the face of the woman inspector expressed a vengeful satisfaction as she said to him loudly:

"Let's go!"

Without getting up, he started explaining something quietly; she hovered over him like a crow, tightly gripping the handrails of the neighboring seats as if afraid that he might run away. Or, possibly, she was secretly hoping that he would. Perhaps in this difficult life, which could be read in her face, these skirmishes with ticketless passengers were her only safety valve, the only way she could release the accumulated bitterness of her daily existence.

For some reason I felt sorry for this unappealing inspector, sorrier than for her victim, who was wiping his reddened bald pate with a clean handkerchief.

Without waiting to see the outcome of this duel, I got out and stopped for a moment to breathe in, to absorb the atmosphere of the street so familiar in every detail, down to the cracks in the asphalt. There is the school where I studied and where Seriozha studies now. The mailbox where in my childhood and youth I would drop letters with the sensation that I was performing some sort of magical act. It seemed incredible that my envelope, thumping just audibly against the bottom of the mailbox, would soon find itself in the hands of a distant addressee.

This spring a lawn was put down in the middle of our courtyard, and now the grass has grown in thickly. This little verdant island, in the center of a grey asphalt gulf crowded by cars, produced a pitiful and touching impression.

Maria Fiodorovna, the yardkeeper's wife, was watering the lawn with a hose.

"Greetings, Maria Fiodorovna!" I said.

She raised her head, nodded, and asked:

"Coming from the dacha?"

"Yes," I answered for some reason. Had I said that I'd just flown in from the North Pole, Kamchatka, or the Antarctic, she would have nodded with the same indifference and continued to water the grass. It's only to me now that my appearance in the courtyard seemed a miracle, a return to my native planet, while all these months, day after day, Maria Fiodorovna has been watering the lawn with a hose in just the same way, and what does it matter to her where I've come from?

"The mailwoman brought the pension letter, but none of you were home."

"Thank you, I'll stop by the post office."

I took the stairs up to the fourth floor. Several years ago they installed an elevator in our apartment house. But at the time when I was still being met there was no elevator, and there, far from home, whenever I pictured my return, I would imagine not an elevator but the stairway, with its scratched wooden handrails, and I would hear my mother's quickened breath behind me and see my father on the threshold of the wide-opened door to the apartment.

But now there was only the stairway. I opened the door with my key and walked into the entryway, which wafted to me the stuffy odor of abandoned residences.

I shrugged off my knapsack and walked to the kitchen. In the sink were two unwashed cups with dried tea leaves on the bottom. The refrigerator was turned off, its door held open by a chair. In its empty interior sat a solitary can of beef stew. No, I hadn't dreamed of a miracle, but something quavered painfully within me when I saw this misplaced can, the spot of spilt milk on the oilcloth, and an empty herbal tea box lying on the unwashed linoleum.

Then I walked into my parents' room, where Seriozha's bed also stood—unmade. Seriozha's presence, his carelessness, could be felt strongly here, and I experienced no tender emotion as I looked at the little batteries and instruments scattered in the most inappropriate places. On his desk, among plastic boats, wires, and tacks, lay a school report, also nothing for me to be proud of. I looked at the final grades: "C," "C," "C," "C," "C." . . . And as a little holiday against the background of these grey weekdays, an "A" in history.

"Passed on to the sixth grade." That's something, at least. We ought to get after him more. This "ought to," by the way, has persecuted my husband and me for many years. Empty words. The boy has been brought up by his grandmother and grandfather, who adore him and spoil him terribly.

I caught myself reflecting that I think about Seriozha not as I would about a son, but as I would about a boy in general. In my objectivity I seem to sense indifference, but it is my Seriozha, after all, who touchingly walks around ants so as not to crush them, who cries over a mouse caught in a trap, and who said about a boy who beat him up: "So what? I'm stronger than he is anyway. If I hit him, it'll hurt him." No, it's quite obvious that he doesn't possess any "pugnacious" qualities. On the contrary, he wants to live in a way that doesn't cause the weak any pain.

I opened the door to my room. Time had stopped here at the precise moment when Volodia and I left it, loaded down with knapsacks. Everything remained in the same place it had been at that moment. The bottle of Georgian wine that our friend had brought for a farewell drink. A crumpled piece of paper that had fallen short of the wastebasket and on which Volodia, as was his habit, had made a list of the little things so that we wouldn't forget to take them with us.

But I was especially struck by a little bouquet of lilies of the valley. I remembered buying it before our departure on the corner by the grocery. I vaguely recalled the appearance of the woman from whom I'd bought it, how I'd hurriedly looked for a little vase, didn't find one, and put the flowers in a simple thick glass tumbler. These were the first fresh flowers that had appeared in our apartment after the winter, and maybe that was why this simple little bouquet had seemed so beautiful. I'd inhaled its fragrance with delight.

And so it had stood in a glass all these months, and now they were no longer flowers but mummies of flowers, pitiful, dry little corpses, a symbol of arrested time. I recalled the luxurious gladiolas that used to be bought especially for my return and felt tears welling up in my eyes. I was surprised; I hadn't cried for a long time.

These tears were the final step on the bridge that joined my two lives. I'd entered city life with both feet, and I was immediately seized by a fever of activity.

Calmly now, without those nervous jumps into the past, I turned on the water. While the tub filled, I opened the can of stew, heated it, and ate it straight from the pan. I felt I had successfully plugged myself into the rhythm of a life that was defined by the expression "there isn't any time," into a life that consists of petty, fragmented responsibilities that have to be connected, each linked to the next, so that the eternal engine of household cares won't misfire.

Mother was sitting on the porch reading Dickens. She raised her head as the gate creaked, and an expression of happy incredulity lit up her face,

"Tanechka? How? Where'd you come from?"

"As you see, I've come. Greetings! Not a bad surprise, eh?"

"I mean, we didn't expect you at all! Why so early? Did Volodia come too?"

"No, no, Mom. I haven't come for good. They've let me go for ten days. The head of the expedition put it down as a business trip. Father gave me such a scare with his letter."

"Oh! Only for ten days. . . . But what a treat, anyway! And here I nearly died. . . . Kolia!" she shouted through the half-opened door. "Look who's here! I felt so bad. More than anything, I was afraid to die without seeing you again. And how could I leave your papa? . . . Kolia!" she called him again. And then she complained, "His hearing has gotten worse. He's in there putting the teakettle on. Go and see him."

"In a minute. But where's Seriozha?"

"He went to a friend's to watch television. What a boy! He's wonderful! We'll drink tea in a minute, and you'll tell us about everything. Is Volodia well?"

"Everything's fine with us."

"Well, that's the main thing."

She picked up a cane that was propped against the armchair and, leaning on it, got up heavily. She looked at me and said in a guilty tone:

"Yes, as you see, nowadays I get around with the help of a crutch. What can you do? I've been up only two days. Papa's exhausted."

"Did Seriozha help out at least a bit?"

"Seriozha is a wonderful boy!" she repeated with feeling.

It was as if she were protecting her favorite ahead of time, placing a cushion under our impending quarrels, which I hadn't even thought about yet, but which she obviously already anticipated and had nervously prepared for—and not without foundation, since someone had to be more strict with him.

. . . And here we sit in the kitchen at a table covered with an ancient oilcloth. We're drinking tea, and Father and Mother are asking me questions from both sides, making frightened sounds and opening their eyes wide. I answer something with my mouth full, tell them about something, and I can feel how glad they are that I'm with them, that they can simply look at me, reveling in the mere fact of my presence.

And at those moments I myself am happy. . . .

. . . It was already dusk when I found Seriozha on the banks of a stream. At first I recognized his bicycle, with its torn-off pedal, lying in a pile of other bikes. Then I saw a group of boys squatting around something that was not visible to me beyond their backs. In the middle of them I saw Seriozha concentrating on lighting some matches that were going out quickly. He was so preoccupied that I didn't dare call out to him. I just stood there and watched, feeling a stupid, tender smile on my face. But then he struck several matches at once; the boys crowded even closer around the object that I couldn't see, then quickly moved apart. There was a rather weak, hollow explosion, a bright red flame flashed, and a white rocket rose into the air, leaving a flaming tail behind it. It flew up quite high, then somehow plunged to the side and fell to the ground. The entire company of boys immediately rushed toward it, picked it up off the ground, and started to discuss something loudly, pushing and gesticulating.

"Seriozha!"

Carried away by the conversation, he didn't turn around right away, but some other boys glanced back, and he also looked crossly in my direction. His thoughts were so far away from me at this moment that even when he recognized me he uttered in an interrogative tone, "Mother?" and didn't fling himself toward me, as I'd imagined in my dreams, but turned back toward the boys to hurriedly finish saying something in a businesslike manner. He took the rocket from a boy's hand and only then strode toward me. He didn't dash forward, he didn't rush; he literally strode. Offended, I dropped my arms, which I'd stretched out to him.

"How did you get here?" he asked.

"Quite simply. I got on a train and came. I decided to pay all of you a visit."

"I see," he said. "And on your way here, did you meet anyone?"

"Who was I supposed to meet?"

"Well, you know. . . . I asked some people to come see the launching," he explained obscurely.

My son was not happy to see me. Not at all. My arrival had disturbed his game, and the rhythm of his life in general. It introduced nonfreedom. He had simply become unaccustomed to me.

"Well, and what are you doing here, Seriozha?" I asked the stupid question cheerfully, trying to hide my injured feelings.

He answered:

"Look at this rocket! I made it myself! Did you see how it flies?"

"You really did it yourself?"

"Well, Lioshka helped. And do you know what makes it work? The heads of matches! We stuff them into cartridges made from heart medicine capsules. Grandpa and Grandma give them to me; they've got lots of them. . . . And there you put a wick. You set it on fire and—bang!"

"You know, my dear, that's a good way to lose your eyes. Who gave you permission to take matches?"

"Don't give children matches, they'll take them themselves," he answered, smiling.

"I'm serious, that's not something to play with. Well, besides rockets, what else keeps you busy here?"

. . . My Lord, what a tone! An onlooker might think that a journalist was conducting an interview with a Pioneer from some school. Yet there, out in the field, I mentally carried on such interesting conversations with him. I told him about all sorts of things that happened and sang geologists' songs for him. . . . What is the matter with me? It's as if I were all tied up. But that's because he feels shy with me and answers my journalistic questions thoroughly and hopelessly, as if he were answering a question at school for which—he's sure ahead of time—he is bound to get an unsatisfactory grade.

"Well, . . . I do a lot of things. . . . We're getting ready to string a telephone from Liosha's dacha to ours. They're selling them in the village store. We go there on our bikes to get matches. . . . Well, and for groceries, too. . . . It costs twelve-fifty. We've already got six rubles."

"Where did you get the money?"

"We earned it ourselves. We hired out to paint some people's fence for twelve rubles. Later we divided it. Lioshka got six rubles and I got six. Except that I lost mine. . . ."

"Lost it?! Like always. . . ."

"It wasn't my fault! It was Lioshka! I had them in a coin purse in a pocket of my shorts. We went out in a boat . . . and Lioshka started rocking the boat, and my shorts fell in the water. . . . I fished them out, but the coin purse sank. . . . And so did the watch. . . . Afterwards we dove and dove. . . ."

"There you have it!" I said. "That's just like you. And I said to your grandfather, 'Don't buy him a watch, it's too early.' And of course, you've lost it! It's simply amazing how anyone could be such a muddler! But then, you only get 'Cs' in your courses. . . ."

"That's enough!" he shouted with tears in his voice. "It's started! She's back!"

. . . What in the world is this? . . .

He marched scowling beside me, walking his bike. I saw that he would like to jump on his bicycle and speed along the streets of the dacha settlement with his former freedom, now lost so unexpectedly and inopportunely.

"Do you know what I've brought you?" I asked in a conciliatory tone. "A collection of minerals. Some of our people went to Kamchatka, and I got them to give you some. There's quartz with little veins of gold."

"Really?" he said stiffly. Then, assuming my conciliatory tone, he asked with interest, "Is it real gold?"

"Of course it's real. And they also gave me two starfish for you. You remember you asked for them?"

"Are they pretty? What color?"

"White. When they dry out they turn white."

"And did you bring me bell-bottoms, by any chance?"

"What? . . . "

"Bell-bottom trousers."

"N-no. . . ."

"Will you get them?" he asked, and something unspoken flashed across his face. Maybe it was apprehension that I'd get "wound up" again or make fun of his request.

"Fine . . . but why?"

"Because all the boys have them, and I don't."

Our conversation was like a talk between diplomats representing two powers in a state of temporary truce. We spoke carefully, now and then reaching sharp corners and cautiously walking around them.

"And how's the camera?" I asked. "Is it still working?"

"Almost," he said after a pause. "The shutter got jammed. Liosha and I took it apart a little bit. . . . But we'll put it together!"

He shot me a frightened glance. What an absolute fool I am.

"What took you so long? We were getting worried."

On the table are slices of watermelon and a cake. Around it sit Mother and Father and a youngish woman with a knot of greying hair. A blood pressure monitor lies next to her on a stool. It's Irina Mikhailovna, the doctor.

"Here's our daughter!" Mother says proudly.

Irina Mikhailovna and I shake hands. What a nice smile she has. I feel a surge of gratitude toward this woman who didn't leave my old folks in dire straits.

"Your mother's pressure is almost ideal," she says to me. "See what positive emotions will do!"

"Have another piece of cake, Irina Mikhailovna!" invites Mother. "Tanechka brought it. Seriozha! Tanechka! Hurry up, sit down! Seriozha, you were dying for some watermelon. Your mother brought some!"

We eat the watermelon and launch into a conversation about the benefits of watermelon, about how harmful cake is for the elderly, about blood pressure, and about how nice the sour cream is in the local store. Although I am completely indifferent to all these subjects, I feel good because my old folks are enjoying themselves. They're beaming. The family is at the table. We're having a peaceful conversation. There's plenty of everything. We all like one another. What more do you need for happiness?

I make my bed on the veranda. Seriozha and I are sitting on the fold-up bed examining rocks.

"That's a spar!" he says. "And that's quartzite. It's even prettier than quartz."

We look at the starfish.

"How hard they are," says Seriozha. "They look like little octopuses. Look how the tentacle has bent. Do they attack people in the sea?"

"Oh, come now. They're small."

"I feel sorry for them," he says. "They were swimming around happily. . . . Is there a sea where you work?"

"No. But next year we may be going to the Okhotsk Sea."

"If only I could. . . ."

"When you grow up we'll take you with us."

"How much do I have to grow?"

"A lot."

I yawn. My eyes are gluing shut. I'm tired after spending the night on the road.

"I think I'll go to sleep, Seriozha."

"Can I stay up and read?"

"Go ahead. What are you reading?"

"*The Three Musketeers*. Have you read it?"

"Of course!"

"And which of the musketeers did you like most?" he asks.

"D'Artagnan, of course."

"Well, I liked Athos. I don't especially like D'Artagnan."

"Why? He's handsome . . . brave. . . ."

"Yes, he's brave. But just look. He fell in love with Constance, but they abducted her. Anyone else would have rushed to find her, but he didn't even look for her. He fell in love with Milady. And when he found out that she'd betrayed him, he fell in love with her servant. That's what I don't like. I couldn't behave that way. Mom! Do you know her name?"

"Whose?" I resurfaced from my sleep.

"Milady's servant's?"

"No . . . I don't remember. . . ."

"Her name's Kitty," he says with an expression as if he were intimating a secret. And he falls silent as if expecting some question.

. . . But I feel so good lying on the clean sheet under a warm camel's-hair blanket. I remember my sleeping bag and the tent, the crackling of wood in a small iron stove . . . and Volodia sitting beside it on a sawed-off stump, the reddish reflections of the fire in his bearded face. . . . I start dividing into two again, but that's because I'm falling asleep.

And that's all the time I had with him that evening. But it wasn't even an evening, only a half-hour before bedtime. I had a lot of things to take care of. After all, I was on a business trip. As I was leaving, Volodia had said, "If everything's more or less in order, try not to delay. The amount of work we have—you yourself know. . . ." Of course I knew, and that was yet another reason I hurried.

In the morning I went to town. I had to convince those in charge to speed up the shipment of two gravimeters, and I had to run a number of other errands. I also had to clean the apartment, order the van for the move, and buy Seriozha a school uniform, shoes for the fall, shirts, and underwear, as well as notebooks and other minor school supplies.

As I approached the village, I suddenly saw Seriozha. He was pushing his bicycle by the handlebars. Walking beside him was a girl. They were coming toward me, and with a purely feminine, jealous curiosity I studied the girl from afar. She was taller than Serezha and looked older. Slim and long-legged, she wore a short dark-blue skirt and a blue boys' shirt. The boys' shirt emphasized her budding femininity. Her light, almost straw-colored hair reached down to her shoulders. She was very pretty, and, to tell the truth, my poor Seriozha didn't look all that good beside her.

Suddenly he recognized me. He gave a confused, embarrassed smile, then frowned, trying to assume an unconcerned expression. But I could see that he was constrained by his shyness and that he was afraid. Yes, that wasn't shyness, but quite ordinary fear on his face. He was afraid that I'd come out with yet another tactless remark, and his fear was not without foundation. It's precisely with your own child that you most often lose your sense of tact. You always think that they're too young. Most probably you don't even think at all, but just blurt out whatever comes into your head.

I answered him with a cheerful, understanding smile. I almost winked at him.

"Hi, there! How are things at home? In order?"

"Seem to be."

"Had lunch yet?"

"Not yet."

The girl looked at me with interest and without the slightest embarrassment. I waved to them and continued walking. I badly wanted to turn around and take another look at my son walking with a girl, almost a young woman. A staggering sight! As far as I knew he'd been horribly shy with girls since the first grade.

Mother and Father were sitting on the porch. They seemed to have been sitting there like that the whole time I was rushing around in the city. They were waiting for me.

The three of us had lunch together. Seriozha hadn't shown up. At lunch I mentioned that I'd met him with a girl.

"A tall blonde?" asked my mother. "That's Katia, Irina Mikhailovna's granddaughter. A delightful creature. But she's older. She's fourteen."

Katia . . . Kitty. . . .

The last evening, when the suitcases were already packed, I asked him:

"You didn't forget the starfish?"

"I don't have them anymore," he answered, "I gave them to someone."

He was silent and added:

"Are you going to yell at me?"

"No. . . . Why should I? . . . They're yours. Whom did you give them to, if it's not a secret?"

"It's a secret," he answered.

In the morning when everything was ready for departure—the things loaded, and Mother sitting in the cab of the truck—Seriozha suddenly disappeared. That is, he'd disappeared earlier, but we became aware of it only at the last minute. I ran off to look for him, but where? I rushed angrily around the village. And suddenly I saw him.

"Are you in your right mind?" I shouted. "We're waiting for you, worrying. I'm running around like an idiot."

He wore the expression of a person struck down by grief. I said no more.

We were sitting on our things in the truck, and as it roared into a turn, two people on bicycles came alongside and passed us. A dark-haired boy in a bright-red jersey and a girl with light, almost straw-colored hair down to her shoulders. Seriozha followed them with his eyes and turned away.

The truck drove out onto the highway. We were sitting on a sofa, facing the traffic. I wanted to comfort Seriozha, but how? What did I know about him? He has his secrets, which he has no desire to share with the woman sitting next to him, this so-called mother who lives two parallel lives and knows nothing, nothing about that unique, that most important life which she herself once created and which now has become alien to her.

. . . In old age we are hurt by the ingratitude of our children. But what is it that they should be grateful for? What did we sacrifice for them? Did we deny ourselves anything as far as they were concerned? On the contrary, we constantly try to fix it so that our children don't disturb us, don't deprive us of our well-deserved rest. We chase them away or yell at them if their interests run counter to ours. Under the guise of educating them, we push them aside, and we're relieved to be rid of them for a time. So then, why should we be offended when, upon reaching adulthood, they start avoiding us? Or talk back to us in words they didn't dare use when they were little? Or pay us back in kind? We give people back what we get from them.

. . . Well, that seems to be all.

"What a treat," says Mother. "What would we do without you? How nicely you've fixed everything up. Even the gladiolas. . . ."

And here again is the platform of the train station. The little bridge rocks, one more step, then another . . . and there, on the shore, will remain an exhausted, nervous creature bearing my first and last name, while I return home. But where am I to hide from the bitterness, the shame I feel for that woman? No, for this woman. . . . I bear my shame, my helplessness, and like a heavy burden, they bend my back.

NOTHING SPECIAL
VIKTORIA TOKAREVA

Translated by

HELENA GOSCILO

MARGARITA POLUDNEVA WAS A FORTUNATE PERSON.
For example, once, in the fourth grade, Vovka Korsakov, the boy
sitting next to her, fell in love with her. Wishing to draw attention to
himself, he threw a heavy metal flatiron at her from the sixth floor. The
iron landed eleven centimeters from her foot. Fate stepped aside eleven
centimeters. At that moment Margarita was fixing a stocking that had
slipped down. She raised her head, saw Vovka at the window, and said,
"Ah—it's you . . . ," and went on her way in her two-peaked dark-blue
velvet hood. She didn't take offense at Vovka. That was the kind of character she had. If he had killed or maimed her, then there would have
been a reason to take offense. But, why take offense at something that
hadn't happened?
Margarita had emerged unhurt, beside a stack of firewood. At that
time firewood was used for heating. She grew up, finished school, and
enrolled in a shipbuilding institute, Shiply for short. And at seventeen
she became enamored of an Arab with the sumptuous name of Bedr el-
Din Maria Muhammad. Two months after their acquaintance, Maria Muhammad returned to his harem. The complicated international situation
wouldn't allow him to remain any longer in Leningrad. He had to return
to the United Arab Republic. Bedr left her the name Margo—instead of
Rita. And also a little son, Sashechka, with black eyes and light-brown
hair, which, practically speaking, was a joy. She could have been left with
nothing.
Officially Margo was considered a single mother, though it was more

correct grammatically to say unwed mother. If a woman has a child, and especially such a beautiful and precious one as Sashechka, she's definitely not single.

In addition, Bedr el-Din taught Margo to eat potatoes with vegetable oil and lemon; it was tasty and cheap. So on closer examination, Bedr proved to be quite a lot of use. More than harm. Especially since he was useful consciously. And harmful unconsciously. After all, he couldn't influence complicated international relations. Love is helpless in the face of politics. Probably because love involves only two people, whereas politics involves many.

Time passed. Sashechka grew and was already enrolled in a boarding school, and on Saturdays and Sundays Margo would bring him home. Margo worked in a design office and awaited her happiness. She didn't simply wait, vaguely hoping; she abided in a state of permanent readiness to meet her happiness and to accept it joyfully without recriminations for its tardiness. For such a long absence.

Once happiness appeared in the form of a Russianized Armenian named Gena. Friends said, "Here we go again." They said that Margo specialized in the Middle East. They thought that Gena and Bedr were one and the same. Though the only thing they had in common was their hair color.

To Gena's credit, one must say that he had no intentions of pulling the wool over Margo's eyes, and immediately, from the first day, he said that he didn't love her and didn't intend to. His heart belonged to another woman, but their relations were temporarily complicated. Gena studied at the conservatory in the woodwind department, and, to express it in musicians' language, complicated love was the dominant theme of his life. Whereas Margo played a subordinate part. His whole life was a symphonic "poem of ecstasy."

Gena was somewhat languid, not like an Armenian at all. He constantly caught colds and coughed like a trumpet. Apparently the damp Leningrad climate didn't agree with him. He said that Leningrad was built on a swamp and he could never get warm there. Margo knitted warm things for him, cooked hot soups, and took him out for walks. As they walked down the street, she led him by the hand—not he her, but she him, holding his soft, limp fingers in her hand. Sometimes they would stop and kiss. That was wonderful.

The dominant theme interwove harmoniously with the subordinate part. In music this is called polyphony.

Margo knew how to live for the moment and didn't look ahead. But Gena was prone to self-analysis. He said that only the simplest infusorial microorganisms reproduce by simple division without looking ahead. A human is a human precisely so as to plan life and direct fate himself.

And so they planned. They got together with the Starostins from the design office for their holiday. They set off for Gagra, but ended up in totally different places: Gena in the grave, and Margo in the hospital.

Margo recalled how they had driven onto a nearby road. Zinka Starostin had switched on "Maiak,"[1] and Pekhi's voice had launched into the old waltz, "Dunai, Dunai, oh, try to find whose gift is where. . . ." Starostin had glanced back and said, "The door's rattling," referring to the right rear door beside which Margo was sitting.

Gena said, "Go faster."

The speedometer leaped to a hundred and twenty kilometers; the car seemed to take off, leaving the ground, and you couldn't feel the friction of wheels at all. Margo looked at Gena, found his cool hand on the seat, squeezed his fingers, and said through tears:

"I'm happy."

That was the last thing she felt—happiness.

Then there was a gap in her memory. And then the surgeon's voice said:

"She's fortunate. She was born under a lucky star."

Margo's good fortune this time consisted of everyone else's having been smashed to death, whereas she'd been thrown out of the improperly closed door and suffered a ruptured spleen.

When a person's spleen is removed, the marrow assumes the blood-producing function, so that one can live as before without a spleen, without noticing whether it's there or not. After all, she could have had a ruptured liver, for example. Or heart. Or the door could have been closed properly.

Margo regained consciousness in the hospital when they were wheeling her into the operating room, and she didn't experience a single emotion: neither fear nor distress. Not even surprise. Apparently that's how the psyche's defense mechanism works. Had Margo been able to fully realize and experience what had happened to her, she'd have died of nerves alone. But she didn't care. Only one thing worried her—where to put her hands: to stretch them out along the seams or to let them hang down from the gurney. Margo folded her hands on her chest like a corpse who'd gone to meet her maker, and the surgeon on duty, Ivan Petrovich, covered her crossed hands with his large palm. His palm was warm, whereas her hands were cold because, on account of her internal bleeding, her blood pressure was disturbed and her end was literally near, for she was growing cold precisely from her "ends," her extremities—the hands and feet.

Ivan Petrovich walked beside Margo without taking his gaze off her, either keeping a professional eye on her or sympathizing with her as a human being—after all, she was young and pretty. No matter when death comes, it's always premature.

In the operating room Ivan Petrovich bent over Margo. From close up she saw his blue eyes and light-brown beard. His beard had been rinsed in some wonderful shampoo, and each hair shone and emitted a gentle fragrance. Through her profound indifference, Margo suddenly sensed that she wouldn't die because life was beckoning to her. She further understood that even right before death she was thinking of love.

Several hours later Margo awoke in intensive care. There were tubes sticking out of her nose and stomach. She realized that she was alive; this neither cheered nor depressed her. She didn't care one way or the other.

From time to time nurses approached and gave her injections, drugs with soporifics. That's why Margo either slept or remained in a rather dazed state. Sometimes she would open her eyes and see Ivan Petrovich above her, but even that fact left her indifferent.

Once Margo awoke during the night and heard one of the nurses telling another that the operation hadn't been successful because Ivan Petrovich had accidentally cut across some very important duct, that during the operation they'd had to summon a special unit, and for five hours they'd intricately sutured this important duct. Now no one knew how things would work out, and her relatives could sue him and he'd be put in prison if Margo died.

Margo thought about the fact that she had no relatives except Bedr el-Din. She'd been an orphan from the age of thirteen. Her friends the Starostins also weren't around. That meant that no one would complain anywhere, and she should tell him so.

Ivan Petrovich came the next morning and started checking the tubes that stuck out of Margo's stomach like flowers out of a modern vase, with every stem pinned in place. Then he placed a can of cranberry juice on the night table beside her and told her to drink two spoonfuls. He raised the spoon to her mouth and stretched his own lips, as if duplicating her movements. The way mothers feed little children.

Then Ivan Petrovich took some manganic solution and cotton wads from the nurse and started carefully washing the traces of dried blood from Margo's stomach, scrupulously avoiding the tubes. Ivan Petrovich was a surgeon, not an orderly, and this procedure wasn't part of his duties at all. But he couldn't entrust Margo into someone else's indifferent hands.

Margo smiled gently, as if to say, "It's all right, we'll make it!" He also smiled, but his smile came out as a grimace. And tears gathered in his eyes. Margo was startled: it had been such a long time since anyone had cried on her account. To be really honest, no one had ever cried on her account, except perhaps Sashechka whenever she forbade him something. Margo gazed at his face, inspired with sorrow, and suddenly she didn't regret her stomach at all. She was ready to surrender both an arm and a leg. Let him cut. If only he would sit like that beside her and cry on account of her.

Next day Margo asked the nurse for a mirror. No mirror could be found, and the nurse brought her a powder compact on the lid of which was written "Elena." Margo peered into the round mirror and saw her face in it. It wasn't pale, but bluish-white, like a blue-bleached pillowcase. And not thin, but simply shrunken to the bone. It looked good on her. A new expression had appeared—of sanctity. She also noticed that her chin and the tip of her nose were peeling. She wondered what that could mean, and recalled that the evening before the trip she and Gena had kissed. Gena had been unshaven, and his cheeks had scraped like a grater. And suddenly, for the first time in this whole period, she realized that he didn't exist. His kisses had not yet left her face, but he himself was no more. Nor were the Starostins.

For the first time, Margo burst out crying and couldn't bury her face in the pillow to hide it. She could lie only on her back. A nurse came over and said that under no circumstances was Margo allowed to cry, because getting upset was bad for her. Margo replied that she couldn't stop right away. Then the nurse dashed to the telephone and called Ivan Petrovich. He appeared literally in two minutes and ordered the nurse not to disturb Margo's crying; Margo should do whatever she wanted. And if she wanted to cry, then the nurse shouldn't forbid it, but should create all the right conditions for it.

The nurse went off in a huff because she'd been humiliated in front of a patient. And patients ranked lower in the hospital than did nurses and even orderlies. Ivan Petrovich brought a low stool from somewhere. He sat down beside Margo, his shoulders stooped. Their faces were on about the same level with each other. He took her hand in his and started breathing on her fingers as if her hand were a frozen bird and he was warming it with his breath. He seemed glad that Margo was crying. It was the first emotion she'd exhibited in all this time. It was a return to life.

He breathed on her hand, raising it close to his lips. He gazed at her with a look as though he were withdrawing a part of her suffering and absorbing it into himself. She really started feeling warmer from his breathing and better from his gaze. And she wanted to sit like that forever.

Two weeks later they pulled the tubes out of her and set up an x-ray. All the gurneys were in use for some reason. Not for some reason, but precisely because they were needed. The hospital observed its own procedures, according to which what was needed could never be found, and what wasn't, could. Ink for a fountain pen, for example. Ivan Petrovich spent half a day on operations, and half on writing up these operations. Who needed this writing? Not the doctor or the patient, in any event. Perhaps it was for the archives. Sometime, many generations later, descendants would have an idea of the state of affairs in medicine at the end of the twentieth century. So Ivan Petrovich spent half the day for the sake of descendants. Although his contemporaries needed his time much more.

There were no gurneys handy, so Ivan Petrovich carried Margo in his arms. The x-ray room was located two floors down, and Ivan Petrovich carried Margo first along the entire corridor, then down two sets of stairs below. She was afraid that he'd drop her and all her seams, both outside and in, would burst, and she held him firmly around the neck, and smelled the delicate aroma of his mustache and beard. Once she'd experienced the same feeling, or one similar to it, at a downhill skiing resort, when she was riding on the ski lift to the top of the hill. A ravine yawned below—and she dangled between heaven and earth, breathless with fear and joy.

"Don't breathe in my ear," he requested. "It tickles. I'll drop you."

"That's okay," she responded," if you drop me, you'll patch me up."

He continued to carry her, on and on, and it was the way not to the x-ray room but to eternity. In the Lord's arms.

No one had ever carried her in his arms. Only her parents when she was a child.

From that day, Margo started waiting for him. She lived from one hospital round to the next. She fell asleep with the thought that the next day she'd see him again. And she'd awaken with a sense of joy: soon the door would open, and she'd see his face and hear his voice.

Margo caught herself imitating his intonation and assuming his facial expression. She didn't see herself in the mirror, but she thought that she looked like him when she wore that expression. That was the beginning of love, when one "I" started becoming identical with another "I." When Margo's "I" didn't wish to exist independently, becoming a part of Ivan Petrovich's "I."

Each morning he would enter the ward at a half-run. Her life would enter the ward at a half-run, and fluids of joy would gush from her eyes and the crown of her head, like little fountains of water from a whale. He'd sit down on the edge of her bed, and he too would become happy because he'd entered the climatic zone of young love and because Margo was getting better and was in some sense like a creation of his.

She was happy. Her soul soared, like a bird that he'd warmed. And from the heights of her flight, difficulties and even physical pain seemed diminished.

Patients and nurses were surprised at the discrepancy between her mood and the seriousness of her condition. Her neighbor Alevtina, with the gall bladder problem, believed that prolonged anesthesia had affected her brain and now Margo "was not all there." Others thought that Margo possessed an exceptionally strong will. But Margo had neither strength nor will. She was simply happy because she loved her doctor, her Ivan Petrovich Korolkov[2] [Kingly], as she'd never loved anyone. This was, of course, betrayal as regards Gena. But she was tired of not being loved by him. Gena had acted as though his very presence were a favor. Margo had continuously entertained him and reminded herself of a nanny who dances and claps her hands in front of a capricious child to get him to eat a spoonful of gruel. But the child looks sullen and distrustfully pushes the spoon away, and the gruel trickles in a thin blob down the nanny's face.

She was fed up with self-abnegating love. Victimizing love. She needed compassionate love. Ivan Petrovich felt compassion for her. He spoon-fed her, carried her in his arms, and cried. Even if to some extent he was saving himself, he also saved her. That meant that their interests coincided. And love is just that—the coincidence of interests.

Ivan Petrovich didn't prevent Margo from loving him. She could love him as much as she wanted. And how she wanted. And he didn't prevent her—because he didn't know.

Her neighbor Alevtina fed Margo vitamins. Alevtina had visitors every day, several times a day, and the whole department could have lived off her parcels.

As a conversationalist Alevtina was a bore, because she was wholly engrossed in her illness and talked only about her gall bladder. Alevtina was absorbed with her breathing, digestion, and swallowing down the next piece of gourmet food; she would dive together with the piece into her esophagus, then would swim down to her stomach and hear how her gastric juices started their activity, and the piece would be processed and digested, tumbling like a jacket in a dry-cleaning machine. Her face would assume a fetal grimace. She loved no one in the world more than herself, and she had nothing left but to sustain and ensure her life processes.

Life in the hospital ran its habitual course. Laughter could be heard from the adjacent ward. Patients laughed, making fun of their illnesses, their helplessness, and each other. The healthy visited and cried. And the sick laughed. Because laughter was a means of surviving.

One fine overcast day, Ivan Petrovich arrived at the ward dressed up and jubilant, like a groom. From under his surgical coat peered a starched shirt and tie. He extended his arm to Margo and said:

"Please."

He was asking her to get up. But Margo was afraid of getting on her feet. In the course of her illness and her acquaintance with Alevtina, she'd had time to grow enamored of life, and more than anything she valued and trembled for her fragile existence.

"I'm scared," confessed Margo.

After the accident her feeling of insecurity and instability had increased, as if her life were an empty shell. Someone was bound to step on it and—crack!—not even a trace would remain.

"I'm scared," repeated Margo.

"But my arm?"

Margo glanced at his crooked arm, which was strong and seemed filled with extra strength. She placed her hand on it, withered like a cypress branch. And she got up.

"Are you standing?" he asked.

"I am," said Margo.

"Now walk."

She took a step. Then another. And he also took a step at her side. Then another. They walked down the ward. They went out into the corridor.

Along the corridor a little blonde nurse was wheeling a tray with medications. Beside her, helping to wheel the tray, was a black Cuban on whose dark face stood out white Band-Aid strips. The black was a patient on the floor above, in the male section, but every day he'd come down because he found the little blonde nurses's company more interesting.

The floor in the corridor was slippery and wet. Margo walked as if on ice. She tired immediately, and large beads of sweat appeared on her forehead. She thought that that was the way it would be now, and it would never be any different. She'd never be able to walk just like that, as before, without expending any effort on a movement, without thinking about every step.

Margo's robe was wound almost four times around her. She was pale, emaciated, marked by profound suffering. But Ivan Petrovich gazed on her and couldn't hide the joy spreading over his face. He gazed on her as no one had ever gazed on her, except perhaps her mother or father when she was little and they were teaching her to walk. But that was long ago, if it had ever been. She didn't remember it.

Thereafter Margo started wandering around the ward: at first bent over double, holding onto her stomach. Then just slightly bent. Then almost upright. And—an amazing phenomenon—with what avidity her young organism was restored. Margo stood at the window, looking at the street, and felt the strength surging within her like juices from the ground along a stem.

Outside it was already November, dirt mixed with snow. People were wearing dark clothes, their heads lowered gloomily. And she was utterly happy because she was alive and in love as she'd never been before, with anyone.

As soon as Margo started to improve, Ivan Petrovich lost interest in her—at first sixty percent, then ninety percent. He hurriedly examined her stitches, said that she had reached the first stage of healing and that she was a real trooper. He would press his finger against her nose as if it were an alarm button and immediately would dash off. Other postoperative patients were waiting for him.

Ivan Petrovich was considered the best surgeon in the department, and all the most difficult cases were given to him.

Margo patrolled the corridor watching for him to appear. He'd appear and, with hand raised, sketch a greeting to her, his fingers scratching the air as if to say "so long," and would walk on. Behind him, like a retinue behind a military leader, trooped the interns.

Two other surgeons worked in the department—Anastasyev and Protsenko. Anastasyev was a good specialist but a bad person. If, for instance, a patient asked him before an operation: "Is it possible not to operate?" he'd answer, "It's possible. But you'll die." When a patient's relatives started asking questions, he would ask: "Are you a doctor?" The other person would reply: "No." "So what's the point of my giving you a lecture? You won't understand anything anyway." Anastasyev had several such witty responses ready, and whenever he had the chance to put them to use, he was pleased with himself. What the relatives or the patient felt— that didn't concern him.

He was good at operating. But when patients were discharged, they almost never said "thank you" to him. And each time he was surprised: why were people so ungrateful?

Anastasyev and Korolkov didn't like each other, like two prima donnas in one theater. Anastasyev—so Margo thought—was somewhat disappointed by the fact that she'd recovered and wandered about the corridor like a shadow of her forgotten ancestors. Naturally he didn't express this in any way, but she divined his thoughts on the basis of his fleeting glance, which barely brushed her.

There was also a third surgeon in the department—Raisa Fiodorovna Protsenko. She was a very sweet woman, though it was beyond comprehension why she worked in surgery and not in the registry or the kitchen. Her patients survived purely by chance, not owing to, but in spite of, Raisa's intervention. It was said that Raisa had got her job through some high connection, and to remove her was impossible. First it was necessary to remove her high-placed benefactor. Margo dreamed of having this benefactor brought in by ambulance someday and having him fall into Raisa's hands. Then the crime and the punishment would meet at the same point, and for a while moral balance would reign in nature. But the benefactor had other doctors. He couldn't come to Raisa. The crime flapped freely, like a sail in the wind.

Soon Margo was transferred to a convalescent ward. Raisa ran this ward. She came on her rounds and examined Margo, painfully pressing down on her stomach with hard fingers, and the expression on her face was one of disgust. Then she went to the sink and washed her hands at length with some slaked lime and carbolic acid so as to wash the traces of someone else's illness from her hands. Margo stared at her back, and it struck her that a human being was an erect animal. He'd been straightened out and left to stand on his hind paws.

After Raisa left the ward, Margo suddenly saw herself through her eyes—a pallid, underpaid single mother, a semi-invalid, without parents and without even a lover. She buried her face in the pillow and started to cry. Now she had the opportunity to do so unnoticed. She pulled the blanket over herself, and no one could see that she was crying. And anyway, that was her private business. Margo no longer enjoyed the privileges of the seriously ill; she was a run-of-the-mill hospital in-patient. As a person who had lost her glory, Margo cried until nightfall. Until she realized that things wouldn't be any different. And tears would change nothing. Instead of enduring it, as the yogis teach, she had to find a way out. Margo realized that her way out was through the door. She should get discharged from the hospital and go back home. And rely only on herself. She shouldn't even rely on Sashechka, for children, as we know, are ingrates.

It was night. Raisa was on duty.

Margo approached her table and sat down on a little white stool. Raisa was writing up someone's case history. Her handwriting was remarkable, simply calligraphic. She should have worked in the passport office filling out passports. Or written out honor certificates. At least future generations won't have to agonize over bad handwriting, but will easily follow the course of operations performed by Raisa.

"Discharge me so I can go home," requested Margo.

"Got to be a bore for you, has it?" asked Raisa and glanced at the blue page of an analysis.

"Not at all. It's nice here," replied Margo evasively.

"It's very nice here," confirmed Raisa darkly. "Simply splendid. Monte Carlo. Roulette."

Apparently Raisa felt offended by someone. Even insulted. But discussing such matters with patients wasn't done.

"Don't do the laundry right away. And don't lift anything heavy. Nothing over two kilograms. Whom do you live with?"

"With my family," replied Margo.

In the corridor lay a patient, a middle-aged woman with a stomach like a dirigible. Margo glanced at her and thought that tomorrow she'd be transferred to the ward. To the spot just vacated.

The next day, Margo called her place of work to ask them to bring her some winter things. But the person who came to meet her wasn't from work; it was Zina Starostin's mother—Natalia Trofimovna, or, as Zina had called her, Natalie. Natalie was an incredibly fat old woman weighing around 150 kilos, with poignant pretensions to sophistication. She stood downstairs with a string shopping bag swollen with items and waited for Margo.

Margo descended the stairs dressed in a hospital gown, holding onto the bannister. Once she stumbled a little, but she kept her balance, and for a few seconds she couldn't bring herself to go farther.

When she saw Margo, Natalie burst into such loud sobs that everyone froze. From the floors above, the curious started leaning over the staircase.

Margo didn't know what to do or how to comfort her. It seemed as if she were guilty of having survived, though she could have died twice, on the road and during the operation. And here she was alive and standing there. Whereas there was no Zina. And yet it could have been vice versa if Zina hadn't sat beside her husband, but in Margo's place.

Silently, with a sense of guilt, Margo changed into her worn leather jacket, which she'd bought before leather jackets became fashionable. She changed into her clothes and shoes and, supporting Natalie, led her out of the hospital.

They walked through the hospital yard. The air was damp and piercingly crisp. Natalie was utterly drained by her sobbing and simply clung to Margo. Margo walked along and expected all her stitches to burst. She was allowed to handle two kilos of weight, whereas Natalie weighed 150. Over seventy times the weight allowed. But Margo didn't feel sorry for herself. Her spirit had plummeted from a great height and lay insensible. And her spirit was indifferent to what was happening with her body.

Margo was so constituted that she could think of herself only in connection with someone else. What's one person? A pitiful half, incapable of reproducing someone like herself.

On official forms, Ivan Petrovich Korolkov wrote that he was Russian, was professionally employed, and had been born in 1937. He enrolled in school early, when not quite seven; he was the youngest in his class, then the youngest in his class at the institute, and also as an intern in the hospital. So he considered himself young until he noticed that two young generations had grown up after him.

Ivan Petrovich Korolkov had a salary of 180 rubles a month. A stomach ulcer without any symptoms. A fifteen-year-old daughter, Ksenia. A fifty-five-year-old wife, Nadezhda.[3] Nadezhda was ten years his senior. Formerly, in their youth, this had been noticeable. It was also noticeable now. Korolkov was thin, frail. Nadezhda was bulky, broad, like a sofa bed placed on its side.

Nadezhda worked as the director of studies in a school for young workers. They had met in the town of Toropets[4] in the Velikie Luki province, where Ivan Korolkov had been sent on assignment. He was in charge of the hospital, she of the school. And in the evenings, when there was nowhere to go, he'd visit her. They'd drink home-brew and sing, accompanied by a guitar, and they sang so well that people would stop outside the window to listen. As a result of these singalongs Nadezhda got pregnant. They were both young, but in different ways: Nadezhda's youth was ending, Ivan's was beginning.

Nadezhda calculated the character of the new doctor, Ivan Korolkov, precisely. His character consisted of two components: conscientiousness plus inertness.

The inertness was virtually guaranteed. He would continue to come and go, drinking and singing, until his assigned term ended. Then he would leave and send New Year's cards. Or he wouldn't send them.

His term was drawing to an end. Awaiting him were Leningrad, a guaranteed profession, twenty-six years, and all of life. It never occurred to him to marry Nadezhda. However, to drop her when she was pregnant would have been awkward: the town was small, it was impossible to keep anything secret. Had Nadezhda made demands and reproached him, had she said that it was his duty, he simply would have dressed in silence and left. But she exposed her throat, like a dog in an unequal fight. And he couldn't go for the jugular.

With a vague sense of shame, he recalled how he'd tried to persuade her not to have the baby. One evening they were walking along the street. Ahead of them towered the wall of a club that the builders hadn't finished constructing.

"If you have the baby, I'll smash my head against the wall," warned Korolkov.

"Go ahead," Nadezhda gave her permission.

Korolkov gathered momentum, threw himself against the wall, and lost consciousness. When he came to, Nadezhda was sitting above him, her face long and doleful and sheeplike.

Korolkov held no grudges against her, except one: she wasn't *the* one. Yet she wanted to take *her* place. She wanted to take away from him twenty-six years and his future life.

Half a year later a little girl was born with a partial dislocation of the hip joint; they put a simple gadget called a brace on her legs. At first she couldn't get used to the brace and yelled from morning till night and from night till morning. In turns they carried her in their arms, wandering the length and breadth of their small apartment. Once the little girl fell asleep at the break of dawn. Through the dawning light he saw the emerging contours of her little face with its look of childish helplessness, her short nose, like a little sparrow's, and then at daybreak he felt a sense of conscience germinating in him, growing like flowers and water plants, and releasing its roots not only into his soul but also into his brain and his capillaries. He realized then that he wouldn't be going anywhere. That this was, indeed, his life.

Fifteen years had passed since then. During that time almost half his friends and acquaintances had got divorced and remarried. But he and Nadezhda continued to live on and on. Those who got divorced wanted to find happiness *à deux*. But a union accompanied by loneliness proved the most durable. With time Ivan Petrovich became used to, and even grew to like, his loneliness, and now he wouldn't want to exchange it for happiness. Happiness—that's an obligation, too. One has to work for it, it has to be maintained. And he had enough obligations toward his daughter and his patients. A surgeon is like an athlete. Always a routine. Always in good shape. Nadezhda created that routine and demanded nothing for herself. Life was comfortable and inert. And even her age was convenient, insofar as it didn't presuppose any surprises, any betrayal.

But Nadezhda understood more and more that, despite having figured out everything about him, she hadn't figured out the main thing: when there is no love in the foundation of a relationship, a person turns nasty. She started feeling sorry for herself, for her life, devoid of affection. She realized that she could have gotten married in the normal way and would have led a normal life. Whereas now—who needed her? A natural selection process by age. And how she wanted to be loved. How chilling it is to live and know that you're not loved.

Awaking in the morning, she felt the heaviness of her face. In the mirror she would see a new wrinkle forming a second layer beneath her eye, resembling an arrow shot into old age. Old age is fatigue. And one wants to age with dignity. Yet she had to pretend all the time.

Not feeling up to dealing on her own with things falling apart, Nadezhda would sit at the telephone and call her acquaintances.

"Rai," she would say to Raisa if the latter was home, "it's me here. I'm calling you. I'm so depressed I can't stand it."

And Raisa would reply: "And who's happy?"

It turned out that nobody was happy. And that meant that she was like everybody and could go on living.

Raisa, in her turn, complained about problems at work. Nadezhda gave Raisa support, saying that free medical treatment was the source of all evil. They sought evil not within themselves but around them, and easily found it. Neither one wanted to admit to herself or to the other that she was not in her proper niche. It was too late to set anything right. A ruined, twisted life.

But people don't write that on official forms.

Ivan Petrovich walked to work. He believed that half of life's illnesses were due to hypodynamics—lack of movement, slackness of the heart muscle.

Five years ago he'd had a car, but he sold it. After a certain incident.

Oksana[5] was nine years old then. They sent her off to camp for the summer. She became homesick and pined, ate little, and cried a lot. But there was nowhere to put her. They had to visit her often. Once Korolkov came during a weekday. The girl on duty at the gates asked: "Are you Oksana's dad?"

He was startled: "How'd you know?"

"You look alike," said the girl and rushed off to get Oksana, yelling as she ran: "Korolkov! You've got a visitor!"

Oksana appeared. She approached quite restrainedly, although she was all aglow inside. Korolkov watched her approach and saw that his daughter resembled his wife, but that didn't stop him from loving her.

"So how are you finding it here?" he asked.

"It's okay. Only not enough affection and stroking."

He took her into the wood, got some early tomatoes out of his brief-case and some first-crop apricots. He started stroking his daughter—for a week in advance so that she'd have enough stroking for the week. He kissed each of her small fingers in turn, stroked the little grey wisps of her hair. And she calmly waited until he finished, neither over- nor un-dervaluing it all. Her father's love was a habitual condition for her, like the earth under her feet and the sky above.

Then she told him the camp news: yesterday they'd had elections to the advisers' squad.

"And were you elected to anything?" asked Korolkov.

"I was. But I refused," replied Oksana with dignity.

"What were you elected as?"

"Sanitary inspector. To check feet before we go to sleep."

Korolkov privately noted that in a collective his daughter was not a leader. A common ant by heredity.

"And do you have dances?"

"Of course, I attend them," bragged Oksana.

"And do boys invite you?"

"One does. Valerik."

Some boys were running down the soccer field. They were chasing a ball.

"Is he here?" asked Korolkov, indicating the field.

"No. He's excused from phys ed."

"Some sort of invalid," noted Korolkov privately. "Also not a leader."

They went over everything. Two hours later Korolkov headed home. Evening was just setting in. The sun was no longer hot. The road was improbably beautiful. Korolkov drove, enjoying the beauty, peace, movement, and the state of equilibrium that replaced joy for him.

The road opened onto a little village. The grey log huts emitted the coziness of a healthy, simple existence. It would have been nice to get out of the car and stay there forever. Or, in any event, for the summer. On condition that a local hospital be nearby. He couldn't do without a hospital. Suddenly he noticed, moving swiftly somewhere from the depths of a vegetable garden, something resembling a small dog, yet not a dog, for dogs don't have such bluish-grey coats. Korolkov realized that in a second they'd meet at some point and that the weight of the Moskvich,[6] increased by the speed, would hit that "something" in the side. He braked sharply. The something also braked sharply and came to a halt on the side of the road. It looked at Korolkov. Korolkov discerned that it was, nevertheless, a dog, which had slept the previous night, and perhaps all past nights, on a pile of coal. That was why its coat had acquired that unnatural hue. And if it were washed, what would emerge was a white little mongrel with a clever, charming face and eyes the color of golden syrup. Korolkov registered the color of its eyes because the dog looked at him attentively and questioningly, as if trying to determine what he intended to do next. To Korolkov it seemed that the dog was making way for him, the superior force: go ahead. Whereas the dog apparently thought that Korolkov was delaying, making it possible for it to run across, since it was in such a hurry. Otherwise why would he have stopped? The dog came to that conclusion and abruptly darted onto the road. Korolkov stepped on the gas and abruptly flung the car forward. They met. Korolkov heard a dull thud. Then he felt his shuddering soul. He didn't turn around. He couldn't turn around. He drove on. But he drove differently. The world had become different. The beauty of the road had disappeared, or rather, it was as before, but it didn't penetrate Korolkov's eyes. His soul wailed like a siren, pounded inside him with its hands and feet, like a child locked in a dark room. Like a mechanical robot Korolkov continued to drive the car, changing gears and stepping on the clutch.

Suddenly in the rearview mirror he saw a policeman on a motorcycle riding behind him. With his small head, short neck, and broad frame, the policeman resembled a bag of flour. Korolkov didn't know whether the policeman was coming to get him or was simply riding along. He speeded up. The policeman also speeded up. He slowed down. The policeman also slowed down. That fact unnerved him, and his nerves refused to accept the additional burden. Korolkov stopped the car. He got out. The policeman rode up to him. He got off the motorcycle. He asked:

"Was it you who killed the dog?"

"It was," said Korolkov.

"Why?"

"What do you mean, 'Why?' " Korolkov didn't understand.

"Why'd you kill it?"

"It was an accident," said Korolkov. "Surely you can understand that?"

The policeman looked at him in silence, and it was obvious from his face that he didn't believe Korolkov.

"We didn't understand each other," explained Korolkov, feeling it necessary to justify himself. "It thought I was letting it pass, and I thought it was letting me pass."

"You thought, it thought. . . . How do you know what it thought? What did it do—tell you?"

"No." Korolkov was embarrassed. "It didn't tell me anything." They were silent.

"Well?" asked the policeman.

"What do you mean, 'Well?' "

"Why'd you kill it?"

For a second everything appeared unreal to Korolkov: the road, the dog, the policeman, the talk with its high degree of idiocy. The only thing real was the rage starting up in him.

"What do you want? I don't understand," asked Korolkov quietly, feeling the rage within himself and fearing it.

"You go back and clear it off the road," ordered the policeman. "You're around when it comes to killing. But when it comes to clearing it off, you're gone. And traffic will be coming. . . ."

"Okay," interrupted Korolkov.

He swung the car round and drove back.

The blue dog lay right where he'd left it. There was no evidence of external injury. Evidently it had died of internal injuries. Korolkov squatted above it and glanced into its eyes, the color of golden syrup. Its eyes didn't reflect fear or pain. It hadn't had the time to grasp what had happened to it and probably had continued to chase someone or escape from someone, only in another temporal dimension.

He lifted it—scruffy, trusting, and foolish—in his arms, pressed it to his shirt, and carried it across the road. Across the ditch. Into the dry birch forest. There he found a square hollow overgrown with thick grass and placed the dog on the bright-green, young June grass. He covered it over with twigs and branches. He stood a while over the grave. Then he went to the car, forcing himself not to turn around.

Before getting into the car he stood a while, leaning against the door. He felt sick. He wanted to vomit up the whole day. And all of his life.

He forced himself to get in and drive off.

Beside the police booth stood the "bag of flour." Seeing Korolkov, he whistled.

Korolkov stopped the car. He got out.

"Did you clear it off?"

"I did."

"So tell me now: why did you kill the dog?"

Carefully, almost stealthily, Korolkov took hold of the policeman's top button and tore it off with a piece of his tunic.

As if he'd just been waiting for that, the policeman actually cheered up and readily blew his whistle.

Korolkov was taken away to a pretrial cell, and the door was closed behind him.

He looked around: there was a small barred window and a bed fastened to the wall like the upper berth in a train compartment. There was nothing to sit on. Korolkov sat on the floor. He leaned his head on his knees. And he suddenly felt that right then he wouldn't want to be anywhere else. He couldn't have gone home, sat down to drink tea with his wife, and then watched TV. He wanted at least some form of punishment for himself. To place a cool palm against the burning forehead of his sick conscience.

Who was to blame for what had happened? Or was no one to blame? It was simply an accident. Chance. A defect of fate. Or was it a preordained chance, inscribed at birth?

Korolkov sold the car; for the first time he was afraid of the steering wheel. Soon he became free of the memories. He was almost free. He was, after all, a surgeon. Death was part of his profession. People die. And how they die! What is one homeless mongrel more than a hundred kilometers from the city?

Time restored the balance between him and his conscience, between his "I" and his ideal of the "I." Life continued according to his beloved and indispensable inertness. But one day when he was on duty, a young woman was brought in, with big eyes the color of golden syrup. She looked at Korolkov, and the expression in her eyes, tranquil and even dreamy, didn't correspond in any way to the seriousness of her condition.

On the basis of her extreme pallor and thready pulse, Korolkov immediately diagnosed internal bleeding and ordered that she be wheeled into the operating room.

"I should call in Anastasyev," he thought for some reason. But there was no time for that. Her diastolic blood pressure was down to twenty. It turned out to be a ruptured spleen. Just as he'd surmised. One doesn't sew up the spleen. One removes it. And technically it's one of the most straightforward operations, even entrusted to interns.

Korolkov performed the operation with concentration, almost artistically, but he didn't experience that special feeling that usually possessed him during an operation. His anxiety and his near-certainty that something would happen prevented that. And when he cut through the pancreas, he wasn't surprised. He thought: and here it is.

It meant that the road had been his preordained destiny. The dog had merely chanced to be under the feet of his fate. And now fate was winding a new coil, and that new coil was called Margarita Poludneva.

During the entire postoperative period, he didn't stir a step from her side. He was afraid of peritonitis. He ate and slept in the hospital department. No one visited her. Korolkov would go to the market himself; he'd steam minced veal and press and squeeze out juices. And when he felt that it was all behind them, that they were out of danger, he felt devastated. He'd got used to looking after her, and he didn't stop suffering on her account. His conscience plus inertness switched on. And it was a dangerous union.

Korolkov suddenly started noticing that something fascinating was taking place in the world. For example, the sky outside was cosmic, as in Baikonur,[7] where sputniks were launched. He'd never been in Baikonur, but was certain the sky there was just like that—gates to the cosmos. He could stand for long stretches and look at the sky, shaken at the insignificance and the greatness of man. Or, for example, the park in front of the hospital with the tame squirrels, shedding their coats after spring. People fed them and cats chased them at top speed—so that the squirrels flew all over the park on their chic tails with their shabby greyish-beige flanks. The cats probably thought that the squirrels were flying rats. But perhaps they didn't think anything—what difference did it make to them what they gorged themselves on?

The park had always been there. The tame squirrels had browsed in it for about ten years. And the sky, too, had existed long ago—much before Korolkov paid attention to it. Only now, however, did he notice all this.

"What's the matter with you?" Raisa asked him as she came off duty. "I think you've fallen in love."

"What makes you think that?" Korolkov became nervous.

"I understand the language," said Raisa vaguely and went off to engage in battle with the world. She felt more self-confident outside the walls of the hospital.

Love—if one were to define it chemically—is a thermonuclear reaction that necessarily ends in an explosion. An explosion into happiness. Or into unhappiness. Or into nowhere.

Korolkov had no faith in himself. What could he give her? His almost fifty years? More accurately, those that would remain after fifty? His salary of 180 rubles, or rather, what would remain from his salary? His intractable daughter, or rather, his pining after his daughter? His symptomless ulcer, which was a danger precisely because of its lack of symptoms and threatened to become perforated? What else did he have to offer the woman he loved?

But, my God, how he wanted love. He'd been waiting for it for so long. He'd been walking toward it for a long time. And he'd encountered it. And he'd recognized it. And he'd got cold feet. Perhaps he'd waited too long and had overstrained himself? Everything in life should come in its right time. Even death.

Korolkov transferred Poludneva to the recovery ward, and each day as he passed the ward he'd give himself the short command: "Move on! Move on!" And he'd move on.

Today he also said: "Move on." And he peeked in. Her bed was empty.

"Where's Poludneva?" asked Korolkov.

"She was discharged," said the patient from the next bed calmly. For her the fact that a patient had been discharged was a common and even happy event.

"When?"

"Yesterday."

Korolkov just stood there, as if waiting for something. The woman looked at him in surprise.

"Did she leave a message for me?" asked Korolkov.

"For you? No. Nothing."

Korolkov went into the interns' room, attempting to arrange all the chaos within him on the shelves. He had the sensation of having been betrayed. After all, he'd carried her in his arms out of the fire, even if he'd been the one who'd shot at her. And she'd left without even saying goodbye.

Raisa was standing in the interns' room. She hadn't yet had time to put on her cap, and her elaborate hairdo resembled a flowerbed.

"Did you discharge Poludneva?" asked Korolkov.

"Yes. She requested it," said Raisa.

Korolkov took the medical chart. He leafed through it.

"She requested it. . . . Her hemoglobin count is forty-five." He looked at Raisa with disgust.

"She'll increase it with natural vitamins."

Raisa had thick brows and restless eyes that sought advantage, like the eyes of a predator. A marten. Or a polecat. Although Korolkov had never seen a marten or a polecat.

"Her type wouldn't fall under a car," he thought. "And she wouldn't roll along with the car." Anastasyev came in. He looked at Korolkov and asked: "Are you dying your hair, Ivan?"

"What color?" asked Korolkov.

"I've no idea. Only it's got darker."

"I've got paler. My face has changed color, not my hair."

"Do you want me to remove your ulcer? Out of friendship."

"Thanks. No," replied Korolkov tonelessly.

Margarita Poludneva was lodged like a bone in his throat. He couldn't swallow her or spit her out. Suddenly he realized that he would choke if he didn't see her. He read her address on the cover page of her chart. He asked: "Who's Vavilov?"[8]

"What Vavilov?" Anastasyev didn't understand, thinking he was talking about a patient.

"Vavilov Street," explained Korolkov.

"A revolutionary, most likely," prompted Raisa.

"Or perhaps a scholar," suggested Anastasyev. "Why?"

"No reason," replied Korolkov.

Anastasyev was surprised at the discrepancy between his expression and the gist of their conversation.

Korolkov left the hospital, caught a cab, and arrived at Vavilov Street. Margo opened the door, saw him, heard a ringing in her ears, as if bells had started chiming, and fell on his chest as if on a knife.

Their souls met, and ascended, and alighted on a little cloud, hand in hand.

Margo gazed, scrutinizing his lowered face. In her whole life she'd never seen anything more beautiful than the face bent over her. A work of divine art. An original.

"All people are the same. But if gradually you pluck out everything that's the same, what finally remains is what a person is in essence. A mystery. You understand?"

She watched his lips moving.

"It's like restoration. You remove layer after layer, and finally you find that which you. . . . Does it hurt?"

"Let it!"

It hurt from the knife that pierced her solar plexus. Tears came to her eyes.

He kissed her eyes. Then her lips. And she caught the taste of her own tears.

"Where did you get this?"

"What?"

"This here. . . ." She kept touching his face like a blind woman, her fingers checking his eyebrows, cheeks, and lips. "Where did you get this?"

"This is only for you. In general I don't have this. I'm totally different with you. It's you."

They spoke in whispers about something for which there are no words. And what happened can't be defined.

"When did you start loving me?"

"I? Right away. And you?"

"Also right away."

"And what did you imagine?"

"I was afraid."

"Of what?"

"I'm old, penniless, and sick."

"So what!"

"Now it's 'So what!' But later?"

"You shouldn't look ahead. There's no need to plan anything. It's enough that he made plans. . . ."

"Who?"

"It doesn't matter who it was. . . . History has a lot of examples. Hitler. Napoleon."

"Did you love until I came along?"

"Now it seems to me that I didn't."

"I ask you . . . while we're together, don't have anyone else. . . ."

"We'll always be together. Don't be afraid of anything. A real man shouldn't run away from love. He shouldn't be afraid of being weak, sick, and penniless."

"I'm not a real one. You're mistaking me for someone else. You don't know me."

"It's you who don't know yourself. You're strong and talented. You're the best person there is. You're simply very tired because you've been living a life that's not yours. You've been unhappy."

"How did you conclude that?"

"Look at yourself in the mirror. A happy person doesn't have a face like that."

"Really?"

"It gives the impression that you've lived your whole life and are still living it through inertia. Living by habit."

"You're still young. You don't have habits. You're not drawn to them."

"I have the habit of solitude."

"Do you like it?"

"What?"

"Solitude."

"Is it really possible to like solitude?"

"I did until I met you. Now I realize that I was really a beggar."

"And I know what you were like when you were small."

"What was I like?"

"Like you are now. You're still small, a child who's turned grey from horror. And you talk, you mutter like a reader in a church choir. You were probably scolded at school."

An old-fashioned clock chimed. Ivan closed his eyes and recalled how he'd been small. How long ago his life had begun. And how much it would still stretch out.

Margo flowed around him like a river, filling in all the bends, not letting either pain or a draft get through to him.

"What are you thinking about?"

"I'm happy. My soul is so at peace. In its very depths it's so quiet. That's all a person needs. Peace in his soul and a devoted woman with a light touch."

"And wrinkles," added Margo.

"And wrinkles that you yourself have put on her face. Wrinkles from tears and laughter. When you made her happy, she laughed. When you made her unhappy, she cried. That's the way a man takes a young face that's beginning its life and draws according to his discretion."

"And what if it's been drawn on before you?"

"I'll erase everything that came before me."

"You won't throw me over?"

"No. Will you me?"

"I'm your dog. I'll follow at your heels as long as you want. And if you don't want, I'll keep my distance."

"Don't talk like that. . . ."

They intertwined their arms, bodies, and breath. And it was no longer possible to disentangle them because you couldn't tell who was where.

"Where are you off to?"

"To get cigarettes."

"I'm coming with you."

"Wait for me."

"I can't wait. I can't stand it without you."

"Do wait!"

"I can't. Honestly."

"Then count to ten. I'll be back."

He got up and left.

Margo started counting: "One . . . two . . . three . . . four . . . five. . . ."

When he returned, Margo was standing in the middle of the room looking at the door. Her nakedness emitted a soft glow because she was the brightest object in the room. He went up to her and said, "You're shining. Like a saint."

"Don't ever go away anywhere again," she requested seriously.

He gazed into her face. She seemed to him like his frozen scared daughter.

His kisses on her face woke Margo.

She opened her eyes and said in profound fear, "No!"

"What do you mean, 'no'?"

"I know what you were about to say."

"What?"

"That you have to go to work."

"That's right. How did you know? Are you telepathic?"

"Where you're concerned, yes. I'll go with you."

"Where? To the operating room?"

"I'll sit on a bench and look at the windows behind which you'll be standing."

"I'll cut somebody up. I ought to belong only to the patient. And you'll be pulling me away. Do you understand?"

Head bent, Margo quietly burst into tears.

"I can't leave you when you're crying."

"I'm crying on your account."

"On mine?" Korolkov was startled.

"I feel so sorry to leave you without me. I'm afraid something will happen to you."

"I'd like to know . . . who's the doctor and who's the patient here?"

Margo raised her palms to her ears.

"There's a ringing in my ears. . . ."

"That's anemia."

"No. Those are bells. Tolling for you and me."

"What kind of nonsense is that?"

"You won't come again. . . ."

"I will. I'll come to you for good."

"When?"

"Tomorrow."

"And today?"

"Today is Oksana's birthday. She's sixteen. She's been growing and growing and has grown up."

"She's a big girl. . . ."

"Yes, she is. But also little."

"I'm scared. . . ."

"But why? All right, come with me if you want to. . . ."

"No. You'll cut somebody up. I'll be to blame. I'll wait for you here. I'll count to a million."

"Don't count. Work on something. Find something to do."

"But I have something to do."

"What?"

"Love."

Smells and shouts drifted through the house.

Nadezhda was setting the table, exchanging abuse with Oksana, who was in the bathroom and answered from the other side of the wall. The actual words weren't audible, but Korolkov grasped the gist of the conflict. Nadezhda wanted to sit at the table with the young people, whereas that was precisely what Oksana didn't want, and she cited as examples other mothers who not only didn't sit at the table, but even left the house on such occasions. Nadezhda shouted that she'd spent a week preparing the birthday celebration and her whole life bringing up Oksana, and she wasn't about to sit in the kitchen like a servant.

Korolkov lay on the couch in his room. His heart gave him pain, or rather, he felt it like heavy cobblestones laid in his chest. He lay and thought about how he'd leave and they'd continue to trade abuse from morning till night, because Oksana didn't know how to speak with her mother, or Nadezhda with her daughter. She brought her up by belittling her. They ignited each other like a match on a box.

Korolkov knew by his own example: from him, too, it was possible to get something only by flattery. No truths. Still less belittlement. Flattery seemed to elevate his abilities, and he strove to raise himself to that new and pleasing limit.

The door opened, and Oksana entered in a new jacket in retro style, what she called a "retree." It's a great thing to advocate "retrees" at sixteen.

"Come on, Dad, tell her," Oksana complained loudly. "Why is she tearing my nerves to shreds?"

"Is that any way to speak with your mother?" Korolkov rebuffed her.

"But, Dad . . . why should she sit with us? I'll be tense the whole time. She's always blurting something out that makes everyone uncomfortable. . . ."

"What do you mean—blurting out?"

"So she won't blurt something out. She'll raise a toast to peace in the whole world. Or she'll start turning people's attention to me . . . or she'll start piling everyone's plates as though they're starving. . . ."

"You've never starved, whereas we did. . . ."

"But look when that was. Forty years ago she went hungry, and she still can't get enough now. The bread starts getting moldy and she doesn't throw it out."

"All right, that's enough, it's disgusting to listen to you," announced Korolkov. "You're talking like a complete egoist."

"Well, I'm sorry . . . but it is my birthday. I'm sixteen. Why can't things be done the way I want them on this day?"

Korolkov glanced at her clean-cut face, with its fresh, sparklingly white teeth, and thought that they'd loved her to excess as a child, and now they'd have to reap what they'd sown. He realized that his daughter needed him not when he had carried her in his arms and visited her in the Pioneer camp. Any decent fellow could have carried her and visited her. It was precisely now, at sixteen, when the foundation of her entire future life was being laid, that she needed her own father. And not in an ambulatory way, as doctors say—coming and going. But as an in-patient. Every day. Under constant observation. So as not to overlook possible complications. And complications, as he knew, were on the horizon.

The doorbell rang. Oksana disappeared in a flash together with her dissatisfaction, and in a second her voice could be heard—taut and tinkling like a stream released under pressure. Everything was fine for her. She had a celebration to look forward to, and life is like a celebration.

Korolkov imagined Margo sitting and counting. She wasn't living but was marking time. And he realized that he first had crippled her body and now her soul. He had knocked her down on the road. Even if accidentally. For it to have been on purpose would have been the last straw.

His heart gave a jerk and started aching. The pain spilled into his shoulder and beneath his shoulder blade.

Korolkov rose and went into the kitchen.

He could hear the noise coming from Oksana's room.

"Mom!" yelled Oksana. "Make us some jam water."

Nadezhda took a can of sugared plum jam out of the refrigerator. They also had strawberry jam, but Nadezhda didn't waste it on guests, keeping it for family use.

Korolkov knew from Raisa that Nadezhda had called the hospital during the night and had learned that he wasn't there. If he wasn't at the hospital and wasn't at home, that meant that he was at some third place. And it would have been natural for Nadezhda as his wife to show an interest in what that third place was. But she kept silent, as though nothing had happened.

"You're a sly one," said Korolkov.

"Give me the sugar," ordered Nadezhda and glanced at him.

He saw her eyes—grey, pluvial, without lashes. Actually, there were some lashes—sparse and short, like a worn toothbrush. It had been a long time—ten years now—since Korolkov had looked at his wife. He'd got used to her the way people get used to their own arm or leg, and he no longer looked at her with an outsider's eye. But now he really saw her. And he shuddered with hatred. And precisely because of this hatred, he realized that he wouldn't leave for any place. Had he decided to leave, he would have felt sorry of for Nadezhda and would have seen her differently.

"You're a sly one," he repeated, clutching at his heart.

"I'm old," replied Nadezhda.

"You weren't always old."

"With you, I've been an old woman since I was thirty-five."

"But you always knew what you were doing. You churned me about like meat in a meat grinder and got the product you wanted."

"Quiet," requested Nadezhda, "we've got guests. What will they think of us?"

"Why are you like that to me? What did I do to you?"

"Don't project onto me. I always did everything the way you wanted it. And I go on doing things the way you want them."

"I don't want it this way."

"Of course. You want everything at once. To permit yourself everything and not to answer for anything. Centaur!"

"Who?" Korolkov was astonished.

"Centaur—half-horse, half-man. And you're half-old man, half-child."

"Very well!" Korolkov was pleased. "I'm leaving."

"Go on!" answered Nadezhda calmly, and he was struck by how simply problems that had seemed insoluble could be resolved.

Korolkov went into the entrance hall. He dressed and left the apartment.

On the third floor he remembered that he'd forgotten his razor and stethoscope. He went back upstairs.

"I forgot my stethoscope," he explained.

"Take it," said Nadezhda.

Korolkov took his old briefcase, which had seen better days; he'd acquired it in Czechoslovakia during a tourist trip. Into it he threw his razor in its case, along with the stethoscope.

"Goodbye," he said.

Nadezhda didn't respond.

Korolkov pressed the elevator button. He went down, then remembered that he hadn't explained anything to Oksana.

He went back.

"I didn't tell Oksana anything," he explained, standing in the kitchen doorway.

"Tell her," Nadezhda gave her permission.

Korolkov glanced into Oksana's room.

The girls and boys were sitting around the table. He knew some of them—Fedotova and Max.

"You're like a Georgian, with your toasts," said Fedotova.

"I'm not 'like a Georgian,' I am a Georgian," Max corrected her.

"Georgians cherish traditions because they're a small nation," announced Oksana.

"Georgians cherish traditions because they cherish the past," replied Max. "Without a past there's no present. Even comets must have a tail."

"But tadpoles manage without a tail," Fedotova reminded him.

"And that's how we live, like tadpoles," replied Max. "As if everything began with us and will end after we're gone."

"Go on talking, go on," requested Oksana and propped her high cheekbones on her little fist.

"Talking? Saying what?" Max didn't understand.

"Anything you want. You talk very well."

Oksana noticed her father in coat and cap, standing in the doorway.

"Where are you off to?" she asked in surprise.

"Nowhere," replied Korolkov and left, heading for the kitchen.

"Sit down," said Nadezhda calmly, standing with her back to him. "Stop running back and forth."

"I don't feel well," said Korolkov, and his face became detached.

"You need to calm down. Have a drink!"

Nadezhda took a bottle of cognac out of the refrigerator. From time to time his patients would slip him these bottles. To take them was awkward. And not to take them was also awkward. It was a form of gratitude, within their powers, for a life saved.

Korolkov poured himself a glass and drank it down as if he were thirsty. He poured a second and drank the second.

He was pouring not cognac into himself, but anesthetic, so as not to feel anything, to wash away all his feelings, down to the last one. Otherwise there'd be a catastrophe, as if a patient were suddenly to awaken during an operation and to start blinking consciously. Music blared from Oksana's room. For a while through the door Korolkov saw them dancing, or rather, slowly swaying, like weeds in water. He just had time to think, for some reason, that youth is an essential condition for modern dancing. Then everything vanished.

. . . He was running along the highway—grey, smooth, and endless. It was difficult to breathe; his heart thumped in his throat, in his temples, and in the tips of his fingers. He felt he wouldn't make it.

But there was the familiar booth. In the booth was the familiar policeman, the "bag of flour." The top button of his tunic was torn off. So he hadn't sewn it on since then. He was sitting and drinking tea with a large bagel that was soft even in appearance. Korolkov knocked on the door as if he were being pursued. "The Bag" rose slowly, approached him, and slid open the bolt.

"Take me to a pretrial cell," requested Korolkov, gasping for breath.

"Why?" asked "The Bag" in surprise.

"I've committed a crime."

"What crime?" "The Bag" wiped his lips, brushing the crumbs from his face.

"I betrayed love."

"That's not a crime," "The Bag" soothed him. "There's no punishment for that nowadays."

"And formerly?"

"Depends when, formerly. Comrades' court, for example. Or a reprimand, with an entry made in your personal file."

"And earlier still?"

"Earlier still?" "The Bag" grew thoughtful. "A duel."

"But whom should I shoot it out with? I alone am to blame."

"So shoot it out with yourself."

"Give me a pistol."

"I don't have the right to. I'd have to answer for it."

Korolkov tugged at the holster and pulled it off the belt, expecting "The Bag" to blow his whistle, and to be taken away to a pretrial cell.

But "The Bag" didn't blow his whistle.

"Only not in the road," he cautioned. "Some vehicle might come along. . . ."

Korolkov went back along the highway, peering into the forest that bordered the road. He thought: "But where should I shoot—in the temple or the heart?"

He placed the pistol against his heart. He pressed the trigger. The trigger was heavy as if it were rusty and moved sluggishly. Korolkov pressed harder, squeezing the muzzle against his chest so that it wouldn't make too much noise. But there was no sound at all. He only felt a strong blow in the chest, and a spot of pain started to burn. Then the fire from this spot traveled to his throat, to his stomach, and in an instant his whole chest was filled with an unbearable burning. He wanted to break open his chest so that the air could cool his heart.

"How painful it is to die," thought Korolkov. "Poor people. . . ."

Three years passed.

Korolkov recovered after his heart attack and as before walked to work and back.

While he lay in the hospital, they discovered that he had never had an ulcer at all. The pain from his heart had been radiating into his stomach.

Korolkov got the job of department head. His administrative duties increased, taking him away from operations. On the other hand, he started getting twenty-five rubles more.

Life flowed on as before. His essential and beloved inertness returned. He didn't think consciously about Margo. He was afraid that if he started thinking, his heart would split along the former seam.

Korolkov had known from his experience with his patients, and now knew on the basis of his own case, that a man wants happiness when his heart is healthy. But when it's like a slow-acting mine with a timer and can explode any second, when his life is in danger, then he wants to live, and nothing more. Just to live and perform operations, both scheduled and emergency ones.

As formerly, squirrels raced among the trees, and as before, cats chased them. But to Korolkov it seemed that in three years everything had changed. The squirrels had shed and aged, as if gnawed by time. The cats had grown more melancholy, and he had the impression that the cats and squirrels had also had a heart attack.

Oksana married, divorced, and was planning to marry again. When Korolkov asked, "Is it serious?" she replied, "At the moment it's forever."

No changes occurred in Margo's life.

Korolkov had said, "Wait." And she waited. At first, each minute. Then, each hour. Now, each day.

When the phone rang at work, she would turn her head and look at the instrument seriously, intently. Her friends laughed at her, and she laughed at herself along with them. But in her heart of hearts she waited. After all, a person can't leave—just like that. And forever. If one believes in such a thing, then to live is impossible.

So that the wait would not be so monotonous, Margo took Sashechka out of the boarding school and arranged for him to take swimming and figure-skating lessons. She loaded his childhood to its limits because childhood is a very important time of life, and one shouldn't rush by it, like an express train past a small station.

In the winter it gets dark early. When Margo returned from work with bags and carryalls, it was already dark.

She and Sasheckha would sit down in the kitchen; and Margo would feed him, and she'd experience pride every time he swallowed, pride that the essential vitamins were going into the precious growing organism.

But Sashechka knew nothing of pride; he simply chewed, and his ears moved and his Adam's apple moved up when he swallowed. Sometimes a totally unfamiliar person would show through in him, and Margo with happy bewilderment would examine the Russian boy with light-brown hair and a Pharaoh's manners. But at other times he was the spitting image of her in her childhood photographs, and then Margo felt as if she were sitting at the table with her own childhood.

Once at a subway crossing, she met Vovka Korsakov, the one who had thrown the iron at her.

"Ah . . . is it you?" Margo felt joy well up in her, and her face lit up with joy at meeting him.

Vovka said nothing and stood there, his face expressionless.

"Don't you recognize me?" asked Margo.

"Why? I recognize you," answered Vovka calmly. "You haven't changed at all."

In fact, there was something in her that did not succumb to time: trust in the world and its individual representatives. Although the representatives left her for various reasons, the trust remained. And it made her resemble her earlier self—the one beside the stack of firewood in a velvet two-peaked hood of the kind worn by jesters in Shakespeare's time.

"Well," Margo didn't believe him, "twenty years have passed. In twenty years even the climate changes."

"Perhaps the climate changes," agreed Vovka. "But you haven't changed a bit. You've only aged. . . ."

LOVE

LIUDMILA UVAROVA

Translated by

REGINA SNYDER

AS THEY HAD AGREED, FILIPPOV CAME TO MARIA Alekseevna's hotel about three hours before her departure.

"I was so worried," she said. "I called the desk a few times to check on the time."

"Can you ever *not* worry?" he replied.

Without asking, he took her valise and opened it.

"Just as I thought, everything dumped in, any old way."

"I do my best. Don't criticize," she said sharply.

"All right, Masha, no need to get defensive," he replied without malice.

He took all her things out of the valise: notebook, underwear, dresses, the rubber-soled shoes which, as it turned out, she had never worn once. He wrapped the shoes in newspaper and thrust them into the corner of the valise. He laid her underwear and dresses on top.

"I'll put the notebook here, in this pocket, see?"

Without answering, she looked into his tired eyes, surrounded by creases. She said, more in surprise than annoyance:

"I can't get you out of my head."

"Same here," he sighed.

"Shall we have tea?"

"Sure."

"Then take out the kettle. It's somewhere in the valise."

"Not somewhere. At the bottom. I put it there myself."

"And the glasses are on the table."

"I see them."

"Do you like the word 'have tea'?"

"It's two words."

"Okay, two words. Don't you find something comforting in them, something soft and cozy, like a cat's purr?"

"I love you," he said.

As if wanting to cool its burning heat, he plunged his face into her palms.

"What can we do, Masha?"

"You figure it out."

"I can't, no matter how hard I try."

"I can't either," she said sadly.

A single star seemed to move along with the train, as if it had made a bargain to stay with it until the end of the journey. The train sliced through the night, trying to escape the darkness, to hide from it. But the darkness was stronger and won out, in spite of everything.

Suddenly something bright and fiery twinkled in the dense blackness—a campfire in a field. For a moment the flying sparks illuminated the faces of the people sitting around it and the huge trees, hinted at in the shadows—then darkness again. It was a long time till dawn, an eternity. . . .

Maria Alekseevna imagined how unpleasant and cold it would be in the field now—and in the forest, even more frightful. The trees would aim their branches at you, like spears, and behind any one of them a malevolent stranger might be hiding. . . .

Closer to home with every kilometer, every curve of the track. Before, not at all long ago, it seemed, she had loved coming home from these trips. On the plane or train she would imagine how she would arrive and go directly to her nice clean white-tiled bathroom, right under the shower, with the warm jets of water hitting her from all sides. Then she would lie on her crackling, pleasantly crisp sheets in her own bed.

Fiodor usually met her. In the taxi on the way home, he would tell her about what had gone on in her absence. At home were their common interests—mainly, Nastia and everything connected with her: her work, her marriage, which, it had to be admitted, was none too happy.

It would seem that everything had been settled and defined long ago, with life going along a path as smooth and familiar as her own palm, always knowing what the future holds. . . .

Not quite.

She suddenly imagined Filippov, his tired eyes, the cleft chin, the soft dark hair, already thinning at the temples. . . .

She hopped down from the berth, opened the compartment, and went into the corridor. The lamps burned with a daylight brightness. Below, beneath the slightly quaking floor, the wheels clacked faintly: "We're going, going, don't know where. . . . "

Filippov had said that if you listen, everything on earth has its voice; you just have to know how to listen. He had spoken with conviction, without a trace of a smile, seriously believing his own words.

"And does a table speak?" she had asked.

"Of course."

"What is it saying?"

"Just a minute, I'll listen."

Filippov's face became attentive; he indeed seemed to be listening to a voice that only he could hear.

"My legs are giving out; it hurts to stand. If only someone would take pity on me."

"What a funny one you are."

"That's the way I am," he replied. "There's no help for it, Masha, just get used to it."

She almost asked, "Why should I get used to it, since we will soon part and won't be seeing each other again?" But she didn't.

This was the first time for her. As many such trips as she had been obliged to make, such a thing had never happened before. She had always wanted to get home as quickly as possible. And this time she thought fearfully, "Am I really going back to Moscow?"

She had come to this little village on a quiet Russian river—a village named Iziumsk[1] (such a funny name, like something from a fairy tale for the very young)—because of a letter.

A teacher at a school for workers' children had written to the editor of the paper that the principal was walking all over her and systematically trying to drive her out. She didn't spare her criticism of him. The letter concluded with: "If you don't remove this insufferable tyrant, you will have only yourselves to blame!"

Maria Alekseevna reread the letter. For some reason she felt an immediate dislike for this teacher. No matter how she tried, she couldn't rid herself of distaste for this woman who was, in fact, a complete stranger.

Remarkable! Her instinct had not failed her; the teacher roused in her a rare degree of antipathy. She was pretty enough, or rather, had a cute appearance; wide, astonished blue eyes, a doll-like rosiness, tiny, squirrel-like teeth in tender pink gums. She was wearing a sheer pink blouse; the hue of it shone on her faintly scarlet cheeks, and she seemed pink through and through, with her bright ringlets at the temples, her small forehead, and her round neck with the tiny hollow at the center.

"I'm so happy that you came!" she exclaimed, putting her palms together. Maria Alekseevna noticed her short fingers with chewed nails lacquered a dark plum shade. Ugly fingers.

"If you only knew how I've waited for you! You in particular!"

"Why me in particular?" Maria Alekseevna asked, surprised.

"I just love your columns in the paper."

"They don't appear that often."

"But I just love them," said the teacher. Her name was Valeria Valentinovna.

"How cute! I can't stand it," thought Maria Alekseevna, and immediately scolded herself mentally for going so far as to find her name annoying. . . .

"But please, just call me Valia," said Valeria Valentinovna, and added with a naive directness which she didn't even try to conceal, "You may, since you're so much older than I am. . . . "

"Of course," agreed Maria Alekseevna. "Now tell me everything in detail, as it happened. . . . "

Oh, how many nasty, insulting terms fell upon the head of the school's principal! Of what sins was he not guilty!

Tiny bubbles simmered on Valia's dainty pink lips as she rushed to get out everything she could, interrupting herself in agitation.

Finally played out, she said in a tired voice:

"Now you finally understand. . . . "

That evening Maria Alekseevna met the principal of the school.

No longer young, a little under fifty, thin, with slightly hunched shoulders. She was struck by the tiredness of his eyes. As if he had taken some burden upon himself, but didn't want anyone to feel sorry for him, since he felt sorry for no one—but his eyes betrayed him.

He asked: "I suppose you were summoned, as they say, by a letter?"

"You're not mistaken."

He took a twenty-kopek coin out of his pocket and deftly tossed it in the air and caught it. Like a boy, Maria thought disapprovingly. It looks as if he's picked up a lot from his charges. She couldn't immediately decide whether she liked him or not. There wasn't the kind of animosity she had felt toward Valia sight unseen. But she didn't notice a particular inclination toward him either. Her relationship to him could be characterized, if you like, in two words: "benign expectation." This was how she related to people at first encounters.

Like many who are kindly by nature, she was prepared to classify each by his best characteristics. That made it all the more painful after disillusionment. She would berate herself mercilessly for blindness, for not being discriminating, but then, once again, the same delusion and self-deceit. . . .

However, with the years she had become not colder, less trusting, but more watchful and a bit restrained. Sometimes she would stop herself: "Calm down, don't fall for this person, don't jump to conclusions!"

And now, looking into his tired eyes (in her mind instructing herself: "Don't feel sorry, be as objective as possible"), she was conscious that her thoughts seemed to flow in two channels. First and foremost, she tried to get at the truth, at what was fair; and beneath that, she thought, "Why does he have such tired eyes? Has he suffered so much, lived through so much?"

She caught herself wishing that all of rosy Valia's accusations would turn out to be exaggerations. Why did she wish that? Perhaps, even though it was unprofessional, she felt sorry for him?

And sure enough, her unexpressed wish came true. Valia turned out to be the commonest sort of disparaging backbiter. Her entire fabrication burst like a soap bubble almost as soon as Maria Alekseevna began to look into it by meeting and talking to the other teachers and colleagues.

All of them praised Filippov in a friendly way; his fairness, his innate tact, gentleness, and responsiveness.

"So it seems that Valeria Valentinovna has spread it on a bit thick?" she asked cautiously.

"Thick, indeed!" The mathematics teacher was indignant. He was a skinny grumbler and probably the most groaning bore you could find. "She's just an out-and-out troublemaker."

"And disgusting!" added the German teacher, a wolf-eyed blonde who looked like a Valkyrie. "She wanted to get Avenir Grigoryevich fired with your help and replace him with her sister's husband."

So the explanation, it seemed, was quite simple. Maria Alekseevna was even a bit offended. How uncomplicated and primitive! Was it worth coming all the way from Moscow to straighten out such an ordinary situation, the kind that occurs, unfortunately, all too often . . . ?

Yes, it was. The pink villainess got her punishment; the other teachers applied to the district office for her to be transferred out of the school. Anywhere, as long as she was not with them, as long as they didn't have to see her anymore!

And then the rest happened. Unexpectedly.

That very evening she spoke to him.

"I'm very happy for you, Avenir Grigoryevich."

"Well, I knew that you'd straighten it all out."

She smiled.

"How?"

"I don't know. . . . I just knew."

"You surprised me a bit."

"Why, how?" he asked.

"You were so detached through the whole affair. I must say that your colleagues were more worked up than you."

"Well, I'm that way by nature."

"How?"

"I don't suffer much when they beat me, and, well, I don't rejoice when—" he faltered, seeking the right word.

"—when they don't beat you?" she said quietly.

He burst out laughing.

"Exactly!"

He bent his head. She saw the narrow nape, his delicate, somehow vulnerable neck. For some reason she was struck with a singular pain at the sight of that neck, rising from a too-wide shirt collar. It was hard for her to keep from touching his head, his neck, his hands. He lifted his face, looked at her, and understood everything. By his eyes she saw that he understood everything, just as it was. . . .

Sometimes he would ask her:

"Why?"

"Do you think I know?"

"It would be better if I had never met you," he admitted once.

She was not offended; on the contrary, she agreed.

"I think so too."

She loved to tease him by imitating his manner of speaking, of waving his hands when pronouncing certain words, of opening his mouth when he was particularly interested in something he was hearing.

"For some reason, I always call you by your last name—Filippov."

"Even when you're talking to me in your mind?"

"Just how do you know that I talk to you in my mind?"

"Because I always talk to you, no matter where I am or what I'm doing. . . . "

Both tried with all their might to be absolutely open with one another, as if afraid to hide the least insignificant incident of their former lives.

He had two children. They were in the ninth grade, a son and a daughter. He called them "little walnuts."

"Why little walnuts?"

"If you could just see how funny, round-faced, and brown they are, well, just like little walnuts. . . . "

"Do they get along?"

"Not very well. Sometimes they even fight. And, by the way, Lialia is stronger than Leshko."

"Oh, he just gives in to her, out of chivalry."

"Oh, no, he'd never give way; the fact is, Lialia is stronger than he is."

"And I have a daughter, Nastia. All grown up. She got married the year before last."

"All grown up," he said.

A little slowly, not at once, she said:

"I'm older than you."

"Nonsense—by two years."

"It's not just nonsense."

"Nonsense. And if you were ten years older? Would that change anything?"

"I guess not."

Not once, not by even a single word, did they mention her husband or his wife. As if they didn't exist.

But just before her departure, while they sat together in the uncomfortable hotel room, he asked:

"Are you going to say anything or just keep quiet?"

"I don't know. You?"

"I'll probably tell her. I won't be able to hold it in."

"And then what?"

"If only I knew."

He took her hand and ran it over his eyes, and she felt their inflamed dryness on her skin.

"Do you feel sorry for her?"

"Who? Lena?"

He had just said his wife's name for the first time.

"It's awful. It's not her fault in any way."

"I wish Fiodor were guilty, too. Of something, anything. Even the most stupid little thing."

Later she asked, "What's going to happen to us all?"

"If only I knew," he repeated. "It's bad to be so spineless, isn't it?"

"Morally flabby." She picked up on it.

"Right. Indecisive."

"Weak-willed."

"Yes, yes. Weak-willed, and—"

"Enough," she said. From her handbag she took a snapshot of herself taken at a dacha with some friends. She wrote on the back: "To the most spineless, morally flabby, indecisive, weak-willed, and beloved person forever."

The train arrived at Moscow in the morning. There was a fine, already typically autumn drizzle. The trees outside the windows of the railway car were being tortured by the wind. The man sitting next to Maria Alekseevna, a sanguine, talkative, unusually self-satisfied fellow with a long mustache, announced loudly: "Arriving in the rain is a lucky sign."

"A lucky sign for what?" asked the little old lady sitting opposite Maria Alekseevna.

"For what?" The man with the mustache began to laugh, although there was decidedly nothing amusing about either the old lady or her modest question.

"For something good, for happiness, for example. For the fulfillment of all your wishes."

He directed his dark, slightly swollen eyes at her, raising his eyebrows, and from beneath his whiskers his even teeth shone with an unexpected whiteness. At that moment Maria Alekseevna saw him as he probably had been twenty or twenty-five years ago, dashing, bright-eyed, charming in his own way. . . .

"A very good sign!" she thought. "What could be better? What next? How will it all be?" Her thoughts were abrupt, chaotic.

The train kept getting closer. The rain-washed platform had already appeared, and she could glimpse the people waiting, Fiodor in the very front. He saw her face in the window, waved, shouted something, ran along after the car. In his hand she saw a little bouquet of wilting asters from the city. He hopped up on the step of the car and rushed into her compartment. She practically tore the withering bouquet out of his hands, with loud and exaggerated delight, just so their eyes wouldn't meet.

But he was unaware of anything, and just looked at her with shining eyes, openly pleased:

"You like the flowers? That's great! I wasn't too sure—they're kind of dead-looking."

"Oh, come on, they're lovely."

Her own voice seemed false and unnaturally lively to her, and she thought that Fiodor would notice.

But he just enjoyed looking at her, simply happy that she was back and that they were together again, and that the flowers had pleased her. In the taxi he told her everything that had happened since she left. However, there was almost no news, except that Auntie Agasha had had quite a scene with her daughter-in-law and had left for her daughter's in Rostov. The Kareevs' dog had recovered from distemper, and the Nikonovs were redecorating.

"How is Nastia?" asked Maria Alekseevna. "You haven't said anything about her at all."

"The same," answered Fiodor. "She threatened to come by this evening."

"I hope we can manage to get dinner ready."

"I've made dinner already. You didn't think I'd forget the most important thing, did you?"

"And what's the most important thing?"

"For example, steak with fried potatoes. If I'm not mistaken, you like steak and fried potatoes. And so does Nastia."

"No, you're not mistaken."

"Well, and how was the trip? How did it all work out?"

"Generally, fine," answered Maria Alekseevna, and once again she noticed with surprise how ordinary and unassuming her voice sounded.

"And I actually missed you, imagine," said Fiodor. His face was sun-tanned, and his eyes in that dusky face looked a particularly bright, un-clouded blue.

"I probably look older," she thought. "We women age faster than men."

She thought of Filippov. Once again she saw his eyes, his untidily cut dark hair, his frail neck. And how he had stood beneath the window of the railway car. She had looked down at him, and he had frowned and looked away. And she knew he was afraid to look at her, afraid he wouldn't restrain himself, would do something shocking—jump into the car with her, go with her, or else drag her back, or burst into tears, not paying any mind to who was watching. . . .

Fiodor said something or other, the fragments of his words reaching her as if from a long way off, breaking through a thick curtain—about the bonus he hadn't received, the unpaid telephone bill, or the weather changing almost every day. . . .

Suddenly he broke off.

"Marusia, what's the matter?"

"Nothing," she replied. She thought: Filippov called me Masha, and I called him by his last name. I liked that so much better. . . .

"No, really, what's wrong?"

She tried to smile, wave it aside—nothing at all, I'm just fine, you're just imagining, but everything's fine—and suddenly, against her will, tears gushed from her eyes.

At first she was frightened. Then she tried to turn it into a joke.

"How do you like that? What stupid nonsense!"

She even attempted to smile.

"I must be crazy. What else?"

But he looked around, frowning, biting his lip, and suddenly it dawned on her—he knew everything.

Amazing! Just as she remembered Filippov knowing everything, so now Fiodor understood at once. Why? How transparent she must be. . . .

But at the same time it was suddenly easier. No need to explain, no need to pretend. . . .

Everything became clear, and in the depth of her soul she needed this clarity, so that there shouldn't be a single bit of falsehood, not a drop of deceit, since what they had, she and Filippov, was real, without counterfeit, without pretense. . . .

At this thought she sobbed even harder, almost hysterically, burying her face in her hands. The startled taxi driver looked back at her a few times, shrugging his shoulders and staring reproachfully at Fiodor.

And Fiodor, still silent, looked at her without moving, his face turning stonier with each passing minute. . . .

THE WALL

GALINA SHCHERBAKOVA

Translated by

HELENA GOSCILO

THIS EVENING IS LIKE ANY OTHER. YESTERDAY'S and tomorrow's, too. . . . Two gas burners are hissing. There's a teakettle on one, a coffeepot on the other. For a long time now she's wanted one of those special containers that are narrower at the top—what's that funny name they have?—but hasn't come across one. On the other hand, what's wrong with the pot? That's all nonsense, whim. As if it makes any difference what you use to boil a glass of water.

Iraida Aleksandrovna and Viacheslav Matveevich wait beside the stove. It's funny for two people to be standing together at one gas range, but who sees them? They turn on the gas synchronically, synchronically carry everything over to the table, and fill their cups synchronically. With a crackle two newspapers are opened at 180 degrees—V. M. has *Soviet Sport*, and I. A., *Moscow Tonight*. This evening is like any other.

When two people are silent, things start to communicate around them (or instead of them?). Perhaps it's some law of the preservation of contacts. The sugar bowl, for example, clearly has kind feelings for Viacheslav Matveevich. It pushes out lumps of sugar onto his spoon, whereas Iraida Aleksandrovna puts her fingers inside it, for she can't catch a single piece with her spoon. The vindictive bowl squeezes her fat, clumsy fingers as they grope futilely inside the thick glass. Ugh, how ridiculous! Can't she finally drink her coffee in peace in this cursed house?

The chairs creak, and the ventilation window lets in a draft. . . . The meter ticks away . . . a tap drips. . . . The lightbulb starts to crackle for some reason, and a polyethylene package has begun to smell offensive and nasty.

Their newspapers—as nowhere else—are on the front line of battle. They serve as both ambush and barricade, a cover for unexpected attacks and a means of defense. The defeat of our hockey players in Prague can be a splendid catalyst for anger. It wells up in V. M. in a hot, youthful rush, and passing through two newspapers—bang! it hits its target: "Hide your pantaloons. . . . Call yourself a woman."

Her knees jerked and drew together. The coffee grew bitter. Ah, she'd forgotten to stir the sugar. She forgets everything, simply everything! . . . The doctors say it's a natural process; though, of course, if you follow a regimen. . . . If you take care of your nerves. . . . Just try to take care of them. Even at home you can't walk about as you like. What does she think about most once lunch is over, until six o'clock? About coming home and taking off her damned French corset—what the hell. And about putting on her old woolen robe with holes at the elbows, spreading her legs freely, as her mother used to do, on the bottom step of the high wooden porch. She used to let her hands drop into her low-hanging flowered skirt, and no one ever said anything to her. No one dared. She would sit if she wanted to, and as much as she wanted.

And *he* knows how difficult it is for her to spend all day in these accoutrements, with her stomach pressed against her spine. . . . She has no choice. She's the boss. She has thirty-seven people working under her, and most of them are men. He knows that very well, and every time it's the same thing; he latches onto something domestic.

Her eyes scanned the column of obituaries.

"Petrenko died." She broke through the two papers. "He was how many years younger than you?"

V. M. grinned. For two minutes now he'd been expecting her to tell him the news about Petrenko's death. Today the guys from the ministry had called to ask whether he'd "go in on the wreath." He'd sent a fiver with the messenger, in an envelope with "Happy holidays!" written on it. Petrenko was two months younger than he.

Today, while moistening the envelope, he'd thought: that means theoretically that two months ago I, too, could have . . . ? That thought later occurred to him so many times in the course of the day that it finally stopped being frightening. Why, right now it was even sweet to think about death. Everything would be over. . . . There'd be peace. *She* wouldn't exist.

Now she'd have to go back on her word, because—no matter what you said—she was afraid that he'd die before she did. She's afraid of staying alone in their apartment at night. The *wall* frightens her. When he's away on business, she calls her former colleague to spend the night with her.

This is the woman she pushed into retirement the moment she reached fifty-five, but the fool comes over anyway, so as to enjoy having something to eat for free. . . . Sturgeon, caviar, real sausages, and instant coffee with "Evening Bell" candies.

You can't fix suppers like that on an ordinary pension. His business trips are a boon for the old glutton. She should pray to the wall that her former boss is frightened of.

"I bought some lamprey eel. It's in the refrigerator."

V. M. titters inwardly. Oh, how well he knows her. She's sucking up to him now!

"We've got fresh cottage cheese. Should I make some cheese blintzes?" *Soviet Sport* quivers in his hands. That's the only response.

I. A. sighs, then pensively pours the coffee from her cup back into the coffeepot.

"Cheapskate!" sounds gaily from behind *Soviet Sport*. "Are you saving the dregs again?"

I. A. looks at him, offended.

"What's it to you? I save them, and I'm the one who drinks them."

But V. M. has already clammed up. He's already said everything he intends to, and she won't get another word out of him. I. A. washes out her cup, places it in the dishrack, and goes off to the bathroom. V. M. listens closely to what she's doing as she turns on the water and clatters in the washbasin. She's locked the door.

He gets up and takes a half-pint from a drawer under the color TV in the corner. He drinks greedily, with pleasure, right from the bottle. Before, he used to do this openly, putting it on the table. And still earlier he used to offer her some. "Want some?" Her thin plucked eyebrows would jump all the way to her hair. "What??!" That would really set her off. . . .

Once, when they'd launched into an argument, he'd unexpectedly looked in the mirror. They both looked so dreadful that he was shocked into complete silence for about ten days. She brought home a doctor friend in the guise of a colleague. He had to speak to get her to leave him alone and stop dragging in outsiders.

But at that time he was really silent, *with his whole being!* Since then he drinks on his own. When he's alone, by himself.

I. A. washes her panties and bra, thinking: "He's drinking now. I saw the bottle in the drawer." She shakes off the soapsuds, bends down, and pulls out the same kind of bottle from under the bathtub. "Everywhere. . . . All you need to do is stretch out your hand. . . . " She wants to pour it down the sink, then gives a dismissive wave of the hand. "To hell with him." She puts the bottle back in place.

Had she known earlier, had she known. . . . Had she known what?

When they lived in a communal apartment, everything was fine.[1] He didn't start until they were in their private apartment.

They say it should be the other way round. Yet for them, the better things are, the worse they get. But nobody knows that, not a single soul! She hates women who moan and complain. Nothing and nobody will force her to speak badly of him. But does he know what that costs her? How badly she wants to yell sometimes! But she can't. She can't allow herself that luxury.

Let everybody think that everything between them is as it was at the beginning. After all, they started well. No one could deny that. They enjoyed perfect understanding. Whoever came home first did the cooking. And they did the laundry together—she'd do the scrubbing, and he'd wring it out. People used to say to her: "That's some husband you've got!" What happened to all that? Surely something good can't turn into something bad just like that? You need to work at it for that to happen! And he'd certainly had a hand in it!

After they moved to the private apartment, he suddenly didn't need anything. He greeted everything she brought home with such sarcasm that you'd think she was robbing orphans. Then he used everything in the nicest way possible. But at the beginning it was always like that! "Junk collector!" He loved this theme of "I don't need anything." He'd have new suits made for himself as if he were doing someone a favor. That was when she decided to shift his attention to the animal world, and bought a dog. He and the dog came to love each other so much that later she gave it away for nothing, glad that someone would take it. "Oh, you!" he'd said to her then. What did he mean, oh, she!

V. M. stands beside the refrigerator, eating the lamprey eel with his fingers. His face is tranquil.

"I drink," he recites his usual interior monologue. "Yes, I drink! And whose business is it? It's after work, and I've paid for it. I'm not doing it in some doorway, but at home."

His habitual monologue, which usually convinced him how right he was, came to a halt. Once again he recalled Petrenko. He'd been such a thoroughly upright colleague. He didn't drink, didn't smoke, never cuddled up with anyone's secretary. He wondered whether the guys would notice his envelope. But what did he care if they appreciated it? . . . He wasn't their subordinate.

What did he care whether someone liked his envelope, his joke? Now it began to seem to him that, in fact, it hadn't been mere chance—there simply hadn't been another envelope handy—but rather, a really daring piece of inspiration. Like the dashing little postcard which twenty years ago they had slipped into the briefcase of the nauseatingly righteous Petrenko. That had been some affair! Who'd have thought that Petrenko would have enough brains to write a report? They all got really nervous then. They were forced to set Shibaev up. Everything was clear where he was concerned anyway: he was in trouble on account of another matter and was changing his mate for the third time. That postcard, with its moral cast, tied in well. And they all wriggled out of it then. Incidentally, Shibaev survived. He went into municipal affairs and now either inspects a cemetery or is in charge of its regulations. He's visited them, a really happy butterball with a beard and sideburns. He uses makeup and already has a fourth mate. . . . He offered to arrange a place for each of them through connections; not in Novodevichye,[2] of course—that would be much pricier—but in Vagankovskoe.[3] Said it didn't cost him anything. And now Petrenko needed such a connection. Ah, Petrenko, Petrenko! Why didn't you drink?

Now, Esenin drank . . . ![4] Yet both died. The difference is that in a week everyone will forget Petrenko, whereas they still mourn Esenin. He'd been at Vagankovskoe—what a coincidence!—and had personally seen real flowers at Esenin's grave.

. . . V. M. didn't even notice how he'd steered over to his customary subject: "It's nobody's business. *She* doesn't like it, you see. But what does she like? Interesting question, if you think about it. What do you like, my dear? I don't give a damn. I drink, so I drink. And that's that." He called on all the objects in the kitchen to testify to his righteousness: the tap, which sniffed in disapproving agreement; the sugar bowl with the lid off, which was always devoted to him; the lightbulb, the meter, and the refrigerator; the chairs and the medicine cabinet on the wall; and the drafty ventilation window. These things understood him, and they voted "pro": for his right to drink at home whenever and however much he wanted. This support encouraged him.

"You should have horseradish with lamprey eel," thought V. M. "This fish still has that look. . . . It's repulsive, the bitch. It's probably really nimble in the water! A long, spineless whore!"

Two wide beds of Arab make. V. M. and I. A. have already retired, withdrawing as far as possible to the edge of their respective beds. V. M. has a copy of *Football* in his hand, I. A. a mystery by Iulian Semionov.[5]

"If they retire me, I'll turn on the gas in the bathroom and that'll be the end," thinks I. A., gazing at the page with unseeing eyes. "Cheapskate, cheapskate. . . . Yet it'll all be left to him."

These aren't even thoughts, but the shadows of thoughts that had been born, had matured and flowered, and now were already desiccated with age. Shadows that exist remind you of their existence, but no longer affect you, because, strange as it may seem, the very thought of death doesn't affect you. So what? There'll be peace. So what that it's eternal?

That's fine! To die, knowing about it a few days in advance. . . . To have time to throw out some junk at home and at work. God knows what she's got in her desk! If she were to have a stroke or a heart attack, what would people think of her? Yet she's afraid of tidying up; she's afraid of it as something that would prompt the consequences of preparation. You shouldn't prompt them knowingly. She simply wants to believe that, in return for her entire life, so full of hard work and activity, she'll be given three days to put things in order. Then she wouldn't take off her corset for three days; she'd wear orlon and nylon, have a pedicure, and fix her hair herself, just as she did when she was young, instead of having it done at a hairdresser's. She'd have to sleep the whole night in iron rollers. Normally she doesn't have the energy for that, and so they make her look awful with teasing and hairspray, as if to say that an old woman like her doesn't need anything else. Other women somehow know how to cope with their age; instead of succumbing to it, they minimize it and look forty, whereas she feels that each of her cells is fifty-nine and not a second less. And in front of the large mirror at the hairdresser's, against the background of those modern girls who cut and dye your hair indifferently, she feels a full hundred and eighteen. That's why if she were given three days for such an event, she'd spend one of them in rollers and would fix her own hair. Without teasing, without hairspray, so that her hair would fall down to her shoulders in a wave, with two locks at the top held up with pins. At one time that used to look good on her. . . .

Of course, he's already noticed that she's not turning the pages. Let him! To tell the truth, she doesn't understand the current habit of reading mysteries. Stupid occupation! Her new assistant, who'd recently been promoted from an outlying district, had brought her this novel. Thirty-nine years old. Right now he brings her popular books and never leaves work until she does. But in a year or two? In a year or two he'll feel cramped in his own office, he'll start writing complaints about her to everybody. Age, he'll say, age. . . . Not the same reactions, not the same ability to think quickly, he'll say, whereas he, with his smaller salary, isn't obliged to take care of her larger one. Anna Berg, from the next department, who had been edged out this way two years ago, warned her: "Just don't get any ideas about making him your lover. I've gone that route. It's the quickest way to the last exit. Under no circumstances should a man learn how old you are like that. . . . He'll remember it when he needs to."

Iraida Aleksandrovna choked with anger at that. To say such a thing —to her! And she said precisely that: "You're saying something like that to me?" Anna threw her grey head back and laughed in a bass. But she didn't say anything, because after she'd been pushed into retirement, it was Iraida Aleksandrovna, after all, who'd given her a position as a consultant. So she preferred to refrain from rudeness and hints. And the hint concerned the late Ivan Sergeevich and the time during the war when they'd just returned from evacuation. Ivan Sergeevich was sixty-five then, and Iraida twenty-five. She needed a room, and it was then that Anna said: "Will it lower you or something?" Ivan Sergeevich helped her at work right up until his death, and he got her a room, and supported her when she came up for promotion. He was a good, kind-hearted man, but ever since then the word "lover" for some reason always conjured up one thing for her: pale naked feet with unclippable yellow toenails, hoarse breathing that signaled the terrible approach of death, and heart drops within arm's reach. Thank God he died soon after the war, did Ivan Sergeevich. And she led his wife in the funeral procession. It happened completely unexpectedly. The old woman trustingly lowered her head, in black guipure, onto her shoulder.

In any case, she should keep Anna's laughing bass in mind. And if the assistant from an outlying district got any ideas about following the example of Anna's assistant, then she'd have to tell him: "My dear man! Don't take me for her! I'm not Anna Berg to you. . . . " Well, perhaps there was no need to say anything about Anna. Everyone knew about it anyway. But "for her" must be said with a touch of satire and steel.

He clicked off the light. And at once *the wall* appeared. A yellow wall, which they don't have in their apartment. They have apple-green wall-paper with a goldish stripe. It's all the damned neon sign opposite. It shines directly through the window, and when they switch off the light the apple-green wall turns yellow. Nothing helps, neither dense blinds nor folding shutters—it still stays yellow. And there are also shifting shadows. Their house is at the foot of a trestle bridge. Before descending, cars find their window and leave a flying autograph on the yellow wall. All night the wall writhes, winks, and dances. V. M. has categorically refused to move the beds. You can't place two Arab beds that make up a set in different corners. And so she's tormented by this honking yellow wall.

She scans the room: the crystal in the sideboard, glittering in the semidarkness, the expensive caulking on the walls, and stares at the darkness of the cheval glass. Beside a powder compact on the night table below stands an old, old photograph of her. She can't see the shot, for it's too far away, but she doesn't need to; she remembers it well anyway. She should throw the damn photo away. Every evening it's the same thing all over again: it's like an encounter with her young self.

I. A. abruptly gets up and goes to the kitchen. The refrigerator isn't closed, and the lamprey eel is hanging over the side of the plate. She bangs the door shut loudly so that *he* will hear. And *he* hears and laughs, pulling the blanket over his head.

I. A. rummages nervously in the medicine cabinet. There are the sleeping pills. She swallows one down without any water, throwing back her head like a bird, then goes to the bedroom. She lies down and closes her eyes tightly so she can't see the wall.

But she can see. With eyes closed, she can see splendidly.

... It's '39. She's sitting on a small wooden log on a river bank. Only it's no longer a bank, but the bottom of the river, which in summer becomes shallow up to the middle. There's a camera on the sand.

Mitia is walking around on his hands. His shirt has come out of his pants, and she's laughing as she sees his thin, boyish, skinny stomach. She laughs to hide her compassion. Compassion, as Gorky said, degrades a person.[5]

Mitia abruptly stands up, then sits down beside her.

"When our son is born he'll be an athlete. I'll make him walk on his hands and run and swim. You know what I mean?"

Iraida laughs and shakes her head.

"But what if it's a girl?"

"Oh, come on!" Mitia is full of indignation. "Why should we have a girl? I'm a son! And I'll have a son!"

"But I'm not a son," says Iraida in embarrassment.

"I have no idea who you are," replies Mitia.[7] "Just answer this question: if you were to die tomorrow, what would you do in the time that's left?"

"I don't want to think about a thing like that."

"Think about it!" he asks. "For example, I know what I'd do. I'd move along really slowly, touch everything with my hands—houses, dogs, grass, stones—and drink straight from the river. I'd ask people everything I wanted to; I wouldn't leave out anything or anybody. And then I'd probably be satiate . . . or satiated? Is it -iate or -iated?"

That's the way he always is: he can erase one thing with another. Well, is she supposed to laugh? Mitia once told her: "You've got no humor, none whatsoever. It's amazing. An inborn defect." Being young, she adjusted deftly back then: if she found something unclear and for some reason unpleasant, she defined it as humor. Later, after a great many years had gone by, she no longer felt ashamed of her "inborn defect." If everybody laughed and she didn't find something funny, she'd ask loudly:

"Was that humor? Was it? I don't find it funny, my friends!"

She liked the way their laughter was extinguished and their smiles disappeared awkwardly, as if snagging on something.

But that was only later. . . . Back then, in the bed of the shallow river, she was still Rada. Only Mitia could have thought up such a derivative name from her strange double name.

"Rada-lada, happy-lappy, rada-ladushka mine." Mitia gazes at her knees, then kisses them.

"What are you doing?" Mitia strikes her as wanton.

"What have I done that's bad?"

"You need to ask?"

"Why can't I kiss your knee?"

"It degrades me."

"Why doesn't it degrade you when I kiss you on the mouth, then? How's the knee worse?"

Iraida looks at him in confusion. Mitia laughs and stands on his hands, and walks around her again, showing the whole world his defenseless stomach. She's a student at an industrial institute, and Mitia, at a pedagogical one. "Does compassion degrade a person?" asks Iraida softly.

Mitia sits down on the sand, breathing heavily. Why does he walk on his hands so much?

"I'm certain it doesn't. I'm certain Gorky personally couldn't have thought that. His Satin[8] could have, or someone else for whom compassion is the last charity. . . . A lifeline to a drowning man. But how's it possible not to feel compassion for a child or an old man? I feel compassion for you, for example."

"Why's that? I'm not drowning. I'm not a child, or an old woman."

"But don't you ever feel compassion for me?"

"No," she said.

"That's strange," he replied. "Really strange. You need to be reeducated."

He was supposed to come and see her in Moscow in August of '41. Before the war, graduates could be sent from provincial institutes to Moscow. She'd been sent there, and Mitia's institute had promised to recommend him to the Pedagogical Academy. In return for this recommendation they asked only that he work a summer in the children's home, the director of which had taken it into her head to have a baby in June. Mitia knew the children's home, for he'd been going there since his first year of study, and he'd spent a lot time with the kids there.

Of course there was no August.

Mitia perished on the fifth day of the war; the children's home was bombed while he and the others were in it. Iraida didn't see it happen, but she thought about it so much that she seemed to know what it had been like, how he had hidden the children and tried to cover them with his own body.

. . . I. A. turns abruptly on the Arab bed. In doing so she trespasses beyond the dividing line, and V. M. instantly moves even farther toward the edge. He's almost hanging over the floor just to keep his distance.

I. A. understands, and she crawls back like a dog that's been kicked.

"What kind of medicine are they making nowadays that you take it but can't fall asleep anyway? Maybe I should have taken two pills."

. . . And yet she'd known that there wouldn't be any August. She'd sensed it. War hadn't even occurred to her, of course; it was simply that that spring Mitia brought Lelka down to the river. The first thing she did was to fasten her skirt between her legs with a safety pin and walk on her hands with Mitia along the sand of the river. Their thin, tanned legs swung loosely against the blue sky, and later they propped each other up with their backs, choking with laughter, and wailed some song. Iraida felt something unpleasant welling up in her which in that instance had nothing to do with humor. She felt as if someone had moved everything inside her and had forgotten to put it back in place, as people do when they're repairing a house.

Kneeling in front of each other—"like dogs," thought Iraida—the two of them counted: "Papin-dore, trindi-andi, iaku-maku, fandi-andi. . . . "

Then they chased each other. When she couldn't run any more, Lelka lay down on the sand, and, tucking the first log she came upon under her head, she said: "Folks! It's already Wednesday. . . . "

"Sunday," Iraida corrected her.

"Wednesday," said Lelka thoughtfully. "It's the Wednesday of our lives."

Then she jumped up, stood like a dog again, and began to chatter:

"Listen! On the average we'll live seventy years. Count them: the first ten are Monday, the second, Tuesday, our age is Wednesday . . . and so on. And we'll die on Sunday evening."

"Wow!" Mitia was delighted. "What an ironclad setup! Good grief! It's already Wednesday! We're already at the halfway point, and we're still playing with sand."

He became seriously upset and moved off, then sat on a hole-riddled boat, and biting his nails, lapsed into thought.

To Iraida it all seemed ridiculous. Life was life. One should live it as the quotation says.[9] After all, a week is a week, and there's no point in comparing. And why seventy? That's really a lot; fifty would be quite enough.

She was afraid of Lelka. She was afraid of her cheerful chatter, which did away with rational logic.

"Eat more seeds," Lelka chirped. "First of all, they're filling, and secondly, it's fascinating to see if a sunflower will suddenly sprout up inside you. Mit, hey, Mit? Are you by any chance a sunflower already? You turn your face to the sun all the time. Irka-Idka!" she jabbered. "You know what you are? You're a savings bank. You're convenient, reliable, and profitable."

"Why profitable?" asks Iraida. "Profitable" and "for profit" are negative, offensive words. They're not Soviet.

"Because you're profitable and reliable."

"And who are you, chatterbox?" asks Mitia.

"Me?" Lelka narrows her brilliant brown eyes. "To tell you the truth, I'm an inkwell. I've got so many different stories inside me. Horrors! Who'll save me from them?"

Iraida saw this as a hint to Mitia. She was saying he should save her. A nasty feeling welled up inside her, a feeling she'd never acknowledge as being jealousy. It was simply a premonition that you could expect anything from Lelka.

And it all came true. Later, many years later, during a business trip, she came across a slender little book. It had no binding, but contained a small portrait of the author. Lelka! The same narrowed eyes and the smile from ear to ear. On top was written "To Mitia's memory," and the entire story was about him. How he used to walk on his hands on the river's sand, and how he loved the river; how he was a "slender sunflower reaching upward," and lived only "until Wednesday." It was written as if only the two of them had walked together on the bank and she—Iraida—had never been with them; as if Mitia had never kissed her, Rada-Lad-ushka's, knee, and hadn't been planning to come to Moscow in August; as if he'd not wanted a son from her, and not from that "inkwell."

From the book she learned that the children's home had made a bust of Mitia. Several years ago, when she was back in the neighborhood on business, she drove over there in a car belonging to the district executive committee. Mitia's bust didn't look like Mitia. In fact, they had nothing in common. Alarmed by the official car, the head of the children's home kept trying to drag Iraida into the dining room to feed her lunch. And she kept asking her to pay no attention to something or other. The funniest thing was that it was the same head who'd had a baby in June of '41. She recounted the story of her journey to her mother's in Elista,[10] and how she'd been saved by staying there and nursing the baby. She'd returned to the children's home only after the war. She'd had to start everything all over again because *those* children and workers had perished, but a lot of new ones had replaced them, and she had a rough time of it. . . . And her son, the child of June 1941, was now a doctoral candidate[11] in technology in Leningrad, and had constructed a cooperative in Gatchina.

On her way back, Iraida Aleksandrovna thought: I should have had lunch at the children's home. Suddenly the old, forgotten irritation with Mitia welled up inside her; he'd always forced her to act contrary to the way she should have and the way she really wanted to. Back then, in their youth, he used to drag her down to the river, even though it was often cold and wet. He used to force her to spend time with that stupid fool Lelka. If the war hadn't happened, who knows how her life would have worked out? Would she have the self-assurance and strength she has now, and also her present position? . . .

Viacheslav's a difficult person to get along with, but he doesn't get in her way. . . .

After visiting the children's home, she parked at the side of the road next to a fast-food joint, and haughtily entered the glass building. The male drivers looked at her curiously, wondering what kind of woman would be riding around in a Volga. She demanded that they wash and dry the fork and spoon they gave her from the cutlery lying on the tray for general use. She was pleased that they obeyed her without a word. She went further, demanding a clean towel and "parsley, more parsley," instead of an egg in her cold kvass soup. Her apple compote helped her wash down the trip to the children's home and the book by Lelka, who was a writer of only local significance. That definition appealed to her, for it clarified what was essential. Lelka hadn't done anything on a large scale, whereas she was someone important in the ministry. And that Volga which the head of the children's home had looked at longingly was a mere trifle in her life.

She carried her triumphant, self-assured strength inside her until nightfall and, apparently, overstrained herself. She woke up in the middle of the night to find her mouth filled with something salty and bitter, and her chest clamped in a hoop. "The cold kvass soup," she thought and fumbled about on the hotel bedside table for her handbag to check whether she'd brought any soda with her. As she was searching, she swallowed a lump of salt. Good God, those were tears! Her whole face and neck were covered in them; they even gurgled in her ears. They streamed and flowed as if something in her had broken somewhere, some pipe in the communication system that was now spilling over and inundating her. And she felt that it would drown her. It was a strange thing for *her* to die from tears. She raised her pillow and lay high on it, giving the torrent of tears a chance to flow freely. And she thought, what if there really is something there, after all? Then she'll meet Mitia and say: "You know, I died from tears." "And why were you crying?" he'll ask. "Your bust doesn't look like you at all. I should know. After all, I remember what you were like." "That's the most important thing, that you remember," he'll say. "Just think, what's a bust? It's only clay. . . . "

At that point she began to feel very unwell. As an experienced business traveler, however, she knew there was no point in pressing the buttons on the panel, for they don't work even in a "luxury"-class room. Did that mean it was the end? Sweet as it would have been to die thinking about Mitia, that part of her which had escaped inundation by tears succeeded in locating the polyethylene packet of medicine she'd been fumbling for. The nitroglycerin settled like a thorn under her tongue. The rustling of the packet stemmed the gush of tears as if by magic, and after a while the hoop grew loose. She got up, paced back and forth, then went out onto the balcony. The air was diffused with a quiet stillness. There was a faint odor of slime. She had a vague desire to go down to the river and sit a while in the shallow bed, but she was no longer crying. She was almost her usual self again, so it wasn't hard to stifle and crush the desire evoked by the faint odor of the river.

"My nerves are shot," she said aloud. "I need a massage. I'll ask for a morning appointment, before work. So I'll get up an hour earlier. Problem."

She removed the wet pillow from the bed, but placed the tube of nitroglycerin beside her. She fell into a heavy, dreamless sleep, and woke up strong.

Now, too, I. A. ordered herself to sleep. Sleep. The Arab springs creaked beneath her, and she started making herself comfortable in businesslike fashion, kicking the dividing line with her foot. That basic strength of hers which raised her above everyone had been aroused. It kept her above V. M., and Anna Berg, and the new assistant ("a clothes-mad snotnose!"), too, and it was pleasant to feel that strength and no longer fear the blinking wall. She knew she'd fall asleep now, and gave a quiet sigh of satisfaction.

How well he knew her, how really well! He'd been waiting for this sigh, the sigh of a strong, masterful woman who, no matter how tired she was, no matter how much she anticipated and feared unpleasantness at work and at home, no matter how she suffered from insomnia on account of that damned yellow wall, ultimately emerged from it all triumphant. And this was the woman, this woman who now occupied most of the bed, whom he secretly respected.

He was even ready to talk with her right then and there, to say that as a matter of fact it was possible to move the beds, that she was wrong to think that he'd dug in his heels like a stubborn ass. He hadn't at all. And he'd say there was no need for her to wear a tight corset. You'll pinch some blood vessel and end up in the hospital. He turned onto his back, softened to the point of kindness, and saw the wall—it was really yellow! He wanted to say so out loud and offer to look for a Finnish plastic blind that he'd seen in a new polyclinic, with slats that fitted together solidly with no slots or gaps. But something was distracting him. Something prevented him from speaking with her in a quiet, conciliatory manner. This something flitted about, alarmed him, and—oh damn!—it also was tied up with the wall. It was reminiscent of something. . . . But what? He pulled the blanket up higher because he'd realized, he'd recognized, what it was. A slender needle, like the ones used for the most sophisticated injections, entered his heart and stayed there. It stayed in the cruelest position: it tormented him, yet didn't kill him. . . .

V. M. isn't sleeping; he's lying, his eyes open, looking at the patches of light dancing on the wall that make the wall look washed-out and dirty. Like that one, the other . . .

. . . wall of the corridor in the communal apartment, with traces of putty and dirt. Nastia, dressed in a dirty robe and clumsy rubber boots, and wearing an old woman's kerchief, is examining it with profound satisfaction. The startled apartment tenants are standing behind her.

"It's child's play now," says Nastia. "Whitewashing. That'll take me two hours. I'll wash the window in the evening, and you'll have a super corridor instead of a barn."

"The last time they repaired anything was before the war," says the old man who's their neighbor. "The Finnish war. A whole team of painters and plasterers worked on it."

"A team?" Nastia claps her hands. "Now, that's hilarious!"

"But how will your husband take it?" A lady in a shaggy bathrobe smiles ironically.

"What's there to take? Will having the place clean make it worse for him?"

"But he's only temporary here, a tenant."

"Why not live decently even if you are temporary?" Nastia moves a table and lithely jumps onto it. He recalls that he didn't recognize her at first and wanted to walk around the table so as not to get dirty. Nastia gave a laugh and raised the whiting brush right up to his nose. He froze, afraid of bumping into the heady smell of whiting and water, and the cleanliness of the bristles.

"What are you doing?"

"Getting rid of the dirt. Slavik, it's hilarious! No one in the apartment knows how to whitewash! For me it's child's play. What does it cost me to do the corridor and kitchen? At home I whitewash the cottage inside and out. It looks like a forge here. As though the war were still on. See how I've caulked everything. . . . And I poured some broken glass into the mousehole; the kids in the courtyard shattered three green bottles for me."

Nastia dances with pleasure on the table. Viacheslav turns pale. The lady in the shaggy robe says: "We all tried to dissuade your wife. We explained that you aren't living here permanently."

"Can you imagine?" laughs Nastia.

"We were prepared to pay. Each family according to its size. . . . But your wife. . . . "

"Can you imagine?" Nastia appeals to Viacheslav to share her indignation and bewilderment. "As if I'm doing it for money. As if it's hard for me. As if I can't do it just to be human. . . . You live here, after all! You have to walk through this corridor, and a cobweb was always catching on your brows."

"They did some repair work before the war. The Finnish war. A whole team worked on it." It was the old man explaining again.

"Can you imagine?" Nastia's ecstatic.

"Get into the room." Viacheslav opens the door. He's broken out in a sweat. He's ashamed.

Nastia jumps off the table, winks at everybody, and follows him, trying not to touch anyone with her dirty robe.

Inside the room Viacheslav can no longer contain himself.

"What are you doing? Have you hired yourself out as domestic help? As a servant? Why are you disgracing me? I'm studying at the academy, and you—it's not enough that you don't want to study, but are you also going to clean up after everybody?"

They could hear everything in the corridor. The lady probably made a helpless gesture.

"Q. E. D.![12] Believe me, he's right! Right, right, right. A woman's position should match the man's. But there's an obvious mismatch here. . . . "

"She's simply a good-hearted woman. She saw the dirt and the mess." That's the old man.

"I saw them, too." The lady becomes indignant. "So what?"

Inside the room:

"The way I envisioned things, I'd graduate from the academy, and you'd start studying so that there'd be no difference between us. I'd planned to talk this over with you. And what are you thinking of? As soon as you got here, you started teaching everyone to fry cutlets. Didn't say a single intelligent word. And now it's beyond the limit . . . you've started white-washing. . . . Don't you understand? This is a communal apartment; there's an order of priority here. Everyone understands that nowadays no one works in somebody else's place. We have a gentleman landowner here, one of the throwbacks, and he washes things when his turn comes. He washes them badly and sloppily, but it wouldn't occur to anyone to do it instead of him. Once you start doing that, some people are going to do the work, while others eat the bread."

"But I'm young and used to it. It's not hard for me, Slava. . . . "

"Look at yourself! A cleaning woman! A slut! People come to Moscow to go to the theater, to museums. Look, look. . . . " Viacheslav pulls tickets out of his pockets. "Here's for *The Dancing Master*, Zeldin's playing. And this one's for *The Queen of Spades*. Nelepp. . . . [13]

"What?"

"It's a singer!" shouts Viacheslav. "Maybe you'll clean the toilet bowl for them?"

"I will!" shouts Nastia. She bangs the door and goes out into the corridor. She no longer climbs onto the table as lightly, but she does climb onto it, stamps on it with her boots, and flourishes her brush.

"You could lose your husband that way." That's the lady making her pronouncement from the doorway.

"If we lose him, we'll find another," replies Nastia defiantly.

"Oh!" The lady is surprised. "That's the kind you are!"

"Aha!" replies Nastia. "Exactly!"

Viacheslav hears this conversation. He starts shoving Nastia's things into a suitcase. Nastia listens to the noise in the room, understands what's going on, and tries to hold back her tears.

The old fellow, wearing a tie and a watch on a chain, his hair wetly slicked down, comes out into the corridor.

"I'll explain to your husband the difference between helping somebody and serving him. He doesn't understand it because he's never had servants. Whereas I, Nastia, am from the aristocracy."

Nastia looks at him with horror.

The lady:

"Cut out the nonsense. What meaning can the arguments of a former gentleman landowner have nowadays?"

Viacheslav leaves the room. He heads for the exit. Nastia stands stock-still, looking at him.

"Viacheslav Matveevich, you . . .," " says the old man uncertainly.

"To hell with all of you. . . . "

"So how did that go down?" The lady in the doorway smiles ironically.

. . . V. M. gets out of bed and goes to the kitchen. He lights a cigarette at the open ventilation window. The wind stirs his thin grey hair as he gazes at the town in the darkness of the night, and sees Nastia leaving. She went to catch the night train on foot and alone. He followed her, and to this day he doesn't know why he did. To make sure that she left? Or did he want to get his fill of looking at her for the last time? He'd said to her:

"I simply can't imagine living with a person who disgraces me."

"I can't imagine it either," she'd said.

The train was leaving. He didn't get too close to it, fearing that she'd see him, but when the train cars moved off—strange thing!—he saw her face in every window. Really, in every one.

He wanted to stop the train with his hand. He was certain it wouldn't take much to do it; he had powerful hands, and if he grasped the handrail of the last car, the train would come to a dead stop. And then he'd say to Nastia, to the thousand Nastias who were leaving at that moment:

"Pardon me, Nastia—incidentally, remember that this word is written with an *a*—if a person is climbing to the top, it's very easy to pull him down. But I don't want that. I don't want to say 'afflúent,' 'ain't,' and 'wanna' instead of 'affluent,' 'isn't,' and 'want to' again. For five years I repeated these words before going to bed. And you're pulling me back into the dungheap or the humus, Nastia, just as you did back there. In short, into serving a former gentleman landowner and all his kind. I'm trying to make something of myself, Nastia. Can you understand that?"

And he'd release the handrail. Beat it! Let the train carry away all those whitewashing, scraping, baking, cooking Nastias. Our paths have separated, yours leading north, mine—south.

Next day he went to the movies in the evening. At that time he had a whole pile of tickets. He met Iraida. She approached him as if she were uncertain or lost. She suited his mood—one of his own kind.

"Do you need a ticket? I have an extra. . . . "

There was news when he returned home.

"Your neighbor died. . . . "

Grand and austere, the old man lay with the joints of his fingers showing white against his black jacket. The lady kept dabbing at her eyes with a handkerchief.

"He was a part of the past. Before the revolution he had an estate near Moscow."

"We'll all die, both past and present," snapped Viacheslav and headed for his room. The lady trailed after him.

"Listen, Viacheslav, grief is grief. But life is life. You could get his room. You know, I've heard they're keeping you in Moscow."

Indeed, they were keeping him there—theoretically. But in practice they'd asked: "You mean you don't have a fiancée in Moscow to help things go smoothly?"[14]

No one in the academy knew about Nastia. They hadn't registered their marriage officially yet, and after the incident with the whitewashing he began to feel completely free.

The old man's death, which left his room empty, the possibility of acquiring it, and Iraida, who'd appeared like fate at the exact moment when he had some extra tickets left—it all happened as a single set of indivisible circumstances.

Back then Iraida didn't appeal to him. She didn't have the strength that elicits people's respect. Everybody was thin after the war, and her teeth were falling out from a vitamin deficiency. She constantly covered her mouth with a kerchief because she'd been undergoing bridgework for a long time with no success. But as soon as the work was finished, she immediately perked up; she even grew taller, as though her new jaws had bitten through something inside her. He could pretty much guess what! Evidently some love affair. From conversations in passing he'd managed to deduce that she'd met a man whose biographical particulars made him unsuitable.[15] Whatever he may have felt about other things, that was one thing he could understand. At that time they were in total harmony without making any formal agreement, and now that she smiled without being afraid of losing her teeth, he enjoyed appearing with her at functions: he was impressed by her restrained severity and the womanliness which she thoroughly suppressed and which Nastia had had in excess.

It was then that Iraida's boss died. Apparently he used to wear her out completely with his advice. Viacheslav had a person like that, too. He noticed that she was pleased, but felt ashamed afterwards. After all, it wasn't nice; a person had died. And she started making a lot of fuss at the funeral. He liked the fact that she felt ashamed of this joy of hers. It showed a good side to her character.

He started to believe in happiness with a woman like her. He even thought: "I'm intelligent. I know what I want. I know how to deal with circumstances and turn them to my advantage. I have a good sense of people." He wrote "Beloved" on a photograph that he gave Iraida. He formed the letters as if he were branding them in his heart, in those places where Nastia could show through irrationally and spontaneously. And he rejoiced that he was able to crush and triumph over what showed through. "Man is the master of fate." He wrote these words down on the cover of a calico-bound notebook. And lower down, "Through horns to the stars."

"We'll move the bed," he said firmly. "We'll do it. We'll lie with our heads to the damned wall."

But she kept silent. He felt rather offended—hadn't she heard? And then he realized that she'd fallen asleep. The fact that she'd fallen asleep without waiting to hear what he'd say, and, what was more important, as if she didn't need to, provoked his irritation once again. She complains of insomnia, yet she's sleeping! Whereas he doesn't complain—he never complains to anyone—yet he can't fall asleep! That's the way he always is, no matter what happens to him. During his army stint, he'd experienced all kinds of things. Something would happen somewhere, and though you had no idea what it was, since you were a thousand kilometers away, you had to answer for it. And he did. He didn't have a uniform or that kind of work now. In his old age he's become an overseer of papers and paper clips. Nonetheless, he fulfills his duties as scrupulously as possible, because he could never take a kopek for doing nothing! He can't understand those modern people who like to receive money without doing their work. . . .

He longed to get up and have another swig, and the imminent act, which was so dear to his heart, invigorated him so much that he leaped out like a young man, right into his slippers. She heard him, and woke up. . . .

She watched him leave the room briskly, and wondered which of the bottles he'd go to—the one in the kitchen, the toilet, or the bathroom? She thought about the fact that one day he'd have a heart attack, and she'd have to pull him "out of there." She'd do it with her characteristic conscientiousness and pull him out.

She had no fear or horror in the face of sickness; she was certain of her own abilities and strength. Of how she'd get all the specialists going, secure a private ward and sick-nurse, and obtain any medicines from any country. It's strange how life works out! She'd had no way of helping Mitia.

She could imagine how she would have protected him with her body. Then both of them would have died. There are cases that are hopeless. There are. And they occur not only in war. Ultimately it had occurred then, in that affair with Valentin Petrovich. She'd known how senseless and dangerous it was, and had made her decision quickly; all she'd needed was one hint.

Once in Kislovodsk she thought that she had run into Valentin Petrovich. He was standing looking at the water. Although their relationship hadn't lasted long, she remembered this passion of his for looking at water. She took refuge behind her parasol, and started observing him: was it he or not? He hadn't gained weight—he was as skinny as ever. He'd not grown bald—his hair was as thick as ever, though it was white now. He looked as defenseless as ever, but. . . . And it was because of this "but" that she finally decided that she'd made a mistake and that it wasn't Valentin Petrovich. The first "but" was his suit, made of a stylish synthetic material that had just become available. It was expensive and could only have been imported. The second "but" was the deputy's badge on his lapel. That's where things made no sense whatever. The third "but" was the young and beautiful woman who materialized at his side and trailed her fingers down his cheek. Trailed them, that's all. He merely gave a slight nod, as if to say "I see you're here," and continued looking at the water, while she remained motionless at his side. Then she started examining Iraida's parasol because she had one just like it. A folding Japanese parasol.

These three "buts" made her reject the idea that it was Valentin Petrovich. Valentin Petrovich couldn't have a suit like that, a deputy's badge, and a woman that age. "It's not he!" she told herself firmly and left, repressing the gnawing sensation of an unpleasantness that she'd forgotten and then remembered.

Thanks to Ivan Sergeevich, after the war ended she was given a tiny room, nine meters in size. Heaven. A palatial residence. The narrow window looked directly onto a church tower, which unnerved her at first. Looking out of the window, the first thing you'd see was a cross. But then she trained herself to look down on the cross, contemptuously, and she fell madly in love with the room. Nothing daunted her. Neither the kitchen for eight households, nor the line to the toilet in the mornings, nor the work she had to put in on Saturdays, like all the other tenants, washing the enormous corridor with a brush and washing soda. Other tenants moaned as they washed, saying that there was a lot of trash, bicycles, suitcases, and boxes, but she didn't care. She was young and strong, and she washed and scrubbed the parquet floors, cleaned out the yellowed washtub, and didn't quarrel with anyone in the apartment house. What was there to quarrel about?

Later Valentin Petrovich moved into the apartment house. Rather, he returned to his room, which had been locked up and sealed until then. Together with his two kids, whom he'd picked up from their grandmother's: a boy and a girl, seven and nine years old. He himself was returning from prison, and his wife had died during the war, so the whole apartment felt sorry for him and his kids.

How well she remembered that line to the bathroom and to the toilet in the mornings. The sleepy boy and girl would go where they needed to without waiting; no one objected. In the kitchen they all tried to pour hot water for their tea from their own kettles. She did too.

Valentin Petrovich was hilariously entertaining in the kitchen.

"May I have your matches? I dropped mine in the saucepan."

"Excuse me, Olga Ivanovna, I didn't get enough butter again. . . . Would you give me a spoonful?"

"I've burnt my macaroni a bit. What do you think, is it a lost cause, or can it be saved?"

Iraida was the one he turned to most frequently: she'd give the kids some of her own food and would even do their laundry along with her own. In the evening Valentin Petrovich would turn up without any warning.

"Ida (that's what he called her), thanks for everything. You did such a good job washing Natashka's dress that I didn't recognize it. I've discovered it has little flowers and berries on it."

"It's nothing."

In embarrassment Iraida would take what she considered intimate things and stuff them away in corners. For example, she didn't think it right for a man to see a powder compact and lipstick, and she would hide them under an embroidered runner on the night table. The cushion cover with open-work embroidery on her pillow also embarrassed her, as if she were some bourgeoise. She'd put a geography map on the cushion cover, but would leave a lightbulb on the table with the stocking that she hadn't had time to finish darning. That had to be hidden, too. And the strips with which she curled her hair at night lay in a chintz kerchief on the sill. She'd hide everything, stuff everything away, and Valentin Petrovich—the naive blockhead—would want to help her. He was so grateful to her, after all. So she'd put the map on the open-work embroidery, and he'd remove it; if order was what she wanted. . . . He didn't understand that order meant that everything had to be strict. It meant her mother with her bibelots and her embroidery. She kept on sending stuff.

A severe black hat with a veil.

"Idochka, that hat really suits you. Let me adjust it for you." He turned down the brim a bit and fixed the veil. Where had he learned that?

On Sundays they'd all drag her out for a walk. They would go along the Moscow River to watch the train suddenly emerge on the elevated subway. Each time it was an unexpected and joyful sight. This stretch of open subway really appealed to Iraida; it moved her and softened the preciseness and efficiency of her movements. But Viacheslav Petrovich would turn aside and move a little distance away from the subway. He preferred to gaze at the water. "It casts a spell on me." And that was their way of going for a walk. She'd look at the subway, he at the water, and the children would run along the embankment, throwing pebbles at each other.

She never thought that a casual observer would take them for a family. But once an old lady said:

"You're not looking where you ought to be, Mrs. Your children will knock each other's eyes out."

It was startling to discover that they were a family. She even started believing that she'd given birth to these children. She'd had an easy delivery with the girl, but the boy had been a breech birth. They'd used the oxygen mask on her nonstop. She imagined that with time they'd change apartments, and everyone would think that. The girl was rather pale; she took after her. And judging by everything, her feet would be large, at least a size eight. As the saying goes: when it rains, it pours. And that's just what happened in her case: in one fell swoop, she suddenly acquired a family, the whole works. "Yes, yes, the boy was a breech. They only just managed to save him and me. But, thank God, the midwife turned out to be very experienced. What was her name? My ungrateful memory. I've forgotten!"

The old lady continued to look at her disapprovingly. She wore a cherry-colored coat and prewar white felt overshoes with worn heels. She had a string bag in her hands, and carrots protruded through the holes in it like pins on a mine. Iraida led the children home, holding them by the hand, while Valentin Petrovich trailed behind.

Her hat with the veil had slipped down to the back of her head. Iraida shook her head, but that made it fall off altogether. The boy started to cry.

"What's the matter?"

"I'm sorry for the ice."

"Why?"

"It'll melt. . . . "

"So what?"

"But it's ice. It wants to be ice, not water. Ice, ice. . . . "

Valentin Petrovich hugs him and explains:

"You're growing and changing, too, you know. You start off as a boy, then become a youth. But you're still you, nonetheless. Water and ice are the same thing."

"No," he shouts, "ice wants to be ice!"

Iraida is embarrassed. Strange children—how did they get such ideas? Nothing like that ever occurred to her.

They drank tea in her room. She made sandwiches with jam and hurried into the kitchen to get the kettle.

That's when her neighbor, Olga Ivanovna, intercepted her in the corridor.

"Idka, don't be a fool!"

"What are you talking about?"

"You know where he's come from? He'll never shake the stigma of prison. And your reputation will be affected, too. You're starting to come into your own. . . . "

"But I never even thought of anything like that."

"Then start thinking. He's latched onto you like a flea onto a coat. . . . "

"You're wrong. . . . "

"Iraida, I'm telling you, he's branded. And his children are branded for life. Don't get involved with him."

Iraida takes the kettle back into the room. The boy rushes to help her. Valentin Petrovich looks at her tenderly. Really, why have they latched onto her?

Next morning the girl knocked on her door:

"Aunt Ida, Aunt Ida! You can go to the bathroom. I saved you a place in line."

Iraida was about to head for the door, then suddenly stopped when she heard a noise. The boy had run up and was peering through the keyhole.

"She's gone," he said in disappointment.

Valentin Petrovich's voice: "Come back in the room! Come on!" Olga Ivanovna's voice: "Why are you children hanging around here?" Then everything died down. Iraida washed with the water from the water bottle, and left in such a way that no one would notice her.

It was evening, and everybody at work was getting ready to go home.

They took their packages from behind the window and stuffed them in their bags, and powdered their noses. Iraida pretended that she still had things to do.

"What about you? You staying?"

"When I got a room," said Zina, who sat opposite Iraida, "I couldn't wait for the workday to end. I used to be on pins and needles. And all the time I used to imagine how I'd come home, open the door, take off my garter belt, and walk around like a slob."

"How many neighbors have you got?"

"I didn't care then. I'd close the door and become a slob."

"And what are your neighbors like, Iraida?"

She shrugged her shoulders.

It was their venomous typist who asked that. For some reason, she was afraid that everyone would get married before she did. So she would encourage everyone to talk about getting married and would try to dissuade them from doing it. That's just what she was doing then.

"You be careful, Iraida. Right now there are all sorts of guys coming to Moscow. They're on the lookout for silly women. . . . "

"Are you talking about me?" Iraida raised her brows.

She wanted to get married. She wanted to for three reasons. First, it would give her a reason to break off with Ivan Sergeevich. The old guy wouldn't dare have anything to do with a married woman. He was a man of principle. "I like being with you, Iraidochka," he used to say. "It's a gift from the gods that you're free. I realize that you're the last woman's body in my life, and it's nice to know that this body is warm and beautiful." He'd run his dry palm down over her stomach and hips, then slide it back all the way up to her neck, and she was afraid that he'd discover the gurgling lump of revulsion in her throat that she kept swallowing down until her jaws hurt. So marriage meant being saved from Ivan Sergeevich.

Secondly, she wanted to have a husband when she visited her parents. She could see the two of them walking along together, both tall and plump. (Yes! yes! plump. It's only now there's an idiotic fashion for skin and bones. Back then, right after the war, only a plump woman in full bloom was considered beautiful.) So they'd walk along, plump and tall, both wearing gabardine raincoats, and both wearing hats, he a green velour one, she a small black one, with a black moire velvet ribbon tied behind in a bow. They'd have two leather suitcases with straps, and she'd have a large bag with a lock that clicked shut. The whole street would watch them as they made their way, and her father would be waiting at the gate, proud of his Daughter, Who Had a Higher Education and Actually Worked in Moscow. He'd be standing, chin up, so that the sparkling little tears of happiness gathered in the corners of his eyes would not run out.

Who else had such a clever daughter? Which of the neighbors drank tea with Moscow cookies? Eh?!! There you are! She wanted to get married for the sake of that, for the sake of her father and mother, for the sake of their happiness. That was the second reason.

Thirdly, there was a woman's reason. After the dry wandering hand of Ivan Sergeevich, she always thought: what are *these relations* really like? Is there any truth at all in what's written and said about them? Of course, this question could have been cleared up without marriage, in any vacation resort or tourist area, but that wasn't the way she wanted to do it. She was certain that that way everything would work out badly: she had to do it differently. Splendidly.

But after the war, admirers didn't exactly grow on trees.

It so happened that everyone had left. The phone rang. She picked up the receiver and heard children's voices. It was the girl and boy.

"We'd like to speak to Aunt Ida, please. . . . "

She replaced the receiver very, very carefully. . . .

At first she was filled with a profound respect for herself. How cleverly she'd got out of it. Valentin Petrovich soon left Moscow. She didn't inquire where he'd gone. Ultimately she wasn't the one who'd given birth to the girl and boy. What if the old woman in the worn felt shoes thought she had? That was her problem. And besides, how could she have turned up at her father's with a ready-made family? Suddenly it became clear that a gabardine raincoat wouldn't look good on Valentin Petrovich, that their neighbors would see their walk down her home street as a gypsy procession instead of a triumphant arrival. They'd simply say: "No one would have her, that's why she got married for the sake of the children." And they would be saying that about her, Clever, with a Higher Education, and Actually Working in Moscow! To marry "for the sake of the children" had always been the fate of plain women, women approaching old age, or girls with a past. But this was she, she, she! . . . She was absolutely brilliant at her job and had the most wonderful prospects, if she didn't spoil them for herself, of course. She had some ideas of her own, and she was saving them until she could articulate them herself. And she would! She was simply overwhelmed with horror when she realized that everything, all her prospects, could have fallen through on account of Valentin Petrovich. That would have been bad for her and for the whole plan— she wouldn't realize her idea, and she'd leave her father standing sadly at the gate, with his chin proudly raised so that his two sparkling tears of pride wouldn't run inadvertently down his face. Because of her. Because of his Daughter. Ah, Valentin Petrovich, Valentin Petrovich, sort out your life yourself. In the final analysis, what am I to you, a buoy for you to grab at? She worked up such an anger that she began to see all her former thoughts as the thoughts of a woman who'd been saved by a miracle.

Later, at the Reruns movie theater, a tall military man approached her and asked, "Do you need a ticket?"

She bought the ticket from him. Everything worked out just as it had appeared in her dream. Her father stood at the gate, and she and her husband walked along the street carrying two leather suitcases with a strap. True, it was summer and they didn't wear gabardine raincoats. But she did wear a silk dust coat, and Viacheslav wore a dark-blue fine wool suit, with a striped shirt made of light, sheer wool. After lunch her father told her that her husband was impressive and had a good name, like Molotov's.[16] Her mother made the rounds of the neighbors in a new outfit: a brown vicuna wool top with black trim along the collar and a flowery crêpe-de-chine kerchief in matching colors. Brown flowers on slender black stems were scattered against a yellow background.

Ah, how good it was back then! The main thing was that everything was substantial. She liked that word a lot. A substantial person was the highest recommendation. A word you could build and depend on. Substance. Substantive. How good it was to sit next to Viacheslav in the theater or when they visited other people. He was very neat, his clothes always pressed. Plus, he was extremely well-mannered! He always asked whether he might light a cigarette, and he would wave the smoke aside with his hand. But she found it sweet! Smoke!

They'd had good times once, they really had. Once, when they were traveling on the Military-Georgian highway, they suddenly discovered that she was prone to motion sickness and got nauseated on the turns. He immediately cut their trip short. Two holiday passes were wasted, but he said: "Who cares?" They stopped in Tuapse.[17] He brought her grapes in a rubbery little container and massaged suntan oil into her back. Later they had a sealskin coat sewn for her by a special tailor. He got access through connections and said to the tailor: "Make it as if you were making it for your own wife." It was a fine fur coat, warm and voluminous. It was the first good thing she'd owned in her life.

Later he had his revenge. He had his revenge for the fur coat, the crystal chandelier, and the silver coffee service. He was capable of saying: "Other people. . . . " What about other people? Other people had already bought cars long ago. "Happiness isn't a matter of clothing." And did she say it was? For her, work had always taken first place, with everyday life second.

When she got married, Iraida took it for granted that they'd have children. If she had a husband, that meant she'd have children. Three years later that notion rather surprised her—why? It wasn't a question of anxiety or disillusionment—there was none of that. She was over thirty, she was in charge of her department, her ideas were being put into practice, and the advantages of not having children were very palpable. That was why at first she and her husband didn't discuss the subject out of bashful delicacy, but later they avoided it deliberately. So they had no children—well and good.

... The young woman with the Japanese parasol could also have been Valentin Petrovich's daughter. Strangely enough, Iraida couldn't decide what was better—for her to be his *woman* or his *daughter?*

What nonsense can keep on bothering you! What on earth did she care? Mistress, wife, daughter. . . . What was it to her? They'd drunk tea three times, she'd washed his children's underwear twice, and they'd been to the embankment. Come on! All the same, what was she to him? She'd come up to him and run her finger down his cheek, and had stayed at his side.

Now, as she rocked on the soft springs, I. A. suddenly recalled her old room, with the cross you could see through the window, and pieces of dark bread on a chipped cheap plate. She was trying to dig some rubbery jam out of a jar with a knife, while Valentin Petrovich's daughter jumped up and down impatiently beside her.

"Come on, daughter!" he said.

The girl threw herself into his arms and began jumping up and down in his lap. Iraida kept on struggling with the damn recalcitrant jam. Natashka sighed and ran her small finger down her father's cheek, along a little scar. Iraida never had the time to find out where he'd got that scar.

That meant it had been Valentin Petrovich's daughter. She felt better, and even thought it funny now. Somehow the other "buts"—the suit and the deputy's badge—faded away.

The fact was that nowadays Iraida felt the deepest sympathy for anybody who had grownup children. She had eyes, and could see. She had ears, and could hear. She knew only too well what grownup children were like. Anna Berg's son would come to visit her. He was young but puny, already was balding in places, and wore his hair long at the back of his neck. He regularly came to hit her up for twenty-five rubles for "personal needs." Anna would utter her bass laugh and give him the money. He was her son, after all! Whenever Iraida saw this, she would rejoice at being free from such disgraceful scenes. But what if she had a daughter? Then she imagined Anna's daughter-in-law, all decked out in stones, chains, trinkets, and pendants, with crimson nails like talons on her widespread, grasping hands. She would also come running to her mother-in-law for ten rubles, a carton of cigarettes, face powder, lipstick, nylons. . . . Unlike Anna's son, she never repaid her debts. Anna's reaction to that was:

"What the hell. I'd rather she didn't give it back to me. Or else some stranger could make a scene with Misha, and he'd get an ulcer from nerves."

Not to have children *like those* is a gift from the gods. Of course, there are other kinds, too. True, she'd never seen them personally. They bleed you, suck you dry, and you're supposed to love them! However, to be fair, she and he are of one mind on the question of grownup children. That's why people say silly things about her: "She's like that because she doesn't have children." That's no argument, dear folks, no argument. You don't need brains to have a baby. It's everybody's personal choice. But what does it become? Frenzy! What kind of job is that? Feeding, dressing, getting set up, marrying off, babysitting. . . . And who's going to do all the rest?

True, there's a woman in her department, Maria Mitrofanovna. She's got the *brains* of a minister. Whenever there's a problem, even when there seems to be no solution, people go to her. When that happens I. A. hates herself. A couple of times she actually rejected a correct solution because Maria had suggested it, but that was too dear a price—an official one!—to pay for pride. It was funny: to get to Maria's brains you always had to pass through some damned luminescence. That's just what it was—luminescence. It was as if she moved in a nimbus of love, love for her children, her grandchildren, books, pictures, birds, dogs. . . . Ugh! They could be calling her from the Central Committee, the Soviet Ministry, or the State Planning Committee; personnel from the Soviet Mutual Economic Aid Fund could be driving over to consult with her, but "en route to her mind" everybody—every single one of them—would have to be thrilled with the photograph of her cat Maksik hanging above her desk. He'd have to chat about her granddaughter Lenochka, who—horror of horrors!—had scoliosis, and to read a composition by her niece Vera, for which the girl had received a prize somewhere. God knows what else you had to do. And they'd do it, so that the hen would finally lay her golden egg. And she knew, oh yes, she knew that they listened patiently to all this gibberish because they needed her for the other thing. She even said: "My friends! Everything else is secondary, only love is primary. This is indisputably true for women, and for the best men, too. Forgive me for digressing, Iraida Aleksandrovna. I haven't forgotten that time is money, but we weren't the ones who thought that up. It was the Americans, and do we really have to follow them to this extent?" And this nature of hers would glow nonstop, it would simply radiate. Yet she had the brains of a minister—damn her! She'd sit a while, mew over the papers—and then would propose a solution. On her sixtieth birthday the ministry was inundated with gifts and telegrams saying: don't leave!

Maria the hen. She and her husband—he's a big wheel, a botany teacher in an eight-year school; in short, buttercups galore—she and he walk along the street with their arms around each other. "The young people were so clever," she says, "to come up with this custom." Zinaida once walked behind them from Trubnaia Street to the Soviet Army Theater. She walked as if she were bewitched.

Just then she remembered something negative, really negative. Zina. They had started together in '41. They'd gone along neck and neck, and then, after the war, Iraida outdistanced her friend. Zina didn't have a sound grasp of essentials. Just one coat for ten years, and one room her whole life. And that wasn't out of modesty, but from lack of drive. And then, she never got married. . . . Lord! If she, Iraida, were to start over again, this time she'd really give a lot of thought to whether this business of "getting married" was worth the effort. Everyone's marriage seems okay to an outsider; but if one were to dig? Zina was a stupid woman, and she had stupid quirks: since nobody wants to marry me, I want "my own pear tree in my own backyard in Kliazma. To lie under it and not think about anything."

Where could Zina have got her own pear tree? That's just what Iraida asked her: where could you get money for that?

Many years later she invited Zina to her dacha. By then Zina was gravely ill. She couldn't walk much, but she toured everything. Slowly, taking breaks, she inspected everything, then sat down on a bench and said, with a great deal of venom (and she had three months left to live!):

"No, Iraida, this certainly isn't Kliazma. There's no pear tree here."

She'd never forget that about her! Like the idiot she was, she'd brought her by taxi to the country, so she could be in the midst of nature. She knew the diagnosis and knew it was a matter of months. She'd wanted to make the woman happy for a while. She'd sent Viacheslav off to Push-kino to get some strawberries at the farmers' market. True, Zinaida did eat the strawberries and drink the cognac. "Now I can have everything I shouldn't." But she didn't care a rap for the dacha and the land around it.

"Don't be offended," she told Iraida. "But you've brought me to a gloomy place. It's meant for positions, not people. Look, even the pines have an official and impersonal look to them. People don't leave any traces here, but pass through like shadows. . . . "

Iraida said:

"And it's a good thing they don't leave any traces. That means they preserve nature."

But Zina made a dismissive gesture:

"Don't play dumb. You have money. Buy yourself a pear tree and plant it. Get a cat. A dog, too. Hang a washstand on the pear tree. Dig a well."

Iraida looked at Zina and thought: She's mad. The cancer has already destroyed her personality completely. Just imagine such a thing—*a washstand on a pear tree.*

Zina died in her arms. At the last moment she opened her eyes and recognized her.

"Ah! It's you! Well? Did you plant the pear tree?"

Right after the crematorium, Iraida went to the dacha. For the first time in her life she didn't return to her job during working hours. She boarded the electric train and left. To hell with all of you! It was fall. The people with children of school age had moved out of their dachas, and only the old folks and people who had no children remained. It was very quiet and peaceful somehow. Iraida roamed around the lot.

What if she really did it—if she planted a pear tree? She started looking for a spot. It was difficult to find one because everything had been planted a long time ago, planted sensibly according to a plan. The empty spaces had a specific function—for drying the wash, for football, for children's sandboxes. "People thought it all out, they really did!" Iraida became exasperated. "This isn't a lot for pear trees. The place has an order of its own."

At that moment that order, whose structure had always made her feel good, suddenly evoked a sense of panic in her. She imagined that she was Zina, who hadn't had a private room until she was dying, or money for a first-class sanatorium, or a husband or a pear tree. And now she herself didn't exist. No trace of her anywhere. For some reason she found it very easy to be reincarnated into the something that was what remained of Zina. There, she doesn't exist. Next summer her successor will be sleeping in her official bed at her official dacha, by the official pines. He'll move something a trifle, just a touch, and he'll hammer two of his own nails on the terrace. Probably one for his raincoat, and the other. . . . He'll hang his racquet on the other. In the course of the summer their spirit will be effaced from the premises. There'll be no evidence of her life and Viacheslav's. The night before leaving, she'll carry the half-pints out into the ravine, and the cream jars and little medicine bottles along with them. And that's all. But at this point her thoughts got side-tracked. You didn't have to die for there to be nothing left of you. Why die? To leave work, to retire, was enough. She became frightened that she hadn't gone back to work after the crematorium. And she ran to catch the electric train. If she made the one that left at four-twenty, she'd arrive right before working hours were over. Throwing off her sandals, she started running, just as she was, in her nylons.

. . . Say what you will, a part of her life had disappeared along with Zina. As it had disappeared once with Mitia. And Ivan Sergeevich. . . . And Valentin Petrovich. . . .

Every time she reached this point, she'd get angry at herself: it wasn't right to list a living person along with the dead. Valentin Petrovich was alive, after all, and was even some sort of deputy. She'd never wished him any harm. She'd wished him nothing but good, and had never done him any harm. But these logical and righteous explanations to herself didn't make her feel any better.

Toward morning, V. M. for some reason recalled that Shibaev's fourth mate was a stomatologist and was undoubtedly loaded. Now, there was a fellow who knew how to stay on top, a real smart guy! Someone else would have gone under time and again, whereas he kept bouncing back, and his situation only got better and better. He has children from each of his girlfriends, but no one would ever write a complaint against him, nor would he say no to anyone. People even visit him as if he were a member of the family. V. M. was overcome by a profound, oppressive sense of mortification.

Right then he decided to drop in on Nastia with the very best of intentions. His visit didn't look like a detour; he hardly went out of his way. All he did was make a stop and hitch a ride for a short distance. After all, it was his home territory, the place he'd spent his youth, so he was drawn to it. No one could criticize him for that. What was wrong with it? As he walked along, he thought: "I'm going there with good intentions."

Nastia was standing beside the house on a stepladder and—you've got it—was whitewashing a wall. She was standing on it when she saw him and broke into uncontrollable laughter:

"Hold it! I'm about to fall off! That's all I need."

Valentin Matveevich's suitcase was light, and he held the stepladder with his free hand so that Nastia could climb down. Her plump white legs and green slip flashed right by him.

"You know why I cracked up," she laughed, wiping her hand on her apron and holding it out to him. "Whenever I whitewash now, I think of you! You recall how I disgraced you? I was remembering it now. Then I look, and here you are in person."

"I'm just passing through." Viacheslav Matveevich's voice was hoarse. "I thought I'd have a look and see how you live."

"Well, well, well," laughed Nastia. "Why all of a sudden? Well, go on, sit down, have a look around. My man will be coming from work soon, I'll introduce you."

"You're married?"

"What kind of a question is that? Of course I am!" She didn't stop laughing. "And you?"

"I'm married." It came out sounding proud, as if absolutely everyone around him were a bachelor, whereas he was married.

"You have kids?"

"We don't have children," he continued in the same tone. "We both work a lot."

"And that's why you don't have children?"

Well, she wasn't going to sidetrack him with a ploy like that.

"We have a different kind of life, Nastia."

"Ah! Museums . . . theaters . . . Zeldin and Nelepp. . . . "

"What?" For some reason that suddenly made Viacheslav Matveevich feel alarmed or offended (it was hard to tell which): what did that have to do with anything?

"We've got three," said Nastia.

"What is your husband?"

"A wonderful man. Our son's already a school director. Our older daughter's enrolled at an institute, and the younger one's in school. That's how we live. Everyone should have a life like ours."

"We live well, too. That means everything's really fine. . . . "

"Why have you come? Come on, tell me, why? To have a look at me, at my children, or for some other reason?"

She looked him over from head to foot. She was small and solidly built, with a cheap comb in her hair, her dress splashed with slaked lime. The thought kept nagging at him: why hadn't she gone to change? After all, he was a guest, wasn't he? He was a man, wasn't he? "She's let herself go!" he thought gleefully. "Let herself go completely."

"I'm just passing through," he said carelessly. "I stopped off on the way. "I'll be going now. My train leaves soon."

"Well, well!" responded Nastia strangely. "Well, well! As you go past the school, have a look at my son. He's playing football with the kids."

"The school director?"

Nastia gave a laugh.

"Isn't it fitting?"

"It's sort of strange."

"Well, go on if you're just passing through."

"You're not so young anymore," Viacheslav Matveevich suddenly said pompously. "You could have got somebody to do the whitewashing. Hired somebody."

"Slava, I've been doing my own cleaning my whole life! Hire somebody! What if I like doing it?"

He didn't remember any more of the conversation. But apparently there was more of it, because some time went by, and several women came out to stand at the gates. They stared, their hands raised as if they were saluting. And the feeling he had, that he and Nastia hadn't been apart since that time in Moscow, couldn't have been born in the space of a couple of minutes. It even seemed to him as if the same lady in the bathrobe were standing in the doorway across from Nastia's house. That's when for some reason he became frightened, as if he had to explain something, to say certain words. He even broke out in a light sweat, though generally he was a man not given to perspiring, of which, incidentally, he was very proud.

He started talking. Everyone has his own road to travel, he said. All of life is a road. And that being so, it's good to have a suitable companion to travel with.

"Ah!" said Nastia. "I understand. A traveling companion. To play dominoes, cards. . . . " And she gave a laugh. "Don't bother explaining, Slavik. What for, after all these years?"

"No, no!" Viacheslav Matveevich got upset. "That's not the right expression. Not a traveling companion. Rather, a comrade-in-arms. . . . Do you understand?"

"I do!" said Nastia. "That's a good expression. I like it. Let me feed you, okay? I really should feed you! I must. I'll feed you as a traveling companion and as a comrade-in-arms, as well as an acquaintance, and I'll feed you even as my first husband." Nastia suddenly grew excited, clapped her hands, and dashed into the house.

But he had enough sense to glance at the black dial of his Japanese watch and stop her. "I'm very sorry, but alas. . . . " He made up some story about having a car waiting for him on the other side of the hill.

In conclusion he made a gesture—he kissed Nastia's hand. She had a strong little fist, tanned and wrinkled.

He left as if he were sailing away. At any rate, that's how he wanted to appear in all the eyes watching him from under the women's saluting hands. He should have headed right out, like a white steamer. . . . But he stopped by the school football field. There was one adult among the group of children. That had to be Nastia's son. He glanced around in surprise, then took the ball and headed for the fence. The closer he approached, the better Viachelslav Matveevich felt: *he didn't like* Nastia's son. Nastia had managed to have a son who was exactly the kind of guy he couldn't stand. Precisely that type. First of all, he had grey hair. Now, why, at thirty? What tribulations had he suffered? What could he have seen? What could he know? Secondly, why that ingratiating glance? What sense of joy could be prompting it? After all, he was nobody to him—neither kith nor kin. Then there was his whole appearance. The sports outfit he wore was expensive, made of pure wool, not rags. So why keep bouncing the dirty, dusty ball against his knee? If you really must do that, buy some tricot for five rubles and forty kopeks, and then you can bounce the ball all you want, keep bouncing it until you drop.

"Whom are you looking for?" asked Nastia's son.

"Why are you, the director, playing ball . . . like a little kid . . . ?"

The guy laughed Nastia's laugh:

"How do you know I'm the director?"

"I just know." He wanted to say something about his outfit, too, and to ask him about his hair. What unbearable sufferings had turned it grey?

"I thought you wanted a light," said Nastia's son. "But I don't smoke."

A nonsmoker, too!

"Go ahead and play!" Viacheslav Matveevich said it as if he were giving him permission, and the guy burst out laughing: that's exactly how he interpreted it.

"Well, thanks!" said Nastia's son and, like a little boy, kicked the ball gracefully with his left foot. He did it like a professional.

When he and Iraida got married, he'd waited for a son, but they didn't have one. Then they actually decided: that's fine. That leaves us free.

But now he suddenly thought: if this grey-haired guy had been his son, it wouldn't have mattered if he'd torn a dozen outfits at one go. Then he, Viacheslav Matveevich, in his stylish synthetic suit, could have kicked the ball himself right now, kicked it so high that everyone would have gasped. And Nastia would have gasped and clapped her hands.

He was in a peculiar state of mind. He had done everything right. He hadn't waited for her husband; he'd kissed her hand, which was the proper thing to do; and he'd left quickly, as if he had business to take care of. He'd comported himself beautifully, and had told the young fellow his opinion about football politely, without forcing himself on him. He'd come and gone as he wanted. So why did he hurt all over?

He felt as if someone had shot him out of a sling, and now he was flying and would land God knows where, stomach first.

Viacheslav Matveevich started drinking in the bar at the station. He drank a lot, greedily, without having any snacks. He overheard the waitress at the bar say to some man:

"Looks like a man with an important position, yet he's a drunk. . . ."

He wasn't flattered by the first half of her description of him, or distressed by the second. It occurred to him that the first wasn't true, and neither was the second. Truth. . . . There was no truth. . . . There was nothing. . . . His whole life. . . . His whole life he'd dreamed of going to Nastia and making sure that *back then* he'd acted right. But it hadn't worked out like that. Nastia had laughed, and his hopes were turned to dust. And that was the way it was. An old man came to see an old love of his, and had nothing to say. Of course, he'd mumbled something about some *course of development*, and she had nodded and kept wanting to feed him.

He was no idiot. For thirty years he'd known that that's *exactly* how everything would be. There was no way to drink that away. No way. Never.

The alarm clock rings shrilly. It's seven in the morning. Both open their eyes painfully. Has there been any night at all? Their backs, necks, and heads ache. Ah, if only it were possible not to get up. . . . At a quarter to eight they're at the table.

"When you were eating the lamprey eel yesterday evening, you forgot to close the refrigerator. It's a good thing I got up."

"You didn't wipe the floor in the bathroom after doing the wash. There was a puddle there the whole night."

They'd had their say, and hid behind the newspapers.

She wanted to lean down over her cup, but immediately the French corset painfully forced her to sit upright.

"Like a trap," she thought and slowly raised her coffee to her lips. . . . How infinitely long a cup of coffee can travel.

THE VIOLIN

LIUDMILA PETRUSHEVSKAIA

Translated by

MARINA ASTMAN

SHE WAS LYING IMMODERATELY, GETTING ENTANGLED in her tales, forgetting what she'd said the day before, and so on, and so forth. This was a typical, easily discernible case of lying, of putting on airs and presenting all her actions as being significant and of great consequence, as a result of which something had to occur, but nothing ever occurred; and yet, with the same important demeanor, she would drag herself through the entire ward, holding in her outstretched hand a pale-blue envelope containing probably just some trifling message, but she would carry it, demonstrating with her whole demeanor the supreme necessity of mailing the letter. The content of her letter was roughly known to all the patients in that hospital ward, but obviously only the intention with which the letter was being dispatched was known, and not the words in which she couched her obvious intention, not the form in which she hid all her pathetic wishes, so obvious to all, or how she had lied this particular time to her heart's chosen one, a certain engineer Valerii who lived in another city.

However, it doesn't follow from all this that she, this very same Lena, was a chatterbox or willingly launched into explanations concerning her present condition. On the contrary, she was laconic and excessively ceremonious; this ceremoniousness became especially apparent during the rounds of the head physician, who liked to converse with Lena while seeing the patients on Mondays. The head physician, frowning in a paternal manner, used to say that everything was taking its normal course, and if henceforth things continued thus, then our little student would recover and would go out for a little stroll before the impending central event; and that she shouldn't be afraid to go outdoors, he would then interrupt Lena, it was absolutely imperative to breathe fresh air before her delivery, to take walks in the park, to store up strength. "And how are your hands?" he asked Lena. "As the hands of a violinist, won't they grow unused to strings and bow, and isn't it generally true that musicians, and especially conservatory students, must practice every day for several hours?" "For four, sometimes five," replied Lena, not in the least embarrassed. "And before the specialized exam, as much as you can without straining your tendons, and that, to be sure, is a matter of stamina."

The professor would move on and finally disappear from the ward, and everybody would carry on with her own business; but Lena, diligent Lena, once again would sit down to write her letter, writing and writing until the moment came to seal up all this scribbling and solemnly carry it through the entire ward to the exit. Or she'd make telephone calls and, in a soft voice, negotiate with somebody; those negotiations seemed to be of a strictly business nature, and you could see by the expression on her face that she wanted to clear up something extremely important and decisive for her. Those telephone conversations took place every day—each time there was the same preoccupied face, the same hushed voice, the same vague, unintelligible questions.

In spite of those exclusively businesslike telephone conversations, and in spite of the existence of somebody who was doing something for Lena, nobody ever came to see her, and, accordingly, there was nothing on her bedside table except an empty glass covered with a paper napkin.

After long days of silent rest stretched out on her hospital bed—she had not been allowed to get up and walk around, as generally was the rule in that hospital whenever there were the slightest signs of complications—after those days of obligatory bedrest, she at last was allowed to get up, and she left the ward, heading somewhere with her usual letter in a pale-blue envelope. She began to pace up and down, and struck up some quiet, meaningful friendships with the nurses and nurses' aides, but it remained uncertain why Lena undertook all those secret negotiations with the nurses and aides, because they yielded no practical results: as before, nobody came to see Lena, and as before, perfect emptiness yawned out of her clean glass, which she sometimes used to get a drink of water. Lena also busied herself slaving over her letters or fixing her hair before the mirror in the corridor, or modestly consuming her hospital dinner. And, one should note, to all of that she attached a kind of supreme, inexplicable meaning.

The only channel filtering through at least some information about Lena was her conversations with the professor on Mondays, during his rounds, when she, all in a blush, lay on her elevated pillows and in a hushed voice answered the professor's questions, although he could have known everything from her health record.

However, the professor asked questions, and Lena answered him, and from those soft, brief answers the ward, frozen in silence, found out, for example, that Lena had fainted on the street and that her girlfriend had sent for an ambulance—and that was all. Further, in reply to the professor's inquiries, Lena complained about her present great weakness, about dizziness, and about occasional pain in the lower back. "Stay here, stay here and rest," said the professor after those conversations.

Each Monday they resumed their quiet conversations, during which Lena monotonously complained about dizziness and some sort of weakness, but her blood tests were excellent, as it turned out, and her heart condition couldn't have been better. And so, one fine day, one of those Mondays, the professor gave orders to have Lena discharged, advising her to move about as much as possible so as to overcome the weakness caused by lying in the hospital, and to start exercising vigorously so as to grow strong and robust and be able to cope well with everything in the best possible way. The professor jokingly invited Lena to come for delivery when he was on duty, asked her, for the hundredth time at least, whether she would send him tickets for her solo concerts, and disappeared into his quarters.

By that day, that Monday, Lena already felt quite at home in the ward and spoke a lot about her husband Valerii, the engineer living in another city who for the time being was unable to join her. Lena also told them that she had spent New Year's Eve at his place and that his parents had treated her splendidly, and so on and so forth.

In just the same way she kept up her diligent letter writing, her solemn procession through the entire ward to the doors, her secret negotiations with the nurses, and as before, she talked on the telephone with her girlfriend in a hushed voice—and all that to no avail.

However, one should note that by that time her bedside table was no longer empty; it was filled with all kinds of fruit and vegetables and food in general. This filling had occurred fairly soon, immediately after the women had guessed the true state of affairs. At first timid and ashamed, but later more composed and at ease, they began to put on Lena's night table all their provisions; Lena, likewise, dealt with those gifts at first shyly and shamefacedly, but later with ever greater ease: she ate without stopping, constantly nibbling, dragging herself to the sink to wash some fruit on a plate and munching again. She ate apples, lettuce, cheese, and Polish sausage, candy, and once even half of a raw cabbage head, which had been brought into the ward for a woman with a stomach ailment.

Now the nurses gave Lena larger helpings, and sometimes, when there was nothing else available, they even offered her a second bowl of soup after dessert. Lena accepted, triumphantly nodding her head, and calmly ate the second bowl of soup, then left to comb her hair or sat down to write the next letter. Incidentally, the envelopes were no longer her own, because, as it turned out, her husband was late in sending her allowance, and her girlfriend could not come visit her. That girlfriend, to be sure, didn't come and didn't come, and the whole month that Lena spent in the hospital, that girlfriend didn't show up until the very end, when Lena was leaving the hospital.

True, before Lena left, the women in her ward negotiated with the doctors to keep Lena for two more months until her baby was due, but evidently that was impossible, and finally that Monday arrived when the professor again conversed with Lena about the difficulties of studying at the conservatory, already knowing that there was no conservatory or violin. Nevertheless, that conversation on the most elevated level took place, and shortly after, Lena left the ward for good, together with her yellow comb, which had become so familiar in the course of that month.

Lena departed from the ward, one could say, fully exposed, yet without losing her solemnity and mysteriousness. And all that after the entire ward had seriously discussed in front of Lena what she could do with her future baby, and whether she could count on help from that engineer who, Lena claimed, was her husband—all these problems immediately came to the surface the moment Lena started to say goodbye. The patients in her ward in a chorus advised Lena to place the baby in a children's home, if only for a year, and during that period to somehow get on her own feet, find a job and living quarters, and only then take the baby back. Lena nodded in her usual dignified manner, sitting on her bed, and then once more said goodbye to everybody and left with her swollen belly; afterwards, she could be seen again as half an hour later she was triumphantly walking away in a crumpled yellow raincoat, arm in arm with her supposed girlfriend. It was clear to everyone that her fainting spell on the street had been faked, and that after some time had elapsed, the two once again would stage something on the street, if only Lena wouldn't faint before they managed to agree on all the necessary arrangements.

THROUGH HARD TIMES

IRINA VELEMBOVSKAIA

Translated by

JOSEPH KIEGEL

IT ALL BEGAN ONE EVENING AT THE DISTRICT HOSPITAL in Guliashi. Supper had already been brought around. The nurses' aides were collecting plates of unfinished porridge, and the lights in the wards were beginning to go out when an old Pobeda[1] ambulance honked at the gates.

A woman had been brought in. She walked along the path from the gate, hiding her pale, bloody face in a shawl, while an attendant, an elderly woman, supported her by the arm.

"Probably a fight," remarked one of the patients who stood smoking in the vestibule of the surgical building. "Drunk."

"Go on, you smokers, get out of here," scolded the attendant as she closed the door behind the woman. "You're always imagining drunks. This is Pania, the postwoman from the Hill. Who's ever seen her drunk?"

Pania was led into the receiving room; the doctor washed his sinewy white hands while the attendant carefully unwound the shawl, which was spotted with dark blood.

"Have I ruined my kerchief?" Pania asked in a low voice.

"Forget the kerchief! Be thankful your head is in one piece. Who did it?"

"Be quiet!" the doctor ordered.

Pania sat still while they cleaned the wound, stuffed something into it, and put in the stitches. Only from time to time she said quietly, "Oh, my heavens! Will you be done soon?"

Then she was taken to a bed, and since she suddenly felt very weak, the aide lifted Pania's feet for her and covered her with a blanket.

Everyone in the ward was already asleep. Pania lay motionless, her bandaged head showing white in the dark. The aide glanced around to see if the night nurse was close by and leaned toward Pania.

"Are you awake, Praskovia? What happened to you?"

"Let me sleep, for God's sake. I'll tell you tomorrow," Pania muttered with displeasure.

The aide left with nothing and Pania dozed off, happy that the pain in her head was gradually subsiding and she could sleep in—not like at home, where she always got up early.

Nevertheless, without any alarm clock or cock's crow, Pania woke up right at five. She realized where she was and why, and couldn't sleep any longer. She took a sizeless flannelette gown from the head of the bed, stuck her quick postal feet into a pair of pancakelike slippers, and went into the corridor.

"Nastia!" she called to an aide she knew. "Take me to wash up. Do you have a mirror? Don't I look just horrible? They shaved half my head."

In the washroom she decided to satisfy the aide's curiosity, to tell who had smashed her on the head. The night staff, however, already knew the whole story. A policeman had come and told them how Pania had been delivering the evening mail. When she knocked at a certain house on Beriozovka, she heard someone groaning. She broke the hook on the door and saw a husband holding his wife by the throat as he flailed her. Not even stopping to throw off her heavy bag, Pania began to drag him away from his wife. He turned around, grabbed a copper tray from the table, and smacked her over the head. But Pania held on tightly to the crazed man, smearing him with blood and giving his wife a chance to run to the neighbors'. She covered her gashed head with a shawl, took her bag to the post office, and called the hospital from there herself.

"You ought to at least give her a reward," the aides told the policeman. "If she hadn't stepped in, he might've killed her."

"I don't know about a reward, but you fix her up a nice little place here," the policeman asked. "She's very decisive. Everybody ought to be so aware. Whenever there's a fight, people always wait for a policeman to break it up."

... In Guliashi, many people on the left bank, or the Hill as it was called, knew Pania. She and her husband used to work at a neighboring lumber company, he as a lumberjack and she in the tool shop. Pania's husband had died three years earlier. They had had no children, and she lived alone. She was nearly forty-three but was still quite a fine woman, quick and easy to get along with, according to her neighbors and coworkers. True, she wasn't known as a beauty, but she did have one inherent quality—vivacity.

When people asked if she hadn't dried her tears for her late husband too quickly, Pania answered sincerely, "I can't really blame myself for anything. I felt quite sorry for him when he was alive. Toward the end he was very ill; he had two operations, and I still always slept near him. He was seventeen years older than me, you know. I was still young when we met, but he had been married twice. I wasn't jealous of that. What business was it of mine? I didn't care who was before me, as long as there wasn't anyone else while I was around."

Pania moved to Guliashi shortly after her husband's death. A stepson had come and asked for his share of the house. Pania knew that as his father's lawful wife she had inherited everything. But she said to her stepson, who was always complaining about his life, "Where is your share? You can't divide three windows and a door. Take the whole thing, it's yours. Just give me whatever money you can spare. I'll live; you won't cause me any hardship. I've got hands and feet, and a head, no matter how poor."

Besides hands, feet, and a poor head, Pania had some belongings that she didn't mind parting with.

"I didn't go a month without a present from my husband. He seemed to know they'd get me through hard times. Now, who could I sell that three-gallon samovar to? Brand new. What good is it to me? I'll use a teapot."

She got a job at the post office, saved ten or twenty rubles from every paycheck, and in a year had bought herself a small house with just one room. Ever since then Pania had flitted around the Hill with a twenty-pound bag on her stomach, knocking on gates and doors, shooing away fat, hissing geese with a switch, and carrying a stick for mean dogs.

"Put your dog on a leash, citizen. If it bites, I'll go for shots and that's it. What do I care? But you'll answer to the law. Our pay isn't much, and if we're going to get bitten in every yard, who'll deliver the mail?"

Yet when Pania was finally caught by some Zhuchka[2] that came out from under a porch, she didn't go for shots.

"Oh, I know that little dog like it was my own. It's the size of a mitten, but it's got puppies and it's mean. I was wearing wool socks, so it hardly scratched me."

One time a gang attacked Pania and tried to take the pension money she was carrying. But she defended herself and raised a ruckus. After that she didn't carry money in her bag. She hid it under her blouse in a special pouch. When she went to a house to deliver a pension, the first thing she did was say, "Turn around for a minute, please."

. . . The hospital stood in a grove of trees on a high, loose bank. To keep the patients from going down to the river, it was fenced off by a low railing, which took no effort to get over. Tilting birches sprinkled the warm September water with their small yellow leaves. No benches were around, but there were several old tree stumps, flat and roomy, that seemed made for sitting. And the grass near them had been flattened by hospital slippers.

Pania rustled through the fallen leaves and sat on one of the stumps, pulling her drab hospital gown over her sturdy knees. The curly shadow of a twisted branch flitted across her face and became lost in her dark eyes, eyes the color of autumn acorns.

Pania sat and thought about what a lovely fall it was, how pleasant it was in the woods, and she hadn't once gone hunting for saffron milk-caps or red whortleberries. Now she couldn't go at all—it hurt to bend down.

Beyond the shore the blue river sparkled, a silvery steamship floated out of the glimmering distance, and the calm birch trees bowed to a light breeze. It was so quiet and pleasant that she didn't even want to remember all that had happened the day before. Oh, some people are crazy!

Then Pania noticed that one of the patients had sat down right on the rough, dry grass not far from her. The man's gown was the same sad color as Pania's. He had a large head with curly hair and a sickly white, swollen face.

Pania hastily pulled down the hem of her gown and fixed the kerchief on her head, gingerly touching the spot above her forehead where the hair was shaved and there was still a sharp pain. She pulled up the straying cuffs of her men's shirt—the hospital was full and the aides were swamped with laundry, so she couldn't criticize them.

It wasn't one of Pania's rules to meet someone and not speak.

"Been sick for long, mister?" she asked and moved closer. "Are you from the Hill or across the river?"

Curly (that's how Pania privately nicknamed him) moved closer, too. He was no longer young, but he was nice looking, broad-faced, and he seemed melancholy.

"Across the river, from the cove. My kidneys are out of whack. I haven't had a drop of salt in two months. I've been eating sweets and semolina like a baby."

"What kind of food is that for a man?" Pania sympathized.

"My health almost turned around," Curly went on loquaciously. "My discharge was coming up, but there was this heart patient next to me. He gave me a homemade pickle. 'If your body wants it,' he says, 'it's good for you.' I knew it was no good, nothing but trouble. But, you see, I couldn't resist. The whole ward smelled like dill! I ate a couple. I'm ashamed to say it! I puffed up again, and the next morning I could hardly open my eyes."

"Imagine!" Pania shook her head. "You don't seem like an intemperate man. That old fellow ought to be kicked right out of the hospital! What an expert! If he doesn't know what's going on, he ought to stay out of it. Giving you advice about your body!"

They sat for a while, and Pania told of her own misfortune.

"I'm afraid that after this crack on the head, they'll make me an invalid. The doctor says that after sick leave I go straight to the medical commission. He hit me hard, you know! If only I'd moved my head to the side a little or put up my arm. You can't think of everything at once."

"I suppose you'll take the troublemaker to court?" Curly asked.

"What do you think? Of course I will. What if I suddenly can't work anymore? If he'd killed me, I wouldn't say a word, but now I can't let it go."

The aides called them to lunch, and they cut their conversation short. They went to their own wards.

Visitors began to come after six. No one called on Pania, and she didn't expect anyone—everyone was busy enough, and she wasn't having a baby or so gravely ill that they should run seven miles to see her. Even so she felt sad when she looked at the others. Near the women's wards, husbands pressed against the windows, which were covered with bug nets, and chatted. The ambulatory patients poured into the garden. There was a young couple over on a bench, and it was clear from the way they acted that they were newlyweds.

There was also a somewhat older couple on another bench. Walking by, Pania heard the beautiful but cyanotic woman say as she firmly squeezed her husband's hand in her own, "Vanka, take the money for the abortion to the receiving room. Or else the next time you come, your credit won't be any good."

Pania stopped, struck by an unusual feeling. "She hasn't even gotten over this one, and she's already planning for the next!" she thought with sad amazement. "She loves him!"

Pania sat down, too, and began to think of her own husband, who was now in the ground. He had been a good man, but somehow they had lived together almost too peacefully. Pania hadn't suffered any pain because of him, or felt a woman's cares. Maybe there should have been some. Was that all there was to it?

Mastering her thoughts, Pania looked around again. For some reason Curly was nowhere to be seen. Perhaps no one had come to visit him, either. Was he sitting somewhere in the garden alone, hanging his shaggy head and staring at the ground?

She found him in the same place. He was sitting on a tree stump, twisting a sheaf of grass in his large hands. He saw her and smiled.

"A hospital is just another prison. At least if you talk with somebody, it's cheerier."

Pania could hear his difficult breathing—the shirt on his chest seemed ruffled by a light breeze.

"You ought to button your collar," she advised. "It's getting late, and a chill is blowing in from the water."

Curly obediently buttoned up. Then he took a little bag of fruit drops from his pocket.

"Have one? It'll cheer us up."

Pania took a fruit drop.

"Why are you so sad? You'll get better! They do a good job these days. They know all sorts of cures. The doctor told me that if my Stepan Vasilyevich's heart hadn't played tricks on him, he'd have gotten back on his feet after the operation."

"So your Stepan Vasilyevich died," Curly said pensively. "That means you're alone? At least tell me your name, my bride."

Pania was on her guard. It seemed that Curly was making fun of her.

"If I say it's Violetta, you won't believe me. My name is Praskovia Ivanovna, but some call me Pasha and others Pania."

"Why wouldn't I believe you? There are all sorts of names nowadays. So it's Violetta. There are even stranger ones."

Darkness was coming on. It was already time to go back to the wards. She and Curly were heading down the lane when a woman with a purse in her hands rose to meet Pania. She looked around in dismay and couldn't decide whether to speak in front of Curly.

"Excuse me, are you Praskovia Ivanovna? I'd like to have a few words with you."

Curly withdrew, and the woman began speaking hastily. "Praskovia Ivanovna, please, don't take my husband to court. He's a drinker, but he's not a bad man. He didn't mean to hit you so hard. It's the wine that did it, Praskovia Ivanovna!"

Pania said nothing, mechanically touching the sore spot on her head. Her supplicant began to whisper even more quickly.

"Here, I brought you something to eat. We have meat and our own eggs. I keep chickens. And if we can compensate you monetarily . . . "

"Listen, get out of here!" Pania said sternly. "I stood up for you as a woman. The hell with your compensation. When your husband breaks your arms and legs, demand compensation from him. And another thing: he doesn't coddle you enough with his fists, or you wouldn't come running here."

Pania got up and went to her building. She saw Curly in an adjacent doorway. He knit his thick brows and smiled, stroking his wide, stubbly chin.

"Hear that?" Pania asked.

He nodded and laughed. "So they slipped you a bribe? Tell them about it at the trial."

"What trial?" Pania waved her hand in annoyance. "The little fool will rush over there, too, and humiliate herself."

Pania was discharged three days later. During that time she didn't see anyone come to visit Curly, although he had told her that he was married. Pania was quite surprised. What kind of woman wouldn't run to the side of her sick husband? And such a fine man, too, talkative and sincere. You'd think she'd stay right by his bed. Yes, life is often strange!

When Pania was leaving, she wanted to say goodbye to Curly. Not finding him in the garden, she looked in the men's ward. He was lying on the bed under the window, very ill, and looking bleakly out at the yellow garden. When he saw Pania, he raised himself up on one elbow, waved to her, and sank heavily back onto the pillow.

"Get well, Grigorii Alekseevich," she said tenderly.

"That's in God's hands now," Curly joked wearily.

"Not God's at all! It depends on you. You've got to keep your spirits up."

"I'm trying, but it's not working." Curly covered his eyes with his broad hand, then held it out to Pania. "Goodbye, Violetta."

His hand was hot, sick, and feeble. Pania, almost burning herself on his powerless hand, suddenly decided she couldn't leave him for good. It would be inhuman. She would definitely be back. It wouldn't be the first time she'd visited a hospital and sat by a mournful bed on a little white stool. There was a reason her late husband used to say that with her character, she should be an insurance agent or a nurse. On holidays, when people were getting ready to go visiting or to a movie, Pania was always taking a package to someone.

Curly was surprised when he saw Pania under his window again. She had remembered that he couldn't have anything salty or spicy and had brought him a jar of stewed fruit and a sweet gingerbread. Curly perked up, threw on a gown, and went out to the garden. He was happy, but Pania detected a certain uneasiness in his sickly, puffy face.

"Why did you come, Violetta? You really came to see me? Well, thank you! How's your noggin, getting better? Good for you!"

"And how are you, Grigorii Alekseevich?" she asked, a little embarrassed.

The bandage was gone from her head, and she had bought a new kerchief. Without her institutional hospital clothes, Curly saw that Pania was very nice looking. All she lacked, perhaps, was feminine spirit, playfulness.

Pania inquired about his health and asked him not to "sin" by eating things he shouldn't. Or there would be no end to his troubles.

"You've got a family," Pania said sternly, although she knew through the aides that the only family Curly had was a wife, and she was a "whore."

She had come only twice in six weeks, and it was assumed that they didn't get along.

"Now, I'll come see you on Sundays," Pania said as she was getting ready to leave.

Curly suddenly appeared embarrassed.

"My dear," he said guiltily, "please come, of course. But you know I've got a wife. Otherwise, really, I'm all for it."

Pania saw that he had completely misunderstood her, and she was slightly angry.

"What does your wife have to do with it? I'm here as a friend. Or don't you men understand that kind of relationship?"

Their eyes met, and they both withstood the look. Curly was silent for a moment and then said, "Come visit. But don't spend a cent on me. I've got all I need here."

But how could she resist spending money? On Sunday there was always a big market in Guliashi. Pania delivered the mail early, and went to buy apples, pears, and rose-colored sour milk. At the appointed hour she was already walking up to the hospital with a bag.

But Curly wasn't waiting for her by the window, on the porch, or in the garden.

"His wife came," an aide told her. "They're walking in the grove somewhere. You should get lost for a while, Pasha."

But Pania didn't get lost. After all, her reason for coming was good. She decided to wait, give him the package, and ask how he felt. The time before, he had said that he was going to have to have a blood transfusion, and that was probably hard on him. She would wait: it would also give her a chance to see what kind of wife he had.

Pania sat on a bench and put her bundle of gifts down. While there was time, she wiped off her dusty shoes with a clump of dry grass, and getting out a mirror, she combed her hair and moistened her light brows a little with her finger. Why had she done that now?

Pania looked around. Curly was walking down the path, and beside him was his wife—very beautiful, well-dressed, with coifed hair and penciled brows. A silk jacket, a dainty kerchief on the very back of her head, fashionable shoes on long, powerful legs.

"You rarely visit," Curly said sternly, still not seeing Pania.

"Come on, Grisha! A round-trip trip ticket is fourteen-eighty."

"A ruble forty-eight. Don't count the old way."

"The old way is better. And every workday lost is fifty rubles."

"You're going to have to bury me, so you'd better get an estimate ahead of time."

Then Curly saw Pania. He stopped and said calmly, "Well, I've got more visitors. She's from the union over in the cove."

Pania rose and said in a voice just as calm, "Hello."

"Hello," his wife answered cordially. Then she was suddenly in a hurry. "Well, I'll be running along, Grisha. Here are some presents for you. Empty the bag out for me."

She left, smacking Curly between his thick brows and then wiping her lips with a hanky. She walked quickly, without looking back, swaying a bit and pressing the sand down with her high heels.

Curly sat next to Pania. He unwrapped the package—half a dozen eggs, bologna, ginger cookies . . . and an open bottle of vodka.

"How thoughtful!" he muttered angrily and then looked at Pania. "If I eat this, I'll be dead by morning."

"But doesn't she know?" Pania asked, looking warily at the deadly gifts.

"I told her. She probably forgot. You take all this stuff, Praskovia Ivanovna. You don't want it? Well, then I'll give it to the aides."

They sat quietly for a while. Pania decided to offer her package to him. Curly absent-mindedly took an apple that was white with juice, stared at it intently, and let his hand drop wearily.

"Things are getting me down."

Pania realized that she ought to say a few cheerful words, that they both needed some kind of release. She felt so sorry for Curly that she was ready to hug his head and press his sickly, stern face to her breast.

"I read about you in the paper, Grigorii Alekseevich," Pania said, gaining control of herself. "In the *Red River Man*. There's even a big picture of you. They give all the details about how you work, everything."

"But that was published last spring." Curly raised his head. "Why read old newspapers?" He brightened up a bit. "Tell me about yourself, Violetta. Do you enjoy coming here and smelling this hospital odor? You'd be better off going for a walk in the park. You should go see a movie. The days are so beautiful!"

"Today is the Feast of the Assumption, you know," Pania said. "We have an altar in our village."

"You're like an old woman—you remember the holidays. But every day can be a holiday for you. You're healthy, attractive. No admirers have latched onto you yet?"

"No," Pania admitted.

"You're probably very choosy. Otherwise you wouldn't be alone."

Pania decided to be frank. "I'm afraid of making a mistake, Grigorii Alekseevich. You can always find someone for the moment, but for a lifetime—that takes a lot of hunting."

Curly nodded in agreement and said sternly, "That's right. It's easy to make a mistake. You put your whole soul into someone and they rub your nose in the dirt." Afraid that he had said too much, he added jokingly,

"Only don't give up, Violetta. We're not all worthless. You'll find a good man!"

"One way or another," said Pania, wanting to change the subject. "But you shouldn't tease me by calling me Violetta, Grigorii Alekseevich. What kind of a Violetta am I? A neighbor gave me that name when I was a girl. I blurted it out to you without thinking."

They both sat for a while in the gentle silence of the early September evening. It truly was beautiful, golden-red and quiet. The leaves on the paths whispered among themselves, casting a spell, and the blue, steadily flowing river was visible through the grove as the trees shed their leaves.

"Go on home, dear," Curly sighed. "It's time for my shots, time for them to stick holes in my hide. You should take this food. When you get home you can fix yourself some fried eggs."

Several days later the rains came, and all the leaves in the garden fell from the trees. Although it wasn't very cold, the patients weren't allowed out, to keep them from carrying wet sand in on their slippers. It also became difficult to talk through the windows because the frames were shut tightly, the latches were driven home, and the sills were filled with pots of yellowing asparagus and misshapen century plants.

It began to get dark at six o'clock, and twice a week at that time they would allow visitors. Pania arrived in plenty of time so she wouldn't be left without a white gown.

"There's my friend!" Curly would rise from his bed. "Sit here, Pasha. You didn't get caught in the rain?"

"Just a sprinkle. Well, how are you feeling, Grigorii Alekseevich?"

Each time Pania waited for him to say that he would be discharged soon. But for the moment there was no talk of that. Curly merely promised to come visit her when he was better, to see how she lived. Well, let him come and see that her place was nice, neat, clean. Curly said he'd get her a first-class ticket to Astrakhan on a steamship. That was a benefit he received as a river man. He had offered it to his wife many times, but she wasn't interested. So Pania could take the trip and see Gorky Lake, the Volga hydroelectric station, and New Volgograd.³ On the other hand, Pania figured that when Curly was discharged their whole friendship would come to an end. She was afraid of that now. She couldn't imagine that Sunday would come and she would have no place to go, no one to expect her. A person needs to be expected, absolutely needs to be!

She was even more terrified when Curly suddenly asked, "Pasha, answer me truthfully, do you resent me?"

"Whatever for?"

"Just don't be mad. You've been coming here for two months, spending your time on me. I can't believe that a woman would visit a man without being interested. . . . "

Pania gathered her will power and looked at Curly sternly.

"Do you know very much about women? There are all kinds, my dear. One you have to take care of, while another lives only to take care of others. Well, I've found myself something to do. Is that so bad? Don't be afraid of me, Grigorii Alekseevich. I mean well."

Curly became quiet. Then he took Pania's hand and squeezed it between his own big hands.

"Well, thank you twice as much then!" He shook his big curly head. "Being ill has really got me down, Pasha. It's awful being out of work, without a home. I'm sick and tired of this gown, this frayed shirt, these slippers! You've never seen me in good health. You know, Pasha, I'm an energetic, sociable guy. I like to dress well, to be fashionable. I've got an accordion, I can play good music."

"That's nice!" Pania said sincerely. "I love it when people play well." She said it, then stopped short. When would he ever play for her?

"Well, I'll be going."

"When will you come back?" asked Curly, this time with special anticipation. "Eh, Pashenka? Drop by!"

She promised to come in three days. Suddenly her heart was pounding.

Pania didn't even notice that those three days, from Wednesday to Saturday, three gloomy October days, were so cold and unpleasant because of the rain and the mud on the streets that she crisscrossed carrying her bag. She thought she had never seen better days. What was it he'd said to her the last time they met? Had he looked at her in a special way? Perhaps a touch more tenderly, more cheerfully than usual, and called her Pashenka. This "touch" had moved Pania so deeply that she felt her whole life was wrapped up in him now, and without him her life would be nothing.

She confidently pictured how she would get him up for work in the morning, not a minute too early, so as not to rob him of sleep, and not a minute too late, so as not to make him rush, but in time for him to shave, eat, and get dressed without hurrying. She imagined him standing in the middle of the yard, healthy and good-looking—a furry deerskin hat on his big curly head, a bright-red scarf smiling from under his yellow sheepskin coat, his galoshes sparkling black in the sun. As he walks to the street, she watches him through the frosty window. In the evening they would meet for dinner—she would eat the same foods he was allowed and cook such wonderful things that he wouldn't even ask for meat. Perhaps around May she would give him some ham, make fried eggs, and go for vodka. If the doctors allowed it, of course.

Pania would think she heard steps in the entryway, the creak of the door. She could see him already, and dared not run to him first with joy, but waited for him to say, "Pasha, it's me!"

There is no law against dreaming. Pania imagined a tiny girl with a round, curly head. She held onto her father's finger and suddenly took her first wobbly step. And he would say, "Pasha, look, our little Violetka has started to walk!"

It all seemed so real to Pania that her heart constricted with joy and the very cares she had not felt before. The fair bird had come, the one that had always flown past her house and landed in someone else's garden.

"Grigorii Alekseevich!" Pania said to herself. "I'd do anything for you! For you, my dear! And ask nothing in return!" On Saturday she didn't walk to the hospital, but flew. A nurse's aide, seeing her out of breath, smiled. "You look as if you were whipped on the way over here." Seeing that Pania was reaching to pour some water, she warned, "Rinse the glass off better. Everybody drinks here. Has something happened to you, Praskovia?"

But Pania didn't hear a thing. As soon as the clock struck five, she was the first to rush into the ward. Curly rose to meet her, but this time there was a certain weary surprise in his eyes, and it seemed too much for him to smile.

Pania, who had blossomed for three days, quickly wilted. She remained silent, waiting to hear what he would say.

He was quiet for a long time, too, as if testing her. Or perhaps he was completely caught up in his own thoughts. Finally he asked, "Listen, Praskovia Ivanovna. Forgive me. Let's go out to the hall. I want to ask you to do something for me."

He shoved a slip of paper with an address on it into her hand and began to explain how to get there—an hour and a half by steamboat down to the paper factory, from there to the village by bus. Lenin Lane, the second house from the corner.

"Take the night boat, you'll make the first bus. Just walk right in. Say that I asked you to find out if my mother has come in from the country. Most important, see . . . whether she's alone. My wife, that is. Look at the coat rack. Are a man's pea jacket and a river cap hanging there? But why tell a woman all that? You'll figure it out for yourself. Here's some money for the trip."

Pania was crestfallen. But she took the address and the money and left. A heavy rain was falling outside. Curly stood in a lighted window splashed with raindrops and followed Pania with his eyes as she walked into the darkness.

In the evening, as if carrying out an order, she went to the pier, bought a ticket, and sat down to wait for the steamer. It was very dark and impossible to tell that a fine snow was already falling. Only when Pania glanced back at a tall lamp did she notice the sparks of snow flying past in a rapid dance to be immediately swallowed up by the darkness.

Pania was born on the river, but she rarely had to travel by water. As a child she had ferried across the river and gone boating with her young friends before she married. Then once she and her late husband had sailed to Gorky, but the weather had been bad and Pania saw only frothy water from her window in third class. She had wanted to look at the shore, the sunset on the river, the green islands and yellow sandbars. To watch couples dancing on the open deck in the evening, to hear goblets clinking in the restaurant, to go in herself and sit down at a starched white tablecloth.

The years had passed, and she hadn't seen anything.

The night was dark, dank. A bleak, poorly lit steamer approached, driving a cold wave onto the shore.

Why had she come? How could she carry out this awful, disgraceful errand? Curly didn't have to love her, of course, but he still ought to have some respect!

It seemed to Pania that everything she had wanted for him and for herself was suddenly sinking into the black water of the river—the baby girl, the room filled with happiness, the green grove they would walk to in the summer. The sun, the birches, everything was sinking, dissolving in the blackness and the cold.

She thought that in her shoes another woman would go without hesitation. She would use the chance to catch a hussy with her lover and then report back to the husband. She would even add some details of her own. But then what? At the moment Pania was at least a person, but after that she would be a hussy, too!

Pania understood clearly that if she went to Curly with an account like that, he would look at her with hatred; he would probably shout and maybe even hit her. She would be ashamed for the rest of her life. How could he send her there, how could he? After all, she loved him. Had he really reached his limits?

God forbid that she go that far, too! No, she was stronger than that. Especially now. At least she had been in love for three days. For three days she had been overcome with joy, and now she knew what it felt like. Life could go on—she would no longer take warmth for passion. Too bad, of course, that it had lasted only three days. No, maybe not just three. Only now could Pania admit to herself that it had started earlier—maybe the first time she and Curly had met beneath the yellow birches on the shore of the blue river.

No, she wouldn't go! She would be happy with just those three days!

Pania threw her ticket into the black water to keep herself from vacillating any longer. She walked away quickly, without looking back at the dark boat. When it roared dolefully, her whole body shook, and she started to run and run.

The river froze at the end of November. From the window of the post office Pania could see kids on sleds darting down a hillside right onto the ice. Then carts of hay streamed across the ice from the other side, marking the road with hay dust.

The day was very clear, the kind of day when the sun can't be seen but is everywhere—in snowdrifts, windowpanes, garden stakes, and even in the smoke above the roofs. The water in the ice holes and by the water pumps looked blue in the sun's brightness.

Pania stuffed the afternoon mail into her bag, wrapped a tapestry scarf around her head, took her warm mittens from the heater, and set out on her usual route. When she banged the first gate, light, fragrant snow sprinkled on her from a rowan tree, and fat bullfinches shot suddenly into the sky.

Pania walked down the soft white street shoving newspapers and letters into mailboxes on gates and fences. As if guessing which were unlocked, she went into yards scraped clean of snow and knocked on frosty windows. The work went quickly. The cheery frost spurred her on, and a draft from the river pushed her from behind. Her worn black bag seemed unusually light.

Along the way, Pania quarreled with the yardman at the kindergarten because the gate was frozen shut and she had to jump over the fence. She chased some boys away from a water pump where they were mischievously pumping water and freezing their felt boots. On the corner of Molodezhnaia Street and Bolshoi Sezd she bought herself some ring-shaped rolls and was already contemplating dashing home, fixing some tea, and frying some sausages.

Suddenly Pania stopped. Curly's wife was standing by a clothing stall at the end of Molodezhnaia Street. Pania recognized her immediately, even in her winter clothes. It might have been the long legs in fashionable high-heeled boots that gave her away.

She had a large, ruddy but cold face surrounded by the fluff of an Orenburg shawl.[4] From her shoulder hung a silver fox with bared teeth that seemed to be running its own dead button eyes over a slip with nylon lace that was tossed on the counter.

"Volodia, should I get the blue one? Do have a look." Curly's wife turned and motioned with her red-mittened hand to a man standing not far off.

He was wearing a pea jacket with bright buttons and . . . a river cap. A strong, pink neck showed through his open collar. The neck of a healthy young man. He smiled condescendingly and calmly, like a man who had been drinking that day and had not yet completely recovered from the night before, and who looked forward to another such night of drunken pleasure.

"Maybe a different one? Pink?"

Curly's wife put a hand into her plump purse for the money.

"Can I talk to you for a minute?" Pania said, touching her wool sleeve.

She immediately looked back at her companion in dismay, but stepped aside with Pania.

"I'm from the union," Pania said. "Tell me, how is your husband, Grigorii Alekseevich, doing?"

She asked it loudly, so the man in the river cap could hear. Curly's wife looked around again. She didn't recognize Pania, but she was frightened of something.

"What's there to tell?" She made a hurt and angry face. "He was discharged just before the November holidays and got stinking drunk. Well, he had another attack, and they took him away. If he's so dependent, how can you . . . ?"

"And he's independent?" Pania asked suddenly, pointing at the river cap.

"What do you want?" Curly's wife asked in a low whisper.

"Nothing," Pania said as quietly. "Just don't be deceitful. It's not good." Adjusting her bag, which had begun to feel heavier, she turned and walked away.

Pania should have stopped at the post office to drop off the undelivered money and notices, but she turned into her own street. Her hands weren't cold, but it took her several tries to stick the key into the lock and turn it. When she finally entered her small, yellow-papered room, she sat down without taking her coat off and hugged the bag to her chest. Her own picture, which was not a good likeness, looked down at her from the wall. It was a newspaper clipping, framed and under glass, with the caption "P. I. Rozumkina, the best letter carrier of the Guliashi Post Office."

"Hardly the best!" Pania thought bitterly. "My head being what it is."

Suddenly she felt a sharp pain, as if only yesterday that awful man had hit her on the head, and only yesterday she had taken the last package to Curly in the hospital. Pania continued to sit in her kerchief and quilted coat, and the snow that she hadn't brushed off melted under her boots.

The clock ticked. Beyond the frosted window the sunshine waned, and the snow took on a bluish hue. The bushes in the front garden were as fleecy as those pictured in a color magazine.

Pania began to rush about. She threw off her coat and old resoled boots, and unwrapped the kerchief that hid her newly grown hair. A coat with a shawl collar—her most recent purchase, made since she had become a widow—and a bonnet appeared from the dresser. Pania knew a kerchief would be better, but. . . . Not having a pair of stylish fur boots, she put on her new slate-black felt ones.

She left her bag at the post office and set out across the river for the hospital. The snow crunched gloomily; the blue streets seemed narrow. The opposite shore seemed far away, even though lights were already burning there.

"Nice day, isn't it, Grigorii Alekseevich?" said Pania as she entered the ward. "Best wishes for a white winter. It's been a while. . . . "

He looked bewildered, but she calmly sat down beside him.

"I didn't have time to buy you anything. When I thought of it, the stores had already closed. I asked an aide; she'll bring you some grapes tomorrow."

Curly tested her with his gaze. But there was nothing in her eyes besides warmth.

"Forgive me, Praskovia Ivanovna," he said flatly. "I hurt you then. I shouldn't have."

Pania shuddered, remembering the cold night on the pier, the eighty kopeks in change Curly had shoved into her hand when they parted, the little white ticket that had flickered for an instant in the black water.

"Oh, how could you have hurt me?" she said as light-heartedly as possible. "I'm the one that ought to apologize. I didn't do what you asked. Can you believe it? I haven't had a chance. They put me on telegrams; there was no one else to deliver them. I've been working two shifts until now. Haven't had a minute free."

He looked at her incredulously, but she went on. "I just ran into your wife. She said you were back in the hospital. I thought I ought to come. I got the time off and hurried over. What's with you, Grigorii Alekseevich?"

Curly frowned.

"Where'd you see her?"

"My goodness, I run all over town. I see everybody!"

He was silent as he leaned his thin elbows on his knees and rubbed his wide, stubbly chin.

"You turned out better than me," he said, and his lips trembled. "And as for a wife, I don't have one. She's gone up in smoke."

Pania touched his sleeve.

"Don't, Grigorii Alekseevich. It'll all work out. Life will go on. Keep this in mind: What woman likes it when her husband mopes around in the hospital because of his own weaknesses? Enough of that. You need to get well, to go back to work. Then you'll both figure things out."

Curly escorted Pania as far as the receiving room. He took her hand.

"Pania, I'm sorry I got you mixed up in this dirty mess, but I knew all along it wouldn't touch you."

"Enough about me," Pania said. "The most important thing is that you get over it."

But everything inside her was throbbing, and she wanted to shout her feelings out loud.

"Goodbye, Grigorii Alekseevich!" she said, carefully pulling her warm hand from his.

THE FAREWELL LIGHT
NINA KATERLI

Translated by

HELENA GOSCILO AND VALERIA SAJEZ

BENT OVER ALMOST IN HALF, THE OLD WOMAN WITH A cane resembled a hairpin. As she walked toward Martynov, he saw her hunched back, with a worn-out light-colored coat stretched across it. He saw the top of her grey knit cap and her hand in a child's red mitten squeezing the knob of her short cane.

The old woman moved as if groping her way along, first thrusting the cane forward, then slowly pulling her body toward it. Martynov mused that in order to see her face, you'd have to straighten her out like a horseshoe.

It was almost the end of February. The wet piles of slushy snow mixed with sand along the sidewalk already made it seem like spring. So did the blinding sun refracted in the puddles and the windows of the trolley buses, and its reflections—the brightly colored oranges in net bags, flashing here and there in the crowd. But what seemed most vernal were the sounds: the crunching underfoot, the noise of the sparrows, the sharp, high note from the middle of the roadway where two workers in yellow overalls were methodically striking the rail with crowbars. A streetcar stood nearby, honking impatiently.

The sky over Sokolniki[1] looked remote and pale.

Martynov looked around to see where he could put his heavy briefcase, then stuck it on top of a trash can and unbuttoned his coat. He wiped the sweat off his forehead and adjusted his cap. It was unbearably hot in the subway, and he felt heavy and unwell, dressed too warmly for the day's weather.

The day had begun with Tatiana, his stepdaughter, saying to her mother at breakfast as she finished chewing her sandwich:

"I need some spring shoes, but I don't need a raincoat. I'll wear Grandmother's. It fits me just right."

His wife glanced quickly at Martynov, and he shifted his eyes. That was a surprise, all right. Give the girl the keys to someone else's apartment—they'd had an urgent need for some documents there—and she goes through the closet and tries on clothes. . . . That's not nice. And it was perfectly clear where those vulgar manners came from.

"Why did you touch Grandmother's things without asking?" asked his wife quietly.

Tatiana tossed her head, looked blankly at her mother for a second, then with a sudden flush leaped from the table. Martynov realized that there was about to be a scene. It would be the whole works: sobs, rudeness, slamming of doors—everything that he and his wife had fought against for the last two years. They'd used both strictness and affection, without any success. Then suddenly it had all stopped when Tatiana enrolled at the university. They'd thought that she had grown up. . . . They'd rejoiced prematurely, for there she stood, skinny, her lips twitching.

"What kind of mother are you? . . . What kind . . . ," she was about to say, but stopped short, tilted her chin still higher, and marched out of the room with a firm step. That was exactly what she did: marched out with measured strides, swinging her right arm just like a soldier on the parade grounds.

A minute later the front door slammed.

His wife was silent. Martynov was also silent. He felt awkward. In a way the scene had taken place because of him. Tanka had put on his mother's raincoat, his wife had sensed his displeasure, and so. . . . Thank God the phone rang just then; his wife answered, and while she was talking Martynov got ready to leave. He already knew that he'd have a bad day. And indeed, immediately after he arrived at the ministry, at exactly 9:15, as arranged, everything went wrong. It turned out that Mikheev, who'd summoned him, had to go to a meeting with the head of the union.

"Don't feel bad," he said, winking at Martynov. "You needn't come back to the institute today. You turned up at the ministry, and that's enough. The weather's nice today, you can call some lady friend and escape to the lap of nature."

Mikheev had a pale face that suggested he'd never been in the lap of nature in his whole life. This jellylike Mikheev, with his banalities, which he pronounced in a quiet voice (as if to say, "They'll hear!"), as always aroused in Martynov an urge to say something rude, but as usual he remained silent. But en route to the subway (he was going to the institute anyway), he mentally composed biting remarks with which he could put this well-fed administrator in his place. The remarks came out feeble and clumsy. Obviously because Martynov could easily imagine how he'd turn red as he said them out loud; sweat would appear on his brow, his face would take on an unnatural, desperate, pathetic expression, and there would be a distinct note of hysteria in his voice. Because of this he grew even angrier and suddenly decided not to go to the institute. "His Excellency himself gave me permission. I'm not a kid, to be sent back and forth by him every day across all of Moscow!"

His wife hadn't left for work yet, for sure. Today she had evening office hours at the polyclinic from two o'clock. It took five minutes to get to Tverskoi Boulevard. But Martynov stubbornly walked to the subway, for he'd suddenly realized that he could finally go to Sokolniki. Home.

Home. . . . For the last five years Andrei Nikolaevich Martynov had been living in his wife's apartment on Tverskoi Boulevard. He had grown fond of the well-kept three-room apartment in the old Moscow house which his wife's grandparents had furnished and lived in; he'd got used to it quickly, and he was comfortable and happy there. Yet he always spoke of this house of theirs as "our place on Tverskoi," whereas he referred to the one-room apartment in Sokolniki, where he'd lived with his mother until his marriage, as "home."

In the morning the city had been winter-bound, but spring set in suddenly. It seemed to happen precisely in the fifteen minutes that Martynov sweated in the subway on his way to Sokolniki.

He finally got outside, and while he was tidying up, the traffic light turned green. It was almost impossible to make it out in the bright sun.

. . . That day, too, the sun had shone brightly. Martynov had very likely stood on exactly the same spot as he'd prepared to cross the street to the trolley bus. He remembered that he'd been going on official business to a local plant, was running late, and had taken the subway to Sokolniki. It had occurred to him that it would be a good idea to drop in for a minute at his mother's, but he hadn't even a minute to spare, and that minute wouldn't work out. He could stop by on the way back, or, better still, the day after tomorrow, on Saturday, because today he still had to return to the institute. They were expecting a call from Cheliabinsk.[2] And just as the thought occurred to him, he'd seen his mother.

Her white raincoat unbuttoned, she was walking in his direction along the sidewalk. She was already quite close when she suddenly turned abruptly and walked toward the subway pavilion. He could have called out to her, but Martynov realized once again in chagrin that the tests at the plant were supposed to start in fifteen minutes. He stood in confusion on the sidewalk curb while his mother walked away from him along the boulevard past the subway. The leaves hadn't yet started turning yellow; September had just begun. Yes, *that* was . . . the sixth of September, precisely the sixth, on Thursday, and the night before Saturday she died.

. . . The traffic light had turned red long ago. The cars had stopped. Andrei Nikolaevich hurriedly crossed the street. He was gasping for breath, and his legs felt heavy. "I'm getting old. . . ." Had his mother been alive, he would have put it differently: "I'm getting sick. . . ." Now, with her gone, he was the oldest in the family.

. . . His wife, as usual, had been right: he shouldn't have gone there by himself the first time.

Turning the corner and walking another half a block, Martynov stopped. He felt a tightness in the pit of his stomach, and the whole left side of his chest hurt badly. Of course he hadn't taken his Validol with him. He'd not taken it on principle: if at forty-seven he was already taking Validol whenever he left the house. . . . But do you want to croak at forty-eight? Ah, that's nonsense! Overanxiety. Hypochondria. And the weather. The atmospheric pressure had dropped for sure.

Forty-seven years old. . . . His mother would have been seventy-four. Mirror reflections. . . . She'd lived alone. In the mornings she'd come down the stairs and go to the bakery. Then she'd go for milk, then . . . ("Come on, what's the matter with you, Andriusha, I walk a lot . . . "). In the evenings, television. Then she'd take a sleeping pill and go to bed. . . . Lord, how many old women there are in Moscow! There went another one: she was without a cane, her hands hanging uselessly at her sides. She could barely walk, and took tiny, uncertain steps. Her eyes were huge, bright, and scared, her mouth half-open, like a fledgling's. It was her heart—it wasn't getting enough oxygen. . . . That's when you first truly feel that you won't be able to escape it, to outwit fate and avoid it, and then it becomes really frightening. . . . And *right now* the old woman, the fledgling, was afraid that she'd suffocate *right now*. . . .

Martynov looked in his pocket for the Validol just in case. What if his wife had put it there? He didn't find it. And that's the way things are, Andrei Nikolaevich, ex-Andriusha, all in a steam, with an edematic face and grey hair, an elderly—yes! elderly!—bureaucrat in the sciences (look at that bulging briefcase). What do you have to fear, you blockhead? What can you lose? In your youth—your youth, nothing!—even ten years ago, you had so many desires. To fall in love. To go to Poros in the summer to do some skin diving. To buy a car. And to be appointed section director. And also to pass the candidate's minimal requirements. And finally, just to go to a restaurant! In your best suit and with a beautiful woman. To the "Prague."[3]

All that and even more came to pass. He visited not only Poros but Naples. He defended his candidate's degree. They appointed him director of the largest and most important laboratory in the institute (even though he didn't have a doctorate!). Up to the age of forty-two he led an active bachelor's life, and then he fell in love with a charming woman and took her away from her husband. As for a car—to hell with it! He owned one and had already tired of it. It gave him no pleasure, only trouble. Everything had come true. . . . And so what? No, there was no reason to provoke God; everything was fine. But where was that enthusiasm, that swooning of the soul that comes when, say, you find yourself in a forest clearing and suddenly you look around and it's so wonderful all around you that tears actually fill your eyes. It wasn't only in childhood that such things happened. However, it was probably just as well; the organism's defense mechanism. With age the soul becomes covered with an armor plate; otherwise it would be impossible. Otherwise there'd be a hundred percent guarantee of a heart attack, because encounters with the beauty of nature are less and less frequent, whereas encounters with functionaries like Mikheev are increasingly frequent.

So what was left? For the soul, that is? Television, like Mother had? Dancing on ice and "Animal Kingdom"? Malicious satisfaction that in an argument with the assistant director it was once again you and not he who turned out to be right? By the way, how many times was that already! And all because the guy was senile. That was yet another horror of old age: a person is reluctant to resign himself to his own uselessness, struggles to the end, hopes to deceive those around him, and above all, himself. In such a situation, of course, one shouldn't be angry but sympathetic. Poor Mother, she also seemed to think that her advice about raising Tatiana contained God knows what wisdom.

Martynov slowed down. He was only a block from his house. There was the small grocery store that his mother for some reason had called the "self-service store." So. Well, we still haven't clarified what kind of positive experiences we have in life. . . . Perhaps next spring there'll be a business trip to Chicago. Do I want to go? You bet! Am I interested? Of course! If it works out I'll be very happy. "Very happy. . . ." And that's all! And if it doesn't work out, I'll make out. I've still got to make it to next spring, incidentally. . . . In the past I wouldn't have slept nights, I'd have dreamed and fantasized how the plane would cross the ocean and the stewardess would announce, "Our plane will be landing any moment now at Kennedy Airport." That was before. Get it?

There was also a cultural life: visitors, the theater. . . . Why not go, say, to the Contemporary Theater?[4] Of course you can go, of course it's possible. . . . However, today there's a major hockey match on TV.

That's now, but what about in another ten years? Poor Mother. The one consolation was that she lived to seventy-four and didn't become feeble. All it took was a stroke—that would do it. And not at seventy-four, but . . . tomorrow even. You'll crawl along, my dear, like that old woman with the cane. She looks like a snail. Or like the other one, with a mouth like a suffocating fledgling's. Mother's gone; your turn's coming, Andrei Nikolaevich. "What do you mean? I never stood here!" "No, I'm sorry, citizen. You stood here, all right. I remember you—plump, with a briefcase. Elderly. Move along, move along, don't hold up the others, others are waiting."

. . . Well, anyway, what other joys are there in life? Now, today? Family happiness? Sure, there is that. There's peace and harmony at home, so you worried for no reason, Mother. And Tanka, despite her incredible "complexity," got into the biology department. I helped her with the chemistry and physics myself, and now she says: "Andrei Nikolaevich, you're simply a genius," and she never mentions her real father. Today's scene at breakfast was essentially nothing, just the usual tantrum of protracted adolescence. And nerves, of course. This hysterical friendship with Liuda can't help but tell on her.

Martynov frowned as he recalled Liuda. He didn't like that friendship, hadn't liked it for a long time now, though on first glance everything looked very noble—you couldn't fault it. Liuda had had a long bout with rheumatic heart disease and had to spend most of her time at home. Tatiana sympathizes with her, which is wonderful. But there's something in her behavior that . . . how can it be put more precisely? Something that's not completely natural, some sort of exultation, of sacrifice. There's a lack of sense of measure. For two years now Tanka's been leading the life of an invalid: she's dropped everything—sports, trips to the country, and the theater. "Liuda can't, so I won't go either." Why?! You ask: "What do you do there for days on end?" "We talk." "About what?" "Well . . . about everything. . . ." There's no need to ask any more—it's clear they talk about nonsense. Empty chatter, hot air. And the result is obvious. The girl is degenerating right before your eyes: the range of her interests is growing narrower and narrower, and she can't even dress sensibly. She walks just like a soldier on the parade grounds. If you take stock of Liuda's spiritual requirements and her cultural level, it all becomes clear: it's the principle of two-way streets. So what's the result? On the surface, you've got a heroic deed in the name of friendship, but if you dig deeper. . . . It's all complicated, because there's sincere compassion there, but there's also a pose, pride, and even vanity. They tried to influence her somehow: "We feel sorry for Liuda, of course. One should help her, but one should do it sensibly! There must be a point to everything, a sense of measure. Mother and I, for example, could try to get Liuda into a sanatorium. That's a realistic solution, whereas self-immolation isn't. You should live a normal life, by the way, then Liuda would benefit more from being with you. And who told you that one may have only one girlfriend? It's a tragedy that Liuda's ill. But why must you ruin your own life? For God's sake, visit Liuda, but have other company besides her. . . ."

Of course, that conversation ended in a scene, with threats of leaving home. They backed off. But Martynov was convinced that this hysterical devotion would come to no good. She was wasting her time, straining her nerves, and saddest of all, sooner or later she would grow tired of her attractive pose anyway, and want a normal life. And then there'd be an argument and a severe trauma for Liuda, while Tatiana would carry a sense of guilt for the rest of her life. How could he explain this to her without offending her? How could he prove that everything should have reasonable limits, that life is not a theater where one can play a noble role forever? It's sad. Tanka's a good girl, intelligent, pretty. . . . All right. Enough of that, nothing can be done anyway—it's a vicious circle. His heart began to pound again.

. . . The sun was finally shining freely; all around him everything began to melt in a rush as it flowed, streamed, spilled, resounded, and glittered, and fell from the roofs with a crash. Dodging the puddles of water that were forming before his very eyes, Andrei Nikolaevich went up to the second floor, and as usual felt through his pocket for the key.

He was frightened. It gave him a terrible feeling to enter the apartment—not sad, but really terrible, as if danger had settled in there and was lying in wait.

He hadn't been there for half a year.

On that awful Saturday morning, he, his wife, and his stepdaughter were calmly drinking coffee when the telephone rang. When Martynov answered it, at first he couldn't understand whom they wanted to speak to, who was talking, and about what. The call was from Klava, a neighbor at Sokolniki. Without greeting him, she immediately began to cry and shout, repeating again and again: "They took her away, they took her away." After asking her three times to repeat what she was saying, Andrei finally realized that his mother was in bad shape and that Klava had called an ambulance, which had taken her away. The ambulance had driven off to the general hospital at Izmailovo.

Martynov ran down the stairs, but forgot his car keys. He raced back, bumped into his wife in the driveway, shoved his hand in his pocket, and found the keys, unlocked the car, and put the key in the ignition. The engine wouldn't start.

In a frenzy he turned the key again and again, knowing that it wouldn't do any good—he'd only kill the battery. At this point his wife flagged down a taxicab.

He had no recollection of the drive to the hospital. He remembered quite well, however, the basement where the admissions room was located: a long, rather dark corridor, and on the left along the wall, some white chairs, on one of which Martynov's wife seated him. For some reason he sat down obediently and waited while she found out what had happened from the flat-faced woman behind the information window.

His wife returned to Andrei Nikolaevich's side shortly, a perplexed and confused expression on her face. With an irritation that was unlike him, Martynov suddenly yelled:

"Did you have to go into details, when a couple of words would have done?! Where and what? What's the diagnosis? What can she have? Chicken? Cottage cheese? What?!"

His wife shook her head, and sank into a nearby chair with a sob.

"It happened in the ambulance," she said, "on the way to the hospital. A heart attack."

Since that day Martynov hadn't once gone to Sokolniki. His wife took over all the funeral arrangements. Even now, after all that time, she still tried to protect him from everything that could cause him pain. One time Andrei Nikolaevich heard her scolding her daughter.

"Stop acting like you're dying of grief! It's tactless. Andrei's lost his mother. He's the one who's really experienced a great tragedy. You should feel sorry for him, not yourself."

"But I feel sorrier for Grandma!" snapped Tatiana and ran out, slamming the door behind her.

Of course, during these days, which were difficult enough anyway, she frankly behaved not quite . . . adequately. And even though Martynov was touched that the girl was so upset over his mother, he realized that her grief was not wholly natural, but exaggerated. When he got married, Tanka was already twelve years old. It was unlikely that in five years she'd come to love so much an old woman who was not her own family and whom she'd seen only a few times. Still, it wasn't worth scolding her. Egocentricity is characteristic of that age. They all sincerely believe that no emotional experiences are stronger and more important than theirs. You have to approach this tolerantly, as he told his wife at the time.

Half a year passed, but no decision had been made yet about what should be done with the apartment, which was still registered in Andrei Nikolaevich's name. Should they exchange it or keep it for Tatiana when she married?

Strange as it seemed, the more time passed, the more uncertain became his awareness that his mother was gone. His crushing grief gradually subsided, and life in the house on Tverskoi Boulevard continued as before. The only things to vanish from it were the telephone conversations with his mother and the short weekly trips to Sokolniki. He would unload the heavier groceries, such as potatoes, groats, and vegetable oil, would look repeatedly at his watch as he had some tea, and then would be on his

way. Next time I'll stay a while longer, I'll come for the whole day. . . .
Yes, recently the illusion that nothing had happened was sometimes almost total. And yet life had changed, or rather, Martynov himself was
changing. It seemed to him now that prior to his mother's death, he'd
never really managed to grow up. With the years, only his physical appearance had changed; but beginning with this September, the process of
internal maturation, or, more precisely, of aging, set in at incredible speed.
From Andriusha, as he always felt he was, Martynov suddenly turned
into Andrei Nikolaevich. Moreover, he began to suffer from old men's
ailments: heart, blood pressure, lumbago. Ideas that he'd never had before
occurred to him about all this nonsense—for some reason even about his
pension, which he'd never been interested in, inasmuch as it hadn't been
part of his foreseeable future. Now the foreseeable future had somehow
become compressed and drawn nearer. His one hope was that all these
moods were only temporary and would be gone in a month or two.

But now he stood on the stair landing, pressing the key in his pocket,
and didn't dare open the door. He felt that as soon as he stepped inside,
his premonitions and fears would all become reality. He'd walk out a
different person from the one who'd gone in. That's where it would start,
"the foreseeable future," immediately after which. . . .

Again he felt a pain in the left side of his chest. His mother had
Validol for sure, and anyway, at home he could take off his coat, lie
down. . . . Mother *had* Validol. . . . "Had" or "had had?" But it couldn't
have gone anywhere; therefore, "had." What do you mean, "had," when
she couldn't have anything anymore? . . . What nonsense! Gibberish. . . .
Martynov decisively opened the door.

As soon as he stepped over the threshold, he sensed again that all
that wasn't right. Nothing had changed here. Even the air had its usual
smell of mothballs and perfume; he remembered the smell from childhood.
True, his mother's bed was made differently, not the way she did it. There
was dust on the table. And on the piano.

Martynov went to the bathroom, where his mother kept medicine
in the medicine cabinet. Something there struck him as strange, but he
couldn't tell what it was. He started looking for the Validol, found it, and
placed it under his tongue. As he came out he looked back and noticed
a toothbrush sticking out of a tumbler and a white comb. That's what it
was; whenever his mother went anywhere, she always. . . . She forgot . . .
oh, hell!

Andrei Nikolaevich returned to the room. Walking past the bed, he
heard something crunch underfoot. It was an empty ampule, which he'd
crushed. They'd given his mother an injection that morning before they
took her away. What kind of injection? How had it all happened? Why
had Klava been in the apartment? Who'd called her? Why haven't I asked

her for the details? He recalled her telling him something at the funeral, but Martynov remembered only that his mother had been fully conscious when they took her away. . . . "When they were putting the stretcher in the ambulance, she said, 'Thank you, Klavochka'—then took a long, long look at the front entrance. . . . " What had she been thinking about at that moment?

Martynov kneeled down and meticulously gathered the fragments of the ampule. Without getting up, he reached for the ashtray on the table and placed them on it. He pressed his face to the rough bedspread for a moment, then stood up, coughed, walked across the room, and for some reason opened the wardrobe.

As always, everything in the wardrobe was neat and tidy. On the shelves lay piles of clean linen. There was an ancient shirt of his, which he'd worn occasionally if he had to help his mother around the house. Mother's blouses, combinations. . . . His wife used to laugh: "You're a typical momma's boy, Andriusha. You call everything by names that were used in your mother's youth. 'Combinations.' Who talks like that now?"

A white raincoat was hanging on a hanger.

. . . As Andrei stood at the crosswalk, his mother walked along the sidewalk, coming straight in his direction without seeing him. She wore an unbuttoned white raincoat, blunt-toed flat shoes, and grey socks ("Not stylish? Nonsense! I'm old, I don't care"). She walked quickly, swinging the brown purse that she held in her right hand in rhythm with her steps. Her left hand was tucked in her raincoat pocket. Andrei rushed toward his mother, wanting to call to her, but she turned sharply and walked on. It was very warm. The sun shone gently, already with the calm unobtrusiveness of autumn. The sky was different, too, not like today. It was deep blue and seemed closer. The leaves hadn't yet begun to change color. Martynov stood and stared after his mother in confusion as she disappeared down the boulevard. . . .

It was thawing outside, and a naked lacquered branch by the window sparkled in the sunlight.

In the middle of the desk lay his mother's glasses. Next to them was a school notebook, which she'd once called the *Diary of a Sclerotic.*

"You know, I don't remember a damn thing! I'll drink my medicine in the morning, and half an hour later I rack my brains trying to recall if I took it or not. I think I didn't, so I go get another tablet. You could poison yourself that way, you know. And an even more obvious example— I put the soup on, become engrossed in my reading, and forget. So the soup burns. I'm going to write everything down. . . . Of course, it's possible to forget to write it down. . . ."

Martynov opened the notebook.

"The compote came to a boil at 2:40 P.M.," he read. "I should turn it off at 3:00."

"3:00. Turned the compote off." He smiled. "I must call Andrei in the morning about the notice from the enlistment office." "Take Gemiton." "Tell Taisia Arkadyevna that the book in the library has been put aside for her." What Taisia Arkadyevna? His mother was always involved in other people's affairs. . . . "Take Papaverin." "Pension tomorrow. Stay home." "Water the cactus Wednesday." Incidentally, where are they, the cacti? They always used to stand on the window sill. . . . Did the neighbors take them? Wait a minute, wait a minute. . . . We recently saw some cacti in Tatiana's room on Tverskoi. . . . But how did they come to be there? "Stop at the Social Security office."

Notes of this kind filled five pages. Medicine. Pension. Social Security. Medicine again. Yes . . . my poor mom. . . .

And suddenly he saw her face. He saw it for the first time since . . . since the day he'd been there last, when he'd brought some groceries. And here's where he sat, he recalled, at the desk, while his mother stood at the window.

Then she turned around and said something.

Now he distinctly saw her eyes, which weren't the eyes of an old woman at all, but bright blue in a tanned, laughing face.

His mother slowly raised her hand (her index finger was stained with dried ink from a ballpoint pen) and fixed her hair. Her thin, light hair, which she wore combed smooth, was totally white.

He abruptly turned a page. The next page was blank, but Martynov absent-mindedly leafed through the others. And suddenly he came across:

March 20.

I've decided to record some of my thoughts and impressions in this notebook. Not for my descendants, of course; who needs senile philosophizing? I simply like to write. It's an old woman's graphomania. One thinks that everything that comes to mind is very meaningful and important, and, what's most crucial, that it's correct. Herein lie all the problems of the elderly, and mine, too. You *know* how one should live and you're in a hurry to share that knowledge with others, for they certainly don't know how to do it if they constantly do foolish things. You want to help them, but they carelessly brush you aside. This causes resentment and conflicts. Yesterday I was thinking about why it is that we old people are so certain that we understand everything correctly, that we see the world as it is. I thought and finally found the answer: we actually *do* see the world as it is and orient ourselves perfectly well in it. Only the world becomes different with age, smaller and with more contrasts; shadings and halftones disappear, and certain sounds fade. Everything that was multidimensional and colorful becomes flat and black and white. Like on a TV screen. It's a small square, but for you it's a universe, and everything in it is very simple, clear and plain. There's no confusion: here's the top, here's the bottom, that's white, and that's black. What kind of vacillation or guesswork can there be? So it upsets you to the point of tears when someone can't understand elementary things and acts stupidly and as a result ruins his life. And above all, when you tell him: "Things are in a bad way, you know!" he even laughs impudently and insists that, on the contrary, everything's very good, in fact: "Grandma, you just don't understand anything!" A madman, that's all he is!

How quickly and completely we've forgotten that once our world was different, too! No, those of us who stare complacently at our microscreen, and he, that little fool dazed by the infinite, resonating, colorful space—we'll never understand each other in this life. There's no point in trying!

March 22.

Our old folks' glass is small, but we drink from our own glass. One shouldn't only grab someone else's or force one's own on someone else. And our world isn't bad, we can't complain!

Today I spent the morning in Sokolniki Park. The sky is so clear, as though it got a rest over winter. The thin, naked branches look defenseless. The sparrows are hopping about the empty walkways.

I want to live to see all of this.

Last night I couldn't fall asleep for a long time. Suddenly, for no reason, I remembered how once, when Andriusha was very small, he was waiting outside for me. It was night and bitter cold. This was during the war, in Sharyia during the evacuation. I'd gone to the hospital late at night; I had to check on a wounded man in the postoperative ward. For some reason I remember his last name: Osipov. He was critically wounded in the stomach, and I feared blood poisoning.

I spent over an hour in the ward, and when I left the hospital it was already night. So I saw it all: the empty street, not a single window anywhere, the white moon in the sky, and the bright, angry stars. The snow glittered, and on the corner across the street stood a small figure. His collar raised, his scarf fastened all the way up to his eyes. He kept shifting his feet in his felt boots, and slapping one palm against the other, like an adult. He'd left the house to run over here and meet me.

. . . Why is it that I can recall only the good things? And so clearly and sharply, as if it all happened just recently.

May 15.

I haven't written anything down for a long time: "intelligent" thoughts rarely occur to me. It will be summer soon. The tender, fresh leaves on the poplar trees have already come out, and the crows outside are making a racket as if possessed. I was dusting the room today when suddenly I heard it start to rain. It came down fast and hard, and hammered at the window ledge. I turned toward the window and was astonished. The sun was out!

Those were sparrows. I poured some millet out onto the window ledge and, of course, forgot about it immediately. A huge crowd of them gathered there, and sat squeezed together in a row as they all pecked at it.

June 5.

Today has been a happy day for me, a real holiday. In the morning Andrei came by to pick me up, and the two of us drove to Ovrazhki. We went to the forest to get some fresh air. My daughter-in-law Natasha and Tanechka stayed home. Supposedly someone was to visit them, but I'm convinced that Natasha simply wanted Andrei and me to spend the day together on our own.

I sat in the front seat beside my son, and the car sped along the highway. I asked Andrei to pass a large truck that was completely blocking my view. He laughed and said: "Mother, you're a daredevil," but he did pass the truck. Then we began passing everyone, even a black Volga that was cruising along the middle of the road. The driver of the Volga gave me a really dirty look. I stuck my tongue out at him. . . .

We passed everybody and rolled along like royalty. Then Andriusha parked the car at the side of the road, and we took the path into the forest.

Today is a grey, cool day, and it's quiet and somewhat dusky in the forest. But it's a special kind of dusk, greenish and smelling of damp soil, grass, and pines. The pines here are very young, and the bark hasn't had time yet to toughen. It's pink at the top and so, even though there's no sun, it seems to shine on the tops from somewhere.

We walked out into the clearing. I stopped and looked around. The tall old trees growing all around us stood quietly and grandly. I looked at them, at the cloudy sky, and at the large unfamiliar bird that was sitting unafraid on a branch very close to us. And I felt a great respect for all this—for the forest, the bird, even the ants bustling near a tall anthill under the pine. I also felt gratitude and a downright puppylike, childlike delight, the kind that makes your throat tickle, and you want to shriek and run around the clearing. . . . What, are you going to shriek here and run around, at seventy-four. . . . No, feelings don't fade with age, there are simply fewer of them; but those that do remain. . . .

June 12.

Andrei visited yesterday and brought me some vegetables. What didn't he bring—carrots, turnips, potatoes. But I don't like vegetables. Or rather, I don't like to bother with them, cleaning and grating them. I have absolutely no interest in preparing dinner for myself. I prefer semiprepared foods. But I can't tell him that; he's always so happy that he's taking care of his mother.

Evening.

I keep thinking about my son. How good it is that he's settled down, even though he took his time getting around to it, and that he has his own family now. Now it won't be so awful for me to die. No, I'm not flirting and showing false modesty: "A lonely old woman, no one needs her anymore." In fact, Andriusha would have been left completely alone, like an old abandoned dog. Recently in the park I saw a large purebred dog. It was totally decrepit, its back sunken in, its muzzle grey, and it was running along the path looking for its owner. I walked around asking if anyone had lost a dog. No one responded. When I went for a walk the next day, I took a piece of sausage and some bread with me, just in case I ran into the dog again. I didn't. I hope everything is all right with him.

Here I am, getting sentimental. I'm moved by birds, flowers, and animals. By animals I mean cats and dogs. I read or heard somewhere that sentimentalism is ersatz, a substitute for real kindness. Perhaps that's so. Kindness is always active, but old age has no energy left for action. What can you do for others? Except perhaps spare others worry about you as much as you can. Incidentally, that's also a great happiness for yourself, for me—to be able to stay independent, to preserve your dignity. If only I'm healthy, if only I'm lucky enough to stay that way to the end. Sometimes such hopeless and gloomy ideas creep into my head.

June 13.

Reread yesterday's entry. What a horrid, sanctimonious old woman! An egotist, too! Sits in a clean, pretty room and feels sorry for herself.

June 20.

After ten, right before going to bed, I went out for a walk. It was cool, and down from the poplars lay underfoot. The whole street was white. I walked along and thought that old age wasn't such a dreadful thing. Of course, there's less and less energy, and it's awful to look at your face in the mirror, but on the other hand, there are some advantages.

"Old age is second childhood" is a true saying, but it shouldn't be interpreted to mean that children are fools and that old people have taken leave of their senses. It's simply that in old age a lot of what one had in childhood, and which later disappeared somewhere, returns. For example, happiness that the first snow has fallen or that the starlings have returned and are making themselves at home in the starling house. That you saw a squirrel. That you fed a large, ferocious dog and weren't afraid. And also that adults talked to you for a long time, listening attentively, with interest, and not out of politeness. . . . In old age, you've got the freedom of childhood, and even irresponsibility, because almost nothing depends on you anymore, you don't have to attain anything or endeavor to prove anything. You don't have to worry eternally about the future, for it's so small now, if it's there at all! It's thought that old people live in the past.

That's not true. We live in the present, like children. Life turned out as it did; you can't change anything now. And that's fine. If, of course, you have a clear conscience and at least a little courage.

Old age somehow resembles a school holiday: grades for the semester have been decided and recorded in the gradebook, and your father has already scolded you for the "C" in arithmetic. But now everything's behind you—including his reprimand and the expression you wore as you listened to the tirade. And what's ahead is the winter vacation! Short, of course, but perhaps that's what is most delightful about it, that it's short.

August 8.

The old drone got sick! Gave everyone a fright, alarmed them. They kept me in bed almost a month. Poor Andrei and Natasha took turns watching over me the entire first week, but after three days I already felt that I'd pulled through and I lay there and played the *grande dame*. Now I can get up and move slowly, and today I even went for a walk.

The day before yesterday Andriusha's daughter Tanechka visited me. It surprises me that whenever Andrei speaks of her he always calls her "stepdaughter." Somehow that strikes me as ... not very good. She's seventeen years old, after all, and five of those years have been spent living with Andrei. That's almost a third of her life. Enough, you'd think, for him to get used to her, to love her as his own. And she also calls him by his name and patronymic. It's strange. I tried to discuss it with him once. At first he frowned, and then he said that he saw no cause to get upset: the family got along fine, and who called whom what had no significance. He should know best. . . .

But I feel sorry for Taniushka. She's kind of quiet, reserved, and very skinny, like a little branch. I offered her some tea, and we watched television together. She's taking her entrance exams for the university right now. She's already passed two of them with an "A." As she was leaving she suddenly said: "Grandma, maybe after the next exam I can stop by again? I wanted to talk to you about something. Just don't tell my parents." Of course I said yes, but now I'm worried about what's happened. She never came to visit me alone before. Of course, I didn't say a word to Andrei, but today on the telephone I asked how Taniushka was doing. He cheerfully answered that everything was fine, she was studying.

August 17.

Taniushka has just left. We talked the whole evening, and I got upset and even had to take Korvalol. So that's what "getting along fine" means! She's decided that after enrolling in the university she'll apply to get into the dormitory or will rent part of a room. She feels that her parents don't understand her. "They think," she said, "that if I'm not rude and I listen to them, if I'm preparing for exams and getting 'A's,' that means that everything's fine. But they don't care that it's been a long time since I talked to them about anything serious, and that I don't tell them anything about myself. It hurts me; I don't want to live with people who treat me formally." "What do you mean, formally?" I asked. "I mean, just so that I don't cause problems. They're prepared to help me with physics, of course, but no one's interested in what's in my soul." "But why don't you talk to them about what's serious?" "I used to tell them things before. For example, how I argued with Liudka, that's my girlfriend, and Mother didn't even let me finish before immediately sitting in judgment. She decided immediately who's right, who's wrong, and who's a bad influence on whom. I don't like the way they always judge." "What do you mean—judge? Whom?" "Why, everyone! Their acquaintances who don't live right. Superiors at work. My Liuda. Even the telephone operator, who combs her hair badly. And also, why do they repeat things a hundred times? I'll be sitting and studying, and mother starts: 'Study properly. That's the most important thing for you right now.' But that's just the way I am studying! And for that matter, how does she know what's the most important thing for me?" "And what is the most important thing for you?"

She pondered, then said, "Probably to be understood. True friendship. To know what someone's like, whom I can trust, how to distinguish when someone's telling the truth and when they're lying. . . . Do you think that's funny?" "Not at all," I said, "I'm interested in things like that too." "But my parents consider all that just idle chatter. You have to take care of practical matters, then there won't be any time left for self-analysis. They never say anything simply, like friends do. Like you or Liudka. But always like parents who've got to bring me up. I'm no fool. I can see that they say the one thing so that in the evening I won't go over to see Liuda, but will stay at home, and the other so that I'll behave properly with boys. If only they said something interesting, but it's always two times two is four. I'm sick of it!"

How could I answer that? I honestly said that I wasn't prepared at all for our conversation; she'd touched on some very serious things, and I'd have to do some thinking. I believe she actually liked that, and she left somewhat happier, promising to call tomorrow. Tomorrow's her last exam, in physics.

August 18.

Tania's taking her exam now. I'm sitting near the phone thinking about what happened yesterday. What should I tell her? How do I explain that it's often as difficult for parents to understand their children as it is for children to understand their parents? That when they "judge," as she puts it, it's most often from helplessness, from the inability to find a common language. And she herself, after all, is also "judging," and ruthlessly so. For some reason parents always forget that children can see them detachedly. "You must respect your parents." A division of labor: "We brought you into the world and fed you, you respect us." Yet, you know, we ourselves don't respect our own child! Otherwise why do we smother her with truisms? Or is it that we lie for "pedagogical purposes"?

When Andrei was small, I "made a man out of him" like that. Perhaps I was the one who broke his character. . . . It's sad. . . . What will I tell Tania? I'm afraid for her. And for my son. If she leaves home, Andrei will blame himself—he's not her real father. That'll make the philistines happy. How should I talk to her? What should I advise? One thing is clear, no "pedagogical considerations," no discounts for age.

August 20.

There's been no time to write. There have been all kinds of things to get done. A lot of domestic chores had accumulated, and then I got an Agatha Christie novel and couldn't tear myself away from it. I read it even during the night.

Taniushka comes often. She's a student now! She and I have a "secret romance," as she calls it. For some reason she doesn't want her parents to know. Maybe she's afraid that her mother will start getting jealous? I don't think so. Natasha is a sensible person.

We discuss everything in the world. Tania seems to be open with me. We engage in "self-analysis." I don't understand what's bad about that. Why is cleaning the house a necessary task, while putting things in order within one's soul is a worthless whim? I can boast that as a result of our conversations, the idea of leaving home has been dropped from what she calls her agenda. To make up for that, we've decided to spend this winter break at the resort in Kliazma. I lived there last year. I'll get the vouchers for the trip early.

I'm glad that Andrei has such a direct, thoughtful, and refined daughter.

August 25.

Tania and I went to Izmailovo Park.[5] Summer is almost over, but the forget-me-nots are still in bloom there. Taniushka and I picked a bouquet.

We fed a squirrel cookies. It came to us by itself and ate right out of our hands. In Moscow animals aren't afraid of people. Tania maintains that in Iasenev a fox ran loose in the streets for several days. And I suddenly remembered that three years ago, when I was traveling along the Volga, I was surprised that, depending on the city, stray dogs and cats behaved in totally different ways. I recall in Saratov, all you had to do was call and they'd come right up to you, trusting and happy. In another city they paid no attention, and somewhere else they would run away from people.

After the walk we returned to my place. I put the kettle on, and Tania went to our "self-service store" for cake. It looked as if it was about to rain, and I made her wear my raincoat, which fit her. She looked at herself in the mirror and announced that we look alike. The eyes, she said, are the same. So's the figure. My figure—that of an old drone!

I looked out the window as Tania crossed the street. She took such big strides, moving freely and swiftly, that she just about flew, swinging her red purse.

Later we drank tea, and right after tea she ran off to see Liuda, who's not feeling well and is lying down. I gave Taniushka a big piece of cake to take with her.

We talked about Liuda all day today. Tania wants me to look at her. But I'm a surgeon, after all, not a rheumatologist. Yet she should definitely see someone. In September Nina Shustova will return from vacation; I'll call her and ask her to look at Liuda. You never can tell, what if it's not rheumatic heart disease? Mistakes do happen. If it turned out that this was, say, tonsilitis, after the tonsils were removed, everything would be back to normal. Nina will figure it out. She's an excellent diagnostician and a great person in general. She joined our clinic as a young girl, and now here she is, the head of a division, a candidate. *Our* clinic. . . . I've been retired for ten years now, and I still can't believe that it's forever. I still miss it. I miss my friends Vladlen and Nina. True, I see them, and quite often, at that. But most of all, I think I miss the patients. There must have been thousands, yet I remember many of them. You recall the face: you walk into the ward two, three days after an operation and the patient's alive, conscious, eating and talking. . . . And you feel so pleased at the sight, so grateful to him! I experienced something very similar to that when Andrei smiled for the first time. We doctors are lucky people.

We certainly must help Liuda. I like the fact that neither our Tania nor, apparently, Liuda has any doubts that everything will be all right. They discuss how next year Liuda will enroll at the university, also in the biology department, like Taniushka.

Andrei called in the evening. There's no change at work, but there's a problem at home: some part went in the car, and now he can't get it anywhere. I think he's just tired, but he doesn't have a vacation until October. How will he make it till then? I feel sorry for him, and I feel awkward about hiding my friendship with Tania. I'm not used to lying, I never learned how. And the main thing is, I'm convinced he'd only be happy about it. But Tania likes secrets, and has asked me not to say anything for the time being, so I keep quiet. She's still a child.

August 28.

Today I didn't leave the house. I felt weak and dizzy. It's gloomy and timid outside, sprinkling occasionally. Summer's obviously over. Earlier in the morning I was in a foul mood, but it's let up now. I've been lying down, reading Tiutchev. It's cozy in the room, and there's a vase on the piano with forget-me-nots that look very fresh and vivid.

Tania just called. She's at Liuda's. I asked her, "What are you two doing?" She replied: "Talking." I immediately understood that it was about something important.

Tania's lucky that she's got a real friend, that it's a serious friendship. She shouldn't be alone at her age. She wouldn't be able to cope with life, for there are so many thoughts, feelings, and questions leaping out at you, and its useless to expect help from adults. They have their own world, their own "screen."

I've got a fine granddaughter. The more I get to know her, the more I like her. Just take her attitude toward Liuda's illness: she doesn't run away from someone else's misfortune, and in this instance it's incorrect to say "someone else's." In my opinion, compassion is one of the noblest feelings, and at Taniushka's age everyone is so involved with himself that sometimes he's simply not up to hearing and understanding other people. That's probably natural. I've noticed that small children feel sorry for birds and kittens and they cry if their mother's in pain, but later all this suddenly disappears somewhere, and is replaced by egoism, and sometimes even cruelty. Usually this passes with age, but sometimes the goodness and openness of childhood never return. They get submerged in the bustle of everyday life, in immediate concerns. The soul withers. I'm certain that couldn't happen to Tania. Even now she's not self-absorbed; it's interesting to be with her. She recently told me that her fellow students had an argument about whether one should be kind. Someone said that it's not essential in the modern world, and that other qualities are more valuable: energy, intellect, quick reactions. And kindness is an atavism. Others said, "No! You must be kind. If you don't feel compassion for anyone, then no one will feel compassion for you or help you."

I asked Tania: "So what did you say?" She replied: "Nothing. I can't answer such questions off the top of my head. But, in my opinion, the question is posed stupidly. How can one ask whether one should be kind? It's the same thing as asking whether one should be beautiful."

Then she added that because of this argument, she got offended at her parents: "I asked them what they thought about it. Mother smiled and said: 'How people your age love to solve world problems.' And Andrei Nikolaevich said that he considers it 'better to be rich but healthy than poor but sick.' "

I kept quiet, though Taniusha's story surprised me, even disturbed me. Why such superciliousness? I badly wanted to call Andrei and "betray" her, but I must keep our secret. Nevertheless, he's wrong, not only in form but in substance. There are questions that a person wants and has a right to solve for himself, irrespective of the fact that they were solved a long time before him. There's nothing strange, and certainly nothing funny, about this. It's normal, that's the way it should be. I know by my own experience. These are exactly the same kind of "problems" that I solved for myself many a time in the course of my life. And the answers weren't always the same.

Evening. 11:00 P.M.

Speak of the devil—Taniushka dropped by just now. "Your voice sounded sad to me on the phone." I sent her home in a taxi.

Still, today was a good day. Right now it's totally dark outside, the sky has cleared, and there are such large, bright stars in it.

September 5.

It's night now. There's a thunderstorm outside, just like in summer. A heavy rain is crashing down, and lightning whips the sky.

It would be nice if the morning were clear: Tatiana and I have agreed to meet at the park entrance. Her classes begin at twelve tomorrow, so I'll have enough time to show her my favorite places.

> Oh, how in our declining years
> We love more tenderly and more superstitiously. . . .
> Shine on, shine on, farewell light
> Of a last love, of an evening glow.[6]

Love of life—that in fact is our very last love, which is both "bliss" and "despair."

> Linger, linger, evening light,
> Stay on, stay on, enchantment.

Of course this refers to the black sky and the poplar branches beside my window. I hear them rustling now and splashing as they're shaken by the water falling on them. And it refers to the forest clearing in Ovrazhki, where Andrei and I visited at the beginning of summer. It also refers to my friendship with Taniushka. It refers to this room, too, where it's so cozy to sit and read in the armchair under the lamp, and to the fact that tomorrow morning I'll get up and go to Sokolniki. And in the evening Andrei will call me without fail.

The rain is subsiding. The lightning is less and less frequent and is moving farther and farther away. It'll be daybreak soon."

There were no more entries.

A bright, even light flooded the room. Martynov carefully laid down the notebook, got up, and walked over to the window.

Snow was falling. Flat, slow flakes resembling saucers floated cautiously to the ground. A white horse unhurriedly pulled a cart past a wooden house with carved casings. From the doorway of a nine-story building, a large sheepdog bared its fangs fiercely at the horse. The sheepdog paid no attention to the cars. An electric train crawled along the railway.

. . . His mother was walking along the sidewalk. She approached quickly, holding her bare head high and swinging the red purse that she was clutching in her right hand in rhythm with her step, like an adolescent girl. Her left hand, as always, was tucked deep in her pocket. Her light hair was disheveled above her forehead, which was tanned by the summer sun. Her raincoat was thrown open. She was walking straight ahead, with long, loose strides, coming directly toward him and looking him right in the eye. The sky was piercing and very close, and summer leaves, freshly washed by the snow, glistened on the trees.

THE EXPERIMENT

RIMMA KAZAKOVА

Translated by

JOHN FRED BEEBE

"HELLO! I'M ARKADII ANDREEV. I'VE BEEN SENT TO YOU to conduct an experiment."

"What kind?" Mariana inquired unhurriedly but insistently.

"Oho! So you like to take charge! Well, that's just what I can't tell you."

"Cute, but not very informative."

Andreev smiled charmingly, "Believe me!"

"I believe you."

"Will you give me an authorization for some money?"

"No."

Andreev burst out laughing.

"Are you enjoying yourself?"

"Immensely!"

"I think we've finished our introductions."

"Are you chasing me out?"

"I can offer you some tea."

As he stirred in the sugar with his spoon, Arkadii said pensively: "I like your city a lot. It's too bad I'll have to leave as soon as the experiment is over."

Mariana politely remained silent.

"They'll finish reequipping the institute in a week. So, as you see, I have only one week. . . ."

"I can count."

"Will you authorize some money?"

"No. And you can't use our facilities."

"How old are you?"

"Twenty-two. I've been lab director for two years. More tea?"

"Mariana," he said simply and seriously, "I'll try to be honest. It's not because they've shut down the institute. I've thought up the most fantastic idea. I want to give my boss a present. The old boy will be so pleased! I'll. . . ."

Mariana brusquely pulled out the desk drawer and slapped the procedure manuals down on the desk.

"Interesting little books. Have you read them?"

Arkadii said unemotionally and dully, "Please forgive me. The fellows in Section Seven have my proposal. I'll go have a talk. . . ."

"And you please excuse me for a certain lack of cordiality. I'm truly sorry."

The back of his neck was strong and blond. The door closed noiselessly behind him.

That night Mariana dreamed of Arkadii. Throughout the dream—like the shadow of a boat along a river—was his sad, half-familiar face: grey eyes with blue flecks, firm lips, rather coarse blond hair, a movie star's smile. At first it was almost as if he weren't even there, and there was only a feeling of something familiar, like him, which vaguely irritated her: he made Mariana simultaneously feel both friendly and hostile. She was angered by his open desire to win her over for the sake of this mysterious experiment.

The dream wavered and trembled with a watery rippling. Arkadii's face appeared to her sometimes elongated, distorted, and unpleasant, and sometimes calm and serious.

When she got to the lab, the first thing Mariana did was send for Arkadii.

"I didn't understand you very well yesterday. What's going on? Why don't you want to submit an official request? Is this some kind of a joke?"

"No, I wasn't joking."

"What? Really, what is this? Do you know what you're suggesting?"

"Yes, I know."

"Then what do you want?"

"I want you to break the rules."

"Listen, Andreev. It's not just a matter of procedure; understand that. I really don't want you to think that I'm an insensitive bureaucrat. Stop playing your little games. You're not some lovesick girl; you're a scientist. Here's the form. Take a dictaphone and read your request. We'll discuss it. . . ."

"Oh, yes, and by tonight Lipiagin will know everything, right down to the exact wording! Thanks, but no thanks."

"Really? And how would he find out?"

"I don't know! It would seep through the walls. My boss is a genius. All he needs is a hint. He let me off to kick up my heels, to have some fun with people my own age—as you know, there aren't many at the institute under fifty."

"Arkadii, I won't allow an unauthorized experiment. That's final—period!"

"Here I had hoped to move a period, and it turns out the period—such a tiny speck—is heavier than a tombstone."

"Let's not talk about it anymore. I like your attachment to your boss, and there's something to your madness. . . . But after the disaster at Karai. . . ."

"Yes, fine. . . . So, all right, if that's how it has to be."

"How are the fellows in Seven?"

"Charming. Naive and talented, like ancient Greek gods."

"I'm leaving today," said Mariana, as she stepped onto the round platform of the elevator. "Have a good day."

And she pushed the button.

That night she dreamed of Arkadii again. They were walking in a meadow strewn with daisies. Arkadii picked a flower and started mumbling something. "What are you doing?" "It's an old counting rhyme. I learned it from my grandma." "Well, go ahead. . . ." "She loves me—she loves me not, she'll spurn me—she'll kiss me, she'll hug me to her heart—she'll send me packing. . . ." "Charming! Now, how does it go? . . . She loves me—she loves me not. . . ." It was quiet and warm. The daisies had a delicate smell. Like grains of pollen on a butterfly's wings, they rested on the soft, warm ground. Arkadii suddenly threw away the daisy. "Mariana, I want to have a serious talk with you about what's really important. Please try to understand. You know, the disaster at Karai. . . . Do you really think that humanity can be safeguarded against human sacrifices? Of course, it's better when there aren't any. No one disagrees! But you know, we're all walking along the edge. We're invading such a sanctum of nature that there are simply no guarantees of our safety. . . ." His face was sweet, sincere; his words, silent in the dream, had no sound, but were simply absorbed by her, the way skin absorbs sunlight, and with them came a feeling of sympathy and inexplicable joy. "And these regulations. . . . For two centuries now we've been saying that humanity is responsible for each individual, and each individual for humanity. In this respect there's no difference between me and an official committee. So, then, why can't I decide for myself the fate of the experiment? Why such a lack of trust? If I were an illiterate tradesman, they wouldn't have given me a diploma. But this way. . . . I didn't tell you the truth about my boss. My boss urbanely and skillfully hides from us his desire to elevate himself to inaccessible heights. Our boldness frightens him, and here the regulations help. . . ." Mariana listened, picking at the petals, and his words were enveloped in something vague and measured, like the pulsation of blood: "He loves me—he loves me not; he loves me—he loves me not. . . ." "Mariana, and you yourself? You're intelligent, and the fellows adore you, but it's not just tea drinking and official prodecures that give meaning to your existence, is it? And what can you do? . . ." "He loves me—he loves me not; he loves me—he loves me not. . . . And how does it go then? . . . He'll spurn me . . . he'll kiss me. . . ." "You're a slave to the regulations too, a slave of the committee, and of two other committees. There are three committees between you and humanity, and this is considered reasonable, such a censorship of thought, of one's very soul! . . ." "He'll hug me to his heart—he'll send me packing . . . he'll call me his own. . . . Funny boy, terribly funny boy. Who's he saying that to? As if I didn't think the same thing. Help him. . . . Only I'm still not ready. It's not all clear. Of course, there are plenty of old fools on the committees. But reckless young daredevils . . . like me . . . we're not really such daredevils. . . . No, no, I can't. This is too serious. Something's holding me back. Maybe we still aren't mature enough for all this. . . ." "Maybe we're still not mature enough for all this? Nonsense! The disaster at Karai occurred after all the plans had been approved and checked three times. False deductions from natural events. . . ." He took her by the hand; she didn't pull it back. "Mariana! I've wanted so badly for you to understand me! I'm sure that you'll agree with me! Let me do the experiment. You know me well enough for that. And the risk? So what risk? I can only tell you that it won't endanger anyone's life. If everything works out. . . ." "And if it doesn't?" "It will! But that's not the point. If it doesn't work out for me, it'll work out for someone else. What's important is the principle. To hell with routine! Mariana, tell me that you agree. Well, Mariana! . . ."

When she woke up, just one thing struck her: she had never before heard this "He loves me—he loves me not. . . ."

Mariana spent Wednesday at the expedition in the mountains. She got tired, went to bed late, and didn't dream at all that night.

The following day there was a conference in Section Seven. Mariana greeted everyone with a single nod, but was glad to see Arkadii near the vacuum chamber. He was standing with his back to her saying something to the technician. The conference ended quickly, and over the noise of the departing elevators, Mariana gaily shouted to Arkadii, "Well, how about it? Am I a good organizer? I've chased everybody away. The fellows from Section Seven have gone to the mountains for a couple of days."

Arkadii, twisting the chain with the key to the aircar, accompanied Mariana to her office.

"You going to town?" asked Mariana.

"Yes, I am. Want to come along?"

"I'd love to, but I can't. In half an hour I'm flying to the expedition. If you get terribly bored, come join us, but it's not really worth it. We're packing up to come back. . . . You know, Arkadii . . . ."

"What?" he asked intently, sensing something new in her voice.

"I wanted to tell you that our last conversation somehow . . . just that I'm awfully sorry that I can't help you at all. . . ."

"Give me the go-ahead—and you'll stop feeling sorry."

"No, we've already definitely made that decision. It's out of the question! I can't do it. Although my heart tells me. . . ."

"You should follow your heart."

Mariana was embarrassed. He was looking at her pleasantly, honestly, and a little sadly.

"I'll do that . . . after you write a paper entitled 'Physics and the Heart.' "

"People have been working on that for centuries."

"All right. Time to get to work."

Mariana jumped up on the escalator step and touched the familiar button, on which she knew every scratch, but suddenly, remembering something, she called Arkadii's name. He slowly walked back.

"Listen, you wouldn't happen to know this old poem, would you: 'He loves me—he loves me not'? . . ."

" 'He'll spurn me—he'll kiss me, he'll hug me to his heart. . . .' I know it, why?"

"No reason. It just got stuck in my mind. I heard it somewhere—can't remember where. . . ."

She pushed the button.

She wanted to have another dream. She got into bed expecting it. She told herself she would have a dream. And she did. This time it was completely without sound, without conversation—like a silent movie. She saw everything that happened distinctly, and at the same time she realized that it was just a dream, created by her own will, and, if she wanted it to, it would stop completely or do something different. It was her own dream, the way she wanted it, and so it was a wonderful, pleasant dream.

Mariana and Arkadii were sitting on a bench in front of the laboratory windows. Yellow autumn leaves were floating down, and there was a smell of damp, moldy earth. The windows were hidden by the tree branches, and the blinds were pulled down. It was late afternoon; the sun warmed them feebly but affectionately. Mariana's right hand felt Arkadii's cool, firm hand. Her whole being was jubilant and radiant. They sat like that for a long, long time, and then he put his arms around her and kissed her. The kiss was also long—infinitely long. It was hard for her to pull away from him; she was afraid to pull away, because she knew, she felt, that the dream would immediately end. How long did it last? A minute? An hour? The whole night? The falling leaves quivered; the warm air shimmered; the warm lips trembled, gently and lightly pressing lips.

The next day Arkadii called on the videophone and asked to see her. When he came into her office, Mariana greeted him radiantly.

"You in a good mood?"

"Wonderful."

"Well, mine is just the opposite."

"Never mind. It'll soon change."

"Not really . . . I have to leave tomorrow."

"Well, so you see, there isn't time for the experiment anyway."

"There will be, if you let me! I'll call the institute and talk them into it. Well . . . I'll break my leg, damn it! I'll think up something."

"You're really positive that the experiment doesn't threaten you in any way?"

"Absolutely."

"Except maybe I'll lose my job. . . ."

"Well, to hell with your job! . . . That is, excuse me, I meant. . . . Well, what do you care for this mechanized saucepan? We'll go to Tulavi; I've read your résumé. You're not just a theoretician. You need real life, room to work, real machinery. . . ."

"Arkadii, let me think till tomorrow."

"It's a deal."

"I'm not making any promises."

"I'm hoping."

He left, but the holiday mood, the feeling of elation, didn't leave.

That night their conversation was repeated word for word. The only difference was that she agreed. When he was about to dissolve, Mariana pulled him by the hand and kissed him herself.

Saturday came. Mariana finished all her urgent tasks before ten and resolutely pushed the intercom button and asked for Arkadii. The person at the desk told her that Arkadii wasn't there. He hadn't come yet. He was getting ready to leave town. "That's strange," thought Mariana. Not hearing any response to this information, the man started to praise Arkadii: "Really got a head on his shoulders, that one. We could use someone like that! Can't you talk him into staying? Even for a month. . . ."

But right then the bell rang, Mariana nodded, and Arkadii walked in.

"Hello. I'll tell you right off: I agree. To be honest, I've been thinking about it myself for a long time. Let everything go topsy-turvy; you're right! How much money do you need?"

"Mariana," he said, cautiously and apparently with great effort lowering himself into the armchair, "I thank you from the bottom of my heart, but I don't need anything. I came to say goodbye."

"What? And the experiment?"

"It's been completed. Everything's in order."

"What do you mean?"

"You see . . . only please don't get angry. Our institute is testing a device which can affect human beings while they're asleep. . . ."

"What?!"

"Just don't think anything bad! The program was developed and approved by all. . . ." He smirked. "By all three committees, and I followed the program exactly. My task was to persuade you, contrary to regulations, to give your permission for an experiment. . . . You see. And exactly per the procedure manual! . . ."

"Exactly per the procedure manual?"

"Yes, of course. Piatkin and Selko were monitoring the procedure. By the way, I'm to thank you in the name of the association for your enormous contribution to science. I don't think it should affect your health in any way, but in September you and another group of participants in the experiment—it was conducted simultaneously on seven subjects—will be invited to Tulavi for the congress. If I'm not mistaken, this is your third paper for the association?"

"Yes," said Mariana distractedly, "my third. This is all very interesting. . . ." She still hadn't recovered.

"I'll leave you the technical write-up, and in a couple of days I'll send a technician and some more background material. Mariana, my dear, believe me, although this is all legal and you were aware of what you were getting into when you joined the association, I still feel like a fool! Our life is so complicated. . . ."

But Mariana was thinking about something.

"Mariana, what are you doing? Say something!"

"Tell me, Arkadii, was it you who recorded that murmuring 'He loves me—he loves me not'?"

"It was, and I was very glad that the signal got through. Otherwise I would have been left in complete ignorance until the end of the week."

Mariana blushed.

"But don't think that it was my own creation! My boss dug up the counting rhyme; you'll find it in the write-up. . . . It's a curious thing, from that ancient time of fortune telling and beliefs in God knows what, but interesting. . . . There's still so much we don't know about human beings."

Mariana finally got up her courage. "You're probably very tired. I don't know the technology, but every night. . . ."

"What! Not every night! There were three sessions."

"Monday, Tuesday, and Friday?"

"There, you see, the experiment really did work!"

"It did. . . . But about human beings—you're right—oh, how little we still know! Not much more than the people with the daisies: 'He loves me—he loves me not. . . .' One more question. In the dream you instilled in me the resolution to disregard the regulations. But, to the best of my memory, didn't we also talk about that when I was conscious?"

"I followed the program. My task was only reinforcement. In other places the experiment was conducted somewhat differently. In two cases, to the best of my knowledge, there was just suggestion, without any direct contact with the subject. . . ."

"And how do you explain such a strange choice of subject?"

"Committee Two is familiar with your report on the work of Class B laboratories. We sort of nudged your thoughts up to the final conclusion, which you weren't quite ready for."

"Oh . . . and generally, what do you think about the regulations and the three committees?"

"Oh, come on, my dear! That's all well and good for an experiment." Arkadii leaned confidingly across the desk toward Mariana. "But in real life. . . . You can imagine what a mess there'd be if you gave the labs free rein!"

Arkadii saw Mariana's frown and interpreted it in his own way.

"I don't think that anything threatens you personally. They'll send you an answer to your memorandum and that'll be the end of it. There won't be any difficulties! You're solid; I can vouch for that, and if it hadn't been for the device. . . . Besides, the association will protect you. It needs you. . . . And now, sad to say, I must say goodbye. They're waiting for me."

Arkadii got up and offered Mariana his hand.

"Wait! Just a minute. . . ."

"What?"

"No, never mind. . . . Goodbye! See you in September! It's been a long time since I was in Tulavi. But, you know, it's not bad here either, is it? Especially our park. And the bench under the oak tree—opposite my windows. . . ."

"I never had the time to get out to your park. So I'll be sure to come back again and sit on your little bench. . . . Excuse me again and—thank you!"

"Well, have a good flight, if that's how it is. Just one more thing. All this time, I had a better opinion of you than I do now. I want you to know that. I even feel sad. The fellow who sent the regulations to hell, and was even ready to break his leg . . . I liked him better. That's what I wanted to tell you."

"Oh, Mariana, my dear, you're amazing. I'd say—old-fashioned. Why, that's charming!"

When the door slammed shut behind Arkadii, Mariana started to swear in a way that wasn't at all old-fashioned.

BE STILL, TORMENTS OF PASSION
LIUDMILA UVAROVA

Translated by

JOHN FRED BEEBE

NASTIA STARTED CHECKING HER WATCH AT SIX-
thirty. At seven she poured out a few drops of Valo-Cordin mixed half
and half with Cor-Valol—in her opinion, the very best mixture there was—
a joy for the heart. However, the joy didn't help at all. By eight, Veronika
Alekseevna still hadn't shown up. Nastia made up her mind, and started
to look up the phone number for the police station.

But just then the doorbell finally rang. She was here.

"Here she is—safe and sound." Nastia pretended that she hadn't been
the least bit worried. After all, there was nothing to get upset about, to
get all nervous over. But actually inside she was radiant, exultant. "She's
here. Nothing happened to her. She's alive and healthy."

It was always the same old story. Veronika Alekseevna, who knew
how Nastia worried, tried to reason with her: "Try to understand, Nastia,
what could possibly happen to me? Just think, the culture club is at one
end of town; we live at the opposite end. You know that I always leave
late; you know how long it takes me to get here across town. Just figure
it up."

But Nastia didn't intend to figure. "OK. That's enough! Why don't
you leave me alone? I'm not going to change at my age, and I don't have
much longer to live, anyway."

That's what she said, but in her heart she hoped that maybe, after
all, she'd live for at least a few more years. Let's say about ten, or even
a bit more. How nice!

Nastia was seventy-eight, Veronika Alekseevna fifteen years younger.

"Why, you're just a kid," Nastia often said. "Do you think you understand anything about life? How could you, you silly girl?"

Almost fifty years ago, Nastia had shown up for work at Veronika's parents' house for the first time. At that time Veronika had just enrolled in a drama school. She was studying with the most famous tragic actor in Moscow. He predicted: "Little girl, you're not going to be one of the worst actresses in the world. Just keep trying. . . . "

And she kept trying. She studied everything that was taught at the school, ran off every evening to the theater, got seats somewhere in the top balcony, and watched her favorite actors. Later on, at home, she would sit in front of the mirror and make faces, frown, get angry, or be wildly exultant, imitating the actors she had seen on the stage.

They say that if you want something enough, your wish will eventually come true. Veronika's wish did come true. She became an actress in a famous theater, maybe the best theater in the world.

At first, of course, she played bit parts, the least important ones, but one day something happened, something rather common in theatrical circles: the actress portraying the lead role in the play *Little Dorrit*[1] unexpectedly became seriously ill. And then Veronika volunteered. "I can do it. I know the part by heart. Dickens is my favorite writer."

"Well, and what does that mean?" the director asked. "I like Dickens, too. And you can cut me and burn me, but I won't be able to play Florence,[2] or Mr. Dombey, or even Little Dorrit."

"But I can play it." Veronika didn't give in. "I learned that part a long time ago."

The director asked, "Why?"

"Just in case," she answered.

Veronika acted well enough. Perhaps not as brilliantly as the main actress, the theater's star, but she was sincerely moving with her young awkwardness, her innate, genuine spontaneity, an almost childish vulnerability, so very appropriate for just this role.

"OK" said the director after the performance, "not bad. Of course. . . . "

He didn't say anything else, but even this was enough. The director was a man of few words. In addition, he was a bit afraid of the star. Everyone knew that for several years now they had been involved in a prolonged, rather boring love affair, in which, as she herself admitted, the best pages had been read. . . .

Several more years passed, and Veronika became the leading actress of the theater.

The envious actresses openly gossiped, "It's easy for her. She doesn't have any housework or worries, not like some people."

Some of them, as a matter of fact, were greatly burdened with the problems of daily life—children, family, household worries. So, sometimes they'd be late for rehearsal, or they wouldn't learn their part perfectly, or they would perform poorly—those things happened.

But Veronika could devote herself completely to her acting. Nastia was able to free her from everything else. And then Veronika's mother, a plump, sickly woman, fell seriously ill. All her life she had suffered from asthma and pneumosclerosis, but she was dying from heart failure. Nastia devotedly, patiently, took care of her, telling Veronika, in no uncertain terms: "You, Vera (she just wouldn't agree to call Veronika anything but Vera, considering that Vera was the proper Christian name, and a very pretty one besides, not outlandish like 'Veronika'), go act to your little heart's content, learn your parts and act. I don't need you; I can manage without you."

About a year and a half later, after Veronika's mother had died and Veronika was living alone with Nastia, she met Arnold Smoliarov, a senior student at the conservatory, and a future star. That's what everyone said about him. Arnold had already performed in group concerts, and always with resounding success. He had a beautiful, tender, yet strong voice, what is called a dramatic tenor. It's true that he was not physically impressive; he was short and fine-boned, with an inexpressive face, its features somehow hastily stuck on, hit or miss. Only his teeth were nice—white, large, fitting perfectly. But it seemed to Veronika that when Arnold sang, he was transformed; he became almost handsome, even seemed taller.

Once Veronika took Nastia with her to the conservatory for a concert by the senior students. Nastia dressed up in her blue wool dress—her old mistress's dying gift to her. She combed her hair out straight, her unusually beautiful hair, silky, thick, a wonderful light walnut color with a gold tint. She sat in the third row beside Veronika, proudly glancing around from side to side. She seemed to be saying: "See where I am; not sitting just any old place in the balcony, not in the back row. But beside the most beautiful woman in the whole wide world."

Then Arnold came out on the stage wearing someone else's tail coat—Veronika knew whom he had borrowed it from. It hung on him baggily, the sleeves too long, the tails almost to the floor. His face was all splotched from excitement, but then the accompanist played the first chords of the introduction. Arnold stepped back a little and pressed his hands to his chest.

> Be still, torments of passion . . .
> Calmly sleep, despairing heart,
> I weep, I suffer torments,
> My soul, without you, languishes. . . .

At first he sang softly, as if confiding to someone his inconsolable emotional anguish; gradually, following the swelling chords, his voice grew stronger, pouring forth:

> I suffer torments, I weep.
> My grief is not assuaged by tears. . . .

He sang, forgetting about the auditorium where his teachers, acquaintances, friends, and Veronika herself were sitting, forgetting that the tail coat was binding him under the arms and the tails were almost sweeping the floor. He forgot about everything except his singing.

> In vain doth hope
> Foretell my happiness.
> I do not believe; I do not believe
> Her deceitful promises.
> Absence steals love away. . . .

Nastia firmly squeezed Veronika's hand.

"Hey, Vera, he's good, isn't he?"

"Be quiet," whispered Veronika, who couldn't have been more pleased. She didn't notice that tears were rolling down her cheeks.

Nastia headed home before the end of the concert. "You surely won't come home alone; he'll escort you," she said. "In the meantime, I'll get supper. . . . "

That evening Arnold and Veronika wandered around the Arbat streets for a long time. He held her firmly by the arm and couldn't take his eyes off her face. Frost stuck to her eyelashes, making them heavy. A rosy flush appeared on her cheeks. Her fresh, slightly puffy mouth was half open.

"I can't live without you," Arnold said. "I realize that I am unworthy of you, that you can choose the most handsome, the most talented. . . ."

"*You* are talented," she interrupted him. "You can't even imagine how talented you are."

He didn't listen to her, but kept repeating the same words over and over: "I can't live without you! I can't imagine life without you."

He escorted her to the entrance of her apartment house. He stood silently in front of her, tiny and freezing. His thin little chicken neck, blue from the cold, was visible through his open coat collar.

She felt sorry for him. She didn't know whether it was love or pity she felt for him, homely, badly dressed, but infinitely talented, and not even completely realizing the full strength and depth of his talent. She knew that he lived in a dormitory. His parents were far away, in a little town in the Urals—in Karabash. Probably he didn't eat well; his money wouldn't last from one scholarship payment to the next. Of course, he had a hard life, but he had talent, the most real, genuine, scintillating talent.

She pulled him by his coat sleeve. "Let's go up to my apartment."

"Where?" he asked and suddenly, understanding what she had said, beamed with joy.

"Let's go, "Veronika repeated. "Nastia probably is already tired of waiting for us. She left early, promising to fix us a delicious supper."

He moved in with her. At first he just couldn't get enough of Veronika. There she was, alive, in the flesh, his mate, his pride and joy, the most beloved, the most desirable woman on earth, right beside him, in the same apartment. Then, since one gets used to everything, both good and bad, he gradually got used not only to Veronika's presence, but also to the warm, clean apartment, to the delicious food, to Nastia's unobtrusive but thorough tender loving care.

Early in the morning, even before he went to the conservatory, Arnold began his warm-up: at first, scales, then sol-fa and voice exercises. Afterwards, he would sit down at the piano, accompanying himself. In the beginning he was bashful about singing, afraid he would bother Nastia, but she told him straight out, "Don't play the fool, Arnold. Sing as much as you want. It's good for you and a joy for me to listen to."

Viktoria Petrovna, his accompanist, came once a week. She knew absolutely all the best singers in Moscow and one time had even accompanied Leonid Vitalyevich Sobinov himself.[3] A stern woman who looked like a gypsy, she constantly smoked strong cigarettes. Long earrings with transparent stones dangled from her ears. Her fingers were adorned with heavy rings, which, strange to relate, did not at all interfere with her playing. When she came in, Viktoria Petrovna would light up a cigarette and sit down at the piano; flashing a bulging dark-brown eye at Arnold, she would order: "Come here. Let us begin. . . . "

She would toss her head, flash the transparent stones of her earrings, and throw her large, strong hands on the piano keys. She would repeat sternly, "Let's begin. . . . "

And Arnold would begin to sing.

Their little family lived modestly and quietly. Veronika would go to rehearsal in the morning. Then she would run home, eat dinner, get a little rest, and rush back to the theater for the performance. Arnold had begun to work at the Stanislavsky and Nemirovich-Danchenko Music Theater. So far he hadn't received any major parts, but he was hopeful, and Veronika thought that his voice would surely carry him through.

Nastia ran the apartment, ran it efficiently, figured everything down to the last kopek. At the market she would frenziedly bargain for each bunch of radishes, for each fresh squash or head of cabbage.

"I've got two of them," she would say. "They both need vitamins, because they have to work terribly hard."

"What are they?" someone would usually ask. "Warehousemen or dump truck drivers?"

"What do you mean—warehousemen!" Nastia would scornfully curl her thin lips. "They are actors; they have artistic work, not for you and me to understand. . . . "

And with that, she would cut them off and end the conversation so she could have the last word.

Meanwhile, Veronika had already attracted admirers—female admirers. She paid no attention to male admirers, and they would quickly get lost, wither away, as Nastia expressed it. But the female admirers were persistent; they would wait patiently for Veronika by the stage entrance and escort her home in a group. Sometimes, when she left her apartment house, she would meet some cute little girl, who probably had been standing outside the building for a long time, freezing, at times even frozen numb, as it happened once in a February cold snap. Veronika couldn't help herself. Even though she was in a hurry, she took the stubborn girl by the arm and ran back into the apartment with her. She told Nastia, "Hot tea, quick, and vodka, if we have any."

There wasn't any vodka. No one in the apartment drank. But in three minutes there was tea on the table, hot and strong. And then Veronika got a good look at the girl she had brought into her home. She wasn't really so young. Probably she was even older than Veronika. But because she was so thin, all skin and bones, and her face so little, about the size of a man's fist, she seemed deceptively young, in her early teens, except for the telltale wrinkles on her temples and the wrinkle around her mouth.

From then on Varia Kashirtsev became almost like a member of the family. They became friends, but not as equals. Varia worshiped Veronika, but Veronika was condescending to her, allowed her to meet her and walk with her, to help Nastia when she could around the apartment, to go to the store for groceries, to the market for potatoes and vegetables, to the cleaners, and to drop off clothes at the laundry. At first Nastia was jealous, but then she saw that no one could take her place in Veronika's heart, and gradually she warmed to Varia. For Arnold it was as if she didn't exist. He rarely noticed anyone except Veronika. Besides, he was constantly depressed—things weren't working out at the theater. From the very first day there had been problems with the conductor and with the director of the theater. . . .

Varia came almost every day. Basically, Veronika was the main thing in her life. Veronika and excursions. Early every Saturday morning, around seven, she would go to the suburban ticket offices of the Yaroslavl, Kursk, or Kazan railway stations for the excursions, for those who wanted to get better acquainted with the Moscow region, and she would go on the organized trips with them, sometimes to the battlefields of the Great Patriotic War [World War II] in Petrishchevo or Ruza, sometimes to Zvenigorod, to the woods there, sometimes to places even farther from Moscow. She dressed unfashionably but comfortably: old running pants, a nearly worn-out sweater, a backpack, and running shoes or rough saddle shoes with thick soles.

Varia worked as a cashier in a savings bank. She had a surplus of free time after work, no family, almost no close friends except for the aunt she lived with, a long way from downtown in the Bogorodskii district, near the Red Hero factory.

Her aunt had a little house with three windows and a tiny yard, but it was all hers—the dill, and the cucumbers, and the radishes and lettuce. There were several rows of plants in the yard. Varia meticulously seeded them in the spring, and in mid summer she would reap her harvest. She would bring the first dill, the first cucumbers and lettuce to Veronika. Nastia would say, "You've got a green thumb, Varia."

"Why, how can you say that, Auntie Nastia!" Varia would modestly deny it, secretly exultant: this time she had managed to please Nastia.

Veronika's star kept shining brighter and brighter. She was already appearing in movies. She had been in two pictures. Her theater work was constantly crowned with success, and when they had to send a theatrical delegation to London for a Shakespeare Festival, Veronika was included.

She came back beaming, beautiful, wearing a new boucle coat and a new style of hat that had just become popular in the West. At the airport she told Arnold, "I've brought you a stupendous V-neck sweater. All the men there are wearing sweaters like this."

"Thank you," Arnold responded weakly. Try as he might, he couldn't hide the bad mood he was in. Things were going so poorly that he sometimes thought that he should try another theater, or better yet, leave Moscow for somewhere in the provinces. He could probably get a decent position there.

But Veronika, intoxicated by her own success, didn't notice or didn't want to notice anything. Laughing, she turned to Varia. "I've brought you a new backpack. You'll be going on your excursion trips, and your old one is just a fright."

For Nastia she brought an oilcloth apron—on a dark-blue background it had red frying pans, light blue pots, and a teapot with different-colored polka dots. A wonderfully beautiful apron. Nastia immediately blossomed, put on the apron, rushed over to the mirror, and flung out her arms. "That's really something! Vera has made my day."

She grabbed Vera by the light-brown bangs above her forehead and gave her a friendly tug.

Soon Veronika was given the role of Lidia in Ostrovskii's *Easy Money*.[4] For days she studied the part, which was complex and multifaceted, as the director expressed it. There were so many different levels of meaning that every word Lidia uttered had to be considered from all points of view and given an implication which might even seem a bit strange. Veronika was busy from morning until late at night, and perhaps that was why she didn't notice the changes occurring in Arnold. And very striking changes were evident—Arnold had begun to drink. One night he came home late, after one A.M. "Hey, what's going on?" Veronika asked in surprise.

He didn't answer. She looked at him and suddenly jumped back. "Nastia," she called, "Nastia, come look, he's dead drunk."

Nastia dashed out of her room, frowning, but fresh, as if she hadn't just awakened, and said sternly, "Stay out of the way, I'll handle him myself."

She took him off to the bathroom and undressed and bathed him there. He submitted to her silently. Then she put him to bed in her room, and she moved into Veronika's room, curling up on the little couch beside her bed.

That night she woke up and listened. Veronika was sobbing quietly, with her head buried in her pillow. Nastia quickly moved over to her, sat down on the bed, and forced her to lift her head from the pillow. Veronika began to cry loudly, no longer trying to hold back the tears.

That was the first time anything like that had happened. Nastia was seriously frightened and decided to call "Emergency." But then she thought better of it and didn't. Veronika calmed down a bit, although she kept repeating, "What can we do? What will we do now?"

In the morning Arnold solemnly promised: "Never again, not a single drop." Sadly he admitted, "If they don't replace the director, I'll leave the theater. He doesn't give me a dog's life, anyway."

"Don't ever let this happen again!" Veronika ordered sternly, and he nodded his head.

And again, several days later, he came home, as Nastia said, three sheets to the wind, and no wind in his sails.

Veronika didn't sleep the whole night. She cried, choking, cursing herself and her misfortune, cursing Arnold, whom she gradually began to despise—not pity; not hate, of course, but despise. She was surprised, but she couldn't help it. He had completely let himself go; almost every night now he came home drunk, and one night he didn't come home at all.

"That's it," Veronika told Nastia. "We've got to put an end to this whole business." There was a decisive ring to her voice; her face turned to stone, and she seemed older, more stubborn, even mean.

"What do you mean? Are you serious?" Nastia was frightened.

Nastia often said about herself, "I'm a simple Russian peasant from near Yaroslavl." And like any Russian peasant woman, who herself never drank, she sympathized with Arnold, felt genuinely sorry for the poor loser, and even burst out crying when she heard Veronika's decision to break up with him.

She tried to talk Varia into using her influence with Veronika, to have her think things over carefully before taking such a vitally important step, but Varia bluntly refused. "That's Veronika's business. It's not our place to try and make her change her mind."

And soon Arnold vanished from the house, vanished as if he had never been there at all; he took his few belongings and said goodbye to Veronika and Nastia. Nastia burst out crying and hugged him goodbye. Veronika didn't have a tear in her eye. She silently held out her hand to him. "Take care of yourself," she said rather calmly.

He walked out of the building, and out of habit he raised his head to take one last look at the windows of the apartment where he had lived for almost two years. Just in case, he waved his hand, as if saying goodbye to someone, most likely Veronika, who, as he thought, as he wanted to think, was following him with her eyes. But not a single curtain in a single window moved. No one was watching him leave.

That evening Veronika had a dress rehearsal at the theater. She was nervous. Her pale-yellow silk dress didn't fit right. They had altered it twice, taken it in, let it out, but the dress still didn't fit the way it should. Besides, her partner, who was playing Vasilkov, irritated her. He seemed a bit old for that role. He should have been playing Teliatyev, but he took on Vasilkov. Along with everything else, the lace parasol, which Lidia never lets out of her hands, suddenly broke. Veronika had to frantically search for another one, and in about ten minutes appear on stage.

But everything worked out great. Things couldn't have gone better. In the end, the seamstresses attained perfect and absolute harmony. The dress fit as if it had been poured on. The stage manager quickly found another parasol. Her partner performed excellently, became inspired, and at the end of the performance received only a little less applause than Veronika herself.

As always, the three of them—Veronika, Nastia, and Varia—went home together. Veronika was excited, humming to herself; then she stopped humming and said, "I'm dying of thirst! Half my kingdom for a glass of hot tea."

"You'll get your tea right away, as much as you want," Varia said, and Nastia, after a minute, asked, "Well, do you miss Arnold?"

"Who? Me?" Veronika was surprised, so genuinely surprised that it was impossible not to believe her. It was immediately apparent that she wasn't acting or pretending; that was really the way she felt. "Why, what do you mean, Nastia?" Nastia sighed, and didn't answer.

So Vera didn't miss him, after all. That meant she was satisfied with everything that had happened, and that was the main thing. She wasn't suffering because of anybody. She wasn't heartbroken over anyone. But just the same, Nastia felt sorry, sorry for Arnold, poor fellow. It happens, and often, a man just can't control himself. He'd rather not drink, but he can't help himself; he doesn't have the strength, the will, the discipline.

But Nastia didn't say any of this aloud. No point. They quickly reached the apartment, talking about something not worth remembering later, in lockstep with each other—Nastia, Veronika, and Varia.

Years had passed since then, almost thirty-seven years. Many changes had taken place during that time. Veronika had celebrated her big anniversary, received the award of "People's Artist" and a good pension, and retired to a well-deserved rest. Actually, she would never have retired on her own, but a new director came to the theater who didn't much care for old people. He himself said, "One or two seniors will do me fine."

Veronika Alekseevna applied for her pension first. She knew that they would have a big farewell ceremony. And that's the way it turned out. There were lots of speeches, kisses, and emotional words, which seemed to come right from the heart. Everyone seemed sorry to see her go, and even the director said sort of off-handedly, "It's too bad you're leaving us, our dear Veronika Alekseevna."

But those were just words. She knew they were just words, that's all.

Veronika was offered a choice—to direct a drama club either at a factory for the overhaul of some kind of equipment or at a textile mill. She chose the textile mill: there were lots of women there, and women are more conscientious than men and, as it seemed to her, they have more ambition. Once they start, they won't drop out. They'll stay active in the club activities.

In addition, she taught an acting course in a drama school, the same Theater Arts School where she herself had once studied.

There was enough money. Nastia, who had aged greatly over the years but wouldn't yield the household duties to anyone, was still the only authorized household manager. At times Varia would help her. Now, just as before, Varia had two strong interests in her life: Veronika and excursions. She had retired even before Veronika, and she visited Nastia and Veronika almost every day. On Sundays she would go on her trips, always wearing her backpack, her running shoes, and her ridiculous, poorly fitting pants. Nastia would make fun of her: "The old woman just won't settle down. It's long since time to give up your trips, and quit tempting fate." But with genuine pity, Veronika would watch Varia cheerfully stride off down the street, wearing an ancient Japanese sweater that Veronika had once given her, a boys' worn cap with the bill turned back, and comfortable boys' hiking boots. She was skinny, and from the back she looked like a young girl—little old Varia.

Veronika fell in love often during this time, as could be expected. As quickly as she latched onto men, she also cooled off. Sometimes she would say to Nastia, "Probably I was just born this way. Men don't mean that much to me."

"And that's a good thing," Nastia would respond, satisfied. Vera wasn't breaking her heart, wasn't longing for anyone, wasn't wasting away. You couldn't ask for anything better.

Veronika worked a lot, often from morning right through the evening. From the culture club at the textile mill she would rush to the Theater Arts School to give a lecture, then on to the conservatory or the theater to watch her students. She had not expected to become so emotionally involved with them, these boys and girls whom she had not even known until recently. She was surprised at herself. Every exam in the Theater Arts School took its toll on her health. But to compensate, there were also joys, as, for example, when her favorite student was accepted after graduation in the same theater where Veronika herself had worked. And the first role given to the student was the part of Masha[5] in *Three Sisters*.

On the day of the premiere, Veronika suddenly realized that she was nervous, probably more nervous than when she herself had performed. She sat in the third row of orchestra seats, hunched forward, her hands squeezed together, involuntarily moving her lips. She repeated to herself Masha's words, which she still knew by heart. You could wake her up in the middle of the night and she wouldn't make a slip, wouldn't forget a word.

The student was flabby, big-eyed, impossibly headstrong, but undeniably talented. She was forgiven much because of her talent. That night she performed well on stage, and when she said goodbye to Vershinin, she cried real tears. When the audience applauded madly, Veronika looked around proudly at the spectators. This was, after all, her student. She was the one who had taught her to forget everything extraneous; who had taught her to live the life of the character whose role she was performing. And yet, when Veronika got home, she couldn't help confiding to Nastia, "I was a different Masha, do you remember? More disheveled, more sincere, I think."

"Everyone knows there's no one better than you," answered Nastia, who, of course, didn't know and hadn't seen Veronika's student perform, but remembered Veronika in all her roles very well.

Veronika also became similarly attached to her club members at the textile mill. There were no particularly gifted individuals among them, but she tried to teach them to love the theater, to understand and value genuine art.

Arnold turned up unexpectedly. Suddenly, early in the morning, while Veronika was still asleep, the doorbell rang. Nastia opened the door and stared in surprise at an unfamiliar man, very thin, in a light summer coat, even though it was the dead of winter.

He stood in the doorway, looking at Nastia, his eyes brimming with tears from the cold. A big duffel bag hung lightly from his shoulder.

"Whom do you want?" Nastia asked coldly. "Why don't you say something?"

"Don't you recognize me, Nastia?" he asked in reply.

She looked closely, recognized him, and gasped. "It can't be!"

"So, I haven't changed so awfully much," he smiled. The smile was bitter. It made Nastia's heart ache, she felt so sorry for him.

"Vera is still asleep," she said, frowning on purpose so she wouldn't cry. "But I've been up for a long time. As you know, I'm an early bird."

She turned around and started for the kitchen. He followed her. He asked softly, but she heard him anyway, "Is Veronika alone, or is someone else here?"

"There's nobody else here," Nastia snapped. "Let's go into the kitchen. I'll warm you up some tea."

He pulled off his coat. Nastia hung it in the entrance hall and thought sympathetically: "It's lined with air, and nothing else at all." But aloud she said cheerfully, "Well now, Arnold, why don't you sit down at the table and I'll brew you some tea, just the way you like it."

"Can you really remember what kind of tea I like?" Arnold asked, surprised.

She answered proudly, "So far I still have my memory."

He sat down at the table, covered, just as it used to be, with a clean, white oilcloth in a tiny flower design. Pans gleamed on the shelf hanging over the table. A red polka-dotted teapot whistled softly on the stove.

Veronika didn't come out of her room for a long time. Nastia didn't stand on ceremony. She woke her up and told her Arnold was there.

Veronika was surprised, but no, not the least bit sad. However, right away she said, "Feed him. Give him some tea."

"Why, of course." Nastia felt hurt. "Do you think I don't know that myself?"

Veronika got dressed, put on a little makeup, and caught herself wanting to look younger and prettier. Sadly she glanced at her face, still pale from sleep. She remembered how she used to wake up rosy-cheeked. Nastia would say, "Just the color of poppies."—And now, look! Old age. There's no getting away from it!

Stepping lightly, almost gliding, she went into the kitchen. She held out her hand to Arnold and said simply, as if they had just recently seen each other, "Well, hello, I'm glad to see you."

He perked up, turning pink with pleasure at her words and answered, "I'm glad to see you, too."

Veronika sat down at the table and turned to Nastia. "Pour me some tea. Make it strong."

Nastia poured her some tea, pushed the glass over to her, and then immediately left the kitchen. "Let them talk to each other," she thought. "They have things to remember."

That same evening there was the dress rehearsal of a play in which two of Veronika's students were performing: plump, rosy-cheeked Aga-fonova was playing the role of the maid, Tania, in Tolstoy's *The Fruits of Enlightenment*,[6] and Lilia Werther, with the last name that sounded so strange to the Russian ear, even though she was a pure-blooded Russian from near Riazan, was acting the part of Betsy.

"If you'd like, we can go together," Veronika suggested to Arnold.

He thought it over, then refused, "I'm tired. I'd better stay home."

"So," Veronika thought on the way to the theater, "home. . . . So that's the way it is. Well, I'll be. . . . Can he be calling my apartment his home? Can he be thinking that everything will be the way it was? Can he be expecting to stay here with me?"

Then, at the theater, she forgot about everything else. She watched the stage, followed the acting of her students, noting every false move, even those completely imperceptible to the layman. She noted every trifle, even those which, one would think, there was no sense in paying attention to.

It wasn't late when she got home, because in the middle of the second act she suddenly had felt extraordinarily tired, completely drained. No wonder. She had gotten completely exhausted these last few years. It was no joke, five years without a vacation. She hadn't once been to a resort. And if you asked her why she didn't go anywhere, just stayed home, she wouldn't know how to answer. Or rather, she would say that she didn't feel like getting ready, getting a ticket for a train or a plane, and then adjusting to a new place. And almost immediately, after only a few days, getting your return ticket. Evidently, this really was old age, a time when you don't even want to move out of your chair.

At home Nastia and Arnold were sitting in the living room, playing fools.[7] Veronika raised her eyebrows archly. "I didn't think you used to be interested in cards."

Arnold was embarrassed; his gaunt cheeks turned pink. Nastia quickly cleared the cards from the table and rushed into the kitchen to put on the teapot and get them something to eat. Quickly she put plates and cups on the table, and a fresh Russian dried apricot pie, and some jam in a little long-stemmed bowl. She went to her room, so she wouldn't be in the way while the two of them talked.

The conversation was heavy and cumbersome. Veronika didn't ask him about anything. He began to tell her about himself. He was unlucky, poor fellow. In the old days things hadn't gone well for him, and he was still having bad luck.

"My God," Veronika said sympathetically. "You were so talented. Everyone was predicting a brilliant future for you. I was sure you would become a major star."

"But it didn't happen that way in real life. The star sputtered and died before it had time to start blazing."

"You know what I think?" she said. "You turned out to have a rather disagreeable personality, to put it mildly . . . ."

"No, no. What do you mean?" He waved his hand. "That's not it at all." He quit talking, cutting himself off in the middle of a thought.

She guessed, "You probably still drink?"

He didn't deny it, but admitted, without looking at her, "It has happened. And, if you want to know, I even got married once—well, not for love, but I just got the itch."

"And where's your wife?" Veronika asked.

"Where?" he repeated the question, shrugging his shoulders vaguely. "Somewhere or other. She's probably getting along, just glad that she's gotten rid of me . . . ."

"That's for sure," Veronika agreed harshly. "You didn't stop drinking, and she probably got fed up with you."

He nodded, "You're probably right." That's the way he had been before, too: direct, truthful, unable to lie, incapable of distorting the truth even a little bit. If it hadn't been for this ruinous passion of his, how wonderful his life could have been, what a singer he could have become. . . .

He pushed away the cup of cold tea and said, without taking his eyes off Veronika, "And you, I think, are just the same; you haven't changed at all."

"Oh, nonsense," laughed Veronika, feeling flattered. What woman doesn't like to hear such words? "What do you mean? Look more closely!"

"No," he said. "Really."

She glanced at him, and by his eyes realized, beyond any shadow of a doubt, that he was not trying to flatter her. He had said what he really thought.

He hesitated a bit and suddenly made up his mind. "Veronika, dearest, I've thought about you all these years. How many times I've wanted to write you and somehow was afraid. . . . "

"No need to be afraid," she said. "We didn't part as enemies. It's just that I understood then that it was better for us to live our own lives."

"No," he objected, "for me, as it turned out, it wasn't better at all."

She didn't speak. What could she say to that? In any case, she didn't regret it and would never regret it!

He began again. "Veronika, my dear, you have always been, and still are, the dearest . . . "

"Please don't," she said frowning. "I beg you: please stop!"

But he didn't stop. "You know that I never lie, and I'll tell you the honest-to-God truth now. I've always loved you, all these years, no one else but you. . . . " He started to cough, and pulled over his cup and took a swallow.

"Can I warm you up some tea?" Veronika asked in a sober, almost dispassionate voice.

"Please don't. I don't want any," he answered quickly. "You know, on the way here, I was wondering all the time if you were alone or if you had someone here. And then, when I get here, Nastia says you don't have anyone, and I'm alone, too, completely alone, and I keep thinking about just one thing. Veronika, dearest, let's start over. All right?" His eyes glistened feverishly. His sunken cheeks, half-shaven, were covered with dark bristles.

"Please don't," said Veronika again. "And let's not talk about it anymore. Agreed?"

He didn't seem to hear her words. "You know, twice I was treated for alcoholism, each time for two months."

"It didn't help, did it?"

He didn't deny it. "Of course, I held out for a while. . . . "

"And then everything was the same as before."

He nodded. "But now, I think, I've got it licked for good. You'll see! Now, never again. . . . "

"No! No! No!" Veronika said. "Absolutely not, Arnold, and let's not talk about it anymore."

He realized then that her decision was irrevocable; her mind was made up. He dropped his head and stared fixedly at his feet. His thin, blue-veined hands, clasped together, trembled—a light, continuous quiver. They were already covered with age spots.

Exerting all her will power, Veronika forced herself not to look at his dilapidated trousers, his rough hiking boots with the little patch on the side, and the frayed collar of his tattletale-grey shirt.

To keep from breaking down completely—her heart wasn't made of stone—Veronika impetuously stood up. "If you'd like, you can live with us for a while. . . . Do you have any place at all to live? Anywhere at all, in any city? Answer me. Why don't you say something?"

"I'm thinking," he answered. "I've made up my mind. I'll leave tomorrow."

"What's your hurry?"

"I've got to be going," Arnold said. "It's time. There's no use staying too long in one place."

She felt like asking what he would have decided if she had agreed to start all over again. Would he have hurried off somewhere, or would he have wanted to stay in one place? But she didn't ask. And he didn't say any more either.

On her way to her room, Veronika turned around in the doorway. "Nastia has made up your bed in the study."

"Thanks," he nodded.

"Good night," she said, closing the door behind her.

He answered, with a slight smile, "Good night."

The next morning, Veronika got up earlier than usual. She wanted to remind Nastia to give him a good last meal, maybe fry him a chicken or something to take along.

Nastia was sitting in the kitchen with her hands in her apron pockets, morosely, fixedly staring ahead.

It was so strange to see her not working. She was usually busy with something. Sometimes she would be getting dinner, sometimes washing the oilcloth on the table or polishing pans. She would be hemming up Veronika's dress or knitting her an unimaginably strange-colored scarf, which Veronika would quietly take off her neck as soon as she got outside.

"And how's Arnold?" Veronika asked. "Is he already up, or I suppose he's still taking it easy?"

In spite of herself there was a hint of irritation in her voice. As a matter of fact, he had just dropped in out of the blue, without any warning, and now she had to worry about him, commiserate with him. . . .

Nastia slowly, as if unwillingly, shook her head. "Arnold's gone."

"But he can't have left yet?" Veronica asked in surprise.

"He left last night," Nastia answered. "You had just gone to bed, and he knocked on my door. So I said, 'Go sleep in the study. I fixed everything clean for you there. You'll sleep like a king.' But he didn't pay me any mind, just said, 'Goodbye, Nastia, it's time for me to be going. . . . ' "

"What does that mean, time to be going?" Veronika didn't understand.

"Just like that, it means he was hurrying somethere on his own business. To tell the truth, I didn't ask where he was rushing off to, and I probably should have."

Veronika pulled a stool over and sat down opposite Nastia. She thought: "So he left yesterday. Where to? After all, he has no friends, no one in the whole world. Most likely he wandered down to some railway station, haven for all the homeless, and lay down there on an empty bench with his duffel bag under his head. . . .

"How can that be?" she asked in confusion. "And I didn't know. It never even entered my head that he might leave yesterday. He told me himself that he'd leave tomorrow, that is, today."

"You should have known," said Nastia.

"Known what?"

Nastia didn't answer. Veronika couldn't, didn't want to hide her indignation. "Who else would say that? And you know everything! Everything was right here in front of you!"

"And, of course, he came here with the idea of staying," Nastia said pensively, as if answering a question of her own.

"Yes, exactly," Veronika agreed. "Only I imagined for a minute what would happen if he stayed here. You can be sure, everything would have started up again, the drinking, the promises, assurances that never again, not for anything, and then, once more, everything all over again, the whole bit."

"And he asked about Varia." It was as if Nastia hadn't heard what Veronika had just said. " 'How's Varia?' he says. 'Is she still going on her excursion trips, or has she completely dried up on her pension?' "

Veronika only looked at her wordlessly.

"His Viktoria died. You remember, the one who used to come here and play for him. He says she died very suddenly."

"So that's what happened," Veronika said. "I met her once last year at the Actors' Club."

"If she were alive, he would have gone to see her," Nastia said thoughtfully. "You know how much she thought of him. She'd say, 'Take care of him. He has talent.' "

"No question," Veronika said. "Of course he had talent."

Nastia picked up the frying pan from the table and started to wash it in the sink with a sponge. Then she pulled open the drawer of the kitchen table, took out something wrapped in a newspaper, and handed it to Veronika. "Take it. It's for you."

"What is it?" Veronika asked.

Nastia shrugged her thin shoulders. "How should I know? Arnold gave it to me. He says, 'Give it to her in the morning. I don't want to bother her now. You can give it to her tomorrow, when she wakes up.' "

Veronika unwrapped the newspaper and saw a small record, with no label identifying the recording company or the artist. She realized it was a talking letter.

"So he recorded it himself?" asked Nastia.

"We'll find out right away," Veronika answered.

She went into the living room, turned on the record player that stood on the bookcase, and prepared to listen. And then it came—Arnold's voice. It was unfamiliar, hoarse, but, nevertheless, his.

"Veronika, my dear, I foresaw everything ahead of time, and that's why I'm talking to you now. I knew that everything would turn out the way it did, that you wouldn't want to take me in. After all, in your own way, you're right, and I know that it's my own fault. You're also right that I'll never be cured. No matter how much I try, nothing will ever work out for me now. But you can't keep me from loving you. Now, when my life is essentially over, I understand one thing—I have always loved, and, to the end, will love, only you, you alone. And I also understand that everything that happened is my own fault. I alone, with my own hands, destroyed our life. I didn't think about the future or my own talent, which you valued so highly, or about anything. . . . "

Veronika felt that Nastia was right there, behind her. And there she was, standing, bent over, her cheek propped up in her hand.

"Well, what do you say to that?" Veronika turned to her. "As you can see, he blames himself for everything; not me, but only himself." She hugged Nastia, hugged her tightly, patted her on the head, on her shoulders, first on one shoulder, then on the other. "Please, I beg you, Nastia, don't take it so hard. . . . "

Nastia wiped her eyes with the edge of her apron and sighed. "Of course, there's no doubt about it. You're right, Vera. No question about it. But just the same, my heart aches for him, and that's the long and short of it, it just aches and aches. . . . "

Veronika got up, carefully took the record off the record player, and handed it to Nastia. "Take it and hide it. You can have it."

"Maybe I *will* listen to it sometimes," Nastia sighed. "If I get in the mood, I'll listen to it."

She looked at Veronika to see what she would say. But Veronika's thoughts were already far away, far away from Nastia and the apartment. She glanced at her watch, startled. Time was short. It was time for her first lesson of the evening at the Theater Arts School. She had to get ready. . . .

HOME

NADEZHDA KOZHEVNIKOVA

Translated by

MARINA ASTMAN

. . . BUT SVETKA SAID THAT, AFTER ALL, SHE WAS already seventeen, and they really should stop pampering her. All the kids in her class were going, why shouldn't she? Yes, she promised to write, in detail, no less than two or three pages. And she wouldn't swim far out, honestly. Svetka's eyes looked so unhappy, Pavel couldn't bear it, and he grumbled: "All right, we'll see. . . . "

But Svetka decided: That's it—he's agreed, and she rushed to kiss him, beside herself with joy. There was nowhere to retreat. And really, seventeen years old. Seventeen! How quickly time had flashed by. . . .

"So, does that mean we should book only two accommodations? The two of us will go?" Pavel glanced at his wife undecidedly.

"That means the two of us," sighed Marina. "All the same, I'll have no peace of mind. And there'll be no vacation whatsoever."

Svetka left for Karelia at the end of July, while Pavel and Marina lingered on for about a week in Moscow. The pavement was melting from the heat, not to mention the people. . . . They barely made it to the day of departure.

Their train was leaving at 6:30 A.M. At this early hour the framework of the city suddenly was laid bare, like a shore at ebb tide: the streets and the sidewalks were empty, deserted and clear-cut, as in old engravings.

The taxi got them to the station in ten minutes.

Prior to departure, Pavel stood at the window in the passageway looking at the platform, at the people who were seeing others off, and at those who were leaving. Porters, suitcases, luggage, conductors in dark uniforms, the unmistakable smell of the station. . . . And suddenly, as frequently happens in a crowd, he felt sad and lonely. He returned to the compartment. Marina had already taken the traditional chicken, tomatoes, and eggs out of her bag.

"I've forgotten the salt again," she said with an air of guilt.

"You know, I figured out how long it's been since the two of us have had a vacation just by ourselves. Svetka was three when we took her to the beach the first time. That means fourteen years have passed since."

"Yes, she's already completely grown up. . . . But when I start thinking about her there all by herself. . . ."

"She's not by herself. There are twenty of them."

"That's just what bothers me. They're all equals, which means nobody is responsible for anything. And if something happens. . . . Maybe we should ask the conductor for salt?"

"Stop it, now. If we take it so hard, we'll be basket cases by the end of the month. And really, she's an adult, you can't keep her pinned to your skirt."

"All right, let's not." Marina sat down beside her husband. "She promised to write, but it probably takes a long time for letters to get here—do you know anything about that? Help yourself to a tomato. Or do you want me to cut it up?"

At the vacation home they were assigned a nice big room with a view of the sea. The transparent curtains were blown out of the windows by the coastal wind and fell smoothly. It seemed as if everything was subject to the rhythm of the waves. And one wanted to breathe in the same measured, even way.

They got up late, glad that they didn't have to rush anywhere. It had been a long time since they had lived this way, probably since the arrival of Svetka. They had forgotten that it was possible to simply look at the sea without searching for their daughter among the swimmers, without worrying that she not swim beyond the buoy. And it was possible to have breakfast in peace, without worrying themselves sick over Svetka's not finishing her cereal. She was so skinny, it was pitiful to look at her!

They had been waiting such a long time for their vacation, the sea, and rest. . . . And happiness.

The sea was there. So was the moonlight. And the music from the restaurants in the evening. But all the time it seemed that something had gone wrong. Possibly it was too late for them, possibly they had postponed the vacation for too long. Or maybe they simply had forgotten how to spend time together? Maybe that was why they experienced no joy from anything?

They went to bed early, at ten o'clock. What else was there to do? Go to the dance pavilion? After supper they took a stroll along the boardwalk and watched the sea in the blue rays of searchlights. They leaned on the parapet without talking. The sea licked the shore with its rough tongue like a dog. Nobody was hurrying anywhere. The mountains, seen in relief from afar, seemed to be made of soft rubber. If you squeezed them, you'd hear a squeak. Everything was right there—but just reach out, and all that sumptuous splendor, which seemed unreal, would disappear instantly, like a mirage.

Yes, it was impossible to vegetate in such idleness for long.

What were they waiting for? Their departure?

Marina went to the post office daily to check for letters—Svetka had sent one postcard. Marina was hurt to the point of tears, but without knowing why, she didn't share her pain with her husband.

They were drifting farther and farther apart.

If something like this had happened in Moscow, it would still be possible to find solace in work, to get lost in the habitual bustle of the city. But here, it was like being on an island. You couldn't run away, couldn't hide.

The first half of the day it was still tolerable: they'd swim way out, then tan in the sun. Silence was justified: who'd want to talk in that heat? Marina watched her husband getting out of the water and was glad that her dark glasses hid her stare: it was impossible to guess where exactly she was looking. Pavel came closer and lay down next to her; he opened a magazine but didn't read. He just turned the pages. They were bothered by the silence, the pauses frequently occurring during their conversations—they felt embarrassed, as if they'd gotten acquainted only yesterday and both still had to find out what kind of person the other was. But each was afraid to hurt the other: after all, they weren't rivals but intimates.

How long had they lived together? About twenty years. What surprises could they expect? They'd thought that when their daughter grew up they could take it easy, live peacefully. Peacefully? It hadn't worked out. . . .

It turned out that Svetka, for whose sake they had constantly sacrificed entertainment, holidays, and friends, had deprived them not only of their freedom, the right to be their own boss, but also of something greater that had disappeared unnoticed, and now was irretrievable.

After lunch, the minute she entered the room, Marina grabbed her shopping bags.

"Where are you going?" asked Pavel.

"To the farmers' market. I'll buy some fruit, peaches."

She left. Pavel knew she was dragging herself through the heat only so as not to stay with him, not to hear the alarm clock ticking in the total stillness. On the window sill was a bowl of peaches that had been bought yesterday. Neither Pavel nor Marina would eat them.

Everything turned out somewhat stupid and painful. Each was looking to escape from the other to hide their embarrassment, their helplessness.

Pavel thought up walks to the bays in the morning.

"I seem to have put on weight," he said one day, looking at himself in the mirror. "At my age a sedentary lifestyle is dangerous." He said that and felt awkward. His age! And what about his wife's age? Yes, she had aged. He somehow hadn't noticed it earlier.

The area around the vacation home had plenty of greenery and shade, but the walk to the bays was along a bare sandbar. In the morning it was still all right, but by midday it was really scorching! Yet the water in the bays was marvelous. Even without a mask you could look through it to the bottom of the sea: shaggy, rust-colored seaweed, silvery schools of tiny fish, motionlessly lazy, as if touched by light frost, and iridescent jellyfish turned glassy. The cliffs beetled low, ready to crash down at any moment, block up the narrow strip of shore, and hurl far out to sea the gigantic boulders resembling fossilized beasts. That had probably happened here more than once. Mossy, silvery green rocks stuck out of the water; it was good to dive from them, only you had to be careful not to get cut by the sharp shells.

Pavel would return for lunch and then lie down to sleep: the three-hour walk in the heat was exhausting. As he was falling asleep, he would think: fine, at least he had something to do. He was going to sleep, really sleep and not pretend. . . .

"Pavel, can you hear me? Do you hear what I'm telling you? Come on, really, wake up already!"

Pavel opened his eyes and saw Marina's angry face. The sound of her voice was imperious, demanding. He was surprised—she'd been rather timid with him lately.

"Do you hear me? Sveta is coming. Here's the telegram, take it."

"'Meet me seventeenth train four car twelve kisses Sveta.' "

"But why?" Pavel twirled the telegram, perplexed.

"Why! It means something has happened. I told you this month wouldn't pass in an ordinary way. Here's the result!"

"Wait a second. Nothing's clear yet. Maybe she just got fed up with that place, got bored."

"Of course! She was so eager to go, and suddenly. . . ."

"Anything could have happened. We'll have to be patient until tomorrow. Then she'll explain herself."

. . . But Svetka didn't explain anything. She stepped off the train in her blue faded slacks, sportsbag in hand. For the first time Pavel noticed that she was taller than Marina, but maybe it seemed so because she was slimmer, more shapely.

"Well, you've got some tan!" Svetka was all smiles. "We had rain the whole time. Got soaked to the skin. Lousy weather."

In the car Svetka leaned out of the window; the wind tousled her light hair, and she raved over everything—the weather, the sun, the sea, visible at a distance.

"I missed you!" she said, cuddling up to her mother.

"And we missed you," Pavel and his wife replied almost in unison.

They decided Svetka would sleep on the balcony and board at the vacation home. Marina went to make arrangements with the management. Svetka, after scattering her belongings all over the room, urged: "Come on, Dad, hurry up. I'd really like to take a dip."

Instead of the public beach, they went to the bay. They had to walk in single file along the narrow path, and Pavel noticed in front of him his daughter's boyish legs, which seemed to break at the knees with each step, and her white, round-shouldered back. He followed her and thought: Why has she come? He was worried and yet glad at the same time—she was there, close to them. . . .

In the bay Svetka threw off her sneakers and rolled-down socks, and rushed to the water: "Cold!" She fastened her ponytail on top of her head and took a headfirst running dive. Pavel stayed on the beach watching her splash around. Her darkened hair, which had come down, trickled down her face like seaweed.

The beach in the bay was on an elevated slope. Svetka, having had her fill of swimming, lay down in such a way that her narrow pink heels were right in front of Pavel's eyes. Lying with her face buried in the palms of her hands, she called: "Dad. . . ." Her voice sounded muffled, as if coming from afar. "Dad, why does everything turn out to be so damn stupid?"

"What do you mean?"

Svetka got up and lay down beside him, and Pavel saw her face: her whitish eyebrows intertwining at the bridge of her nose, her lids bulging over her closed eyes as if she were sleeping, and her pale Negroid lips.

"Daddy, I've realized that I can't live without you two." She sighed. She put her head on her outstretched arms. "Probably that's the whole point, I love only you two, and it's impossible, simply impossible, for me to be with guys. You see, all of them are . . . sort of rude. . . ." She was quiet for a while, then looked sideways at her father. "They look at a person, me, for example, and perceive me just the way they see me at a given moment. They don't give a damm about all the rest. How can you understand another person if you don't know what happened to her earlier? But they're not interested in that, you know, not interested." Again silence. "And also, I keep thinking, are looks the most important factor in human relationships? Is it possible that if your looks don't attract someone, then nobody will care for your intelligence, your soul? Dad, tell me. ..." Svetka, half-rising, looked at Pavel directly in the eye. "Tell me honestly, am I ugly?"

She waited. But Pavel hesitated; he didn't know how to respond.

"You're pretty," he finally muttered and turned over on his back to avoid Svetka's intensely attentive face, her widely parted light eyes, her somewhat flat freckled nose. What answer could he give her? Was there any answer at all? At that moment Svetka was disturbed not by the attitude toward her of all her friends her own age, but rather by the attitude of someone specific, a chosen one, who apparently had remained indifferent. She yearned to understand—why?

Why! Try to answer that. ...

Svetka awkwardly turned over on her side.

"Dad, how does love start? You ought to know; you love Mom, don't you?"

"Well, that's complicated. ..." Pavel felt driven into a corner: "Oh Lord, why is she doing this to me? Why didn't she wait for her mother to join us? Marina would have an easier time talking to her frankly, woman to woman. ..."

"Complicated?"

"You see," Pavel glanced at his daughter, "our mom is an unusual person. I really fell in love with her at first sight. But love, genuine love, comes later. And nobody can foresee how much he's able to feel love. I thought that I loved your mother very much, that it was simply impossible to love her more. Yet it turned out that no, you can love more, and in a more complex way. In such a complex way that you sometimes wonder whether it's love at all. But it is love, only love that has come a long way. ... Your feeling grows and expands gradually, and then, when it's choking you like a lump in your throat, when your heart is heavy, and everything, every movement, every glance, reverberates in you, both with joy and with pain—that's love. And then, I think it recedes a little, but not because it's disappearing; oh, no. It's simply in you like blood, like oxygen—you live by it without noticing it."

Pavel listened to himself and felt: oh, no, he wasn't saying the right thing, the right words. Svetka touched his elbow.

"I understand, one can't express that in words. ... But if I hadn't known how much you two love each other, I would have thought all along that there's no such thing as love. And that one could easily live without it, quite comfortably and painlessly. It's not there and that's that. No one's hurt. But it's just that you, my parents, are living at my side, and you—we, the younger generation, know—had that thing, love. Maybe we're out of luck. Why don't we come across it? What's changed so much in this world? Or have we ourselves changed? There's no use waiting, it

won't come, there won't be love anymore. Dad, give me an answer! . . .
The people who once loved will disappear, the very feeling will disappear,
even the memory of it. And how can you retrieve it? Retrieve what? It
can't be defined in words. You yourself, Dad, can't define it. . . . Tell me,
when you were young, did it happen to you that after meeting a person
by chance, you were ready to follow her anywhere? Yes, it did happen?
But we, our generation," Svetka twisted her lips, "we have a lot of everything. Good-looking girls and boys, and holidays, and fun. Why should
we look especially for someone? You'll meet him anyway, with less trouble. Without fail you'll meet handsome boys and girls who are intelligent
and cultured, and who don't have the faintest idea about love. Some boy
of that sort might follow you. But if you suddenly turn into a side street,
he won't change his course, that's for sure. Because even by a route he
finds more convenient, he'll meet hundreds of girls resembling you. And
each girl will be your equal because such a boy doesn't need to know
anything else besides that resemblance. . . . You know, Dad, I probably
behave toward people this way because I measure all of them against
you. That's why it's difficult for me, you see. When children don't see
love in their family, they don't understand what it means to love. The
way blind people can't distinguish colors. But maybe something like that
is inherited, like hair, and nose, and eyes? Look," Svetka stretched out
her hand, "my fingers are just like yours. I noticed it when I was little."
She put her palm against Pavel's palm and smiled. "They're exactly the
same, see? And will I also fall in love sometime? And somebody will fall
in love with me. . . . Since you both gave birth to me, I must be happy,
mustn't I?"

"Yes, said Pavel. "Even now you're happy, but you don't realize it.
And you'll be even happier, believe me."

"Dad, I like talking to you so much. You know, when I got off the
train today and saw you, I even envied you. There you stood, and you
even looked alike, just like brother and sister. You were looking for me,
and you were turning from one side to the other in exactly the same way,
as if you were tied together with a string. Then, all at once, simultaneously, you smiled at me. . . . Dad, I wish the same thing would happen
to me. I want the man at my side to be reliable, just like you and Mom,
and for us to love each other in that same way."

"It'll be like that." Pavel rose to his feet. "Do you want to go in
again? It's time to go, Mom will be worried."

"Okay, let's go." Svetka got up, brushing the sand off her knees.

There was a dry crackling of shrubbery, an astringent bitterish smell
of wormwood, and the sea darkened as if from within. Meanwhile, the
sun had set and the air was cooling off.

Pavel walked in front along the narrow path. He wanted to turn around and ask his daughter why she really had come, what had happened over there. He wanted to know for certain, he wanted details, but he didn't inquire, since she hadn't said anything herself. Marina probably would find out everything. Yet he had found out what was intended for him. Children make their own choice as to which parent they disclose their secrets.

Pavel involuntarily accelerated his pace; Svetka had a hard time following him. He was in a hurry to get back to Marina, home. . . .

STAGE ACTRESS

MAIA GANINA

Translated by

HELENA GOSCILO

1

THE COURTYARD WAS FLAT AND OVERGROWN with short yellowed grass, its walls surrounded by sky. On a line that marked off a third of the courtyard sat an old woman, legs outstretched, with a large white kerchief wound squarely around her head. On the hem of her long skirt lay some bread and cucumbers. She would peel the yellow rind off a cucumber, then cut off a round slice and slip it from the blade right into her mouth.

All the surroundings harmonized: the creamy-white square of the stone walls, the flat reddish courtyard, and the white church in the center, as if counterbalanced by the figure of the old woman sitting with her legs comfortably outstretched. It doesn't hurt a tree to have its roots in the ground; it doesn't get cold. The old woman likewise sat on the ground as if she were used to it, as younger people who grow up on asphalt usually don't sit. Agrippina's mother had also known how to sit on the ground like that.

There was a tranquility and silence of lines here. Agrippina moved closer to the wall, removed the kerchief from around her neck, and, tying it so that it covered her cheeks unattractively, lay down on the grass. In the chipped wall of ancient plaster, which once had been mixed with eggs and milk, the rosy brick, which was also ancient, showed up dark.

A wonderful, naturally golden light extended all the way up to the tall sky. Agrippina felt the warmth of the light; she liked the dry smell of the ground in late summer, and she liked being on the ground.

Now she was inaccessible not only to the direct contact of strangers' glances, but even to the contact that takes place when someone remembers you just like that, and knowing where you are, seems to touch you, and disturbs you with that touch. The nervous tension that she'd felt for so long was receding.

The lines around her were complete and silent; she heard that silence and savored it. Something was slowly building up inside her, and she joyfully sensed this accumulation. It was a renewed sense of the invulnerability of her existence in the universe, the happy premonition of genius she'd experienced before.

2

Agrippina dozed. At first she was aware of her surroundings through her slumber, but then she fell into a deep sleep. In her sleep she saw herself photographing someone walking down the street, rushing to take more shots before he got lost in the crowd. The person was moving off; she wanted to hide her camera in its case, and saw that she'd been shooting with the lens cap on. In her sleep that seemed to be something irreparable: she recalled how wonderfully the unknown person moved, his shoulders bent, long legs swinging at the knees, elbows tensed. She'd delighted in anticipating her stolen joy as she would examine the photographs, shot by shot, interpreting each one as if they were hieroglyphics, listening to the sound of discord, the disharmony of the lines, which, however, were united in their essence.

She gazed at the round object lens covered with the black cap and suddenly started sobbing furiously, uncontrollably, as she'd done as a child. She was crushed by the irreversible tragedy of what had occurred and by her failure. And just then someone strong pressed her wet face to his chest and stroked her hair with a heavy hand. A happy sense of being protected permeated her. She felt a sweet and grateful desire to surrender to the person comforting her.

With this sweet desire, which never visited her so strongly during her waking hours, she awoke, and without rising or changing her position, she thought about the person comforting her. She thought about his male kindness, which forgave and justified everything, and about the fact that during her waking hours nothing like that would ever happen to her now.

Then she remembered about the next day's play. The play had been put on only thirty times in Moscow, and had got its rough edges smoothed out without becoming played out and losing its ability to communicate. She had good feelings about it. It was her forty-second role, and her eleventh as a lead. She almost always saw it as her most successful role, the one that more than any other drew on aspects of her own nature. This time she was playing a businesswoman, a business manager; there was almost no lyricism in the lines she had to deliver. Yet she knew this woman through her own self: engrossed in her work, intelligent, strong, unappealingly harsh, she awaited in vain the time when it would finally be possible to become vulnerable and gentle because she had someone by her side.

That aspect of the role wasn't made explicit, but it was there in the pattern of the movements. She always looked for a pattern intuitively, but she instantly memorized what worked and afterwards would repeat it with professional preciseness because she was always strictly aware of what she was doing.

One time, many, many years ago, even before she became an actress, she saw how body movements which were involuntarily subordinated to a person's inner state suddenly became a sound, a phrase that could be more profoundly moving than one composed of words. A friend of her mother's was walking aimlessly down the street. Everyone knew that the lover with whom she'd lived for eight years or so had recently become involved with a young woman. To this day Agrippina saw her shoulders, unnaturally erect in her humiliation, the toss of her head, and the rapid, irregular twitching of her hands. The striking fingers of one hand were held tensely and awkwardly straight, as if the woman were leaning on something and pushing herself away from it. Agrippina stored that gesture in her memory, afraid of wasting it to no effect, and had repeated it only quite recently in a similar situation in one of her roles. Almost all the critics who wrote about the performance noticed it, but the main thing was that she felt the audience react to it every time.

From that remote time on, she'd been collecting unusual gestures, convinced that a seemingly incongruous but precise gesture at the high point of a performance has a striking effect. She began to watch how people experiencing one or another emotion suddenly change their walk, how some of them bow their head or tilt their chin, hold their elbows, and move their shoulders. And like a city dweller who from childhood has spoken a jargon that has five hundred words for all of life's events and, suddenly discovering that her native language is infinitely richer, starts to assimilate these riches with the enthusiasm of a neophyte, Agrippina realized that the actor's usual repertoire consists of only a small fraction of the diverse movements common to all mankind. She started to collect and classify those movements. At first she sketched them from memory; then she got the idea of taking photos on the street, and that became her passion. She interpreted and deduced what transient emotional experience could have given rise to a particular captured gesture or pose—she would pick them out.

Once she came across a book with photographs of Hindu religious sculpture. While examining the shots, she suddenly realized that what she'd considered her own secret discovery, which no one would ever believe, because it was impossible to prove and explain, had been known to people living three thousand years ago. Looking at the numerous variations in the poses of the many-armed Shiva,[1] she went through them as she did her hieroglyphiclike stills, and she knew that the sculptor who'd shaped the joyful god had heard pretty much the same thing as she did. He acted on the viewer through the phonation of lines, and anyone who had mastered the rudiments of sound-movement heard this representation the way a musician hears a score.

Agrippina started to search for and collect numerous editions of Hindu religious sculptures with photographs and sketches, surprised that even in the seeming immobility of Buddha there was an asymmetry, a movement, and a phonation of lines that obviously had been given to him consciously.

Once she went to the Pushkin Museum[2] to look at some copies of ancient sculpture. With chagrin she discovered an immobility and silence of lines even in those works that were supposed to represent the most impetuous movement. Subsequently she realized that those sculptures incarnated the harmony of flesh and spirit, the serenity of a concept that had penetrated the inner essence of things, and that was why there was an equilibrium and silence about them. Hindu sculptures also had flesh, often more generous and always more shameless than that of the Greeks, but there was no harmony in the sculptures and there couldn't be, just as there couldn't be any harmony in everyday life, as opposed to a life conveniently devised for one's own use. The Hindu sculptor sought the meaning of existence; he understood that it was impossible to attain it and grasp it, but he still sought it. When Agrippina came to know more about Indian art, she saw that the Indians had also had a period when they were influenced by the Greeks, but it had lasted briefly, and only a few of the sculptures reflecting this influence still existed. Everything else was distinctive, unique; its origins couldn't be traced back to anything anywhere.

Agrippina became fond of attending performances by Indian female dancers when they were in town, especially their solo performances. She interpreted the classical religious dances of kathakali and bharata natya[3] in her own way. As attentively as if it were a text in minute print, she'd follow how one sign, which had been ritualistic from time immemorial, and was possibly no longer comprehensible to the performer, worked with another: the large toe bent, with the heel resting on the floor, the arms ungracefully, crudely bent at the elbows above the head, and the head flung back one moment, then abruptly dropped the next, now like a gull, gliding along the line of the shoulder left to right, right to left, and suddenly the heavy leaps on legs spread shamelessly, bent at the knees: then again—a foot extended sideways, with the weight on the heel, and the hip thrust out crudely and wonderfully, while the fingers shook and the palms of the hand—one elbow above the head, the other below—were drawn close toward each other: that's the sign of the lotus and the butterfly fluttering above it. That's how they explain it. In actual fact it's the period in a sentence, the end of a chord, an idea that was started and completed. The sharp jingle of the ankle bracelets with bells and the drone of the tabla[4] can also be recorded as lines instead of musical notation. Everything is inseparable here.

The people in the seats around her kept glancing at Agrippina as if she were a lunatic: oblivious to everything, she would strain forward, sigh convulsively, smile with satisfaction, and sometimes swallow a quick "Ah! . . . " She didn't care what the people sitting next to her thought: she'd come to enjoy herself, and she did.

Once she attended such a performance with Zhorka, after she'd tried to explain to him beforehand her theory of sound-movement. Zhorka was an actor by God's grace. During a performance he'd often do intuitively the kinds of things that another actor who was a skillful professional couldn't approach, even if he were to die in the attempt after endless rehearsals with the most sensitive director. He himself moved wonderfully; his hands were especially beautiful and expressive. Moreover, he was no fool. But either her homegrown theory was really nonsense and self-delusion, or Zhorka lacked the kind of spiritual depths with which people perceive those phenomena that cannot be perceived and explained with the usual rational faculties. She recalled with displeasure how Zhorka had grinned, hummed, and made some jesting remark, as if he were talking with one of the little actresses from their theater. To this very day she hadn't forgiven him that condescending smile. Zhorka didn't like the Indian female dancer: he liked classical Russian ballet.

3

It grew unpleasant and dry, and a dull weariness suddenly washed over her. She recalled the actresses from the theater who hadn't liked her and had envied her, actresses and actors from the theater who had always interfered with her acting at difficult points in a performance. People usually say that actors are children; Agrippina could have added: nasty children. Everything that had happened to her in the theater was already irrevocable: it couldn't be set right; it was impossible to start from the beginning and do it right. During her forty-two years, of which twenty-five had been on the stage, she had changed theaters seven times, twice in Leningrad and once in Moscow. The same thing repeated itself everywhere, almost as soon as the acting company got used to her. She should have come to understand that the problem was not with the company, and in general she did understand that, and sometimes tried to be different—lighter, somewhat simpler.

A wind started blowing. Agrippina sat down and leaned back, her arms extended behind her, her legs outstretched. The old woman had already left, and the yard of the monastery was empty and dismal now. The sun was obscured by a cloud. Agrippina was hungry, but she had no wish to go somewhere where there'd be people. Then she recalled that next to the bus stop she'd seen an ethnic diner that had looked completely deserted, and she went there.

It was a weekday and between mealtimes, so all the wooden tables in the diner were empty, and when Agrippina settled down comfortably in a far corner, no one appeared right away to take her order. But she was in no hurry.

Midges sparkled as they moved up and down in the wedge of light that the open, heavy wooden door let into the semidarkness of the diner. The light recalled something cheerful, and the dark wooden barnlike room, with its earthen floor and crude tables and benches, brought to mind paintings from old books that she'd seen while she was still at the age when there's no difference in the way something that's actually happened and something you've seen in a painting become a part of you.

Agrippina smiled slowly and gave a happy sigh, experiencing that healing sensation inside her once again. She took her cigarettes out of her handbag, and without hurrying, savoring every movement, she lit one up and started to wait, gazing through slitted eyes at the vibrant golden light outlined by the crude jamb of the door. Finally a waiter came up, and she ordered a jug of wine and roasted lamb liver. The dish had some exotic local name, and the waiter had used it, but Agrippina forgot it immediately because she didn't remember words that didn't have some basic association for her. She found it difficult to learn parts that had a lot of words like that. While the exotic dish was roasting, they brought her the wine in a black clay jug with a black clay tankard, and some goat cheese and vegetables. She drank the wine, ate the cheese and vegetables, and thought about herself.

If she weren't a failure, people wouldn't interpret the lack of simplicity in her relations and her uneven temper, with its erratic shifts in mood, as talent. Prima donnas, the minions of forture, are forgiven everything. But she was a hereditary failure; talent and failure were passed on from generation to generation in her family. That was why although they acknowledged her talent even in the theater, it was as if it were something insignificant, even something obtrusive, immodestly setting her apart from other people. They wouldn't forgive her volatility, or the barrier erected by her lack of simplicity, which always stood between her and those around her whether she wanted it to or not.

She sat motionless, getting drunk, with a half-smile on her face, as she squinted at the light swirling in the doorway and adjusted her short light hair with her hand. She felt calm and self-assured, and genius seemed about to burst out of her again, as it did during her best performances. At first that used to happen in all her performances, though it wasn't always noticed by the cognoscenti. Later it happened only on rare occasions—and wasn't noticed by the cognoscenti either, because if earlier she'd lacked the skill to reveal and communicate that rush at her throat to an audience, then later she had sufficient skill to hide its absence. Now that absence was perceived only by the rare unsophisticated member of the audience, the sort who attended a performance "with his gut open," "exposed," and he would experience her performance gratefully "with his gut" and be sincerely sad if he didn't feel what the performance was trying to get across.

In their nasty moments, actors, directors, and even critics reminded Agrippina that she'd had no schooling, and she would retort that she thanked God she'd had no "schooling." That meant that she had no clichés and lacked the layer of dust that covers the graduates of these "schools" like stale chocolate. Yet that wasn't entirely true, for something had been lost. Thank God that she'd been on the stage, on the professional stage, from the age of seventeen, and had had wonderful teachers.

Actually, she'd started with amateur performances, with the theater studio at the Palace of Culture[5] at the Stalin automobile factory in Moscow run by Sergei Ivanovich Dneprov. She was sixteen then, the war was on, and she was working as a coil winder at the Dynamo factory. Until the studio tryouts she'd never recited either poems or prose to anyone. She wasn't even a real theatergoer, for she didn't have enough money to attend premieres regularly. To see a good show, just as to see a new film, you could buy a ticket from someone only by paying more than it really cost. However, she liked the Mossovet Theater,[6] then located in the Hermitage,[7] where you could see performances with Mordvinov[8] and Viklandt.[9] She sometimes would stand in a crowd of female fans just to see Nikolai Dmitrievich in a long black coat and hat, without makeup, but with an unusual face, weighed down by talent. Nonetheless, she'd never auditioned in front of anyone, and had decided to go to the studio tryouts only because she'd seen the show *Vaniushin's Children*[10] at the Palace of Culture and had liked it. She'd liked the fact that the amateur actresses playing the female leads hadn't been pretty. She wasn't beautiful or pretty either, although she had an unusual face.

Agrippina liked to recall those times when everything was just beginning, when she was trusting and kind to people, though even then her character was already uneven, volatile, and sometimes somber. She liked to recall her trips to the front with the concert crews, when she wore an ankle-length velvet dress made from an old coat of her mother's. Despite the incongruous outfit, which didn't go with her red hands and adolescent's face, the audience greeted her performances enthusiastically. Encouraged by that enthusiastic applause, wearing her only, incongruous dress, she once joined a group going south. At first she rode on the footboard, then on the roof, and explained to anyone who asked her that she was an actress. She arrived in Alma Ata,[11] and walked across the whole town in her long velvet dress, convinced that that's exactly the way actresses dress and that she did everything like a real actress. Apparently it was just that unswerving certainty, like the trajectory of a shell, that helped her get into a Russian drama theater where there were a lot of actors and directors just then who'd been evacuated from Moscow and Leningrad. They took pleasure in teaching the obsessed, uncouth girl some sense. Like dry moss, she absorbed everything, got used to the theater, and on stage felt normal, unique—that was where she belonged.

In Alma Ata she married an actor twenty-six years older than she. To her he seemed wise, kind, and handsome. And in fact he was kind and knew a lot. He was invited to Tashkent,[12] but the young wife of the artistic director there played the roles that Agrippina could play. That was why the next season Agrippina's husband, who was a well-known actor, went to Odessa, and then to Stalingrad. Agrippina finally got into repertory with serious roles, and people started to notice her. In Stalingrad she married a second time, another actor, because she thought it wasn't possible to love more passionately than she loved and was loved. Three years later, however, she married a set painter, divorced him after five years, and left for Leningrad: the late Akimov[13] had invited her to his theater. She didn't marry again, and until Zhorka she didn't even have any affairs. It was on account of Zhorka that she'd moved to Moscow two years ago. Agrippina saw him in Leningrad when he was touring in the role of Tsar Fiodor; he'd known her a long time ago, while she was still in Stalingrad. Things between them were fine for two years, but now that too was apparently over. For some reason it had vanished somewhere, like everything that she'd had earlier. . . .

The waiter brought her the exotic liver, she ate it, finished the wine, and paid the bill. A half-empty bus was standing at the bus stop, but she didn't want to go to town and the hotel yet. She wandered off along the dusty bystreets between the tall clay houses, making her way down to the monastery. Through the old fretted doors that were open in the houses, she saw trees hung with orange fruit, grapevines winding around the trunks, and heavy dark-blue clusters hanging from them.

She didn't go into the monastery yard but walked past its walls and sat down above the overhang. She gazed at the wide, shallow river and the hills, yellowish-brown like the unfaded coat of a camel, that extended all the way to the horizon. The sun was setting.

4

Red like an albino's eye, it was suspended between dark-blue strips of cloud. It was a sphere, a crimson sphere, a revolving planet. It lay, reflected twice in the smooth, shimmering white water of the river: before the pale-yellow spit in the river's channel, and farther on, in the river's branch beyond the spit.

A dense indigo blanket was pulled up from below over the fiery sphere. From behind the bluish-red shoals of the hills emanated a crimson light. It was thick and pulsating, like someone's body, someone's strong, mysterious, living body, like a free flow of blood, like the breathing of a young lion playing in the desert.

Agrippina sat there, opening herself up to the spectacle so as to take it in. She felt tears rising to her throat and gave a smile. She smiled so as not to jinx it: she was very afraid of these states of sweet receptivity in herself because afterwards something terrible inevitably occurred. Although, strictly speaking, what terrible thing could happen to her? . . . She and Zhorka were splitting up; they were still dragging things out, but they were splitting up, and Agrippina wasn't losing any tears over it. Her fellow actors didn't have it in them to spoil tomorrow's performance, even if they turned themselves inside out or made utter fools of themselves. She felt the movement of divine waters within her, which were destined to bless, to engender creative concepts while she was on stage the next day, and no one here could interfere with her or had it in him to do so.

She reached the outskirts of the small town by bus and got off so she could walk along the shore to the hotel. There was no reason to hurry. Small and slight, she roamed tirelessly along the edge of the rising tide, the breeze tossing her short fair hair and revealing the dark roots. She felt good and smiled as she walked along, the sea lapping at her side.

Reaching the campsite where the unofficial vacationers were staying, she suddenly saw a crowd and, in the center of it, the white peaked cap of a policeman. Curiosity drew her in that direction. She ran into a fat tanned woman wearing a striped swimsuit and a man in swimming trunks who were heading down toward the sea.

"There's nothing to be afraid of," the woman was saying. "We'll go on living and no one will touch us. . . ."

Agrippina squeezed through to the middle of the crowd, expecting to see a corpse: she was hoarding her reactions to everything. But there was no corpse, only a policeman in a light-grey shirt and white peaked cap standing there. He stood with his back to a motorcycle, his head slightly tilted and his chin drawn to his neck; he was leaning back on his outspread hands against the steering wheel and the seat of the motorcycle. Even before she heard what he was saying, Agrippina realized from his pose and the movement of his head that what was involved wasn't a killing or a crime, but something that didn't matter to the policeman (and that meant it didn't to her, either). Perhaps something terrible had already taken place, but that didn't frighten him personally, so it didn't frighten her, either.

"I'm telling you, they'll soon be closing this pass, too," repeated the policeman, bending his head down to the person who'd asked him a question. "I've been informed that it's open for twenty-four hours. You can leave. Go on, leave! But I can't say what'll happen in twenty-four hours." And he started listing the resort towns located nearby to which access was already closed.

"What's happened?" Agrippina asked the woman next to her, simply so as not to leave without finding out what it was all about.

"Cholera," replied the woman and gave an embarrassed and trusting smile. She smiled to keep from looking anxious.

Agrippina also smiled, as if at something incredible, some interesting, awful game into which she was being drawn. She moved on, walking along the shore to the hotel.

The door of the room where Rita Sarycheva and Liza Nilina were staying was open. Iura Vasilyev was playing the guitar, and Vovka Bratun was singing. Vovka was drunk, his kind, handsome face flushed and full of reckless, dashing strength. Agrippina had a protective affection for Vovka and considered him a gifted actor; he never permitted himself to fool around on stage. Vovka sang well, and Agrippina stopped to listen.

Vovka saw Agrippina in the doorway; he got up and bowed, with such a beautiful movement of the hand as he glanced up at her that Agrippina actually gave a smile of pleasure. If Vovka hadn't grown fat recently, he'd have been the best-looking actor in the theater. But Zhorka, of course, moved better than anyone. Where talent and skill were concerned, Zhorka was simply in another class. Compared to everybody else, Zhorka was like a symphony orchestra in a conservatory as opposed to jazz played skillfully at a restaurant.

"Do you know there's been an outbreak of cholera?" asked Agrippina.

"We do!" smiled Vovka. "That's why we're drinking, because we'll all die soon. Have a drink with us, Agrippina Vasilyevna."

"Red!" called Zhorka from the other end of the corridor. "I've been waiting for you for ages."

5

He sat down in an armchair, raising his thin knees high, his hands splayed along the armrests. To Agrippina it always looked as if his hands had a lot of joints instead of the usual three—they could take on any curve, any form. Zhorka's clever, mobile, eloquent hands were three-quarters of his value as an actor, of his means of expression. Even now they reminded her of Tsar Fiodor's hands—white, delicate, and uncertain; that was the way he'd sat on the throne, his arms hanging limply in despair, only his hands slightly raised, the fingers barely drawn together, like "the lotus flower." . . . Lord, how she'd loved him then. Even now her heart contracted when she remembered that love.

Zhorka watched silently as she changed her clothes, went into the bathroom, and came out, then got cheese, a plate of fruit, and wine out of the refrigerator. She grinned.

"Maybe I shouldn't eat fruit now? After all, the cholera's going around."

Without replying, he took the glass with the yellow wine, swallowed half of it, and asked:

"Where did you rush off to?"

"I took a ride. On bus number three to the end of the line. It's about a forty-five-minute ride."

"Why didn't you take me along?"

"I wanted to be by myself for a while."

"The play's tomorrow, isn't it, not today?"

"What's the play got to do with it? . . ."

On the day of an important performance, Agrippina tried to avoid being around people; she kept silent till evening, saving herself for the performance. She had a condescending contempt for those theater colleagues who were capable of coming to a play in a "happy" mood right after a friendly drink.

"I understand, then. . . ."

Zhorka rose and walked over to her dressing table. A postcard with a reproduction of Iaroshchenko's portrait of Strepetova[14] was tucked behind the frame of the mirror.

"What a woman!" he said mechanically for the umpteenth time, then sat down on the floor beside Agrippina's armchair, slumping as he hugged his tall knees.

The folding doors to the loggia were open; noise could be heard from the street that ran along the beach, and the sea looked black as it tossed, sparkling with orange highlights. Invisible clouds lightly covered the horizon, and a hazy, roseate moon was suspended above the sea. For a long time they sat like that, without touching each other; then Zhorka stirred, his bones cracking, and said in a stiff, injured tone:

"Well, I suppose it's time for bed, right?"

"Yes, the play's tomorrow," agreed Agrippina in a cheerful tone and turned on the light.

But after Zhorka had left she felt oppressed, as if dry sand had settled on her heart. She was seized by a premonition of trouble.

She slept in the loggia on a spring mattress that she pulled off the bed, covering her head with the pillow before going to sleep so as not to hear the noise of the resort. And in the morning she didn't really sleep, but dozed, hearing the movement of the sea through her doze and the resounding song of the birds in the cypresses, as the sun touched her white sheets with rose.

She awoke at seven, her vague mood of the previous evening gone. She did her exercises, took a shower, and went down to the snack bar without any fear of meeting her colleagues. They went to bed late and got up just as late. As she opened the door she sniffed the air: it smelled sweet and repulsive.

"Chlorine . . . , " Agrippina noted with surprise, and remembered, "the cholera. . . ."

She took a glass of sour cream, some sausages, and coffee, and had started to eat when she suddenly felt someone looking at her. She turned her head and met the gaze of a man who was sitting at the next table. He immediately shifted his eyes, and Agrippina recalled that the man had stared at her just as intently yesterday morning.

"He's trying to remember where he's seen me," Agrippina thought indifferently. Without being spoiled by the kind of fame enjoyed by film actresses, whom passersby would pester on the the street with their attention, Agrippina nonetheless believed that people recognized her, that she also had her admirers, who remembered her when they saw her in person.

As she left the snack bar she glanced back, her movement mechanical now. The man was fairly short, had dark eyes, and was, if anything, elderly. Dressed in a dark-blue short-sleeved silk shirt and shorts, he sat gazing pensively at Agrippina, his elbows resting heavily and clumsily on the table.

She left, cheerfully taking away with her his serious glance, which had nothing playful about it. Sometimes such glances and flattering words were simply essential to her. It was essential to know that there were people who understood her and accepted her.

As always on the day of a performance, she wanted to lie down and stay locked in her room until evening, but her inner anxiety drew her outside.

The sun was at its highest now, and the sweltering heat was almost paralyzing. Agrippina walked along the sunny side of the street with her head bare, and without any sunglasses. Her silk pantsuit hung lightly on her without touching her body, and cooled her off. She liked the sun and wasn't afraid of it. She ran into suntanned, half-naked people cheerfully preoccupied with carrying fruit wrapped in cellophane, eating ice cream, and drinking carbonated water at the stands. The women she met commented loudly on Agrippina's outfit, which was still unusual. A woman with a string bag full of fruit was coming from the market and bent her head to bite into a juicy peach.

"There's an outbreak of cholera here," thought Agrippina, "but everything's just the same. And people's tongues are wagging the same as ever. Or was it a dream I had yesterday that there's cholera going around? . . ."

She returned to the hotel, put on her swimsuit and a fluffy robe, grabbed a towel, and went to the beach. The beach was red with hot, strong, generous human flesh. People were swimming, yelling to each other, listening to transistors, playing cards, and eating fruit by the kilo—eating fruit as if each of them were a machine made to process fruit for the winter.

Feeling a headache coming on from irritation and despair, Agrippina threw her towel down on an empty spot on the beach beside an elderly blonde with two unattractive black children—a boy and a girl—and lay down, covering her face with her robe. The noise of the beach brought her some relief, and she lay there, basking in the sun, greedily feeling her light muscular body crackling beneath the piercing rays. Then she took a swim and went to the hotel room. En route she caught a phrase uttered authoritatively by the inevitable fat woman in a bikini:

"They can have white children only after the third or fourth marriage. Otherwise they're black. . . ."

"Oh, God, everybody pokes his nose into everybody else's business and has to analyze everything!" thought Agrippina, and entering her room, she locked the door with two turns of the key, closed the glass shutters of the loggia, and drew the heavy curtains.

She lay in the dark, thinking how strange and absurd it all was. That very evening she'd be giving everything she had, pushing herself to the limit, for the sake of exactly those people past whom she'd walked just now with such distaste. . . .

As always, she arrived at the theater an hour and a half early. The makeup rooms were still empty: even Zhorka usually came only an hour early. She stripped to her panties and bra and slowly started putting on her makeup. She felt the onset of nervous uncertainty and irritation—her usual state before her favorite plays. She let them rise to her throat, keeping track of how her face changed, how her skin flushed painfully under the dark makeup. In the mirror her face looked old and coarse, but it would look different to the spectators. She recalled, or rather, all day she'd been carrying around inside her, the man who'd looked at her that morning, and now she allowed herself to recall him clearly. Pleasure surged in her like bubbles in a glass of water, giving her a warm feeling.

Zhorka glanced in and gave a gloomy nod. Then Olga Bogatenkova arrived; the makeup room was a double. Olga chattered, while Agrippina remained silent, reluctantly saying "Aha" from time to time. On the day of a performance she permitted herself to be particularly disagreeable. Liza Nilina threw the door wide open:

"Girls, we've got a full house!"

"I should hope so!" said Olga seriously. "The cholera's going around. . . ."

"Why?" asked Agrippina in surprise and bewilderment. "What's the connection?"

"People are scared. . . . It's scary being on your own, Agrippina Vasilyevna; everyone wants to go where there are people." After a pause she added just as seriously: "I'd like to leave before they impose a quarantine. If, God forbid, there are cases of it, they'll close off the exits. Can you imagine? And then you'll have to sit here and wait till you kick off, too. . . ."

Applying blue mascara to her eyelashes, Agrippina said:

"Oh, come on now. . . ."

She shrugged her shoulders. Surprisingly, she felt no fear.

All the bells on the relay started to ring, and the director's assistant announced that it was time to go on.

Agrippina put on a skirt, a windbreaker, and boots, ran downstairs, and took her place in the wings. Zhorka came up from behind her and put his arm around her shoulders.

"Good luck, little one!"

"Okay. Let's start."

The music to the prologue ended, and Agrippina quelled her usual sense of confusion as she stepped into the circle of light and strode quickly across. Still feeling empty inside, she stopped, leaning sideways against the office desk. Without seeing anything, she stole a cursory glance at the audience—a hotly pulsating world, a heaving, fragmented entity. She sensed something reaching out from it toward her and hesitating weakly in the air without direction. She made a gesture with her hand as if to take hold of it and subdue it, then turned abruptly and sent a wave of herself out there, into the hot abyss.

"Well, comrades?" came her first line. "Whom are we waiting for? Go on, Piotr Semionovich, give us your report on how the construction is coming along."

She didn't look at Zhorka. During a performance she didn't see her colleagues directly, but with her peripheral vision, so as not to break her circle. She heard him move a stool and rustle pages as, unhurriedly sustaining the pause, he started to deliver the dry, wretched lines in such a way that there was nothing but attention down below—no coughing or shuffling.

And they were off. Her boots covered hundreds of meters all over the circular stage before she left to wait in the wings for her cue to return to the circle. It didn't matter that the script was sometimes dreadful and inconsistent. She invested it with a different significance, subordinating it to her own internal script. She told of the arduous, wonderful lot of her generation, her own lot. "Lord! . . . You know, we forget about each other in the comfort of everyday life." She mentally shouted the naive but sacred idea to the audience. She felt it reach them: a two-way flow of blood was infusing whatever it was that linked the audience to Agrippina. She was the heart, cleansing and renewing whatever flowed across to her and sending it back renewed. Everything inside her was unbearably compressed, as if life were leaving her with this outflow—she loved self-sacrificially, as if she were everyone's penitence.

"I've had no friends? Yes, perhaps I haven't. . . ." As she spoke her lines, her lighted cigarette froze in midair, her hand quivering.

God knows what gesture was supposed to accompany the author's stage direction of "She lights a cigarette and acts nervous." The point, however, wasn't the cigarette, but how she held her hand—playfully, with bravado, yet with her hand shaking, drooping, and impotent, for the woman couldn't control a tremor. For the first and only time her heroine showed weakness in front of her subordinates, in front of an audience. First the hand—and then the tears flowed down her smiling face. Zhorka in the role of Piotr Semionovich bent his head so as not to see those tears.

"I was happy, nonetheless," her lines continued. "No matter what lay ahead, I was happy. Do you understand, Piotr? I love people, you understand? You don't believe me? I'm ready to die for them. . . ."

"The whole secret of her 'sincerity,'" she suddenly caught Iura Vasilyev's voice backstage, quiet but clearly audible, "is that she's always talking of herself and about herself. And right now about Zhorka and shattered hopes. . . ."

Iura knew that she'd hear him and that the circuit of currents would be broken inside her now, at the show's finale. He knew that right then, in her wrenching sincerity, this was a low blow. Why did he do it? He couldn't explain it himself: she was more talented than he, but was she any happier? . . . Agrippina glanced quickly at Zhorka: had he heard? Of course he had: something resembling a grin of comprehension crossed his face. The grin didn't come from within, it wasn't really his—that would have been forgivable—but was directed backstage: "What can you do, old man, love comes and goes . . . " and so on: the usual male complex.

Yet she held the pause to the end, dropped the hand that was holding the cigarette, then drew on it and flipped away the butt, watching to see that it didn't fall someplace where it might be a fire hazard.

She sustained the pause again, said her last lines, then joylessly accepted the applause, the five curtain calls, and the flowers that some woman offered her. With an ironic half-smile on her lips, she took her bows, although she wanted to burst into tears or hang herself. The point wasn't what Iura had said, but why he'd said it. Why had he done it? During her whole life as an actress, she'd never even exchanged harsh words with another actor; she was capable of answering rudely, but not in the way young actors abused each other and called each other names and then made up again. . . . She'd not beaten anyone to a part; she hadn't taken an extra twenty rubles from anyone's pay. She was paid—indeed, she was underpaid—only what was hers. So why had he done it? . . .

Zhorka caught up with her out on the street, and fell into step with her. She was silent, but finally stopped and said in a voice shaking with fury:

"Leave me alone! You can see for yourself that I don't love you, I don't want you anymore! You can explain that to your pals any way you want, but I don't love you anymore. I don't love you—try to understand that!"

Zhorka tried to hold her back, catching her by the elbows. She broke free.

"I'll scream. I'll call a policeman. Go away!"

Passersby turned around to look at them. Zhorka shrugged his shoulders and walked off. She went down to the sea and walked along the shore, and the fury that had seethed inside her gradually calmed down and gently subsided. Who cared? . . . What could she do—she wasn't one of their kind. . . . But she didn't need Zhorka anymore. She'd had enough of quiet betrayals, not verbal ones, but those that consist of a smile or a shrug of the shoulders, a pause, or a movement—the same movement that had the exaggerated phonation he didn't believe in. He was seven years younger than she, but as usually happened with her, he'd sought her out, not the other way round. It was pride. . . . Yes, pride—and God would punish her with solitude and the hatred of the people around her. Hatred, but for what? For not being one of their kind. . . .

The illuminated sky of the town receded behind her, the sea undulated inaudibly, invisibly, and even the stars didn't shine through the cloud-laden black sky. A smoky red light glimmered ahead, followed by hazy splotches of pink, dark-blue, and orange light, as if someone were scattering old lampshades illuminated from within all over the hillock. She entered the campsite and paused without being noticed or disturbing anyone. A municipal house, which had been broken up into semitransparent apartments, lay around her. In each little tarpaulin apartment, people were cooking their meals, speaking their thoughts, and listening to their music; no one was nosing into anyone else's business.

Three loaded Volgas stood there, and dark figures puttered around them, checking to see that everything had been put away. Perhaps they'd decided to leave because of the cholera before the last pass was closed off, or perhaps their vacation was simply over.

6

Next morning she awoke at her usual time, but she didn't get up. The morning was overcast and cool, so she lay with her eyes closed, trying to fall asleep again. She felt defeated, weak, and devoid of all will. Although she didn't try to recall the previous evening, it had stayed with her. Her mind was sober and functioned with efficient clarity as she thought painfully about the senseless, incoherent life she'd lived: What for? She wouldn't even leave any children behind. At first she hadn't wanted them, and later she could no longer have any. Though in her good moments she would comfort herself by saying that if one person left a performance thinking about how badly he'd lived until then, then the half-year that she'd spent working on the role wasn't in vain. Now she realized that it was. He'd start thinking, suffer pangs of conscience for a while, and continue living as he'd lived before. . . . Of course, among a billion human fates, her unsuccessful life was a drop in the bucket, a minuscule meteorite that had burned out as it entered the atmosphere, but she felt sorry for her unsuccessful life.

She had to get up and go to the first reading of a new play, but she didn't want to go. She already knew there was no role for her in it, and she didn't want any more roles or plays. Yet she had to go so that they wouldn't say again: there she is, acting as if she's something special; of course, Madame feels that she's a prima donna. . . . She'd had enough of exchanges like that.

As she grasped the handle of the door to the snack bar, she felt sorry that she'd got up late: the man had already had breakfast, of course. Indeed, he wasn't there, and everything inside her was extinguished completely, even the hope for a ray of hope. As she was finishing her coffee, however, the man entered the snack bar, and glancing over the people eating breakfast, he went up to the counter and asked for cigarettes. She didn't know whether he'd seen her or was looking for her at all, but when he made his limping way to the exit, he stopped for a moment and glanced specifically at her. He immediately withdrew his gaze, as if something connected them now and it was awkward to stare openly. He left, and Agrippina's spirits lifted—she didn't understand why. She wasn't a flighty, vain woman, and was usually irritated by intent male glances; she could even be rude in response to a glance like that. This man could even be called unattractive: he was short, sinewy, and had a limp. And his face wasn't nice; it had hard lines, and his lips had a stern cast to them. True, it was a clever face. If anything, he moved rather poorly; however, his movements very tight and spare, either because of his limp or because of an inborn or professional reserve. She didn't really need anything from him, yet Agrippina went outside with that serious dark-eyed glance in her lightened heart.

She walked quickly. She was running late, and, a warm drizzle had started to fall. There were droves of people at the town's railroad ticket office. A sizable crowd was always gathered there, but today there was a real commotion.

Although she was afraid of being late, she was one of the first to arrive at the theater. She sat down in a far corner of the rehearsal room, opened a volume of Williams, and started to reread *The Glass Menagerie* so as not to look at anyone.

Iura Vasilyev came in and greeted her cheerfully, his voice exaggeratedly loud. She looked at him with limpid eyes, then nodded. Lord, why should she bother about them—little girls and boys who were nasty, without knowing what they were doing. It was all so stupid.

Zhorka came in, sat down beside her, took her hand, and kissed the palm. And this, too, was to prove something to someone in little-boy fashion: to himself that he was decent? To his colleagues . . . ? But it was all over with him; there wasn't even a trace of pain in her heart. Yesterday's performance had given her the right to break it off, and for that she was grateful to the performance.

Olga Bogatenkova arrived and said that in the two neighboring vacation resorts they'd officially registered the presence of cholera. There were two, perhaps three, cases, and one victim had already died. They were quickly evacuating the campsite and all the unofficial vacationers, and today or tomorrow the town would be closed and quarantined.

A shudder of joyful horror stirred Agrippina's heart: was it really true? . . . She wanted to participate in the tragedy that had befallen people, just as once when she was a girl she'd stubbornly forced her way into a division that was going to the front. Perhaps it was to become an eyewitness, to store everything in her memory and then to act it out afterwards? . . . She always found it easy to act the part of a woman of the war period because she'd seen so many of them, of all kinds, and she'd memorized faces, voices, poses, stories. . . .

Everyone fell silent, exchanging glances.

"Yes, my dear," drawled Vovka Bratun with an ironic smile, scratching the back of his head histrionically. "Don't you think we should clear out? . . . Eh?"

"Maybe . . . ," uttered Zhorka softly and looked at Agrippina.

It wasn't clear to her whether he was joking or looking for sympathy.

The artistic director arrived with the play, but they didn't start reading right away. Instead they discussed what and how, if, and so forth. Then they started reading and continued for two hours with a break, then discussed it listlessly for an hour. The play was boring. They needed a village topic, but the topic was presented very trivially. Nevertheless, the artistic director and the artistic council insisted on including the play in their repertoire. They agreed listlessly and listlessly assigned the parts. The artistic director unexpectedly offered Agrippina the role of an old woman who stood for truth, but she said that at her age she should either switch completely to old women roles or avoid them in the meantime. The director didn't try to insist. He didn't like to argue with her, and it was only when a lot of such incidents, which were humiliating to his self-esteem as a director, had accumulated that he would remind her of all of them: he'd be spiteful and offensive as he dredged them up in an effort to humiliate her.

The meeting broke up. Agrippina stopped by the hotel to have dinner: there was a restaurant on the second floor which wasn't frequented by people coming off the street. After dinner she wanted to go and see the campsite being evacuated. She sat down at a table and opened her volume of Williams to while away the time until they brought her order. And just then she saw her stranger, making his limping way along the passageway. There was a free seat at her table. "Lord," Agrippina suddenly got scared, "if only he doesn't sit here! We'll start talking, and it'll all fall apart." She had the definite feeling that all they had to do was say a few unnecessary phrases, and something would vanish. This schoolgirlish enchantment of getting to know each other without any words would be ruined. The instant memorization of movement and facial expressions, the eye contact, and the interpretation of a pose—they all help you know a person, tell you more than you'd get from a long exchange. Conversation, tone, and words are always a mask, a game, a smokescreen created out of embarrassment or the desire to make an impression. Movement, however, is unadorned information about what is within.

Her stranger was only one table away from her when he sat down in a place that had just been vacated. His eyes quickly made contact with Agrippina's, and then he turned away, his face expressionless as he picked up the menu. He sat ungracefully, like a peasant over a bowl of cabbage soup, his elbows on the table and leaning forward, his shoulders hunched. "I don't have the camera!" thought Agrippina with sudden regret. "Just look at how he sits! Freely, like a master. He walks stiffly, but here he's unselfconscious and is sitting as he would at home at the head of the table where his wife, sons, and grandchildren all eat, all get fed. . . ." And she smiled: wasn't that precisely the kind of family, precisely the kind of life, that she'd always harbored within her, in the back of her mind? In her present life, which was a rough draft, done in a hurry, she was an actress and everything that entailed, but there was still a brand-new life to come, and that was the real one. God would choose an ungracious man just like this one for her, but he'd be her husband—her one and only, the father of her many children, and she wouldn't be lazy or find it hard to bear his children until old age. . . . The men with whom she'd parted so lightly had been lovers, even though in their passports they'd been officially registered as married. They'd been lovers, and she was waiting for a husband to whom she could submit and to whom she'd have to submit, and simply be a wife, a woman. . . .

Agrippina finished her dinner, paid the check, and got up with an effort: she wanted to sit longer and silently observe the man, to read his face. It wasn't a kind face, but it wasn't unpleasant, either. It was simply a shuttered face, its window closed, and behind that window she sensed a lot of all kinds of things, of complexity. . . . It was difficult to know who the man was. He held himself aloof, in solitude. And judging by everything, he no longer had any connection with village life. His pose at the table was an instinctual memory. . . .

She stopped by her hotel room, took her camera just in case she suddenly came upon something that she should snap, and set off along the shore. They were doing an old show today, so if she returned by four or even four-thirty she'd be able to catch her breath and collect her thoughts.

A lot of the tents had already been pulled down, revealing the trampled, dead yellow stubble, the straw that had been thrown down, and the patches of ground that had served as homes. They looked forlornly naked and abandoned now. It all resembled the site of a fire, a conflagration: people were pushing just as senselessly, nervously, and haphazardly. She snapped several of these haphazard, confused poses. Most of the campers who had cars had gone their separate ways. Those who remained resembled snails that have to lift their houses onto their shoulders, but they didn't know how to act, where to go, and what to do about their vacation. Like many people in a situation like theirs, they tried instinctively not to disturb the arrangements that had been made, on the off chance that things would work out in the end. Policemen and the volunteer patrol walked among the tents that remained stubbornly in place, and pulled out the pegs. Where a house had stood a moment ago, now there was only a faded rag. . . .

"But where will we go?" a woman who'd taken down her tent yelled at a volunteer patrolman. "Are we supposed to hang around the railroad station? There are thousands of people there!"

"There are three regular trains and three additional ones. You'll leave!" explained the volunteer patrolman. "Whoever doesn't get to leave today will be assigned an apartment with water and gas, whereas what have you got here?"

Sitting on old boxes in the middle of the campsite were the chief of the militia, a major in the border guards, and three soldiers with automatics. Their faces all looked dull and bored. The major was listening to what a fat, tanned man in swimming trunks was telling him, and he was nodding inattentively, whereas the other man's face was excited and even wore a servile expression, though it also looked proud. One could "read" his pose, too: he also sat on a box, his knees spread wide, his shoulders flexed, with the fingers of his fat hands folded to form a tent, as if to say: "I'm on an equal footing with the higher administration, and I'm really something in my own right!" . . . Agrippina recalled guys just like him from her distant youth who were traveling south for some reason instead of going to the front. They also used to speak with the conductors as equals, and the conductors would nod just as condescendingly, while they listened with half an ear. But later they'd let them onto the platform of the railroad car anyway, and even into the compartment for official personnel. Whereas she rode on the footboard and later on the roof, but they wouldn't let her onto the platform. What did this guy want? What was he trying to get out of the major? Permission to stay till the evening? Instructions to load him and his things out of turn onto a truck or bus that was transporting people without cars to the railroad station? Or perhaps he didn't need anything, but since there was a disaster he was instinctively trying to establish contacts with the administration?

A boy with a wheelbarrow was going around the field from one abandoned patch of ground to another, collecting empty bottles.

"Look at that," said the major suddenly, and his face became animated, transformed into a knowledgeable, humane face full of many memories. "For some people it's a disaster, but for others it's a real break. . . ."

Agrippina glanced at her watch and started to hurry in alarm: it was four.

She arrived at the hotel at four-thirty, lay down, and stayed like that in the darkness for an hour, marshaling her energy. Yet she couldn't shake off her confusion and edginess, and the ravaged campsite kept whirling before her eyes.

"Where did they get their water? . . . If there really is something, this is a place where things rot quickly, it's a breeding ground. There'll be no avoiding an epidemic. . . ."

Then she recalled her stranger—What was he doing? Was he preparing to leave? Was he scared? And who was he? . . . And finally, where was he staying, on what floor? She suddenly wanted to see him. She mentally went over their four brief encounters, and suddenly was flooded with shame: he'd not sat down at the same table with her because she'd started staring significantly at him; he'd got nervous that she'd latch onto him! . . . She felt as if someone had splashed her innards with boiling water, and she squirmed on the bed, angrily feeling her inner humiliation. She hated herself, her foolish fantasies in her old age. If she should run into him again, she wouldn't raise her eyes. When it came down to it, what did she need him for? . . .

With that thought she got up, dressed, and went to the theater. The play went well, though in the second act the girls in the company started getting in her way again: someone revived the game of "freeze," which they'd found entertaining while they were still in Moscow, and now they took turns "freezing" at the most inappropriate moments. In the next-to-last scene she actually cut short her line and said calmly and quite loudly:

"If you don't stop, I'll leave right now! Then you can cope on your own any way you like!"

That frightened them in earnest, and they finished the play normally. Once again there was applause, bouquets of flowers, and curtain calls, as always. Agrippina was very sensitive to the number of curtain calls and the enthusiasm of the applause.

The show ended at nine-thirty, and she set out for the campsite. The small hill was deserted. Several people moved about like black shadows, burning the trampled grass and the straw that had served as a sheet. Red flames and smoke crawled along the ground toward the sea. Amid the flames and the darkness stood a table assembled from boxes, and a man was sitting at the table with what looked like a jar or bottle in front of him. The sky behind him was a radiant dark blue, like a backdrop, illuminating the ridiculous silhouette of a man at a table in the middle of a burning field. . . .

A girl in white slacks and red sweater was sitting on some backpacks; no other campers were left.

As Agrippina approached the large bonfire, she suddenly saw her stranger. He was talking to a man in a peaked railroad cap with a red band on his sleeve. When Agrippina drew near, the stranger looked at her in surprise, but true to her decision, she glanced indifferently past him and walked away.

As she was coming back along the shore, she thought she heard the shingle behind her creaking beneath uneven footsteps, and she felt the urge to stop and say something. Conversation is easier and more frank in the dark: you don't have to assume expressions. But she went on.

She'd already gone to bed when there was a knock on the door. Agrippina opened it and saw Zhorka.

"I've come for just a minute, little one," he said nervously.

He came into the room, sat down in the armchair, then took Agrippina's hands in his.

"I'm scared," he whispered with a grin, and rubbed her hands over his face. "What the hell. I'm frightened. . . . I'm frightened and keep checking myself all the time to see whether I'm sick or not. It's driving me crazy. . . . And I already think I've got a stomachache. . . . Two hours ago they took away three people from the hotel. They had some gastric symptoms."

"It's not necessarily cholera. All kinds of things can go wrong with the stomach in the summer. . . ."

Agrippina suddenly felt sorry for Zhorka. He was no coward, and if he had to take a gun or a knife and fight someplace out in the open, he'd go and fight. But the degrading waiting, when you don't know where something's going to happen, what to be afraid of. . . . She went up to Zhorka and stroked his hair. With a shuddering sigh he pressed his face against her and pulled her robe aside. His face was cold; his blood vessels had evidently contracted from fear. He was talented, and he was afraid that suddenly he'd die ridiculously without being fully recognized and his brilliant future wouldn't be realized.

"Can I stay with you?" he asked pathetically. "I can't stand to be alone. You understand. . . ."

7

Zhorka left toward morning. She dozed on until seven, then got up and took a long cold shower, dried herself vigorously until she turned red, and put on her nightgown again: it was still cool. She went up to her makeup table. As a rule, she hardly ever looked in the mirror during the day and never put on makeup, feeling that she had enough of the professional grooming that took up one and a half hours every evening. Now she sat there for a long time, examining herself, then combed her hair with a straight part, and saw the large forehead, blue eyes, and high cheekbones of a north Russian peasant. Her mother was from Krasavino,[15] which was on the Northern Dvina. She'd done seasonal work from about age ten until she left for the city and the famous Krasavino factory, where they wove wonderful linen fabrics, tablecloths, and napkins—the kind you couldn't get anymore nowadays. She worked in the winter, and during the summer she labored in the field, at home, and on their plot, as did the whole family. . . .

Evidently her daughter was also a peasant at heart, and now, as her womanhood was drawing to a close, her blood began to yearn for her native roots, for the firm soil under her bare feet, for her own folk, and for real work, the kind that breaks your back and puts solid calluses on your hands. That was why her entire life she'd also approached her hard idleness seriously—just as she approached harvesting, hay mowing, and the demanding field work during the summer—without a light touch. And people didn't like her for that. "She's overdoing it. . . ." And, in fact, she did overdo it and tried to change humanity. . . .

She went out into the loggia. The crowd on the beach had thinned out noticeably. If earlier they'd been lying there like a single solid mass, now you had to walk to get from one outstretched body to the next. And suddenly, not far off under a tent, she made out a familiar silhouette: a man was limping toward the water. Her gaze followed him as he swam off, without speed or grace, but confidently. Then she went down to the snack bar, hurried through breakfast, hurried back to her room, put on her swimsuit and robe, and grabbed a towel. She kept justifying herself, rationalizing that after a bad night she also needed to refresh herself. She had a difficult performance today.

She reached the tent, and glanced surreptitiously at the spot where she'd seen her stranger, but he wasn't there. "He's gone. . . ." Agrippina immediately lost her desire to stay, and actually felt a pang as her gaze swept over the people tanning themselves. He stood a little farther on, watching her, and of course had caught both her expectation and the disappointment on her face, as well as the grimace of pain. . . .

"Who cares. . . ." Agrippina barely managed to contain a smile as she lay down on the hot stones. "It'll be over soon anyway. What's the difference whether he realized or not. . . ."

She basked in the sun, went for a swim, then basked in the sun again. Glancing sideways now and then to check whether he'd left, she was calmly aware all the time that he was there, too.

"Fiodor Sergeevich!" she suddenly heard a loud voice. "Why are you on your own? I thought you'd be with some girls. . . ."

Agrippina raised her head slightly to see who was speaking and to whom he was addressing this nonsense. Her stranger replied:

"Why would I need girls during the day? The day's exactly when I love solitude, golden solitude. . . . At night—that's something else, at night I. . . ."

"Stop!" Agrippina requested mentally, recalling Serenus Zeitblom.[16] "Be quiet, my dear! Your lips are too pure and austere for that. . . ."

She wasn't a canting hypocrite, but questionable comments didn't suit him. What he did at night was his business, but to chatter about it didn't suit him, and he probably realized as much himself because he fell silent just in time.

"Fiodor . . . ," mused Agrippina. "When I first saw Zhorka, he was also called Fiodor. That name's fatal for me. . . . And how well he speaks, rolling the *o* just like my late mother. That's my native dialect. The guy's from the north, one of us, obviously. . . ."

She lay with eyes closed and recalled his face: somewhat pale (either because he was unwell or because for some other reason he didn't tan), with a knot of muscles bunched alongside his austere lips. . . . Well, it was thanks to him that she was experiencing it again—the desire to think about someone, the desire to see someone, and the bittersweet dependence on someone. . . . And she didn't need anything else, there couldn't be anything else in such a situation: they weren't the people for it. . . .

By two o'clock she was back at the theater for rehearsal. The play announced for the following day was Anuev's *The Lark*, and the director wanted to run through it and revitalize their old performance of it, which had become sloppy. Agrippina was playing Zhanna, a role she liked a greal deal.

They were already on the third scene when Olga turned up. She was playing Agnes, Karl's mistress. Zhorka was playing Karl.

"I was at the clinic!" she snapped in response to the irritated comment of the artistic director, and explained angrily: "I'm pregnant." Raising her voice above the smug guffaws that rippled through the actors, she continued: "The doctor said very specifically that there were five cases of cholera, and tomorrow they'll be closing the town and imposing a quarantine."

Right away everyone fell silent: it had prowled around somewhere in the distance, had circled as it drew closer, then retreated. It had teased and unnerved them—and finally it was here, right at their side. It was somewhat frightening. . . .

Zhorka threw aside the toy he'd been playing with, walked over to the edge of the stage, and made as if to jump off, then sat down, dangling his legs and leaning back against the floor, with palms outspread:

"We've got to leave today," he said. "You can go crazy waiting for it to get you. Well, if need be, I'll leave without a ticket, even if it means traveling on the footboard." Zhorka's hand sketched one of his splendid gestures expressing nervous confusion, and Agrippina realized that he wasn't joking.

"Let the administration worry about that," shouted Iura Vasilyev.

"Where can we go?" wondered the artistic director. "Being on tour makes things difficult. We'll be in the hole as far as finances are concerned. We won't have anything to pay salaries with."

"To hell with the salary!" grinned Zhorka. "Life is dearer than any money, Boris Nikolaevich."

Once again everyone started expressing his opinion and imposing his views; someone ran off to get the administrator and the managing director, someone else started speculating along with the artistic director whether it couldn't be arranged to have the tour extended in Penza. They'd originally intended to go there during the winter, and then the administration had managed to arrange this tour in the southern sea town.

Agrippina got up and burst into quick, angry speech, saying how she couldn't understand why nowadays young people had a visceral fear of death, even though there hadn't been as much as a hint of death yet, and nothing certain was known about the cholera. Olga was notorious for spreading panic.

"I believe you and I are the same age, Boris Nikolaevich? Do you remember the fall of '41 in Moscow, when there was typhus, dystrophy, and bombings? Death really walked at our side, but who thought about it? But that's not what I'm talking about, ultimately. How on earth can we leave now? If it's really cholera going around, they won't let us leave anyway. What if it's not cholera, though, but simply panic? Not everyone will be able to leave town. How will people pass the time? We're on tour, and so's a group of guitar players from Leningrad."

"Be quiet!" cried Zhorka. "If you want to die on the cross. . . ."

"On a cross in flames," corrected Iura. "She's Joan of Arc, after all."

"Don't talk nonsense," Agrippina dismissed the comment. "This is serious, you won't get me going today!"

She went on explaining, impressing upon the artistic and the managing directors that during the war, for example, even those soldiers who had never read anything would read the leaflets from the front. Art is essential for people at times of disaster; it helps them think, unites them, and gives them faith.

"You told me," she shouted at Zhorka, "we're clowns for their amusement. . . . Perhaps in peacetime some spectators do see us that way. That's why—and this is the only way I can explain it—you allow yourselves various little stunts during a performance for which you should be disqualified and forcibly run out of the theater! But people need us now. These aren't elevated words," she retorted to Iura's snide rejoinder, "but the truth. Why did you become an actor?'

If he only knew why he'd become an actor! . . .

She got what she wanted. The administrators and the artistic council decided that the theater would stay in town. Especially since, really—where could they go now?

They put on another performance. Fewer people attended than usual; the audience was excited and nervous and didn't listen well, though the group worked earnestly and well, either because they'd grasped the play emotionally or because they'd got scared.

"So they need us, do they?" said Zhorka during intermission. "That's your fantasy! Right now all everyone cares about is himself. They're not listening at all, can't you see that?"

"Yesterday you cared only about yourself, too," said Agrippina, "and yet you came to me. They come to see us for the same thing. So as not to have to face disaster alone, for the comfort of having someone at their side. So as to figure out how to act, what to do. Besides, if they're not listening, it's simply because you're not working well. You should be in control of their reactions. . . ."

The second act went better, and, quite unexpectedly, the audience responded to them as they'd never responded before. They stood there, applauding, and wouldn't leave. They were simply too anxious to sit quietly.

8

Upon leaving the theater, Agrippina headed for the railroad station. Olga had said that three more trains were supposed to leave that night.

She walked along, happy to be wearing soft flat shoes, so that her heels didn't clatter. She walked through the quiet town as silently as a shadow. She ran into few passersby, the windows with drawn curtains were dimly lit, and only three solitary customers sat in the lighted glass booth of a café, drinking something. Agrippina recalled that Zhorka had said that all the dry wine in town had disappeared, even the dry champagne. A rumor had spread that the cholera bug couldn't survive in acid, that in ancient times they'd actually treated cholera with dry wine. Although, on the other hand, it wasn't likely that during the 1935 epidemic the Italians had stopped drinking their acidic chianti. But that hadn't helped them much then.

She ran into some volunteer patrolmen with red armbands who looked her over suspiciously and asked: "Where do you live, miss?"

"At the Shore Hotel!" replied Agrippina cheerfully. She felt a strange excitement, a nervous boost of energy.

The patrolmen went on.

At night the town looked cozy and old: the houses of yellow shell rock, with tall, black, old-fashioned doors, the cobblestone roadways, the pavements of sunken stone slabs, and along the pavements, acacias with clusters of enormous pods rustling among the lacy leaves on the branches. These pods also crackled underfoot. Agrippina imagined the pink flowers, with their sickly sweet perfume, which just recently had been where the pods were now, and she regretted that she hadn't caught them in bloom. She really loved the smell of acacia.

Behind the semitransparent blinds in the houses an independent, separate life flowed on, and quiet voices spilled out into the street. Once again Agrippina recalled the war and how the apartment doors in their house had opened immediately. During a bombardment they weren't allowed to lock the doors as long as the alarm lasted, in case a fire suddenly broke out somewhere, and the curfew patrols could come at any time of night to check for outsiders. They felt that the empty shell protecting immovable property was pointless—in the face of death no one cared about wardrobes and clothes: they quickly sold off their clothes at the market, and the wardrobes and chairs blazed away in the small stoves.

"Why do I constantly remember the war?" Agrippina suddenly thought in surprise. "The vivid, pure, and unclouded part of my life was my youth, and it coincided with the war years. Later there was chaos—chaos, slaps in the face, and fatigue. . . . And here I am, trying to tie in this little misfortune with the significant one. . . ."

She entered the street where the railway was located, and from the hill there, she saw the square in front of the train station. The square was jammed full of people, and a steady, confused noise, like that of the sea, floated down the quiet street. The neon streetlights were on, and in their modern white light everything below shifted and swayed, as the huge flow of tense human bodies scurried about back and forth.

Agrippina joined the bustle without being noticed by anyone, and instantly became lost in the huge crowd. Now wasn't the time for curious glances. She smelled the odor of hot sweat and felt the electricity radiated by tense bodies, but nothing irritated her. She found it all understandable, for it all reminded her of something else long ago.

Fighting her way to the platform, she stood at the gleaming white wall and looked around. Along the whole platform, as far as the eye could see, people were sitting on top of their things. They weren't dressed in bright resort outfits, but in grey clothes that wouldn't show dirt easily and that were somewhat warmer; the evening was cool. The children were tired out and slept, though several of the older kids kept pushing each other among the seated people. But nobody got irritated. A boy of six or so came up to Agrippina and suddenly took her by the hand, by her bracelet.

"Wow! That's interesting. . . . What is it?"

"A bracelet," explained Agrippina. "It's a sort of ring."

"Oh." The boy moved off.

A young couple sat nearby. The woman held an open powder compact, and the man was shaving himself with an open razor as he looked into it. Agrippina wasn't surprised at that, either: she merely stored in her memory the flaccid, patient poses of the people sitting around her and the erect, narrow back of the woman holding the little mirror, as well as the way she would touch her husband's or lover's cheek now and then with her fingers.

"Right here, Kolia . . . here, too. . . ."

A group of young guys and girls with guitars, dressed in ski jackets and sneakers, were sitting on their backpacks. One of the guys smiled as he caught Agrippina's eye.

"Come and join us, Red. You can come with us!"

Another guy glanced around and asked:

"Have you got a reserved seat? We've got a group ticket. But where are your things?"

"I don't have any," Agrippina smiled in response.

Next to Agrippina, a woman with short hair and a tired, elderly face was sitting on the lid of an expensive suitcase, crushing it. A boy lay asleep in her lap; she had let her arms fall limply with fatigue, and the boy lay twisted uncomfortably, his knees spread apart as he breathed hotly through his open mouth. Another boy, somewhat older, slept in a kneeling position, his face pressed against the lid of the suitcase.

The train began to crawl silently along the tracks. People stirred, and started getting up.

"Red!" shouted the group of tourists. "Come on and join us or you'll get crushed."

She moved mechanically toward them, but the stream of people pushed her back. The train finally stopped, the doors opened, and people started boarding. But no one got crushed; people waited their turn with somber patience and dissolved in the darkness of the doorway. Through the windows she could see shifting shadows and catch glimpses of the faces inside: the people who had seats were looking out at those still left.

Suddenly Agrippina caught sight of her stranger. He was standing at the back of a crowd that was heading for one of the train cars; he stood half-turned toward her and didn't see her. He was dressed in a dark suit that didn't fit well, with a raincoat over his arm.

Agrippina smiled as she felt a pang. Who was he to her? Nobody. And yet here she was, feeling sorry that he was leaving, as if something that had really existed were disappearing.

The crowd in front of the train car cleared; the stranger picked up his suitcase and headed for the entrance, showing his ticket to the conductor. As he passed through the door, he looked back and noticed Agrippina. A wry expression crossed his face, either of alarm or pain, and he made as if to go back. But he was being pushed from behind, and shaking his head and smiling, he passed his hand over his face, as if smoothing out the muscles along his lips. Agrippina also smiled at him with her eyes and nodded. She looked to see where he'd gone, but couldn't make him out through the windows of the car.

The train moved off. Agrippina didn't bother to wait until it left, but went out into the square by the train station. A lot of people were still milling around there: the next train was supposed to leave at two A.M. Passing through the square, Agrippina ambled along the dark, quiet streets to the hotel. It looked as if no one was left in town. As she walked along, she thought about how good it was that she would stay through to the end, see how things developed, and experience it all just like everyone else.

BETWEEN SPRING AND SUMMER

NINA KATERLI

Translated by

JOHN FRED BEEBE AND REGINA SNYDER

1

AS HE WAITED FOR THE STREETCAR, VASIA GOT chewed out twice because the dog wasn't wearing a muzzle. But what was interesting was that both times it was not women but strapping young men who complained. One ugly mug threatened him with some sort of town ordinance—a nitpicker. He hollered, of course, not on account of the ordinance, but because he was scared. Didn't even mind doing it in front of the girl he was walking with. The dog kept fussing, sniffed the ground, and again began to whine and yelp. Kenka, of course, would go out of her mind—and rightly so, since she was the one who had to do all the cleaning up.

Vasia distinctly pictured himself just tying the dog to that post right now, and walking away. His heart suddenly began to thump. No excitement. Doctor's orders. The streetcar appeared.

"C'mon," Vasia said and tugged at the leash. "Let's go home, Athos."

The dog was about to obey, but suddenly changed his mind, dug all four paws into the ground, and lay down.

"Get up, stupid," Vasia urged. "Hey! The streetcar will leave without us!" And the dog, as if he understood, got up.

It was the same car that Vasia had taken to get here, to the market. And it was empty again. Vasia tore off two tickets and settled into the back seat. The dog sat down next to him quietly, except that occasionally his whole body shivered. Then Vasia would lightly pat his warm back.

Houses and trees floated toward them past the clean windows. During the past two hours the branches seemed to have gotten greener. A summertime crowd had lined up in front of a barrel of kvass with cans. The Neva suddenly swept into view, all in sharp, crisp little waves, with the little white river tramway and the Summer Gardens visible far off on the opposite shore. Clouds appeared, and a little breeze came up. The dog gave a sudden loud sneeze.

"Bless you," said Vasia.

He was trying not to think about how his heart had begun hurting again and seemed to be swelling up in his chest. Nor did he think about what Ksenia[1] would say when she got home. He stubbornly pictured Iazvitsy, the summer, the clearing behind the garden, and how he and Athos would run together every morning through the damp grass to the river.

2

"I love you."

"You read too much romantic fiction."

"Well, loving also means romanticizing. It isn't really love if you think of 'positive' and 'negative' qualities. You don't love for a quality. I love you because you are you, that's all."

"You're very unlucky."

"No, I'm not."

"Not because I treat you badly. Just. . . . "

"I know all about it. Why must you make excuses? I'm a very happy woman. I don't need anything else from you, only that you understand how much I love you."

"But why?"

"Don't you dare! I know that I sound silly and tongue-tied. That's the way I always talk to you. This time it doesn't matter; you did promise that you'd hear me out. But usually when we meet we talk about nonsense: 'How is Viktor Sergeevich?' 'Have you seen Nadia recently?' I look at you and hear how cheerful and false my own voice sounds, and my stupid little jokes—and I just think to myself how time is flying, and I wait for you to start saying goodbye. I never remember later what I said. I just know it was stupid."

"Well, there you go, romanticizing again."

"I don't give a damn about Viktor Sergeevich. I want to grab your hand and bury my head in your sleeve. And just talk about important things. So that if I ask you how things are going, you'd tell me what really matters to you. But you talk about Viktor Sergeevich; of course that's simpler. If only you'd understand how I feel, that's what I want—it's as if something huge and awkward has been dragged into your house. Something—unnecessary. . . . "

"An elephant."

". . . But I want you to believe me. I don't plan to drag anything into your house. But you must understand what kind of thing it is."

"You really should write poetry. I'm twenty years older than you."

"Well, that's just fine. At least it's not so embarrassing for me to declare my love twenty times over."

"I have a son your age. Anyway, you can't fall in love with someone old enough to be your father."

"You know perfectly well you can. Listen, it's as if—as if I suddenly had—as if I had—well, the Northern Lights. Yes—my own Northern Lights."

"Oh, my. How beautiful."

"Since I have the Northern Lights, I can't live like other people. Right? Thinking about when to wash the floors, complaining about having to stand in line, gossiping about my girlfriends. I have to live up to the Northern Lights, to be romantic, like them. Do you find that funny?"

"No."

"I love you."

"Stop crying or I'll leave."

"Do you believe me?"

"I believe you, only don't cry. And it's already late. You should go home."

"I love you."

3

The morning was so quiet that Vasia felt like washing the windows. He would have done it, but yesterday the doctor had clearly ordered: No physical exertion! And Kenia, too, on her way to work had said: "Lie down and rest!" The day before, at work, he had been seriously ill for the first time in his life, almost losing consciousness. Things swam in front of his eyes, and he no longer knew which was the floor and which was the ceiling. And his legs got numb. But he didn't pass out completely; sitting on a stool, he heard Nina calling the emergency service in a frightened little voice. The nurse and doctor rushed in, hustled about, and pulled off his work jacket to take his blood pressure; then the nurse gave him an injection. And the feeling left him, though his legs still didn't feel like his own, and there was still a kind of hum in his ears. The doctor told him to go home, and wrote out a sick-leave slip and a prescription. But there wasn't much left of the workday, only an hour plus a few minutes, and he sat out that hour on a stool, giving Nina instructions: Check whether the mass was properly formed, turn off the furnace, turn off the heating unit of the mixer, then the main electric switch, put the flammable cans of mixes in the steel safe. Without a word, Nina did as she was told, all the while glancing at Vasia in panic, until it even seemed funny to him.

"Why are you looking at me? I'm alive—I haven't croaked."

"I'm going with you. All the way home," she said severely.

"Oh, sure. Right now."

"Well, as far as the streetcar."

The girl stubbornly insisted. They walked arm in arm to the streetcar. She helped him in, and then was going to climb up after him. He had to click his tongue in protest. She relented. Not a bad sort, that Nina—though of course to Vasia she was Nina Georgievna, engineer, his immediate superior. There you are—what a laugh.

Nina had come for work experience last fall, fresh out of the institute. Just a girl. Younger than Vasia's Alka. A little thing, with curly hair. What was her patronymic[2] again? Indeed, nobody ever called Vasia by his patronymic, even though he was in his fifties, since it was such a tongue-twister: Panteleimonovich.

Vasia didn't wash the window, but with an effort, turning the handle and jerking it toward him, he tore off the paper that had glued it shut for the winter and pulled open both panes. At once the noise and smells of the street came in. Out there it was really spring, the very first such day this year; the April weather had been bad, and on May Day it had snowed—on May Day! Just yesterday the town had looked grimy, and you couldn't really tell what season it was. It could have been fall—bare trees, puddles underfoot. The only difference was that it was still light in the evenings. Now the sun was burning hot; everything had dried out and seemed clean and new. Vasia thought: On days like this it seemed cleaner outside than in the apartment, because it was stuffy and dusty in the house no matter how much you vacuumed, and mainly the dirty window panes. . . . Okay, okay. The sick-leave slip was good till the end of the week. There would be time to do the windows. He could still rest today. Vasia turned on the television set. It blared out like a lunatic, and he had to turn down the volume. Their neighbor was likely still asleep. Why shouldn't she sleep? She's retired. Vasia turned the sound down completely and listened through the wall on his left. The neighbor's apartment was quiet. Asleep. Though it could be that she'd gone out. Quiet as a mouse, that woman. You never noticed when she went out. He'd had good luck with this neighbor, never any confrontations. It was almost like not being in a communal apartment. Vasia could have signed up long ago for a co-op. He could have found the money. But why should he? These were two good rooms: light and warm, on the Petrograd side. As they say, leave well enough alone. Otherwise they'll give you an apartment way out in the sticks. Vasia turned up the sound. The neighbor had probably gone out, to the store. Or to church. Kenia had said not long ago that she thought the old lady sneaked away to the Vladimir Cathedral. Suddenly, for no good reason, she had become a believer at the age of sixty. It was, of course, her own business—all kinds of things happen. He could understand it in the case of, say, Auntie Nadezhda, a village peasant. As long as Vasia could remember, she had hung an icon in the corner with a lamp burning beneath it. But this one, no matter how you looked at it, was a city person, a typist by trade. Kenia thinks it's all the fear of dying. In church they tell you about the world beyond the grave, and that's just what old ladies need. To be comforted. Vasia had argued with his wife more than once: what comfort was there in that? Just out-and-out lies! And mainly lies about the "other world." Here people are, casually zipping around in space, and not once has anyone seen any sort of "paradise." Personally, he would have all those churches closed, so that people, particularly young people, wouldn't be led astray. Vasia himself never thought about dying. It comes when it comes. He wouldn't be the first to go, or the last. Still, after that stupid attack yesterday, watching how Nina fussed over him, he thought to himself: "Well, that's probably how it happens—everything swimming away, weakness, darkness. . . . " Well, what of it? So long as it's quick.

They were showing morning gymnastics on the television. He wondered, who for? Again for the old ladies. The clock showed 8:40. People had left for work an hour ago, but for them: "Heels together, toes out."

Vasia suddenly realized that he had been angry about something all morning. Because of his illness, maybe? He couldn't think of any other reason. The weather was good. Alka had come in late, but to make up for it, the sly puss had been extremely affectionate—"Daddy" this and "Daddy" that. She knows which side her bread is buttered on. . . . And the day before? Of course, all that yelling of hers couldn't have been what brought on his attack, but he'd certainly been awfully upset at the time. Mostly because he had really just felt like batting her one on her pretty painted face, but how could he hit her? The girl would soon be twenty-five; she's a teacher, with a college education, damn it. But what did her education have to do with it? Even when she was little, he had never once touched her with his little finger, the imp. If she'd been his, you see, he would've whipped her, but the way it was—he just couldn't, even though Alka didn't know anything, and, God grant, never would find out anything. She didn't know, but he *knew*; although it was true, he almost never thought about it. He only thought about it when he seemed to be being unfair to the kid.

All this thinking about his daughter made Vasia feel queasy, and his head felt as if he had a hangover. He lay down on the couch. Well, why not? If you're sick, lie down.

That time Vasia hadn't meant to insult Alka. He had just said what he thought about that one, about the old goat Iurii Petrovich. "Don't you dare run down my friends!" So that's it—her friend, the love and friendship of a spider for a fly. As a result of this friendship she'll be left a single parent; all her girlfriends got married long ago. Vika Ivanov has a two-year-old boy, and this one is just wasting her time with an older man, a family man. Well, what had he said? Her father's heart aches for her. He's not made of stone, he has feelings. And she started to yell and rush around. And the things she yelled at him: Our lack of trust, you see, really hurts her badly. Her father and mother don't know anything except that two times two is four. They don't know anything and don't want to. They're always butting in where they're not asked. They imagine that they've devoted their whole life to her, Alka, and that that gives them the right. . . . And she doesn't need that—do you hear?—she doesn't need them to devote their lives. She only asks for one thing: Let her live her own life, and don't bother her! Don't interfere! She's heard it a million times—they don't have anything except her. That's something to be proud of! Her pupils' parents have also talked her ears off: "Please realize, Alla Vasilievna, nothing else means anything to me except little Sasha. . . ." Well, then, what can a mother and father give their child morally and spiritually, if they don't have anything else except their little snot-nosed kid? Why should he respect them? Well, they've given him life, thank you! They feed and clothe him. Is that really the main thing in life? Usually when people say that they live for their children, it's just pretense, deceiving themselves and those around them, trying to justify themselves. They just go along living catch as catch can. They don't read, they don't think, and they hide behind their children. "We don't have time to read books," they say. "We live for our children." Phew! . . .

She went on and on. . . . Her lips were trembling. She was skinny and pale, her eyes big and swollen. He couldn't stand to look at her. Vasia just grunted and turned away. But she didn't relent. "It's disgusting," she shouted, "to watch how some old daddies elbow people aside and climb in the streetcar with their kids as if they were entering an enemy fortress with banners flying." He didn't answer. He realized that she was shouting from pain, that she was not arguing with her father but was proving something to herself. Iurii Petrovich has two children, even though they're grown up. He is, as Alka herself had told him, a loving father. It's clear that he'll never marry our little idiot. And thank God—the fellow is in his forties! Besides, children are children, as they say, our future, and destroying someone's family is the last thing one should do. Vasia didn't want to say this. He hung on with all his strength, but no, she went too far and he gave it to her.

"How can you!" She started to yell and cry so loudly that Kena even came in from the bathroom, where she had been washing clothes. And then Alka really let them have it: If, she said, someone should tell her that by the time she was fifty she would be like her parents, would think the way they think and live the way they live, she would immediately jump off a bridge into the river.

"Hysterical little fool," Kena said calmly and went off to wash clothes. But Alka grabbed her coat and galloped off to spend the night with Vika, her girlfriend. For a goodbye present she managed to shout that now she knew what she should do, but she hadn't expected this from her father; she had thought that he at least somewhat understood her, she had confided in him. But he was—under his wife's thumb!

That was the day before yesterday. And yesterday she had shown up a little after eleven, quiet and affectionate—maybe she had just seen her Iurii, or maybe she had realized that her father was right. Or had Kenia told her about the attack? All right. She was nice, and Vasia, of course, was nice to her. Are you going to stay mad at your daughter?

The phone rang in the hallway.

Vasia got up and in his bare feet—Alka should see him!—plip-plopped out of the room.

It was Alevtina Petrovna, his boss at work. "How can you do this, Vasia?" she chattered away cheerfully. "Our only man, you know, our pride and joy, and then to go and get sick. Tsk-tsk-tsk! That's not the thing to do. When do you expect to be back?"

"After lunch I'll come and pour the mix," Vasia said gloomily.

"What nonsense! Don't even think of it! We've decided not to pour today. Nina Georgievna is having a general cleaning day at work. Well, and tomorrow, some way or other, working together. . . . "

"Working together"—that means Nina will bust her butt and the other one will tell her what to do. Only they don't need to move the material at all. Engineers are birdbrains! . . .

"Tell Kislov to load up in the morning. Tell him I'm asking it as a personal favor. And after lunch I'll come and pour."

Kislov was the lathe operator in the shop, Vasia's buddy. He wouldn't refuse, but he'd want some liquor in return, and he'd want it then. Right on the spot. But right now that wasn't Vasia's worry. Alevtina would understand what to do.

"What are you talking about, Vasia?" she twittered. "Why, who is going to let you come to work with a doctor's slip? You've been prescribed bed rest, so go ahead and rest. And just think about pleasant things, love, for example. After all, you're still our interesting male. . . . "

"The key to the safe is in my pocket, in my work coveralls. They're hanging there in the corner," Vasia interrupted her gloomily.

After this conversation he was in a bad mood again. "Ta-ta-ta, rest and think about love." Whew! What are people thinking about when they rattle off words like that? No . . . frigging sense! It's like talking to a halfwit. Alka's the same way. And Nina. No, Nina's another matter. When it comes to work she does what Vasia says, without any ifs or buts, because at work it's not her and Alevtina, not even the director himself, it's Vasia who's the boss and in charge. Just last winter, for example, the minister came to visit them at the institute. For a week they washed and mopped everything. Alevtina made Vasia clean the inside of the furnace with a chamois. She was scared stiff. As if the minister were going to crawl into the furnace?! No help for it—he cleaned it. Nina washed the floors and dusted. She knows how to do that, thank God, even if she is an engineer. Alevtina herself told them where to move what, saw to all the little details like a hired servant, and then brought a chart—their technological process—and hung it on the wall for decoration. But maybe she was scared that she would have to tell the minister how the machinery worked. Anyway, when the minister came, he didn't even glance at their decorations, and he didn't really pay much attention to them, either. But with Vasia it was all on equal terms: he shook hands when they met, asked him his patronymic, and addressed all his questions only to him. Without using the charts, Vasia explained everything to the minister, showed him everything, and Alevtina champed at the bit beside him, shaking and jumping up and down—she wanted so much to butt in. Once she did jump in—Vasia said, by mistake, that to repair the molds he used bauxite tar, and she immediately said, "epoxy tar." She corrected him, but with a silly grin, as if to say, "Excuse me, Comrade Minister, sir, I'm just uneducated trash." But he didn't give her the time of day. He thanked Vasia and shook his hand again, while he only nodded to Alevtina and Nina. And he left. A solid fellow, along in years, and you wouldn't think he was a minister— just like an ordinary person. . . . And he understood. Really, if you think about it, what does Vasia do at work, and what does Nina do? (Alevtina doesn't count. She doesn't do anything except move papers around in her office.) In the morning Vasia loads the powder in the mixer. It's called monomer, a hundred kilograms; he turns on the heat, then the mixer, and watches the temperature—there's a special device with thermocouples for that. In exactly two hours he adds catalyzer, pours it slowly, and knows that if the least little thing isn't just so, the whole thing may explode, and surprise, you won't be able to find all your bones! Okay. He's poured it in. After ten minutes, hook up the hose to the mixer and pump this whole mix, the whole hundred kilograms, into the mold, and the mold is in the furnace, and it's two hundred degrees Centigrade there, and once again the steam may become explosive. So you have to add some nitrogen from the cylinder, and if you forget, then cash in your chips. That's if you're lucky, because there'll be such a boom that the building'll be gone—and the one next door, too. . . . That's the kind of work Vasia has, and if it comes to that, that kind of responsibility. And now—what does Nina do? Nina records in the book the temperature in the mixer, the temperature in the furnace, when they poured in the mass, and after how many minutes it hardened in the mold. That's her whole responsibility. Of course, Vasia understands: it's an experimental unit, developing new procedures and so on. Otherwise he could do the recording himself. You didn't need an extra person for this or a college degree. Vasia knows how to write, thank God; he's not illiterate. And why did they need an engineer on his job? Or even earlier, at the factory, where he had worked before the research institute—why did they need so many of them in the shop—so many half-wits? Like a pack of dogs. And whom did you need in a shop? To get the work done? Well, a boss—that's fine. Trained workers. They're not going to sit around without anything to do, of course, and loaf. And designers? And technicians, who are always twisting their brains over little scraps of paper? Maybe five, well—to stretch the point—ten designers and technicians are needed in the whole factory, but they've got a whole devil's army! And every single one of them is so smart, knows everything, wants to teach you, only none of them can do anything themselves. Any ordinary worker can make any part without their blueprints. And then there's the payroll clerks! And the quality control women! And the women who set the quotas!—Here it was obvious. . . .

Vasia irritatedly turned over on the couch with his face to the wall. The sight of the new, freshly hung wallpaper had a calming effect on him. Well, good luck to them all, to Alevtina, to Nina—to all dames, even Alka, although, of course, to tell her parents that she'd rather jump off a bridge than live the way they did was really rude and stupid.

He closed his eyes and wanted to doze off, but he couldn't. He wasn't used to sleeping at this time of day. He used to be able to when he was doing shift work at the factory. Then he could sleep either in the daytime or in the evening. Now he was out of the habit.

He swung his legs down onto the floor, put on his slippers, and went into his daughter's room. He fumbled around in her bookcase, dragged out one of the thicker books, and came back and sat down at the dinner table.

He liked the first story. Even though it was short, it was good, about the war. Vasia had a special feeling for the war. He considered himself a kind of participant, even though he'd been only ten years old at the time, and he was convinved that someone who had lived through the war, even as a child, was radically different from those who were born later, from those for whom the war was not part of their lives, and it's all the same to them whether it's the First World War or the Second. As he read, Vasia in one place even wiped tears from his eyes. That was when the war was already over and the fellow was returning to his farm, walking away from the station across a field at daybreak. A real-life story. But he quit the second story without finishing it. Slammed the book down and felt himself beginning to get mad again. Everything seemed to be true to life: and the fellow it was written about was just like Vasia, a worker, even the same age—born in 1931, only there was something there . . . just like in Alevtina's voice a while back. Vasia took a look—exactly! It was a woman writer. And she's beside herself with joy—just look! A simple worker, uneducated, had only finished a factory training program, but what a model citizen! He doesn't drink, and he loves his work and his wonderful coworkers, and he thinks about life, well . . . like a human being, like you and me.

Vasia took the book back and put it away. He remembered that the woman doctor had told him to take his medicine four times a day. He took it. And just as he was going to the kitchen for water, his neighbor came back. All prim and proper, neat and clean, with a scarf on her head, she smiled at him.

"Did you pray away your sins?" Vasia asked her benevolently. She didn't answer. She went to her own rooms, took off her coat and scarf, and turned up in the kitchen. Wearing her military order, her medals, her badges, and with a new permanent. She told him, "We had a meeting. It'll soon be Victory Day, and we're going to go to the Oranienbaum foothold, to Martyshkino. And, yes, sir, I'm going to go to church, too. A church is still for people, not for animals." And she smiled, the old woman; she had made her point. Vasia knew she hadn't needed anything in the kitchen. She had just come to show off her medals and her hairdo. And he had seen her medals—he had seen them a hundred times, but, to tell the truth, he was surprised every time. Such a little old woman—just breathe on her and she'll blow away, and still she's a soldier. And really, there are so many of them, women like that! Every May 9, Vasia went to Mars Field, and when Alka was little, he had taken her with him. With every passing year, of course, there were fewer and fewer veterans, and what was especially noticeable, there were more and more women among them. Soon you'd be inclined to think that only dames had fought in the war. But there's nothing surprising in that—fellows die off earlier. . . . Well, he should ask Alka her opinion on that—has our neighbor, Elena Aleksandrovna, wasted her life, too, just like us? Oh, Alka, Alka. . . . If only the devil would take your Iurii, even if he is a professor, no matter what he is! . . .

It was only eleven-thirty, and Vasia was already worn out from thinking about it all. He didn't know what to do with himself. He took a broom and swept the floor. When he bent over, there was a ringing in his ears and his chest hurt. He wiped the dust off the sideboard and sat down to rest.

. . . So, that's the way it was. First, that he and Kenia know only one thing: two times two is four. That had been when he reminded her about her health, that it's the main thing and that ruining it at the age of twenty-four is the last thing she should do. He had been right to tell her that! Although, to be honest, that wasn't what he had wanted to say, but that she shouldn't be seeing a married man every night! And, really, what was so bad, even if he did say, "The main thing is your health"? Why yell and make fun of him? And then, if you please, this heart attack got him yesterday, and he's sitting around like a sack of shit. And the windows aren't washed, and Kenia will come home from her shift all tired out. . . .

Vasia got up. He decided that he should at least go to the market and get some potatoes. That'd be something useful, anyway. His head was still as heavy as before, but his legs held him up all right. He slowly put on his clothes. Everything started to swim in front of his eyes again when he bent over for his shoes. Well, try to tell snotty Alka about health, when she, thank God, is never sick! . . . His heart suddenly started beating so hard that he broke out in a sweat and sat down on an end table by the door. He sat there quietly and waited it out. No, without your health, life isn't worth it. That's for sure. There's your . . . what did she call it? . . . your "middle-class morality, invented by old people for old people."

His heart gradually quieted down. He stood up and went out into the hallway. The apartment was quiet.

4

Outside, many things had changed since yesterday. One might even say everything. Summer had come today. Vasia walked along, and in every way he felt that it was summer. Long ago he had noticed that there are special feelings—a feeling of spring, of summer, of fall. . . . And it wasn't just that the sun shines and warms up everything in the summer, or that in the fall it smells like rotting leaves, in the winter there's snow, and in the spring, maybe, the day is longer. That's right and it's not right, and you can't explain it in words, just as you won't be able to make someone understand what pain is, or, let's say, love, if they've never once experienced it.

In front of him over the buildings there was a slender lightning flash, and, after a slight pause, a clap of thunder. Somewhere far off there was a thunderstorm.

5

The whole morning had been hot, and now it was raining outside. The window was wide open, and big drops splattered on the window ledge. The thunder was close, as if someone were dumping boards off a truck around the corner. It smelled like fresh leaves, although there weren't any on the trees yet.

I'm standing by the window. Today I finish work at noon, but fifteen minutes ago he phoned and said he'd be waiting for me at one-thirty in front of the Titan. There's a French film playing there. So there's no sense in going home now.

He phoned me. Himself. After everything I said yesterday. He phoned me. He said that he'd gotten tickets, in a tone as if we'd been going to the movies together our whole lives. Which movie it is, I didn't quite hear, and anyway, it was hard to understand him. The rain had just started.

. . . There they've got a French movie. And here we've got rain. Today for the matinee we have—rain. . . . It's pouring, coming down in columns. For fifteen minutes now—column after column, a short gap, and again, marching down the street. There's a banner over one column. Spread across the sky. It's a heavy, wet banner, faded by the rain. And the column keeps on going. It has filled the whole street. The pedestrians make way for it. They squeeze against the walls. I'm happy. Of course, you can't say something like that out loud. It's awkward even saying it to yourself. I just can't believe that it's happened to me, to the skinny beanpole (like my father), who people always said had that stupidity, which is worse than thievery. . . . Of course, if I told her everything, Mama would burst out crying. For her, happiness is the Marriage Palace and a wedding with a thousand guests in the Orbita Cafe. She's long ago laid aside the money for my "happiness." So that everything will be like decent people. She and Father always have everything like decent people. A nice boy (my dad) became independent—he got a good trade and good pay. He met a nice girl and took her to get a marriage license. They got legally married, and then they got a nice family: in a year there was a little baby, and after that. . . . After that? After that was Life. "You can't just think about today; you have to think about Life." My today is worth ten "Lives" like that.

The rain has gone around the corner. The street is deserted. The sound of its footsteps is dying out. Some stragglers dash past my window. That's all. The rain has passed. Just some wet traces, its footprints, on the pavement. The edge of the banner is disappearing behind the buildings. It's quiet. The sky is blue again. I am happy.

6

The rain faded. Vasia took off his raincoat and tossed it over his arm. His head felt better, and walking became easier. "Faker," he thought, and made up his mind to wash the windows anyway when he got home.

Though the right thing would be to have Alka do it. Let her learn how, since she doesn't like housework; she turns on the phonograph and sits there like a statue. As if you couldn't listen to a symphony and scrub the floor at the same time! It's even more fun with music.

"Why crawl around with a rag," she asks, "when we could call someone from the cleaning service? Are we too poor? You throw away money on junk, but you're stingy when it comes to the most important thing—saving time." Vasia pictured it in detail—he and Kenia lying side by side on the couch, watching TV, while some stranger crawled about on all fours—pictured it, grunted, and even jerked his head.

. . . I could easily walk to the market. It's only two stops. But it could rain again, can't rule that out; the streetcar has a map, so I won't get lost; besides, I'm not used to walking when I don't have to. . . .

And so, when he came to the streetcar stop and an empty car pulled up right away, Vasia got on. The car had just come from the station. The floor was wet; the windows, their panes freshly washed and sparkling, had been left slightly open here and there, and a breeze was blowing through them, smelling of warm dust. It occurred to Vasia that he couldn't sit around on sick leave too long. Soon it would be time to figure out his vacation days and go to Iazvitsy to plant potatoes. Auntie Nadezhda lived at Iazvitsy, and for almost a quarter of a century now Vasia had spent his yearly vacation there. In two parts. First, a week in May, getting ready for the summer season; spading up the garden, repairing whatever needed it, fixing up the house. Auntie Nadezhda's house was getting old; the year before he'd had to replace two tiers of logs in the cabin, and now it appeared to need a new roof. But there was no point in starting on the roof in May. That'd be in August during the main part of his vacation, when Vasia would come for a long stay with his wife.

Vasia pictured Nadezhda's house. It faced the road, and across the road was the Sovkhoz potato field, and beyond that the overgrown piney woods. In those woods they'd go mushroom hunting all day, starting at daybreak. They took only the good ones, the whites and orange-cap boletus. And if they wanted to get just any mushrooms for frying with eggs, then Kenia would dash across the stream. Behind Nadezhda's garden was a clearing, and beyond that a narrow meandering stream, swift and cold, cold enough to give you leg cramps. As a boy, though, Vasia used to swim there as early as May. Forget-me-nots, thick and bright, blossomed along the banks in summer, and in spring the clearing was strewn with yellow swamp flowers, water lilies; since his childhood their subtle smell had meant vacation time to Vasia. A board had been thrown across the stream. It was only by crossing this narrow board, which bent right down to the water, that Kenia could get across to the scrubby, boggy woods on the other side. Here, in season, in only half an hour, you could get all you could use of the russidae, brown-caps, and thin-stemmed and damp swamp boletuses.

So many times in recent years, at work, Vasia had been offered various free vacation packages: to a family resort hotel, tourist trips to the south, even diesel excursion boats down the Volga. But for him there was no better vacation than one in Iazvitsy. In the past, when she was going to school, Alka would come along. She always had plenty of playmates there— half the village, it seemed. You couldn't keep those children in the house. They'd be at the river, or in the woods picking berries. Vasia had set up posts in the garden and hung up a swing. But nowadays—no way.

As soon as vacation came, she'd grab her knapsack and take off for the mountains. It used to be the Caucasus, but now Alka and her friends had taken it into their heads to climb some Khibins[3] and feed the mosquitoes. It's in Karelia,[4] or someplace like that. They go climbing, and their parents can't sleep nights. It's true Alka always sends telegrams; better if she didn't. She comforted them last year with: "Returning defeated flow ice avalanche danger cracks going Uchkeken."[5] On account of that "Uchkeken" her mother nearly went out of her mind. The devil only knows what kind of a thing Uchkeken was, where it was or how high up. And how do you think they felt—another telegram from Uchkeken: "Level five trail ice trough approaching summit impassable icefalls obstructing badly." They didn't sleep the entire night. In the morning her mother ran to the professor in Apartment 37 for information.

When Alka returned that time, they told her: "That's it, you've done your gadding about. On your next vacation you're coming with us to the country!" No way! "It's boring at your Iazvitsy. I'm tired of it. What kind of vacation is that? Weeding the garden. A vacation needs new impressions and, by the way, it wouldn't hurt you to take a trip somewhere." And that was the conversation.

But Vasia considered Iazvitsy his home, although he was born in Leningrad and both his parents had been city people. He got to Iazvitsy at the age of ten, in the summer of 1941. He and his mother were being evacuated. They traveled like everybody else, in a heated freight car, but they didn't know themselves where they were going. They didn't have any relatives anywhere. One morning at dawn the train stopped at a small, unfamiliar station. The last few cars were disconnected, including Vasia's. All day they crawled along in a cart, first through a sleepy, dusty little town, then through some fields, through a woods, and past some settlements; finally, just before evening, they found themselves at Iazvitsy. (Today Vasia could get there by bus in forty minutes.)

He and his mother had been assigned temporary quarters that day at Auntie Nadezhda's, but they ended up living there until the war was over. This was where they got his father's death notice, and later on, in 1946 or 1947, they always came for summer vacations. Toward the end of 1947 his mother died of pneumonia. After that, Vasia didn't go to Iazvitsy for a long time. But he wrote occasional letters and always sent holiday greetings. When he got married, he came with Kena and one-year-old Alka. Alka, by the way, called Auntie Nadezhda "Grandma."

It took twenty-four hours from Leningrad by train, less even—twenty hours. You'd get on at ten in the evening, and by six the next day you were there, in time for supper—in Iazvitsy. It was farther south, so now there'd probably be leaves on the trees already. But here there's just a greenish haze, like fog, on the branches.

"Finland Station!" the woman conductor announced into the microphone. Vasia suddenly came to: I've missed my stop. Stupid idiot. I was daydreaming about the countryside. Slept through my stop. Now there's no sense in getting off and changing trains. I'll just have to go on to the Kondratyev Market. Moron.

He bawled himself out, mostly because he thought he should. He wasn't really upset. What was so bad about rolling along like this in an empty streetcar through the clean, sunlit city, sitting in a soft seat, looking out the window, and not hurrying anywhere? All in all, things were fine, and even that sick leave had come at a good time, like an extra vacation. Maybe I could go to work tomorrow and finish out the week and take these days off later, when it's time to go to the country?

No matter how you looked at it, it was really good that Auntie Nadezhda's house was there, even with its creaky floors, dark ceilings, and narrow door (if you didn't bend down you'd bump your head on the crossbeam). It had the real smell of an old country farmhouse, with its little barnyard overgrown with soft grass, a real pleasure for bare feet! No matter how hot it was outdoors, in the house it was always cool and kind of dark. And when you went out on the porch you'd be blinded by the light. And then there was the vegetable garden, enclosed by a fence that Vasia had built. On the fence, pans were hung out to dry, and in the center of the rows of plants was a scarecrow dressed in Vasia's old jacket and his old green Sunday-best hat. There was all that, and in winter, when you were freezing and waiting for the streetcar in the morning, or running to catch it with your collar turned up, all of a sudden, for no reason, you thought of Iazvitsy and it seemed that even then it was summer there and you could smell the honey, the newmown hay, the ozone from a thunderstorm that had just passed. No, the most elegant southern resorts with their palm trees were nothing to Vasia. They never entered his mind, even though there, really, it was summer almost all year round.

7

Only once in his life had Vasia been south among the palm trees, more than twenty-five years before. It was the year he met Kena. In those days she wasn't called Kena yet, but "Ksana," that is, Ksenia. They met on the beach early in the morning of his very first day at the Agudzera Hotel, just below Sukhumi. At that time Vasia was working at a factory, and in August he was given a free stay at the Agudzera. The plane, he recalled, was late, and it was almost midnight when he arrived. He couldn't make out anything in particular that evening. He noticed only that the darkness was somehow strange—flat and totally black, impenetrable. He also noticed that the air was damp and sweet, with a strange smell, and in the grass there was a chirring, like the sound of lightbulbs about to burn out.

Later, back in his room in the small wooden cottage with a window in back facing the park, after drinking a bottle of wine with his roommate to start their acquaintance off right, Vasia listened to the unfamiliar murmur and thought: The sea must be somewhere nearby; I should get up and have a look. He thought and thought and then just dozed off. In the morning he went out into the park and was dazzled. Everything sparkling, everything strange—palms, dark blue, not light blue. To be exact, the sky was deep blue, and beyond were the mountains, green when seen up close, but in the distance violet-grey with snow on the crests of some of them. Just like a postcard! And besides that, roaring beyond the trees, no more than a hundred meters away, was the sea.

That morning Vasia went for a dip three times. The first time he didn't swim out too far, but then got more daring and went out past the buoys, lying on his back and stretching out his arms. The water supported him, just rocking gently. It was salty. He immediately checked it out by tasting it with his tongue.

When he had turned over and was swimming back to shore, he caught sight of a girl swimming quite close by, wearing a yellow swimsuit and tanned like an African. She had a pretty face and reddish hair curling from beneath her bathing cap. Vasia swam up behind her, and together they came ashore. He staggered once, not used to walking, but the girl ran across the sand in just her swimsuit, without drying off, to a cottage which was just like Vasia's, next door. She was small and thin, like a baby bird. She ran comically, on straight legs, and in that yellow suit Vasia thought: "Just like a canary." That's how she later became "Kena" instead of Ksenia.

Two days later they were introduced. There was a special "get acquainted party" just for that purpose. Everything was arranged: dances, a guessing game (name three authors whose name and patronymic is Aleksandr Sergeevich), and another game—he didn't remember what it was called—the girls standing in one circle and the fellows forming another one outside so that there's a ring within a ring. The accordionist plays and everyone walks, one ring in one direction, one in the other.

Then the emcee claps his hands and everyone stops, and each fellow introduces himself to the girl he is opposite and asks her to dance.

After that, they went for a swim together before breakfast every morning. Kenia was a better swimmer than Vasia. He did a sort of dog paddle, while she swam like an expert. When she was a student at a technical school, she had taken swimming lessons and gotten a certificate. They managed to go on two excursions before her departure, to Novyi Afon[6] and later to the mountains and caves. Vasia hadn't liked being in a cave. It was dark, damp, and low; they finally had to crawl on all fours. He did like it, however, when they lit a bonfire in the clearing, the driver and the emcee roasted shashlyk, and everyone ate and drank a lot of Georgian wine. It was like vinegar, of course, but with the meat and in the open air, who cared? Then they took snapshots. Vasia stood between Ksana and an old grandma from Moscow—an amusing old girl, he remembered. Completely grey, her face as tan as Ksana's, and big blue eyes in that tanned face; lively and inquisitive eyes. She behaved like a young woman, wore slacks, sang louder than anyone else around the campfire, even danced the "lezghinka"[7] with the Georgian tour guide, a young fellow. The guide kissed her hand and kept calling her "Mama." He wondered whether she was still alive. Probably not—so many years had passed. . . .

After the shashlyk they all went their separate ways. Vasia and Ksana went up into the mountains, along a narrow, rocky path. Blackberry bushes grew there along the edges. Ksana kept laughing at something, throwing her head back and talking. That was when she told him that she was a skilled worker at a factory and had gone to a technical school specializing in synthetics. The job was a hard one—reinforcing hoses with metal casing, and so much noise that you had to yell into people's ears to be heard. Everyone was on edge, and they regularly kept a bottle of valerian in the shop office. Vasia said she'd better get out before it killed her, that a job like that would ruin a girl, and she'd better look for something else.

"I'll find something!" Ksana tossed her red curls.

. . . But she didn't quit, and now it looked as if she'd work there until she retired. No matter, she had gotten used to it; she had been shift boss for seven years. But she had gotten hoarse.

That day she said she had come south to get over a broken heart.

"Well, and did you get over it?"

"It's all gone, like apple blossoms in the spring!" she said, and laughed again.

They got back to the hotel just before supper, and that evening there was a dance. Vasia and Ksana went out into the park; the song that was playing was "When you go to meet your love, take the shortest path," and they kissed under a cork oak. Again there was the chirring in the grass, but this time Vasia recognized it—cicadas. Three days later he cut two pieces of bark from the cork oak with a penknife—one for himself and one for Ksana, as a souvenir of their meeting and of farewell.

"And here's hoping we'll meet again in the future!" he said. They were standing at the bus reserved for the main party of vacationers. Ksana's things were already inside, and she was wearing a dress he hadn't seen before. She stood next to Vasia on the scorching pavement under a eucalyptus tree. She didn't say anything. The night before, she had been strange and quiet and seemed almost frightened. Vasia even thought: "She doesn't want to leave, and maybe—who knows—maybe she's sorry to leave me." But today, when he mentioned seeing each other again sometime, she didn't answer but just offered her hand and got on the bus. Vasia went to the beach, since he had a whole ten days left.

He spent them pretty well. He went with his roommate to Sukhumi, and in the evenings they'd go to the movies. His roommate turned out to be a nice fellow, a physicist from Moscow. He had brought a book on astronomy, and he and Vasia would go down to the beach before bedtime, and he'd show Vasia the constellations. It was curious: if you gazed at the sky and didn't look for anything in particular, all the stars seemed alike and seemed to have been thrown up there at random. But when you knew what was what, you could see that the stars themselves were different from one another and the constellations were like pictures. And then, there it was—Libra the Scales, Aquarius pouring water, and over there the Swan with its neck. . . .

But it just wasn't the same without Ksana. Vasia was even glad when the vacation was over. As soon as he landed in Leningrad, he phoned her at the factory, right from the airport. There was a crackling on the telephone, and he had to shout as loud as he could for them to go fetch Ksenia Ivanovna; then he waited for a long time and heard noise and someone's voice, and finally her voice, faint and distant. And the sound of her voice flustered him. He suddenly forgot the witty remark he had thought up on the plane and simply said: "Ksana? I'm back. Have you forgotten? From the vacation resort. Remember? Ksana, it's me . . . ."

He thought she'd be glad to hear from him, but she said she had no time to talk right then. Vasia asked when they could see each other, and she replied, "I don't know," and hung up. He, of course, didn't call again for three days and didn't intend to. On the fourth day he called, and again she said she didn't want to see him, there wasn't any point. A stupid excuse. Vasia stood it for a week, then, one day after work, he went to the city directory and got her address. That very evening he showed up with flowers. That was the first time he entered the apartment where he had now been living for twenty-five years, where Alka was born. . . .

Ksana was alone; she seemed afraid of something, and at first wouldn't invite him in. She said at the doorway: "I told you in plain Russian! There's no reason for us to see each other. So don't come around." Vasia had looked at her and had seen that something was wrong with the girl. She wasn't herself. Her eyes were sunken, and because of her suntan, she looked jaundiced. Vasia didn't leave; he sat right there until Ksana's mama came back from a visit, at eleven o'clock. The next day he took time off, bought flowers again, and met her at the entrance gate when her shift was over. . . . They were married a month later, though his mother-in-law didn't care for him; she thought he was too simple and had no prospects. She herself was a manicurist and worked at that time at a salon on Nevskii Prospekt; not very old yet, still fortyish. She always dressed with style and dyed her hair. Still does. Still earns a living; has her own clientele. She refused to live with her daughter after the marriage and moved, instead, to Vasia's old room on Karl Marx Street: an "intrafamily exchange." He was glad. She thought Kenka was throwing her life away for nothing. Here she was, a skilled worker, taking on a husband you wouldn't even want people to know you had. And she hinted that no wonder Vasia had been in such a hurry; he didn't want to miss his chance. Ksenia might have had second thoughts, so he did his best down south, and Alka was born prematurely.

8

It didn't seem that long ago that Vasia had met his wife at the maternity hospital. He'd bought everything, brought everything, even a pink nylon ribbon, but he'd left Kena's shoes behind, and she had to come outdoors in hospital slippers, size eight. Vasia remembered how sunny the day had been and how he had carried the pink-ribboned bundle to the taxi. The bundle was surprisingly light, but there was a stirring and wheezing inside. And now she yells at me and says I'm under my wife's thumb.

Under her thumb? What was he, some old rag with no mind of his own? His daughter had blurted that out, of course, because of her own married Iurii, that's a fact. Lately, all her thoughts and conversations were only about him. . . . Although, if Vasia really thought about it, there was some truth in what she said. No matter how you looked at it, Kenia was the head of the house. She was the one who made all the decisions.

Vasia had never even given it a thought before. Personally, he was happy at home. And, in fact, he didn't park himself in front of the TV set like some people. He helped his wife with everything. He brought home more money than she did—salary and whatever extra he made on the side.[8] While the rubber mass was cooling, he would cut out and glue brake shoes and vulcanize inner tubes. People with cars would sign up for appointments, just as for a dental technician. If a man had a pair of hands, there was always something useful to do with them. So, no matter how you looked at it, he had never been a drone in the family. It was true that he did mostly what his wife wanted, but that was no one else's business, not even his daughter's, since it was of his own free will. When it came right down to it, he even liked it that way. But why? Well, now that he thought about it, in the other families he knew, the woman was usually the head. And how many men—just take that same Kislov—were always bitching that their wives were forever nagging, wouldn't give them room to breathe? That family life was like a jail sentence, and if they had known what it would be like, they would never in their lives have gotten married? There had been a lot about this in the papers lately, explaining the situation, saying that women now had equal rights, were financially independent, ran the household themselves, so why should they "obey and respect" a husband if he was like a blank space around the house and couldn't even hammer a nail?

Equal rights. Of course. But equality had turned out to mean not only that a man was no longer the master of his home, but that he was the least important person in it. What had happened to men? And where had these women come from who ran everything, whether at home or on the job? And suddenly Vasia understood what had happened. War had happened. Not once, but three times. And remember, all three right in a row. And what was the result? The men had been killed off, and the women were left with the kids. Who was the head of the house? The strongest? The smartest? Who was the protector? Who knew how to do everything? The mother. Okay, now the daughter grows up and gets married. How will she handle herself in her own family? Naturally, like her mother, since she hasn't known anything else. Not that she would have to nag and yell at her husband. She would just treat him the way a mother treats her child, teaching him, making him do things her way, wiping his nose. And he'd like it just fine. At first. Poor fellow. It was what he expected, was used to. His father had been killed, his mother had raised him, and the first thing he looked for in a wife was a mammy, to fuss over him, cater to him, baby him. Then suddenly he'd slip the leash, be independent. Of course! And the mammy would feel sorry for the orphan, would look after him with her last bit of strength. . . .

Well, no, for Vasia personally it was wrong to feel this way. His own mother had been a clever woman, though she had tried to give him the choice morsels. But she'd brought him up to know the meaning of work, so now he helped his wife without complaining, and there was peace at home. What else could you expect? He had been an obedient son and had become an obedient husband. But what about men who were completely spoiled? Their mothers would forgive them, but their wives would think twice about it. And the result? Scenes, drinking bouts, fights, the breakup of the family. And playing around with other women. But if you think about it, what were they running away from? Not just for that, but to rest their souls, to feel like a real person. Of course! At home, he was nobody; but with a lover, at his first word, food and drink would appear, the beds were all made, he didn't have to do any housework. So he'd play around, just play around a bit, and then, all of a sudden, he dumps his wife with a kid or two. And it was no big deal. "My mother raised me all by herself, and it was all right. I grew up!" So they get a divorce and here we go again, fatherless household, female upbringing, and the whole thing starts over again. There it was: the war. So many years later, its influence could still be felt! The war, the war. That was the whole problem, not that girls started wearing pants or that guys had long hair (although that was disgusting to look at). And it wasn't equal rights. Quite the contrary. Equal rights were good—our big achievement. But raising kids without fathers—a disaster.

9

Vasia strode across the vacant lot toward the market, where crowds of people milled around on their day off. Dogs and cats were sold there, and fish in tanks, and across the street, a little farther up—cheap knitted junk. In a word, a flea market. Just like in wartime.

The crowds were sparse today in the vacant lot. A plump woman was selling puppies, roly-poly and red. They slept cozily in a basket. "Hunting dogs!" she called out shamelessly. Even a blind man could see they were purebred mutts. A little boy clutched a skinny, bedraggled kitten. His mother had apparently chased him out to market with the beast he had dragged in from the stairwell. Wouldn't let him keep it in the apartment. Kenia wouldn't have animals, either—there'd be a roomful of fur from them. But that wasn't the main reason. The main reason was the responsibility: If you took it, you had to take care of it. And who could care for it when everyone in the family was busy?

Vasia couldn't stand this "animal market." He tried to cross it as quickly as possible, not looking to either side. If there were just dumb little pups and kittens, well, bad enough, but when there were fully grown ones, or, God forbid, old ones. . . . But today nothing like that was going on. At the very edge, by the exit, a crowd had gathered. Over there you could hear shouts and laughter. Vasia walked over, too. It seemed like a good idea at the time! Some guy who'd been drinking was showing off his dog's training, an old dog, a sort of bulldog or boxer. Vasia had never liked dogs like that. They were frightful to look at. Almost hairless, with chopped-off tails and hanging jowls. And its master was apparently not just an ordinary guy. He looked like an actor or some kind of artist, handsome face and stylish clothes. But he was dirty, somehow—greasy hair, dandruff on his shoulders, shiny trousers, and his shoes—well, they were pretty far gone. In that shape, Kenia wouldn't even let Vasia out in the courtyard with the dishwater.

Spectators clustered around the artist while he smartly gave commands: "Athos!" The dog bowed his head and wrinkled his brow. Black, intelligent eyes. And sad, almost tearful. Maybe the big beast was thinking: "Why all this showing off?" But he obeyed his master, did all he was told, tried.

And the guy, this artist, keeps jabbering, won't shut his mouth: no, he wouldn't sell the dog for any money, you see. But he and his wife had gotten divorced, and now he's going up north to look for work, can't drag the dog along. After all, at first he'd have to live in a hotel, and hotels don't take you with four-legged friends.

"Humph. Needs a hotel. Needs to go first-class," thought Vasia, with unexpected malice. "What's wrong with a bunk in a hostel, thank you very much."

He started to move on, but he suddenly heard a sarcastic young voice right in his ear: "And how much do you expect to get for this fleabag, Pops?"

Vasia looked around. Beside him was a tall young man in a leather jacket, twirling a keychain on his finger. The fellow was as bald as a behind, but with a greasy red beard and grinning from ear to ear.

"You can have him for fifty," said the artist, "but he's worth more than two hundred. He's won medals."

"Me-dals!" the baldy boomed nasally. "Well, what do you know! Did he get them in the last century? Grandpa, he's on his last legs. Looks like he's all moth-eaten." The fellow guffawed like an idiot, and Vasia felt the spray on his face. He wiped it off and was about to say a few choice words to the baldy when the latter, slapping the actor on the shoulder, announced:

"Listen, Pops, take some good advice. Beat it to the dog pound while the streetcars are still running. They take this sort of medal-winner there. They don't pay you, but to make up for it, it's painless."

The fellow whinnied again, but worst of all, the artist giggled, too, the son of a bitch. The mother. . . .

Vasia said nothing; he shoved the bald guy with his shoulder and headed toward the market building. Why the devil had he come to this slave market? And the artist? The artist. . . . Damn drunk.

Vasia hated drunks. In their time they had caused him a peck of trouble. Seven years back, it was because of them that he'd had to leave the factory where he had spent all his working life since he finished his apprenticeship program. Last year he got with a work team that wasn't good enough to spit on. All drunks. The least little excuse, they'd go toss one down. So what? Good luck to them. But since he didn't drink, he was, for them, a money-grubbing miser. And the main thing was that even the journeymen and the boss thought of him that way. A good worker, but he loves money. If he doesn't drink it away, that must mean he loves it! Couldn't change their minds if you stood on your head. Why work two shifts in a row and on holidays? "Vasia, help us out!" They called him back so many times from vacation. . . . That proved it—a money grubber. There you are. Turns out the one who does the work is a money grubber. He got fed up. . . . He resigned and transferred to a research institute. There the team was basically female. Funny thing, though, the first thing they did was pour drinks: "Vasia, you pour!" A hundred grams of liquor. If you didn't take it, they were surprised, even offended. But now they're used to him. And who knows, maybe even they think he likes to squirrel away his money. . . .

The potatoes Vasia bought were firm and dry. He asked the old lady where they were from and she said Estonia. Healthy prices they were getting these days at the market, but Vasia didn't get indignant as some people did. After all, what was the big deal? You don't want it, don't buy it. He knew well the value of farmers' work, and paid now for his own laziness. He was perfectly able to go to Iazvitsy in winter and bring back a sack. Nadezhda had suggested it more than once.

Vasia and Kena always used to stock up for the winter; by the beginning of summer, they would still have at least a dozen jars of last year's preserves on hand. Dried root vegetables, too, and fresh and pickled ones, in jars. And all sorts of mushrooms, big deal. The cabbage wasn't used up till March. He kept two barrels on the balcony. Of course someone would be envious, and again it would be "money grubber." Shoot off their mouths, don't use their hands, and still want to have it all. Spoiled rotten. . . . What kind of life will Alka have? That one can't do anything. When she was little, the whole family worked. You didn't have to ask her. She tried to help all on her own. And now? Gets mad, proud; you can't say a word to her. Who'd she take after? Kena's mother, the aristocrat? No, not at all like her. . . . Vasia's mother, who had passed away, said that her father had been a peasant. Couldn't get near him—a nasty temper. Alka's always asking about him, her granddad. She's really interested in who her ancestors were. A disgrace, she says, not to know where you come from. It's like being a mankurt.[9] What's a mankurt? And if you ask her, she'll make fun of you.

Vasia had never even asked Kena. Not who, not where he was from, not—how it happened. Once, just before the wedding, she insisted, "Let me tell you . . . " He wouldn't hear of it. Wouldn't even let her tell her mother. And now, thank God, it's been twenty-five years, and not a word about Alka's natural father. He never existed—and that was that!

Some of the potato money was still left. Vasia thought a bit and bought two jars of nuts. For his daughter. Like to give that Iurii's face a good swipe, he would!

It was hot as an oven on the street; it made him want to take off his suit jacket. He looked down the street toward the beer stand. There was a long line there. Where did they come from, all these beer drinkers? After all, it was still during working hours, and not a holiday. . . . He suddenly felt really tired, his head like iron, white spots in front of his eyes. He stopped, put the bag of potatoes on the ground, took a short rest, and then slowly strode off across the vacant lot toward the streetcar stop. And then someone called to him, "Please excuse me. . . . "

He turned around. The artist with the dog was standing beside him, nodding his head and smiling happily, as if to an old acquaintance.

"Excuse me, please, I have a little favor to ask. I'll just be gone a minute. Won't you hold him for me? Literally a minute!" He nodded toward the store across the lot, and Vasia understood: "He can't hold out any longer, can't wait." And, although he didn't approve of the drinking, he felt sorry for him. He thought for a moment and agreed: "Just make it quick."

The artist fumbled, thrust the warm loop of the leather leash into Vasia's hand, and swiftly trotted off toward the store. When he saw his master leaving, the dog immediately whined and tried to follow him. The leash stretched and almost broke.

"Quiet!" Vasia ordered sternly. "Sit. He'll come back, your artist. He won't go anywhere." But the dog kept pulling and whining, then began to bark. Not meanly, but shrilly and piteously, like a puppy.

"Sit, Athos!" Vasia said. The dog sat down, breathing heavily, whining and looking in the direction where the drunk had disappeared.

"Now, now . . . it's okay. Just wait a minute," Vasia soothed him. Athos squinted at him and wrinkled his brow as he'd done before, cocking his head to one side and letting his tongue hang out.

They waited a long time. The sun was burning furiously. After thirty minutes or so, already knowing that he'd been had, Vasia nevertheless decided to make a trip to the store. Of course it was closed for lunch hour. He and the dog dragged themselves over to the beer stand. The actor wasn't there, either, and to go looking for him would be just stupid. Well, what can you do? Such a bastard! An artist! Right. A con artist. And Vasia was his dupe.

10

. . . and I wrote the day before yesterday, too, though there hasn't been a letter from you for more than a week. But I'm not really waiting. I know that when you get back down, day after tomorrow, you'll immediately send me a telegram as you promised. And at the same time you'll get my letters at the post office. I'm constantly imagining the Caucasus and your route, and everyone—Mishka and Leshka and Nadia and Aleksandrov. By the way, Leshka did send me a telegram before going up, the usual mumbo-jumbo—utter babble. I couldn't understand any of it, and it even scared me a little. My poor parents. Last year I was sending them even worse telegrams than that. I love you.

My life at Iazvitsy flows along its old familiar channels. You see, I thought I'd die of the blues here, but nothing of the sort: it's nice to see how pleased my parents are that I'm with them. Particularly my father. Generally, everything is fine, except that I miss you terribly. Father's getting better; he's almost the same as he was before he got sick, except that he doesn't dig in the garden anymore like one possessed. Mother won't allow it. Since early this morning, though, he's had it in his head to fix the fence, and he's been nailing on some little boards. Mama says that as soon as it gets hot out, she'll shoo him into the house. But so far it's not hot. Today is a quiet, greyish day, and I feel quiet, too. Lately Mama doesn't yell at me at all. Just when I sit down to write, she'll say, "Silly fool!" and wave her hand.

Just as we used to, I go for a stroll with my father every day before bedtime. Of course we take the dog with us. By the way, today Mama said that I don't wash his dish well: "Once you've got an animal, you have to take care of it." That's really progress. Before, she would make a point of not noticing Athos and considered him the cause of Father's heart attack. Interesting. While Father was in the hospital, I was the one who fed and walked Athos, but just the same he thinks that only Father is his master, and he won't obey anyone else.

He's afraid of Mama, though. He and I are on friendly, though not equal, terms. He looks down on me. In my opinion, he thinks I'm a dog, too, but another breed. And younger than he is. He's the boss! Grandma Nadezhda keeps trying to sneak him morsels. She feels sorry for him. "Poor critter—just have to—he's so scared of folks." Right then Mama started to throw in that it would be better for Athos to live at Iazvitsy all the time, but Father raised his eyebrow so, she shut up at once and that was that. Mama doesn't argue with Father anymore.

Here everyone says about me, "Daddy's girl—the same face." They think that if the daughter looks like the father, she's happy. It's true. I love you.

A while ago my father asked: "Well, what are you planning to do?" I answered, "I don't know yet." But I really do know. I plan to love you. I haven't and can't have other projects and plans. There simply wouldn't be any room for them.

This is turning out to be a silly letter. I remember how I used to suffer through compositions in class. It was an absolute necessity for me that when you corrected them, you'd be impressed at how bright and smart I was. And when we went hiking in the mountains, I would always do things the hard way, to show that I was the strongest, the boldest, the toughest. If someone had told me then how things would be between us, I wouldn't have believed it at all. Even now I don't believe it. Here I am, writing to you so intimately, but we'll meet and still I'll be tongue-tied.

I still haven't told you that we have new neighbors, a married couple from Moscow who have a dacha here. Both of them are about forty. I haven't really sized up the husband yet. He disappears on the river, fishing from morning till night. The wife, Valentina Ivanovna, quite the opposite, doesn't go anywhere. She sits for days on end at a table in the garden, writing. Mama has already explained it. Valentina Ivanovna is an associate professor, a biologist, just a shade away from being a full professor. She's writing her doctoral dissertation. By the way, she's a very attractive woman, tall and stately. The day they arrived, she dunked the bucket in the well and Daddy was helping her pull it out. Mother got terribly upset; she ran up shouting that she'd get the bucket herself, and that she didn't need another heart attack in her house. Father, of course, pulled it up by himself, and afterward, as you would put it, there was a "stew." Now Mama keeps telling us that scholarly prestige is all very fine, but it's not normal when a healthy woman hasn't even once washed the floors, to say nothing of the windows; doesn't make preserves, doesn't pick mushrooms, and so on, and so on. In effect: "A woman should, first and foremost, be a woman." Of course I argue with Mama, but to tell the truth, I don't know whether it's right for a woman to give herself up completely to her work, even interesting work. Sometimes I think that if it were for your sake, I could happily scrub and wash and learn to bake pies. If, . . . but that will never be, and there's no point in complaining.

By the way, the fence Daddy is fixing is between our yard and the neighbors', not far from the spot where Valentina Ivanovna is sitting. He's trying to hammer as quietly as possible, all the while hushing Athos to keep him from yowling at the crows. I'm sitting in the house, at the window. There's the smell of roses—right beneath the window a rosebush is blooming. Grandma Nadia is dozing on the porch, and Mama is sitting beside her, knitting a sweater for Father. For some reason, she thinks that since the heart attack, the main thing is not to let him catch cold. All the while she's watching him like a hawk. It's comical—to be jealous of our Daddy! He's like me. He's a one-woman man.

Time to end this letter. Otherwise I could go on all day writing all sorts of silly things. You know what—I love you. . . .

11

Athos got bored sitting around with nothing to do and started furiously digging in the dirt with his front paws: dust spewed up, and dry clods flew in all directions. The clouds dispersed toward evening and the sky was black and starry.

"Look there. See it? That's Cygnus the Swan. He's stretched out his neck, spread his wings. He's flying. Seven little stars in all. The brightest one is Deneb. And that star over there is Altair, in Aquila the Eagle. Do you see the Eagle, flying to meet the Swan? And over there is Bootes the Cowherd—in the three-cornered hat, smoking a pipe. . . . You cold? Let's go home. Mama's probably starting to worry."

"Mama's baking a pie," Alka replied dreamily. "A raspberry pie." Alka was wearing a thin dress, and her father put his arm around her shoulders. They walked off like that, side by side, both tall and slim. Alka held herself erect, while her father was slightly stooped, and Athos dashed ahead of them. . . . He, too, was hurrying home for the pie. He ran so friskily you'd never guess that he was an old dog.

There was a bright light on in the neighbors' house. Through the curtainless window they could see the room and the dining table. Near the table was Valentina Ivanovna, with her glasses on, bent over her papers.

"Writing!" said Alka. "What a night! But just the same I don't understand. . . .

Across the river in the woods a night bird cried out. Someone, indistinct in the darkness, was drawing a bucket from the well, making the windlass creak.

Vasilii Panteleimonovich paused and dropped his arm from his daughter's shoulder.

"A bird flies. Stars shine. A tree grows. . .," he said, looking at the lighted window.

"What?" Alka was surprised.

"Oh, nothing. Don't bother your head about it."

From the potato field came the smell of warm, dry soil.

MANIA

LIUDMILA PETRUSHEVSKAIA

Translated by

HELENA GOSCILO

IT SHOULD BE SAID AT THE OUTSET THAT, UNATTRAC-tive as Mania was, she nevertheless had glorious ash-colored curls and the wonderful figure of a tall, even somewhat too tall, woman of the north.

However, glorious ash-colored curls aren't everything. They're not enough, not in the sense that you should have something else besides the curls. No, they're not enough insofar as natural curls in themselves are precisely the thing that's no good, that is hardest of all to do anything with, and with real curls, even when they're as big as Mania's, it's hard to do anything with your head, particularly since these curls simply didn't do anything for Mania's looks. Everyone knows that some curly-haired women choose to undergo a complicated procedure at the hairdresser's—having their hair pulled and straightened—but even for that, you have to know a special hairdresser, and in general you have to have something in mind, to somehow plan your appearance and for its sake follow a specific course so as to obtain the desired result.

And here we are forced to conclude that the natural beauty of Mania's hair in our day and age only prevented Mania from being on a par with others, at least as far as the beauty of her hairstyle was concerned, not to mention anything else. And in fact, nowadays Mania with her glorious ash curls couldn't do anything, however hard she tried, and she always went about any old way, with stiff curls over her forehead, when at all costs she needed to have at least a straight lock of hair over her forehead, and not a pile of curls.

As regards straightening her hair artificially, some people advised Mania to do it, and even gave her the name of a stylist, but Mania didn't do anything even after getting his name and address. And this happened, as we are forced to conclude, owing to the inertia of her nature, to a forgetfulness, a constant procrastination, and, to put it more simply, from an absence of immediate motivation to do something for some reason. Everyone around her saw that there was no reason for Mania to do all this, because Mania at her age of thirty plus didn't expect anything from life.

Yet even when it became essential to do something with herself—for Mania fell in love with a long-time coworker of hers—everything remained as before anyway, as if Mania had frozen still, had stood too long in one spot and couldn't move in a better direction even though that was essential. And you could bet your life that that wasn't a position of principle—of leaving everything as it was so that she, as she really was, would be wonderful for some one individual alone. No, everything was much simpler in Mania's case; she would have been happy to do something, but it was as if she got confused, and at the most critical moments, if she was indoors, she would simply not take off her fur cap, which looked a little strange. Yet Mania's cap suited her more than did her own hair, and everyone agreed about this and reconciled himself to it, and Mania spent almost the whole winter of her love in her cap.

Now, about this love: everything was absolutely clear to everyone from the very beginning, but nobody tried to warn Mania about anything, to point the obvious facts out to her, to open her eyes to what was really happening. No, everyone seemed to shun the topic, avoided speaking about it, and the only thing they sometimes permitted themselves was a discussion of Mania as a person. They said that she was a kind, hardworking girl, faithful and devoted to a fault. That basic trait of hers—fidelity—was mentioned most often in conversation. They said she was an utterly normal, healthy person—and that also had a large significance in this couple's relations, and later it will be clear why, when we speak of the other, opposite side, about the coworker with whom Mania was in love.

Moreover, they said about Mania that it was strange that such a nice girl was bypassed; that it was a generally acknowledged fact that Mania was really a very good person, a favorite in the department, that perhaps, on sober reflection, there really wasn't a better woman than she. It was enough to look at Mania during work, it was enough to spend just half an hour in that room to realize how almost tenderly her coworkers treated Mania. They even thought up a name for her themselves, though she was really called Marina, and following their example, everyone around started calling her Mania too, and it became a fashion that everyone shared and that united everyone in a single impulse of calling Marina Mania. It was, as it were, a kind, good, humane impulse, it was almost a password, and upon uttering it, a person seemed to enter an atmosphere of almost familial familiarity, of pet names and the like.

In short, no one said anything to Mania concerning her behavior; no one turned her attention, which was sad to begin with, to some glaring dismal facts. She was received affectionately wherever she appeared—whether in the room where her coworker Iura worked, or even in the corridor opposite his door where she and her girlfriend sometimes waited for him to come out to chat about something, to arrange something, as if there were no time outside of work, as if there were no evenings after work and no telephones on Mania's desk or Iura's. Nevertheless, they would see Mania in the corridor opposite his room, and Iura, who was always very busy, would come out to join her for a minute, and as was crystal clear to everyone, Mania was waiting in the corridor, and Iura would pop out for a minute to discuss some urgent matter on account of which Mania had come to see him!

As everyone could see, and there wasn't even anything to see here, it was enough simply to glance in passing at the two of them as, let's say, the two of them walked up the stairs together, not getting to work until eight-thirty, she with her pocketbook and wearing a cap, he with a briefcase, and how cheerful and loud his voice sounded, and how she would be silent and lower her head as they climbed up the stairs! There was no reason to think that they had arrived at work together, and there was absolutely no reason to think that they had come to work from the same place. And even if that were so, Mania's whole demeanor refuted that set of circumstances, so hopeless and at the same time timid was her demeanor.

No one ever accused her of simply spoiling everything with her funereal demeanor; no one said to her that precisely one's demeanor, one's behavior and pride, often decide the whole thing, that in any circumstances one should walk proudly and cheerfully, and the worse things are, the better one should look and dress, and comb one's hair. This didn't fit the incident with Mania, for in Mania's case everything was as naked and banal as it could be: Mania was utterly transparent, and everyone could see right through Iura, too. No one placed great hopes in Iura, and the only thing that could have moved things along was the fact that Iura passionately yearned to have a child from a healthy woman. Iura's former wife was a big woman who couldn't have any children and with whom Iura had suffered through many years before finally deciding on a divorce, and everyone knew of his yearning for a child, even if only because it was cited in the divorce papers as Iura's grounds for divorce.

Precisely because of this, her coworkers paid close attention to how

Mania felt, how she was eating, and how she looked. Once Mania artlessly said that she felt nauseated, she didn't know from what, she felt nauseated all the time. Moreover, Mania had kind of a distracted air about her, or perhaps she really felt bad and she was treated like someone sick. True, according to some sources, Mania couldn't have anything, nothing but food poisoning and stomach ailments of a similar sort. Mania herself at one time told a girlfriend of hers, of whose connection with Mania's coworkers through a network of acquaintances she, Mania, was ignorant, that Iura amazed her by the fact that he always talked very well with her, and that for him conversations were not a pretext for attaining something, not a means to something. Iura amazed her precisely by not demanding anything from her, by courting her prettily in the real sense of the word, without permitting himself anything at all, as if he were protecting her. It was a wonderful romance, Mania told her friend, even with roses in December, and so forth, and the girlfriend, completely unaware that she was doing so, passed all of this on through her network of friends to Mania's coworkers, and thus many of them reacted with distrust to Mania's admission that she felt nauseated.

Month after month went by, and nothing changed in Mania's situation. Mania continued to be timid in the same way, continued to wear her cap indoors in the same way, and felt abashed about her curls, while Iura in full view of everyone unfailingly continued to go out into the corridor for a minute in the same old way to have a chat with Mania, who'd come to him for a rendezvous—so ludicrous a thing in the context of the corridor.

You could say about the situation that Mania had completely lost her head, but then, everything was like that from the very beginning, and nothing had changed, that's what was strange. That was the strangest thing—that everything continued just as it had started, without intensifying or diminishing. Here, it's true, you had to know Iura's character. From the very beginning Iura had lent too concrete a character and too committed and elevated a level to his romance with Mania. Such things happened with him; he always harmlessly exaggerated everything a little bit from the start. In scandals at work, for example, he would start right away with a great outcry—that was his way. And then, in friendship, he always exaggerated somewhat at first, was ready to give up everything down to his last shirt, and only later, as you'd expect, he'd become bitterly disillusioned. That's why his long-standing friendships with those he met during his business trips were always so solid. On those infrequent occasions when they came downtown, his business-trip friends would immediately receive everything from Iura that he could possibly give them, such was his generous and hospitable nature.

And that's what happened in Mania's case, too: from the very beginning, what contributed to this was the fact that they found themselves on the same business trip, and on business trips Iura literally knew no restraint, he made a fantastic impression. His roses in December—that also, incidentally, was the consequence of a business trip.

All of Iura's boundless kindness descended at once on Mania, as did his insatiable desire to take care of and look after her, and Iura's amazing ability to speak. When he got carried way, Iura could speak for hours if nothing interfered. He was a tremendous storyteller, like a writer, and with ready-made plots, with unexpected twists, and such details as only a really, authentically talented person could notice and retain.

One didn't have long to wait for the end result. Almost the first day after they arrived, Iura took Mania home and introduced her to his folks, and they liked Mania. Mania, in fact, couldn't not be liked; there wasn't a person on earth who wouldn't like her. Then Iura introduced Mania to all his groups of friends, and they liked Mania, too. Iura literally never missed a chance to introduce Mania to yet someone else, and he would say almost sincerely that she was his fiancée. Among the married households they visited, the women sometimes congratulated him and wished him fine, healthy children, and he'd answer: "That's just around the corner, old girl." In short, at times it approached a wedding atmosphere, and just then Mania would walk around like a lost soul in her perennial fur cap, and this demeanor of Mania's could dishearten anyone.

So it all dragged on without ending in anything, and everyone had foreseen all this, precisely such a turn of events. The only thing they didn't know was how it would end, what would be the finale, and it ended quite ordinarily—Iura was transferred to another job, with a promotion, with a sizable promotion for such a young worker, and for the last time Mania came to his office door with her friend to say goodbye, and in front of everyone he held out his hand to her and then to her friend as he said goodbye, and invited them to visit him at his new place of work, and these goodbyes couldn't have been said more calmly, not as usually happens in those cases where women cry and men maintain a gloomy silence, and so on.

So everything ended absolutely the way everyone had foreseen it would, but everything ended so exactly that way, so precisely, without any deviations, and without anything at all peculiar, that everyone was left with the sense of an inconclusiveness, an expectation of something greater. However, nothing greater happened.

THE ROAD TO AKTANYSH

ANNA MASS

Translated by

MARY FLEMING ZIRIN

LIDA WAS AWAKENED BY A DISAGREEABLE FEELING OF nausea and chills. She wrapped herself tighter in a government flannel blanket that didn't give much warmth. Her dormitory mates—women from nearby geological parties—were still asleep.

"What's wrong with me?" thought Lida, wincing. "Was it the canned food?"

She stretched out in bed and breathed in and out deeply several times. As if that could help.

Today their detachment would leave for the work site—in the settlement of Aktanysh,[1] some three hundred kilometers from Tuimazy.[2] The seismological expedition in which Lida was the senior engineer had spent two weeks in Tuimazy regulating their instruments.

Lida put on her robe, threw a towel across her shoulder, and went to the shower installed in the most secluded nook of the base camp. A narrow little path led to it, on both sides of which dense dark-green nettles stretched upward and bent under their own height. The sun had risen, and the moist earth and the thickets of nettle emitted a warm, stupefying aroma.

After her shower, Lida went to the communal kitchen to make breakfast for her detachment. In Aktanysh they would find a woman to cook for them, but here Lida, with nothing better to do, had volunteered to do the cooking; so far she was the only woman in the detachment.

True, yesterday another one had arrived—the wife of Felix, the boss of the detachment. But Lida hadn't seen her yet. All she knew was that she was very young, just out of school. She was curious to see what the girl was like. . . .

Lida had known Felix for many years—they had studied at the same institute and for the last three years had worked in the same organization. She also knew Felix's first wife, Tamara: they had married before graduation and were divorced a few years later. Now Felix was thirty-two, just Lida's age.

Lida set a large pot of water on the gas stove, used a damp rag to wipe the badly worn oilcloth covering the long, crudely built table, set out bowls, and opened three cans of stew.

Once again a feeling of high spirits, energy, and physical health came over her—on expeditions she always experienced a sharp sensation of life. It was as if she plunged into a clear river, and all her nervous excitation (her "mastication," as her husband Anatolii called it) was washed off and carried away in the stream.

Last winter life had gone badly for her; she'd been irritable. Her relationship with her husband had deteriorated. On the surface, however, everything was going well: they'd gotten a two-room apartment and paid off their debts, and Lida began working for an advanced degree by correspondence. And yet all the same, all the same. . . .

An anguished thought came to her ever more often: What was it all for? For whom? She didn't confide in Anatolii, and he said nothing.

There had been a time, after all, when she'd felt sorry for her girl-friends from the institute who were forced to quit work to care for a baby! Why all that education? . . .

Then they had envied her. And now she was envious of them. Almost all of her friends had returned to their old professions, and they hadn't lost a thing; on the contrary, they had become a hundredfold richer in spirit, while she. . . . She could have a seven-year-old son or daughter. But she didn't. . . . And now she probably wouldn't. And Anatolii understood—that was why he had turned cool. . . .

She shook her head to drive out those unwelcome thoughts and went to the men's dormitory to rouse her helper, Uncle Vasia, the driver. The old man was a pensioner who had taken a job on the expedition for his own pleasure—as he put it, to work for the two months permitted by law and see the world. Every morning when she came into the room she found Uncle Vasia sitting on the bed reading a thick, filthy, worn book he'd been poring over for a long time, *Grim River*.[3] As if embarrassed, Uncle Vasia explained, "It's hard to put down. There's a very attractive woman in it, Anfisa. It's all about love. . . . Very frank!"

Again today Uncle Vasia looked at Lida over his glasses and said, "I've been reading since half-past four. They killed off my Anfisa, however. It's a pity."

"Time to go, Uncle Vasia," said Lida. "You pour the macaroni into the boiling water, and I'll rouse the boys."

The boys—students from the Geophysics Technical Institute, Boria, Nafis, and Timur, who had been hired as workers for the detachment—were already up and washing.

Kolia, the operator, was doing pull-ups on a homemade bar. The gravimetrist, Igor Sergeev, went out with a towel across his shoulder.

They were all already seated at the table when Felix appeared, permitting a pretty, plump girl in a short bright dress to enter before him. She was embarrassed and shifted from foot to foot as she saw the curious gazes fixed on her.

"Here she is," said Felix. "Meet Masha, Maria Ivanovna. I hope you'll take kindly to her."

He himself seemed embarrassed. Lida smiled involuntarily—it was so out of character for him. . . .

Hesitantly Masha sat down at the table beside Felix. She kept glancing at him as if trying to guess from his expression whether she was doing the right thing.

"A real baby," thought Lida with a trace of envy and said, "Hold the bowl."

"Perhaps I should help?" asked Masha and once again glanced timidly at Felix.

"Dig in," he answered with a slight wry smile. "You'll get your chance. . . ."

After breakfast they all scattered to pack. Lida stayed behind to wash the dishes and collect the cooking utensils. Tomorrow she would at last take up her real duties—a part of the expedition was already in Aktanysh and had undoubtedly found a place for their laboratory.

Masha came over to her. "May I wash the dishes?"

"Go ahead," agreed Lida and set to work with a twig broom. "Well, what's your first impression?"

"Oh, I don't know!" Masha dropped a bowl, blushed, and glanced at Lida in fright, and Lida thought again: "Good Lord, a real baby!"

"No, overall, so far I like it very much," Masha began again hurriedly. "You know, Felix picked such a marvelous bouquet for my arrival. Felix looks so stern, doesn't he? And actually—oh, he's so nice! It's really completely different when they meet you with flowers, isn't it?"

Lida nodded. She was the one who'd thought of the flowers. She'd dropped by the veranda where Felix was staying, seen the dirty floor and his scattered belongings, and said, "What are you doing? Your wife's coming, and you've got a real mess here. You could at least pick her a few posies."

"Listen, old lady," Felix answered, "I'm up to my ears with things to do. Perhaps you . . . could you take care of it? Pick the flowers and all that? . . . Not as an obligation, as a friend?"

She'd shrugged her shoulders, but she'd gone out in the fields anyway to pick flowers for Felix's wife. And there was really nothing special about that. He really didn't have time. But all the same, it was somehow . . . well, he could have asked her to clean up or wash the floor. But the flowers. . . .

"Have you known him long?" she asked.

"Two months already. Well, what of it?" Masha started speaking rapidly, as if to ward off objections. "That's not the important thing, after all, how long you know each other! Sometimes it's a long time, and then they get married—and it all goes wrong. But sometimes it's love at first sight, and it's for life. That's the way it is with Felix and me. But Mama and Papa don't believe it. They don't understand, they have such old-fashioned ideas. Papa got me a travel pass to Sochi, can you imagine? He thought he could tempt me with the sea. As if the sea were what I needed!"

"And where did you meet?" asked Lida.

"At the conservatory, at a Harry Brodberg concert. And have you known Felix long?"

"Yes. We were students together."

"A-ah!"

She undoubtedly wanted to ask more questions about Felix, but she was too shy, and Lida didn't volunteer anything. Once again, as she had that morning, she began to feel sick, probably from the smell of the kitchen. Hastily she gathered up the utensils and the cans of stew. She and Masha carried it all out to the truck, where the folded tents, cots, and rucksacks were already lying.

Masha went to collect her belongings, and Lida sat down on a folding chair that hadn't yet been tossed into the truck bed and lifted her face to the sun. Uncle Vasia was rummaging about in the engine.

"I don't like her!" he informed her from under the hood.

"Who?"

"That girl Masha."

"Why on earth not, Uncle Vasia? She's a pretty little thing."

"She's the feeble sort. You're prettier."

"Well, now!"

"It's true, it's true. You're full of life and sturdy. I life 'em that way. In fighting trim."

Lida burst out laughing and looked at Uncle Vasia gratefully. He was stout, slow-moving—an old hand on the buses. He'd driven bus number five, the one that Lida took to work every day. She'd probably seen the round nape of Uncle Vasia's neck more than once through the window of the cab and never imagined that they would have a chance to get to know each other and become friends.

It was after one o'clock when they left.

There were three vehicles in all. The supply truck went first, its high-sided bed piled to the top with baggage and boxes of equipment. Felix rode in the cab. After it came the seismic station driven by Uncle Vasia. Igor Sergeev and the operator, Kolia, were his passengers. The lifter, just back the day before from a complete overhaul, brought up the rear. The boys made themselves comfortable on sleeping bags in its enclosed bed. Lida and Masha sat with the driver in the spacious cab.

The lifter's driver was Valentin, a tall, solidly built lad in a soldier's tunic; he looked to be just back from the army. The tunic testified to it, but mostly it was his face—young, but with that expression of having been around, of maturity, which sets apart those who've done their service. He was married—on the fourth finger of his right hand shone a wedding ring which looked bleached and out of place on his strong, roughened, abraded hand. Just before they left, Valentin brought a thick board and put it under Lida and Masha's feet.

"Otherwise the floor gets awfully hot," he explained.

Felix's truck took off quickly and was lost from sight.

The lifter, roaring evenly and rolling softly over the ruts, followed the seismic station. It was stuffy in the cab. Hot air from the radiator scorched their feet.

The feeling of breadth—of horizon and thoughts—she'd experienced so often before made Lida happy. In the limited space of a room, a street, or a city, thoughts sometimes stumbled against the walls of urgent business, obligations, worries. But when there was a long road ahead and the earth and its life were flowing past before your eyes, thoughts were unbounded, they were like a sudden flood overtaking you—and you could splash around in it as much as you liked.

With half-closed eyes, Lida lingered in anticipation of the flood, calling to mind one image after another, rejecting, choosing the main channel along which her thoughts would flow.

And now she'd chosen the path, and her thoughts began pouring out, picking up speed, discarding on the bank everything disagreeable, everything she didn't want to think about, and leaving only what wouldn't disrupt her peaceful state.

This happened to her only on the road and only on expeditions. It was a feeling she'd had many times before, and still she looked forward to it every time.

This time, surrendering herself to the road, Lida thought about the fact that she wasn't eighteen any more like Mashenka, who sat beside her nodding drowsily, and that, to that same Mashenka's way of thinking, she was no longer young. But the sensation of youth was still very strong, and she thought that this was undoubtedly a general trait of character: as you got old, you felt younger.

Somewhere she had read the phrase: "Youth comes with the years." That might well be, but how could you explain it? Perhaps with the years the greed for life increases, because a person becomes aware of much that earlier he neither noticed nor valued. And he hastens to experience things experienced long ago because he's afraid that time is running out.

Mashenka hadn't yet learned that fear. She found it stuffy and jolting, and she squealed when a gadfly flew into the cab and began buzzing and beating against the windshield.

"Look at that lake!" exclaimed Masha. "But why is there black water in it?"

"That's not water," answered Lida. "It's oil. That's how they store it."

"Custodians like that should be prosecuted!" remarked Valentin. "There isn't enough storage, and this is what they come up with."

"What's wrong with it?" Masha didn't understand.

"The most valuable substances evaporate, that's what! And how much dust and dirt fall into it?"

The seismic station traveling ahead of them came to a sudden stop. Valentin braked and swung the door half-open. "What's wrong up there, Uncle Vasia?"

"The engine stalled, blast it!"

While Valentin and Uncle Vasia rummaged in the engine, Lida and Masha got out of the cab to stretch their legs. The boys also got out and lay down on the grass.

"Aren't you suffocated back there?" asked Lida.

"No, it's okay," answered Nafis. "We're lounging on the sleeping bags like kings. We have the window open."

At last the engine started up again.

"Get in, we're off," said Valentin, climbing back into the cab. "That's an old wreck, not a vehicle. The carburetor's gone bad. How on earth the old man's going to make it, I can't imagine."

Once again the road stretched before them. Gas torches shot scarlet tongues of fire high into the air.

"How lovely!" said Masha.

"Whenever I see that, it makes me furious," objected Lida.

"Why?"

"It's such a waste of valuable materials. Millions of cubic meters of gas burning up for no good reason."

"Why do they let them burn then?"

"To increase the oil pressure," explained Lida reluctantly. She thought that none of this mattered to Masha: she had come here to spend her honeymoon; she needed Felix, and that was all.

As if in answer to these thoughts, Masha said, "Everybody thinks I came here because of my husband. But that's not the only reason. I'm going to work, after all. And then—how else would I get to see all this? It is worth looking at, isn't it?"

"Of course it is," agreed Lida and thought about Masha: "She's a good kid after all!"

She tried to remember what she'd been like at eighteen.

Suddenly it seemed to her that she'd forgotten. Not the events—those she remembered well enough—but the inner feelings, the thoughts, the spiritual life of those years.

But then she remembered—and she was astonished. She'd been hardly more than a child. It was all games, droll crushes. She would hardly have been capable of making an independent decision. On two months' acquaintance, to announce like that to her parents, "I'm getting married," and leave the warm nest? No, she surely couldn't have decided on that when she was eighteen.

. . . Uncle Vasia's engine kept stalling from time to time, and Valentin would drive right up to the seismic station and push it gently with the radiator of his vehicle. The engine would start up and run for a while, then stall again. Both vehicles were barely crawling; the cab was full of dust, and that was undoubtedly why Lida began feeling sick again.

"Carsick?" asked Valentin, glancing at her ashen face. "It's about five more kilometers to the settlement of Bakaly. We'll rest there and have dinner."

"No, stop now," she begged him.

Felix was waiting for them outside the dining hall in Bakaly.

"What took you so long?" he asked, displeased. "We've been standing here for an hour already."

"Standing!" answered Valentin irritably. "Couldn't you come back to meet us? If it took us a long time, it's because something went wrong. You're the boss of the detachment, you should keep in touch. And you ran off ahead! 'We've been standing here for an hour!' Would you have stood around until nightfall?"

Masha jumped in front of her husband as if to protect him from the driver's attack: "Well, what of it? What does it have to do with Felix? How could he know?"

Valentin burst out laughing. Felix smiled, too, and hugged Masha's shoulders. "My defender! How are you, little one? Tired?"

Valentin muttered, "Damned if I'll follow Grandpa again. Am I a nurse or something? You'll have to tow him, that's all there is to it."

"Put yourself in my place!" retorted Uncle Vasia. "That wreck belongs in the dump, and you put a man in it!"

Lida went up to the counter. She wasn't hungry—her head was aching off and on, and she felt a bit chilled. She took two glasses of warm stewed fruit and sat down at an empty table. Felix and Masha were eating goulash at the next table.

"Do you want some stewed fruit, Mashenka?" asked Felix tenderly. "What would you like? Maybe I could buy you some tomato juice?"

Masha, worn out from the trip, could barely manage to swallow. The boys, stuffing themselves heartily, kept looking furtively at the newlyweds and laughing.

After dinner, Kolia the operator came over to Felix.

"Are we going to wait for Zinaida Pavlovna, or should we go on?"

Felix coughed and glanced at Masha. "She isn't here on time—why should we wait for her? Let her take the bus."

"I could drive over and get her. I know where she lives."

But Zinaida Pavlovna, with a little suitcase in her hand, was already hurrying to meet them. She was a pretty woman, thirty-five years old. She lived with her mother and daughter here in Bakaly and hired on during the summers as photo technician for the detachment. Everybody loved her for her rare kindness. She was like a nurse or sister to them all.

Lida glanced curiously at Felix. He caught her gaze and frowned.

Zinaida Pavlovna, flushed from running, her chestnut hair with its clearly visible streaks of grey caught in a disheveled knot, smiled joyfully as she came to a stop in front of the boss of the detachment. "Hello, Felix! You've lost some weight since last year."

"Hello, Zinaida Palna," Felix answered drily without looking at the woman. "Let's go, into the vehicles right away. You've delayed us as it is."

The smile gradually slipped from her face. She glanced at Masha, who was standing beside Felix, and then back at Felix again.

"Felix Petrovich, I was here once already waiting for you," she began again in a new, somewhat guilty tone. "I thought you must have changed the departure day. And then the neighbors' boy came running and said you'd arrived. Well, I came as fast as I could. . . . Felix Petrovich, who's this—your wife?" she asked suddenly with a kind smile.

"My wife. But you'll get acquainted later, there's no time now. . . . Everybody to the vehicles!" he shouted and got into the supply truck, and once again his vehicle tore out in front and disappeared around a curve.

Valentin sped up to try to pass the seismic station, but there wasn't room: Uncle Vasia was stuck between the logs of a shaky wooden bridge. Valentin had to back up, pulling the truck free with the towline.

"Oh, I'm so tired," complained Masha. "If only I could lie down for a while."

"Change places with one of the boys," suggested Lida. They walked around the vehicle and knocked to get the boys' attention. They opened the door.

"How cozy you are here!" said Masha.

"Come join us," suggested Nafis cordially. "Here's the most comfortable spot."

Masha lay down on the sleeping bags and put her palms under her cheek like a child. "Pure bliss!" she muttered and closed her eyes.

Boris and Nafis settled down beside her on boxes. Timur moved to the cab.

The seismic station was barely crawling, and Valentin was forced to crawl along behind it. Their throats were raw with dust.

Thoughts like dreams once again clustered around Lida. Perhaps they were dreams, though. She suddenly felt irresistibly drowsy. Her eyes closed by themselves. She leaned back in the seat. For a minute longer she felt the vehicle jolting, Timur's sharp shoulder, and Valentin's strong, warm one. Then everything vanished.

It seemed to her that she barely slept at all, but when she opened her eyes there was darkness beyond the windshield. The vehicle was standing with its headlights pointing at the bed of the seismic station.

She jumped down off the high running board and went over to the group of people crowded around the seismic station. "What's wrong?"

"I'm out of gas," answered Uncle Vasia gloomily.

The canister of gasoline was on the supply truck, and the supply truck was undoubtedly long since in Aktanysh.

"Why did he have to rush off ahead?" snarled Kolia. "We're traveling as a detachment, after all—that means we should stick together."

"Do we have a bucket and hose?" asked Valentin. "We can siphon some gas from my tank. I've got plenty."

But both the bucket and hose were on Felix's supply truck.

"I'd take bosses like that . . . " began Uncle Vasia.

"Easy, now, you mustn't." Igor Sergeev stopped the old man by nodding his head toward Masha, who was standing nearby, withdrawn in her shame and chagrin. She was nearly in tears, and Lida thought that now she hated them all for daring to abuse her splendid, extraordinary Felix, who was better than any of them.

Fortunately, there was a village not far away. They were able to get a bucket but not a hose, so pumping out the gasoline took a long time.

Lida and Zinaida Pavlovna strolled back and forth along the road. There was no way they could help anyway. Masha cuddled up on the sleeping bags again.

"How ashamed I am!" Zinaida Pavlovna broke out. "Why on earth did I go up to him? And then I asked him about his wife. . . . "

"He's the one who should be ashamed," answered Lida. "He talked to you like a real boor."

"No, Felix isn't really a boor," objected Zinaida Pavlovna sadly. "I understand, you know. . . . Here I am getting close to forty. . . . And he never promised me a thing, he never swore undying love. . . . "

"Let's go sit in the truck," suggested Lida. "I've been feeling bad all day, and I'm drowsy."

Zinaida Pavlovna glanced at her with interest. "And I was just about to ask. I thought of it as soon as I saw you. Do I have a sharp eye, or don't I? How long is it now?"

"How long—what?" Lida didn't understand.

"You know, the month—how far along are you? Me, I remember feeling sick right up to the fourth month—I couldn't eat a thing. And was I ever sleepy!"

Lida stopped. She suddenly felt hot.

"Zina!" was all she managed to say.

And she had always thought of herself as restrained! She began crying and laughing at the same time; she hugged Zinaida Pavlovna and kissed her.

Of course! Why on earth hadn't she guessed before? She should have guessed long ago! She simply didn't believe that it would ever happen.

"Dear Lord, is it possible?"

"What, didn't you know?"

"Oh, Zina!" repeated Lida through her tears.

Joy rose from the depths of her being—a joy still timorous, still distrustful, but already so strong that it seemed to fill every corner of her soul.

What a fool she was! All her life she had aimed at something that she thought was happiness, and she had thrust aside the most important thing. What was it anyway, that happiness? Making wishes come true? But whatever you accomplished, you couldn't be content until you fulfilled the most important law. The law of continuation of the species. The law of life.

"Can it really be happening?" she thought.

"Should I send a telegram to Tolia? No, it's early yet. I'll write him. How happy he'll be! Tolechka, dear one, oh, how he would have hugged me tight, kissed me, whirled me around the room! Never mind, it's all to come.

"I'll change jobs. That's enough traveling. I'll bring Mama from Lvov. Mama! How delighted she'll be!"

The dreams she had held in check for so many years broke free at last; she couldn't have restrained them even if she'd wanted to. In her thoughts she picked up and hugged close the tiny body of her own dear child.

It was completely dark by the time the vehicles drove into the village. Zinaida Pavlovna stayed in the village; she had a sister living there. The vehicles rolled down the wide, dusty street past sturdy houses with windows already darkened and stopped beyond the outskirts in a large clearing.

White tents stood in two rows. To the right a hill loomed; to the left a river glinted. A full moon illuminated the camp. Mosquitoes whined.

"You can sleep in the library tonight," said Felix. "I've put your belongings in there already. Tomorrow we'll figure out living arrangements."

"And you?" asked Masha.

"I have things to discuss with the boss of the expedition. Do you want to wash up?"

"Yes."

"Let's go."

He led Masha away. Lida went down to the river. The water was warm. She thought of taking a quick dip to wash off the dust of the road, but she couldn't quite bring herself to do it. She washed her face and hands and returned to the tents. After the roar of the engines, the silence seemed particularly profound. Even the whine of the mosquitoes acted to intensify rather than disturb it.

Lida went into a spacious tent furnished with tables and stools. Room had been made in the corner for several folding cots and sleeping bags. "Which is mine?" thought Lida. "Oh, who cares? Tomorrow we'll sort them out."

She climbed into a sleeping bag and stretched out blissfully. Silence and tranquility were all around her, and within her as well. She closed her eyes—and the derricks, the fields, the pumping installations, the faces of her companions, Valentin's hand with the wedding ring on his finger at once swam up. . . .

There was a rustling at the tent door. Masha came in and began spreading a sleeping bag out on the cot. She was sobbing and sniffing.

"What's wrong?" Lida asked.

Masha didn't answer.

"What's wrong, Mashenka?"

"Felix said . . . he's going to buy me a ticket. . . . And tomorrow he's sending me home! He said . . . that I was behaving like . . . " Masha burst into loud sobs.

"I can't understand a thing. Calm down and tell me clearly what's happened."

"Because . . . I went and joined the boys! And the others might think . . . "

Lida burst out laughing. "What might they think? What's wrong with him?"

"As if it were easy for me, riding all day," wept Masha. "You're all used to it, but I got tired! How can he not trust me? And I thought that he. . . . But he! . . . "

Lida got out of the sleeping bag and sat down beside Masha, hugging her trembling shoulders. How could she soothe this little girl, in whose soul that very minute, before Lida's eyes, the image of a courageous, extraordinary hero, a fusion of all the most romantic images from books and movies, was dying.

But he was an ordinary man, not someone out of a book. Not particularly bad and not particularly good. He was no hero. But let Masha understand that later, gradually, not now.

"It seemed to you!" Lida began to speak warmly. "Well, what on earth have you dreamed up, little fool? Felix—he's a pretty special fellow, after all. Don't you know how they all respect him? Felix! You can lean on him like a stone wall. So what's all this you've made up? You've just had a misunderstanding."

"Do you think so?" Masha uttered uncertainly. She was still sobbing. "Yes-s! Oh, but what if he really does send me away tomorrow. . . . "

"He's not going to send you anywhere! He was just joking! You're at the very, very beginning now, and there's so much ahead. . . . Everything's going to be just fine; you calm down and go to bed. Tomorrow it will all be settled."

"No, I'll go see him!" Masha said in agitation. "If he's the man you say he is, he'll have to understand!"

They heard footsteps outside, and Felix's voice called guiltily: "Maria Ivanovna!"

She started joyfully, got up, and left the tent.

Lida listened to their steps fading away, smiled, and went back to bed.

"And there's a lot ahead for me, too," she thought as she fell asleep. "But I'm luckier than that little girl, because I also have a lot behind me. . . . "

Even in sleep she was surprised by the strange, illogical thought. But that was exactly the way she felt.

The mosquitoes were droning, and to Lida their sound was like beautiful, exultant music.

BETWEEN HEAVEN AND EARTH

VIKTORIA TOKAREVA

Translated by

HELENA GOSCILO

NATASHA SAT AT THE AIRPORT WAITING FOR HER flight to be announced. The plane kept being delayed, at first for three hours, then four. A Bulgarian circus was going on tour to Baku on the same flight. The circus performers freely made themselves comfortable, like gypsies—on the floor and in armchairs. Some Bolognese toy dogs, freshly washed and groomed, all the same age and size, ran around them. Their show probably included a vaudeville dog act.

A tall man walked past Natasha; something about him distantly resembled her first husband. She had a lot of time on her hands, her head was vacant, and to while away the time, Natasha recalled her first marriage. Otherwise she wouldn't have thought about it.

They got married when she was eighteen and he twenty. And they parted immediately. Well, not quite immediately. They did manage to live together about eight months. Their marriage was shaky. As soon as their passion subsided, their river became shallow, the bottom was exposed, and on the bottom was all kinds of garbage and worthless junk. They started abusing each other, constantly and for no reason. That was because their love was ailing; it coughed up incompatibilities and finally died. But for a long time after they separated, they continued to meet and abuse each other. They couldn't live together and they couldn't live apart. The subject of their arguments was more or less as follows: Natasha considered her husband a fool, incapable of acting in a way commensurate with her beauty. She thought that beauty in and of itself ought to give one additional benefits in life, like, say, a free ticket to a New Year's party. But her husband said that beauty was temporary and fleeting. In about twenty years it inevitably would leave with a wave of the hand. But his capacity for steadfast feeling, called "fidelity," was forever: It didn't lose value with time. So he was a husband for future maturity. He didn't quite suit her right now, but then, later, he'd be just right. But at eighteen it's impossible to think about later. Life seems excessively long; it looks as if there'll still be plenty of everything, as if everything lies ahead. . . .

They divorced and met again twenty years later. He had remarried and had a daughter, whom he'd named after her. He lived in a different town. Natasha happened to be in town on official business. She knew that her ex-husband lived there somewhere. She dialed 09 and gave his surname, and they gave her the number. Natasha dialed the number and heard her first husband of twenty years ago. His voice hadn't changed. The voice is the soul's instrument, and the soul doesn't age. They talked with each other in their former young voices.

"Hello," said Natasha. "Just don't be surprised."

"Who is this?" he became guarded.

"This is your wife number one."

There followed such a long pause that Natasha thought: "We've been disconnected."

"Hello!" she called.

"I'm coming over right now," said her ex-husband. "Where?"

She named the hotel and gave her room number.

After hanging up, she became nervous. She couldn't understand why she'd called, why she'd summoned him.

She put on a white French top. Then she changed her mind and switched it for a black one—it suited her figure more, but her face less. She had to choose between her face and her figure.

The knock on the door came sooner than she'd expected. She opened it and saw him. In twenty years he had broadened slightly, but the expression on his face and his entire being remained as before. That being gazed openly out of the windows of his large hazel-green eyes.

"You've changed . . . ," he said and nodded several times, as if to confirm that he'd been right: her beauty had passed, like a station, and in those same twenty years about which he'd warned her honestly.

"And you're just the same," replied Natasha, transparently hinting that he was still the same fool he'd always been.

Natasha really had changed in twenty years. If one were to compare her beauty to nature, then previously it had resembled a meadow, but it had become like a field. But who knows what's better: a meadow or a field.

Something else was amazing: they began to argue, taking up where they'd left off twenty years ago. As if those twenty years hadn't existed and they'd parted only yesterday with the same grudges.

Later they went downstairs for dinner at the restaurant. They drank some wine. He started telling her how long and tormenting his sufferings had been over his breakup with her. He'd got married because he was afraid of becoming a drunkard.

"But you got over it," Natasha soothed him, moving away from the unpleasant topic and letting it be understood that all the negative elements were behind him. In the past.

"But I did have a hard time of it." He emphasized his "hard time," insisting that a long segment of his life had been devoted to suffering.

"To suffer is useful." Natasha seemed to be justifying herself. "Suffering forms the soul."

"Nonsense," he disagreed. "I don't remember who it was that said, 'Happiness—now, that's a university.' Suffering dries up the soul. And nothing worthwhile grows from the drought. All kinds of weeds like malice."

He really did prove capable of steadfast feeling. At first he had loved her. Then he had hated her. Now he wouldn't forgive her. That meant that she was always with him.

They drank some more. Natasha told him about her dissertation. She was studying the hereditary mechanism of the little drosophila fly. Drosophila are the ones that love fruit. And little drosophila flies that fly around fruit resemble dust more than they do living organisms. She interbred them, studied them, and came to serious conclusions concerning mankind.

He told her how after passing his medical exams he'd begun specializing in denture work. He had marvelous foreign porcelain materials, and the demand for his work exceeded his physical capabilities. Beneath all this was the implication that he had money to burn and that Natasha had been in too much of a hurry then, twenty years ago. Now he would have been just right for her.

"Are you married?"

"Yes," lied Natasha. She was married, but not exactly.

"And are you unfaithful to your husband?"

This was a fundamental question. Fidelity was his major requirement of a woman, and if Natasha met that requirement it meant that his loss was irreplaceable.

"You should be ashamed of yourself!" said Natasha in surprise.

"So is it yes or no?"

"Never!"

He got upset and wilted. What had settled and calmed down in him since they'd divorced floated up anew from the bottom of his soul, as happens when you stir a pond with a stick—and slime and dirt rise to the top.

Then they parted. And that was for another twenty years. The town in which he lived and worked was small, business trips there came by chance, and that, moreover, was not the point. The point was the mutual uselessness of it.

Natasha thought that after divorcing her husband she would remarry quickly. All she had to do was go outside and shout: "I want to get married!" And immediately crowds would congregate and form a long line. But she was naive in her self-confidence. Everyone's busy searching for happiness, but few find it. At most dozens . . . or even hundreds. But what's a hundred out of all humanity? . . . With time, however, Natasha succeeded in falling into that hundred and even dozen, when she fell in love with Kitaev, a biochemistry professor and author of fourteen brilliant discoveries and hypotheses about the age of the Earth. His head seemed to contain not brains but some superpowerful electric power station that generated ideas, charging the people around him with them. He would give away his ideas left and right; he was generous, like every prodigy, like a speckled hen that lays golden eggs and doesn't grudge any of them. She knows the next one will be golden, too.

In appearance Kitaev was somewhat bald, somewhat sallow and dry; he looked like an old woman. Natasha didn't notice that. She'd already had a looker. She saw Kitaev in her own special way, and beside him all other men appeared pale and unintelligible, like the tenth copy of an original.

For a long time Kitaev couldn't believe that Natasha loved him. Then he came to believe it, and after many years he grew used to her, as to a wife, though Natasha wasn't his wife. Another was his wife. But this other didn't interfere with anything, and Natasha made no demands, and it became possible not to change anything. Constant change swirled in Kitaev's golden brain, but he was indifferent to external changes.

Sometimes Natasha thought that he'd propose the next day, precisely the next and not the day after—so profound was their *growth* into each other. But sometimes she thought that it would never happen. She could have stopped predicting and asked directly, but questions and words have a certain concreteness. And love, like music, should be beyond words. At any rate, beyond questions.

That morning, when Kitaev called her from Baku, where he was attending a symposium of Asian and African countries, and summoned Natasha to join him for a couple of days, she didn't ask why. It was clear without words. He missed her. He couldn't survive the remaining days without her. But out of those two days, nine hours had already been stolen. She was sitting at the Moscow airport, he at the one in Baku—forced into idleness and waiting, and surely regretting that he'd initiated the whole hasty operation.

A metallic voice above the waiting room announced the boarding of Natasha's flight. The circus performers stirred, and the dogs simultaneously began barking, as if they'd understood and were rejoicing.

Natasha fastened her seat belt. She felt nauseated from fear and the takeoff.

The airplane kept lurching and then settling somewhere below, and each time it settled, her heart would leap into her throat in anticipation of the end. She feared not so much the end itself as the route to it. And the route promised to be a long one, thirty seconds, and what was most unpleasant, a conscious one. Natasha had a distant relative, Valik, who'd been buried in a mine. Forty tons of rock fell on him, and it took a lot of trucks to dig him out. When they dug him out, he had white brows, though he was a young man. That meant that for a time, perhaps about thirty seconds, and maybe even sixty, he went on living, understanding what had happened to him. His wife, Nadka, fell on his coffin in a sincere frenzy of despair, like the great Italian actress Anna Magnani.[1] In those southern regions funerals are performances of a sort, a catharsis, a purification, when your screams expel all your despair, your disagreement with fate. And the people around you, infected by someone else's disagreement, also cry and expel their own, so as to ease their soul and live on. Nadka kept falling on the coffin, and people kept dragging her away. A photographer captured these moments. Yet a mere week later, some Petko was already spending the night at Nadka's. It turns out that he had been around even while Nadka's husband was alive, and they had barely managed to wait out just that one week. The neighbors were displeased, and the phrase "still warm in the ground," referring to Valik, made the rounds. But above all it was Nadka's mother, Valik's mother-in-law, who suffered on account of Nadka's betrayal. She would come to their house and ask Nadka's teenage daughter: "Did he spend the night here?" "Uh-huh," the girl would reply sullenly. "In bed?" Nadka's mother would ask fearfully. "Where else?" The girl would be surprised. "Under it, ya think?" Nadka's mother would start to cry, wringing her hands: "But he *has* been . . . he *has*. . . . And she's acting like he never has. . . . " Nadka was behaving as if Valik had never existed. And yet he had . . . he had. . . . And that instant forgetting frightened Nadka's mother more than anything. It was as if Valik had been buried under rock twice. Once alive, and the other time dead. . . .

Natasha feared the same thing. She knew that live people think about the living. And if right now she were to crash with the plane, then Kitaev, without forgetting her, but sliding her into a rear drawer of his memory, would gaze into other eyes. Forgetting is yet another, additional death.

The plane climbed higher. Natasha moved her seat back and closed her eyes. The plane no longer soared upward. Her heart didn't leap into her throat. She decided to see what was happening below and around her.

Everyone around her was sleeping, and the large number of sleeping men recalled the painting *The Field after Battle.*[2]

Beside her sat a young man who looked like a basketball player; he was a head and a half taller than Natasha, who herself was fairly tall. She glanced out of the window and saw cosmic blackness and a fire emanating from under the wing of the plane.

Her brain became totally numb, and in that numbness only one word sounded—"unpleasant," as if it had been recorded on tape and set in her empty head. It was as if some bystander within her were saying dispassionately, "unpleasant." Not a word was said in her brain about Kitaev. But her body reacted according to its own laws, independently of her head. She seized the arm of the basketball player sitting beside her in such a way that her fingers met on his arm.

"Ouch!" said the Basketball Player. He'd found both the pain and the very touch unexpected.

"We're on fire," said Natasha, with relative calm in light of her information.

The Basketball Player leaned forward toward the window and looked outside attentively.

"That's the signaling system," he said. "Wing markings."

"What are they for?" Natasha didn't believe him.

"So that another plane won't collide with us."

Natasha pressed herself to the window again. Indeed, the lights flared at regular intervals, as if they were pulsating. A fire, by contrast, is more elemental in appearance and nature.

A stewardess went through the cabin—in a businesslike and dispassionate way. That's not how people behave during a catastrophe.

The lights in the plane were extinguished. Apparently the passengers were being invited to sleep. Natasha closed her eyes. The Basketball Player also moved his seat back, and their heads ended up side by side. It was as if they were lying in the same bed. He emanated warmth, sent it out like a stove. She wanted not to move away, but to draw closer so that it wouldn't be so lonely and frightening between heaven and earth. He moved his elbow toward her—just the slightest bit, half a centimeter. But she felt that half-centimeter. And she didn't withdraw her arm. Energy flowed from his elbow like the current in a magnetic field. That energy enveloped Natasha, and they flew together in the same cloud. It was dark and still, but she heard his heart beating in his chest, like a hammer in the stillness. He lowered his face into her hair. Now their hearts beat together, and it wasn't at all frightening to fall. Just so it would be to-gether.

"Are you from Baku?" asked Natasha.

She had to interact with him somehow. It was awkward to remain strangers in this situation.

"Yes, Baku."

"But you're Russian. . . . "

"Russians live there, too."

"What business do they have there?"

"It's a fine city. . . . "

"What were you doing in Moscow?"

"I was at a training camp."

"You're an athlete?"

"Yes, I am. . . . "

They spoke in whispers because passion obstructed their throats. And they spoke only to somehow distance themselves and pull back from their irresistible attraction. It was precisely that—irresistible; to resist it was impossible.

The Basketball Player leaned down and kissed Natasha. His lips were careful and as soft as a horse's.

Her heart leaped to her throat—as if the plane had hit an air pocket.

Natasha had never experienced anything like it in her life. Other serious fulfillments, which in adult language are called love, had nothing to do with this condition. Like words and classical music. Like a text and Rachmaninov's Second Concerto.

"Do you have anyone?" he asked.

"A fiancé. I'm flying to join him."

"Yes. . . . You're still young. . . . "

In the darkness he hadn't made out how old she was.

"And do you have a girl?"

"A fiancée. Snezhana. I treat her divinely."

"She's Bulgarian?"

"Yes, she is. I treat her divinely. But what I feel for you I've never felt for anyone; I never even knew that it could be like this."

"And what do you feel?"

"I don't know. It's like sunstroke."

Natasha drew aside and glanced at him. She hadn't even seen him yet: a young face with tightly drawn skin and troubled eyes. She felt that seeing him wasn't enough, and she stretched out her hand to his face and ran her fingers over it like a blind woman trying to remember features through sensations. He wasn't startled. Everything that was happening between them seemed natural, and even the only thing possible. As if it weren't the airplane flickering its lights in the night, but their souls sending signals to each other.

"What's your life like?" asked Natasha.

"Torturous. I'm in torment."

"What are you tormented by?"

"I want to resurrect my mother. Is it possible to resurrect a person from the dead?"

"No. It's impossible."

"And how do you know?"

"I'm a biologist. I know that for sure. It's the one thing that's impossible to achieve. Everything else is possible."

"But they resurrect ancient horses, after all. Tarpans. They inbred them, matched, and resurrected them. And now there's a whole herd of tarpans roaming about in Ascania Nuova."

"They resurrected the biological form. But you can't resurrect the specific individual. A personality is inimitable."

"But, you know, some people believe it will be possible to resurrect ancestors through descendants. To resurrect the individual personality."

"Nature is interested in the succession of generations. People are born, grow old, and die to make room for the young. The wheel of life can't be turned in the opposite direction."

"But Mother didn't grow old. She died young. She didn't live out her life."

"You have to reconcile yourself to that."

"I can't reconcile myself to it. I can't live without her. I even wanted to follow her. . . . You think I'm crazy?"

"No. I don't."

His desire to resurrect his mother didn't surprise Natasha. Rather, it surprised her, but she understood what prompted it. His motivating force. Nadka had parted with her husband Valik before he was killed, and the fact that he perished had changed nothing. Whereas the Basketball Player hadn't parted with his mother even after her death; on the contrary, he'd merged with her into one, and he perceived the forced separation as unnatural. Rather, he didn't perceive it at all. He sought a way out, either to join his mother or to get her back. He had settled on the latter.

"We had nobody else in the world: I had only her, and she—me. Father abandoned us when I was a month old and she was nineteen. I don't even know if he ever existed. I never saw him. We weren't just poor—we were destitute. Sometimes we had only a bowl of watery soup a day. And once I stayed home all winter because I didn't have warm shoes. . . . "

Natasha lay back on her reclining seat with her face toward him, inhaling his voice and words.

He told her how his mother had graduated from a theatrical institute, but not a single theater had been interested in her. She must have been a very weak actress. She earned money illustrating lectures given by the "Knowledge" society. A lecturer would speak on Maksim Gorky's works, and she would come out in a floor-length dress with a long gauze scarf and recite "The Stormy Petrel," depicting with her scarf the storm and the sea in turn. His mother probably could have come out in a normal outfit—a skirt and top. But she was an actress to her very core. She had a need for theatrical performance and self-expression. But her need did not coincide with reality. Her talent was minor, and she didn't want to believe that. It's a rare person who, infected by the microbe of creativity, can say to himself, "I'm not talented." A special mind and special courage are needed for that. And then she fell ill and died. In a hospital. It happened a year ago. He, her son, stayed with her continually, day and night. His pockets were stuffed with crumpled ruble notes to slip the nurses, but he did everything himself. Once the doctor treating his mother said: "Hold on, it won't be much longer, about two or three days. . . . " And the Basketball Player looked at him without understanding what he was talking about. . . . He was ready to live the rest of his life like that: without food, without sleep, without even a moment's rest, if only his mother would go on breathing and blinking. But one day he went out onto the stairway in the morning to have a smoke, and when he returned, at first he couldn't understand a thing. His mother was there, but she was no more. She'd gone off somewhere, leaving her body, as people abandon their homes in the country.

There was another woman in the ward, his mother's neighbor. She pointed a shaking finger and said in a whisper, "She's dead. . . . " "Yes, . . . " he responded also in a whisper. "Tell them so they'll take her away." "I can't do that. I'm not allowed to touch her." "Why?" "Those are the rules." He was hoping that she could still be brought back, recalled from wherever she'd just gone. "But I can't stand it. I'll go crazy." "There's no way I can help you." "But call someone." "I'll call. But it won't do any good." The woman spoke calmly in a whisper, and he also replied in a whisper and tried, or so he thought, to make her understand. But it was a conversation, conducted logically and in a whisper, between two people who had lost their minds from shock.

Then he went to the doctor, first to the one who had treated his mother, then to the department head, and implored them to resurrect her, and kept apologizing all the time for bothering them. They gave him an injection and sent him home. At home he slit his wrists.

"And Snezhana?" asked Natasha.

"She wasn't important. I didn't even think of her."

They fell silent.

"Do you[3] think I'm not in my right mind?" asked the Basketball Player again.

"No. I don't. You're simply young and can't tolerate grief. You haven't yet learned to endure."

"Perhaps that's so. But Mother shouldn't have died. It's not right. She lived little and badly. She knew only humiliation both as an actress and as a woman. And what's her compensation? Death?"

"Everybody reaps what he sows. That's cruel, but it's a fact."

"She sowed gentleness and naïveté. . . . "

"That means she sowed them in the wrong cornfield."

"What?" the Basketball Player didn't understand, and he brought his face, tense with incomprehension, closer.

"She chose the wrong profession. She had the wrong man's child."

"The wrong man. But the right child! I loved and love her more than anyone."

"That's fate. . . . "

"No!" he cried in a whisper. "That's not right."

He clenched his fist, pressed it against his teeth, and began to shake with sobs.

Natasha had never seen a man cry. True, her first husband had cried several times when he was drunk, but those were tears of a different kind.

Natasha removed his fist from his teeth, opened his fingers, and lowered her face into his hand. She wanted him to feel that she was there beside him, and she wanted them to hold onto each other between heaven and earth.

"Marry Snezhana," said Natasha. "Have a daughter. Give her your mother's name. What was her name?"

"Aleksandra."

"There. Call her Aleksandra. That's a wonderful name. It can be shortened to anything you want: Alia, Sandra, Shura, Sasha. . . . She'll look like you because daughters look like their fathers. And boys, like their mothers. Through you Sandra will look like your mother, and you'll resurrect her . . . "

"And what's your name?"

"Natasha."

"The plane is preparing to land," announced the stewardess in conventionally feminine tones. "Return your seats to their original position and fasten your seat belts."

The lights went on. The passengers stirred, fastening their seat belts. Natasha glanced at the Basketball Player, thus giving him the opportunity to have a good look at her in the bright light. But he didn't see the age difference between them. The sunstroke seemed to have effected lasting changes in his brain.

"Will we see each other?" he asked.

"No," said Natasha. "That's impossible. I'm with someone."

"So what? Perhaps you'll find some time?"

"Perhaps I will. But what for?"

He made no reply. What can one say to that?

The airplane descended, its belly wailing. It landed bumpily, just as it had taken off. A nauseating unsteadiness oscillated beneath its wings. Apparently the plane's captain was not a natural-born pilot, but had simply been taught to fly.

The airport was separated from the city by an iron fence.

Kitaev stood on the other side of the fence; tense, he was staring intently at the door through which Natasha was supposed to appear, and at that moment he resembled some noble, rapacious beast.

Natasha didn't go through the door, but stopped beside the iron bars of the fence, looking at Kitaev from the sidelines both literally and figuratively. Then she called softly:

"Kitaev. . . . "

He turned quickly, walked up to the fence, and, thrusting his arms through the bars, embraced her and gave her a forceful and agitated kiss. His lips were thin and hard. The kiss didn't reach her heart, but stayed on her lips.

While they waited for the luggage, Kitaev complained about the delay in her flight. The night had been wasted, and it had dragged an incomplete day in its wake. She could have said: "What's that got to do with me? You shouldn't have asked me to come." But Natasha kept quiet, her demeanor guilty. Kitaev didn't know what she was guilty of. But she knew: she hadn't thought of him at the moment of deadly danger, and she'd spent the night with another. A double betrayal.

The luggage arrived. A wide belt revolved slowly around the circle. Suitcases, portmanteaus, and bags spilled out onto it from the darkness, as if from outer space. Those who had recently been passengers, but now were simply people who'd not had enough sleep, stood around it and with a bewitched gaze followed the belt the way one gazes at Santa Claus's hands, although they couldn't get anything besides their own suitcases.

At that moment Natasha saw the Basketball Player. On the ground he had an air of great plausibility about him: straight, tall, with a beautiful head on a strong neck. Animated cartoonists draw such necks on Ivan the Tsarevich and Ivan the Fool. He was staring with frank bewilderment at Kitaev and couldn't understand: Why was Natasha leaving him for this dried-up fellow approaching old age? Why wasn't it possible to get some water of life and resurrect people from the dead? Why couldn't he win his princess away from Koshchei the Deathless? . . . His navy sportsbag, which was undoubtedly heavy, sailed by him several times, knocking and piling up against the suitcases around it. And the questions within him knocked and piled up against each other, and his eyes grew larger and darkened.

Kitaev took Natasha's familiar tan suitcase from the belt, and they left the luggage claim area. They showed the airline agent Natasha's luggage tags.

Before exiting, Natasha turned around. The Basketball Player twisted his head like a bird. He had eyes like a gypsy child's.

There'd been a certain incident in her life: once during the summer she and her mother were staying in their dacha, and a gypsy woman had come into their yard. In her arms she held a bedraggled little gypsy child of unparalleled beauty holding out a grimy open palm. The gypsy woman demanded food, clothing, and money. She demanded the maximum because she knew that to get a ruble you have to ask for ten. Natasha's mother went indoors and brought out what she didn't grudge, or not very much: a meat pie, money, and an old robe. In the gypsy child's hand she placed a potato just recently boiled in its skin. Then she became alarmed that the potato hadn't cooled off enough, and she roughly snatched it from the little hand. The gypsy child's eyes instantly dilated with hurt and tears, and he started crying—quietly and bitterly, like an offended adult. He didn't understand that the potato had been taken away for his own good. The Basketball Player also didn't understand that Natasha was leaving for his own good. He had the same staring eyes.

People and obligations are intertwined with each other, as are the earth and the trees. The roots of trees, like gigantic arms, reach deep into the earth, hold it and hold themselves up, too. The earth needs the trees, and the trees need the earth. Obligations exist not only between the living and the dead but between the living and the living. After you pull up a tree, you must be certain that you plant a new one in its place and that it will take root and grow. Otherwise you'll pull up one tree without planting another, and you'll stand over the upturned hole and look at your handiwork.

Natasha was leaving, following Kitaev, but the Basketball Player's gaze pierced the back of her head like a hardened ray. And for a long time afterwards, for almost a week, she felt his gaze as a point of pain in the back of her head.

Yes . . . and what does the first husband have to do with this? Absolutely nothing. It's just that then, at the start of life, it didn't cost anything to tear up roots that hadn't taken firm hold, to pull them up and throw them out. Then it seemed that everything was still to come and that everything lay ahead.

A THREESOME

INNA VARLAMOVA

Translated by

HELENA GOSCILO

1

HE RETURNED FROM THE CEMETERY, WHERE he'd spent the whole day making a fence and a small bench beside the fresh grave. He fell into a chair and let his arms drop. His nylon shirt stuck unpleasantly to his body. The heat outside was incredible—everything was melting: the asphalt, the butter on the plate, and the thoughts inside his head. "My poor Khristi," he thought foolishly, "at least you're cool there, below the ground...." He shuddered. Recently he'd been foolishly forcing out pathetic words and then becoming horrified. He'd loved his wife; while she was alive and seriously, grievously ill, he'd felt not a husband's but a great maternal compassion for her. And when he saw her seemingly fall asleep on that very same chair, without reading her sister's letter to the end, he instantly sank into a stupor, and from that moment he'd spoken and thought only nonsense, or so he believed. "Are you comfortable?" he asked Khristina, lying at peace and remote in her lonely coffin. "Aren't you scared, my love?" He listened hostilely to his own words. "So I'm a groom now, try to find me a bride!" he smiled to his friends who came from the plant to the funeral meal for Khristina. "What nonsense am I spouting?" he thought, ashamed of his inability to suffer decently, not realizing that this inability and the nonsense he was saying were just that: an expression of real suffering.

In this same state of stasis, which he simply couldn't overcome, he suddenly decided to go to Plebanovka. The thought had actually occurred to him a few times previously, but life always proved full of a thousand tasks that were most important and couldn't be postponed. Now, however, when he still had a week's leave left and had buried Khristina, from whose side he hadn't stirred for several years because of her illness, Roman Iosifovich Tykhoniuk decided that it was just the right time to take off, since he was so taken with the idea.

His young neighbor dropped by; she was scared when she saw his vacant face, thrown back and staring at the ceiling. "Hey!" she called in a whisper. "Hey, you wanna eat?" But he replied with a frown that he didn't need anything and went into the kitchen. What caught his eye immediately was the pan, with its caved-in sides, as if dented with a hammer, containing the remains of burnt onions and carrots—the very same pan in which he'd been heating a sauce while his Khristina, her pale temple nestled against the letter, was leaving life. "Well and fine!" he said to himself and began to sob maliciously. "Khristina," he kept repeating as he scraped at the bottom of the pan. "Khristina, what is this? What am I to do now? Khristina?!" Speaking for the first time about himself, about his loneliness and fear, he no longer shied away from words and almost rejoiced that he was trembling and crying. Enjoying the grief that he'd finally allowed himself, he threw against the floor the pot that he'd not finished cleaning.

The next morning, in the same mood of inwardly sustained bitterness that lessened the pain, he set off for the station. In the streetcar with him were some gypsy children—a boy and a girl in rags. The girl, in long torn skirts worn one on top of another, supple and elegant as a wanton woman, with mysteriously fiery eyes, shook her tattered shoulders and asked for charity; the boy swiftly and aggressively shot a lightning series of glances in all directions. At first Roman Iosifovich observed them with the indifference of experience—he'd seen gypsy kids, after all, hadn't he—but then, noticing their chapped black feet with red spots stamping on the roughly latticed floor of the car, and the estrangement of the children from the well-dressed city crowd caused by their awful rags and the endless restlessness, he thought, "It's a good thing I'm going; it's essential that I take a look at my Plebanovka. . . . How's it doing, how are things there?"

It wasn't that there, in that distant Plebanovka of sixteen years ago, he'd seen such people in such picturesque tatters—there, people's misfortunes were genuine, and no one paraded his poverty, but the isolation from the world was as great as these gypsy children's. . . . He sighed, sank into reverie, fell headlong into the past, and smashed himself against it. . . .

2

"Khristina! I'm leaving," said Roman Iosifovich when it grew completely dark.

"Sweetheart . . . don't go," his wife answered from the bed. "When you leave, I get very, very anxious!"

"Khristina, I saw them today standing in a threesome behind the storage shed. I passed by and greeted them, but they didn't respond. I turned around—and they were standing in a row looking at me."

"Rommy, my dear, maybe they were just standing there, not meaning anything."

"No—they watched me in silence after I passed them, just like forest beasts, like grey wolves! I'm going."

"All right then. God be with you. And may the Mother of God watch over you, my love."

He went out into the darkness, down the village road, and set off at a run by the ravine along the road already covered with autumn frost. His footsteps could be heard from far off—small puddles crunched under his boots. He carried a sheepskin coat on his arm and didn't turn around, for he knew that if he did he'd instantly imagine that he was seeing people behind the wattle fences and the corners of the huts. A week ago there had been a mysterious killing in the village—of the former team leader, whom he didn't particularly feel sorry for because of his nasty temperament, but now he saw the victim as his best friend, whom he'd lost and not saved. Thereafter Roman Iosifovich no longer spent the nights at home, but hid in the stack in the field until daybreak.

Now he ran along the field with its sown winter crops. They had already sprouted and showed gently silver in the stillness under the moon, which occasionally displayed its white noseless skull from behind the clouds as if purposely wanting to make its victim visible to his enemies from a distance. "Ah, damn you," muttered Tykhoniuk. "You have the damned mug, you corpse, of a wicked creature!" And when the moon peered out again, mischievous and mocking, he raised a fist toward the sky: "Go away, you devil, take cover, go away, hide!" and he ran as hard as he could to the stack, along the silvery, still lake of young shoots.

The stack was black, heavy, sagging, with a gap in the side—they'd already begun hauling the hay from it to the farm. The hay lay scattered about in untidy heaps. Trembling and cursing, Roman Iosifovich pulled it up to the stack so that the supply wouldn't go to waste, hurriedly dug out a shelter for himself, and crawled into it; spreading his sheepskin coat under him, he pulled some hay on top of his burrow and then grew still. No sound could be heard anywhere, but there was a ringing and pounding in his ears, and the noise lay loud and heavy on his heart.

Why had he agreed to accept this awful, tumble-down kolkhoz, where no one wanted to work and no one believed in anything? If he'd stayed at home in Khmelevka making calculations on the abacus, and another martyr had attracted attention, he wouldn't have known worries and misery! But people in the district had noticed the modest, efficient, hard-working accountant and offered him work in the Red Star, flattering him and promising their help. And, my God, what did he find there! Starving horses, every one of them suspended on belts, for if they lay down, they'd never get up. Hay that was rotting black, as if it had been gathered from a village roof instead of the field. Neither mixed feed nor silage—nothing, and they were already losing cattle. And what about the future? They still had the whole winter ahead of them! There was no one to depend on—the local militia of young volunteers, the village activists from the fighter battalion, clearly were also playing the same game as Bandera's[1] men; and then the murder! It was a warning shot, that was clear. They were showing him what was what. There was only one consolation—Khristina. What would he have done without her, alone against everyone? These people were an alien and ignorant lot; they all seemed suspect.

Roman Iosifovich couldn't get to sleep for a long time. The clouds moved out and the moon shone evenly and clearly, but Tykhoniuk was no longer angry at the silvery radiance—from his shelter, behind a thin curtain of hay, he had a sweeping view of the field, which for some reason looked to him like floodlands. Perhaps it was because the moonlight was cold and flashing, just as spring water in the meadows tends to be cold and sparkling. He no longer heard a pounding in his ears, and he lay in utter silence and thought that this time, too, the danger seemed to have passed.

Far from it, though. There was the sudden crunch of footsteps very close to him, behind him, on the other side of the stack. Someone was speaking loudly without trying to hide. Roman Iosifovich couldn't make out the words, but it was clear that there were several of them. He huddled up and grew stiff, like a beetle feigning death. Even his thoughts grew stiff, and he couldn't imagine what he should do now. But without thinking through or understanding a thing, he abruptly threw back the curtain of hay and clambered out of the shelter, and pulling out his Mauser on the run and slipping in the piles, he rushed off toward the nocturnal visitors without worrying about camouflage.

From behind the stack he caught sight of the people, who'd scattered in all directions—black figures, waving their arms, were running along the winter crop in the moonlight, everyone in a different direction. He shot twice, without knowing whom he was shooting at, and of course he missed, thank God (even to this day Tykhoniuk wasn't certain that these weren't kolkhoz workers who'd been driven to the brink, who'd come peacefully to profit by the hay), and no longer hiding, but upright, with his Mauser lowered to the ground, he stumbled off home.

"Sweetheart," said Khristina, her warm arms enfolding him, "warm yourself up against me. Go ahead, my love!"

He never spent the night in the stack again. He was pleased that he'd leaped out upon hearing the noise, though possibly it would have been more sensible to wait it out and clarify what on earth all that had been. Thievery or banditry? And who were they, those people—were they killers or simply the folks whom he'd been called upon to feed and restore to life? For some reason he believed that he didn't need to know that at all. It was better that way. It was better that way for him because his fear had disappeared; it had dissipated.

3

On the train Roman Iosifovich found himself in young company. Some students from Lvov were going home on leave after completing their stint of practical work. The car in the long-distance train had seats; they all had to get off in three hours. The shortness of the trip kept the passengers in a state of elation; the conversation didn't subside. From his senile little world, as it now especially seemed to him, from his darkened little corner, where he'd immediately hidden, he heard what a girl with hair cut short and with bare protruding ears and bright strands on her flushed cheeks was saying. It was about the sciences, which he didn't understand both out of personal ignorance and because he shared with his whole generation of people close to fifty the general failure to keep up with rapid progress. Something about quantums, about photons and the mass of inertia, but when she happened to mention Vapniarka, which was the village neighboring on Plebanovka and where her parents lived, he grew excited and moved forward to get a better look at her. How old could she have been at that time, during his stay in Plebanovka, this girl with her fashionable haircut? Five, six? Doubtless she used to run barefoot with a long switch, driving the cow to pasture, if they still had a cow then, for, after all, it's possible they didn't have one.

A dark, handsome boy was talking with her; he also spoke fluently, cogently. Putting together his separate phrases and exclamations, Roman Iosifovich deduced that he'd already completed his military service, then had made his way dashingly into the university, where he now was one of the Komsomol leaders. Again Roman Iosifovich felt a blow to the heart, and the old Plebanovka local militia arose before him. But for some reason he couldn't remember a single one among them who'd looked as capable, who'd been as independent and quick in his judgments, to whom the happiness that played and pulsed in the young man's black eyes had come easily! He involuntarily recalled Stakha Muravko, who instead of vigilantly standing guard over kolkhoz property with his gun, stole a bale of hay and was caught at night at the cherished stack, which had fallen apart by spring and which Tykhoniuk then didn't know how to prize.

Beside him on the same seat, listening to the students quietly and without a word, was a thin, blond boy with blue, vacantly lackluster eyes, unattractive, shy, dressed in a decent though cheap suit. And of all of them, Roman Iosifovich understood only him, for in his wistful downtroddenness, his fixed and envious attention, he resembled the local militia of those days long gone, and perhaps also Roman Iosifovich at that age. Perhaps because he wore shoes—enormous adult shoes on feet grown disproportionately large; but then, even in those times they had managed to get shoes when they went on a long journey, for a trip "on a licker," as trains were called then. And it used to be the custom for a fellow as soon as he left the city boundaries to take off his pride and joy on his own initiative, without any reminders, to retie the laces together, and throw the shoes over his shoulder, so as to cover the remaining kilometers barefoot.

"And where are you going?" Roman Iosifovich asked the boy, who readily turned his long-nosed mournful face to the older man.

"I took the exams but didn't make it," he replied.

Everyone looked at the boy with sympathy and bombarded him with questions: "Where?" "What part did you blow?" The topic was one close to them; it was up their alley, for they were young, too. They were depressed only by the village boy's appearance, which contrasted so starkly with their aura of success.

"I took the history exam. I've always had straight As in history, and my dream was to go into journalism. But they want you to have something published, and who's going to publish me? I wrote a good essay, but didn't answer the question in history. The competition was terribly rough. They flunked almost everybody in a row." The boy grew animated as he told them about it, but even his animation was lackluster, and precisely because of that it seemed endearing to Roman Iosifovich, the way a gossamer September day that is still warm but hazy can be after a bright summer.

"What did they ask you?" inquired the girl from Vapniarka.

"Questions that weren't based on our program. The Thirteenth Party Congress, and we didn't go over that. Also why the Swedish king came to be in the Ukraine, and—get this!—who designed Peter's monument, the one in Leningrad, the famous one. Forewarned is forearmed," he concluded in adult fashion. "I didn't answer a single question; I just stood there and stared. . . . Then I looked it all up and read it, but there's no use swinging your fists after the fight's over!"

The students started to comfort the boy, but he sat, shoulders slumped, and Roman Iosifovich imagined his return to the village where his parents, who'd supported him so many years, would receive the news with shame and pain.

"Is your dad old?" he asked, for some reason imagining as the boy's father the stableman Budnyi, tall, with dimpled cheeks, a grey mustache, and hair tangled in knots under a threadbare Polish service cap, the same Budnyi who then, at the meeting, at one in the morning, had risen and said, "Folks, folks, let our boss go, and God be with him! . . . "

"Yes," replied the boy. "Very old, and my mother's old; I'm their last child."

"Ah, my dear boy!" exclaimed Roman Iosifovich and closed his eyes tightly.

He hid in his dark corner again, abashed at the feeling that welled up in him from the depths of his being, and at the tears that he instantly concealed tightly under his lids, or so he thought, but which he later felt spilling down his unshaven cheeks. He didn't know whether he was crying more for the boy or for his dead Khristina, who that year in Plebanovka would spend hours waiting for him at the office, to force him to have at least a bite, and would pull warm boiled potatoes out of a sack. Or was he crying for himself, for being left alone now, for going off to recapture his youth, when he'd been ardent, filled with the desire to alleviate other people's sorrows as much as his strength permitted? . . . He didn't have enough strength. He'd squandered it in the Plebanovka cornfield; all the strength he'd had—all of it—disappeared. Then, running off—cap in hand—to Lvov, though he worked at a factory and even became an adjuster, he never again fanned the golden, pulsating, stirring flame that had burned within him as if under a stove cover.

4

While still at the district center, Roman Iosifovich learned that the chairman of the Plebanovka kolkhoz to whom he'd handed things over sixteen years ago lived there now, sick and in retirement. He went to the address indicated, and behind a fence, in the shade of some apple trees, he saw a Volga. Shubalyi sat on the porch of a brick house with an attic and a small balcony, and his puffy face manifested irritated, inveterate boredom. His eyes, animated even if only by the expression of boredom in a face made immobile by the swelling from his illness, looked like raisins sunk deep in dough.

"Iakov Nesterych!" called Tykhoniuk in a low voice from the wicket gate. "Don't you recognize me?"

The other man half-rose and, bending down, peered at him.

"Well, buddy. . . . Where'd you come from? Dropped from the moon?

You sure look older—ah, youth. . . . I've forgotten your name. I only remember your surname, Tykhoniuk.''

It was obvious that Shubalyi was glad to see his guest. He started fussing, but his movements weren't elastic and smooth, as they used to be, but jerky, sharp, as if broken down the middle along the spine. One hand, with violet-colored fingers that didn't belong to a workman, hung down limply as if in an invisible sling. He dragged one leg, and his mouth was noticeably lopsided: he looked like someone who'd taken offense at something or eaten something sour.

"Well," he said, "take a good look at me. Did you ever see such a thing? And if you knew how it all started! We went on an exchange to Bulgaria, and I got thrombosis of the intestine there. They operated on the spot. I thought that would be it, kaput, but I had good doctors; it was okay, I was on the mend, and I'd just recovered, when zap! I had a stroke. I lost my power of speech—I'm a complete invalid, I sit on the porch. . . . I'd like to work a bit more, but the bastards won't let me. Relax, they say; what do you want? Well, I want to live. I can't just sit!"

However miserable Roman Iosifovich was, however crushed and deserted he felt, he sensed here a confusion and loneliness worse than his own. "Yes," he thought. "He's really been through it . . . Is this Shubalyi? What's going on? Sweet Mary, he's had it rough!"

"Come in, we'll have a glass of something, reminisce about those golden times!" Shubalyi roused himself, and dragging his leg up the steps, he led his guest into the house.

"So how d'you like that? Golden! . . . That's the way it is: to him they seem golden, to me, lousy!" thought Roman Iosifovich, recalling how he'd been sixteen years ago—young and sinewy, yet exhausted, at the end of his rope, and he recalled Shubalyi, sleek and well-built, who with serene self-confidence had despised his luckless predecessor. Not so much for his social rank, which was low in comparison with his, as for his foolish behavior from beginning to end—with everything. It wasn't that Shubalyi, a district vet, considered any kolkhoz chairman beneath him. Like everyone else in the area, he distinguished clearly those who were his equals among chairmen from those whom it was accepted to call "buddy," "mac" in local parlance. And Roman Iosifovich understood that for Shubalyi he was mac, whereas Shubalyi, who'd taken over the semiruined Red Star kolkhoz from him, remained what he had been, a worker on the district level. They even dressed accordingly: Shubalyi wore a tunic, riding breeches, and box calf boots, whereas Tykhoniuk wore a lambskin cap with worn patches, an unbuttoned quilted jacket, dirty plus fours, and worn-down farmer boots.

It was clean inside Shubalyi's house, which was richly appointed in urban fashion. The radio droned faintly from the bedroom; apparently it was never off. A sofa stood in the living room, and the spangles on the dark-blue plush tablecloth covering the table sparkled iridescently. Perched in a corner, like a goat on black legs ready to leap and butt you in the stomach, was a cold, angry television with the horns of an antenna. But Shubalyi led his guest into the kitchen; he took out some vodka and some liver covered in sauce that was still warm in the frying pan, which he placed on the table.

"Have a bite," said the host after drinking the first glass and tearing off a piece of bread. "I had dinner a little while ago, but you've been on the road. Tell me, what business has brought you here?"

"What business . . . ," replied Roman Iosifovich. "I don't have any business. It's just that I buried my wife, and, well, I have some leave. . . ."

He couldn't explain himself more clearly. In fact, everything seemed clear to him as it was, but he suddenly realized that Shubalyi didn't believe him: he was staring at him searchingly as if, having got the basic facts from his companion, he was now mentally processing them.

"Well, well," said Shubalyi, "you've kept yourself in pretty good shape. You were such a puny thing. . . . But now you're not bad, sort of okay. A shirt, a suit. . . . Where do you work?"

"At a plant. As an adjuster. I'm surprised myself—I've turned from a corn grower into a worker. At the beginning, after I left here, I got set up as a house manager; they gave me a room, I got a foothold, but then I went to a glass factory. I learned the trade and make a so-so living. No one bothers me. I work my seven hours and then I'm free."

"Your wife, you said. . . . What was wrong with her—cancer?"

"Heart."

"Yes, health is very precious. I'd give up everything in exchange for health," said Shubalyi. "In Plebanovka . . . the chairman's a broad now. My former agronomist. How much work I put into the farm—I'm afraid to even say. That's essentially where I left my health—in the grain storehouse, in the garages and the fish pond and the apple orchard, in the cowshed and the pigsty. And I don't know whether the people there now remember to whom they owe it all. And all the credit goes to her, the fat-assed woman. She's been made a hero! As soon I see her picture—it's like someone's squeezing my heart with pincers. My wife's started hiding the papers from me. How unfair it is, Tykhoniuk, I tell you—you'd think they could have found a use for my experience. How many Shubalyis are there?"

Shubalyi's face became completely distorted as it grew lopsided from resentment, but the swelling gave him a look that was so childlike it was almost funny: a big, offended, sick baby sat in front of Roman Iosifovich. "Is this him?" Tykhoniuk thought again. "Him, the iron Shubalyi? A former partisan, a security man who once got rid of gangs of Bandera's men?"

"I've got it!" said Iakov Nesterovich suddenly. "Let's go down to Plebanovka. I'll give you a ride in the Volga; you'll see what it was like before and what it's like now. You won't recognize it, my dear fellow. You left the farm in ruin, in complete ruin . . . and I transformed it, you know. . . . Come on, let's go!"

Roman Iosifovich helped Shubalyi open the gates. Shubalyi pushed the Volga out onto the road, and they got in and drove off. Tykhoniuk glanced sideways at Shubalyi, who behind the wheel looked almost exactly the way he'd used to. Pale, concentrated, his dark little eyes glued to the road; grand, with his lifeless hand on the steering wheel and his lifeless foot on the pedal. Tykhoniuk suddenly felt a stab of envy. "A real man," he thought. "No matter what, he's a real man. When I was in charge, the farm was falling into ruin, but he set it on its feet. I only knew how to feel sorry and to suffer; but he didn't feel sorry and didn't suffer—he drove them and applied pressure; and so he has a pond and a cowshed, whereas I had neither a pond nor a cowshed, but a loss of livestock—sixty-nine head during the winter—and the public prosecutor's approval for my arrest. . . . And here we're driving to the kolkhoz we used to share, and again he's the boss, and I'm the odd man out. He's at the wheel, not me."

5

The piles of grain stirred on the threshing floor. The grain—lemon-colored oats, yellow barley, and pink wheat—stirred, shifted, breathed, moved, and was alive. All day from morning till night, the grain here was poured from one place to another, was driven away and delivered; the mechanical arm of the winnower shot it out, metal teeth seized it, and a conveyor carried it. People rested on it, fell into it up to their knees, and chewed it. Grain. It is heavy, mighty. It contains peace. It contains right, truth. There it is, grain. Touch it! Bite through it, chew it up!

Shubalyi and Tykhoniuk drove to the Plebanovka threshing floor, parked the car beside the Volga belonging to the chairwoman Katerina Panasovna Osadchaia, and started watching the people at work. Osadchaia herself, with a taut, suntanned body encased in a brilliant dress of modern material, with plump cheeks on her monumental face and with vivid dark-brown eyes, stood up to the ankles in grain, her large legs with taut calves planted widely apart. She exuded health and joy of life, and Roman Iosifovich thought that even in grief this joy would still be radiated by this beautiful woman of its own accord and independently of her. He gazed at her with annoyance, yet was dazzled—her orange dress, with golden threads, burned and sizzled like a sliver of the sun fallen from the sky.

Noticing the newcomers, Katerina Panasovna straightened her dress, adjusted her kerchief, and made her way toward them, but the kolkhoz workers kept intercepting her to ask her something, and several times she changed direction, going to the storeroom one moment, then returning to the winnower the next. Whenever she disappeared through the black doors of the storehouse, full of chaff and dust, it was as if the source of light faded from the threshing floor. Finally she firmly cut off all the people laying claim to her and approached her visitors, treading solidly with her coppery feet coated with a bluish film of dust.

"Hello, Iakov Nesterych." She shook Shubalyi's hand, and a shadow of embarrassment at her own health and joy flitted across her face. "Well, we're coming to the end. There are two days left to harvest the biggest one, if only it doesn't rain." She glanced up at the sky, reminiscent of an enormous red-hot cauldron overturned above the ground, with the ingot of the sun at the bottom.

"Don't worry, you'll make it," gritted Shubalyi. "Katerina, let me introduce you! You'll never guess who this is. The same poor devil who was in charge before me: Tykhoniuk."

"I've heard about you." She bent her heavy head, with its tall tower of hair, gently toward her shoulder. "Have you come to have a look?"

Her words and tone suggested delighted surprise at some marvelous spectacle, and Tykhoniuk quickly nodded in response.

"Yes, yes, I'm looking now and I don't believe my eyes—it's simply a miracle!"

"Miracle!" Shubalyi pounced caustically. "It's not a miracle, but work, great, colossal work invested in all this!" He gazed, squinting, at the rows of identical farms painted bright green; at the scales onto which a dump truck loaded with grain was driving just then, while a second waited its turn, provokingly blaring its horn; he gazed at the garage under the new red roof, and again a feeling of guilt and sorrow dimmed the ripe cherry-colored brilliance of Osadchaia's eyes. It was as if she were asking helplessly, "But what can I do? Where can I go? Here I am, forgive me for existing!"

She smiled and said to Tykhoniuk: "Everything you see here was done by Iakov Nesterych; he did it all on his own, it's his achievement!" And she lowered her eyes.

He melted instantly, softened and cheered up, and again he seemed a big baby to Roman Iosifovich, only placated, fed his fill of sweet kasha.

"Come on, I'll show you everything; we'll tour all the land, we'll see them stacking hay!" he suggested to Tykhoniuk.

"Don't forget to visit the pond," added Katerina Panasovna. "And when you return, please come and have dinner at my place, all right?"

They'd already reached the car when they noticed a young girl in a short skirt and white shoes run up to Osadchaia, clasp her, and whirl her around.

"What? What is it?" asked Osadchaia, moving away and laughing. "Is everything all right? Well, tell me, my little misery."

"Her daughter," explained Shubalyi.

"Yes, Mom, yes, Mommy, yes, yes!" rejoiced the girl, tanned and taut, just like her mother, with the same cherrylike moist eyes, the same vibrant joy that was independent of her in her whole manner. "They made the announcement first thing this morning and they've already sent us to work on a construction project for two weeks,[2] until classes begin. I carried bricks to the second floor—the small of my back is breaking, and look, see, my skirt's had it, it really has!" She burst out laughing, her head thrown back.

Everyone nearby turned around, smiling and listening, and Shubalyi, who'd already opened the car door, also watched and was in no hurry to leave.

"So did you pass?" he asked.

"Yes! Yes!" cried the girl with glee. "I'm so happy, Iakov Nesterych, and if you only knew, Mama, how many people failed, and one of the boys, who was dirt poor, a local, had his father waiting for him—a mac, the kind you rarely see nowadays, and the boy ran out of the lecture hall to his father and they both started crying—honestly!"

"What, didn't he make it?" asked Katerina Panasovna, feasting her eyes on her daughter.

"Oh no, no, he did, he made it! That's the point, but they both cried so hard that I cried along with them, I swear!" She was telling the truth, of course, but it was difficult to believe that tears could flow from those eyes, even the sweetest of tears—of tender emotion at her own kindness.

"Whereas he returned with nothing!" Tykhoniuk remembered the boy on the train.

Arms intertwined, mother and daughter headed for the threshing floor. Shubalyi got behind the steering wheel, and they left.

"Of course she passed! They hired a tutor! They may even have greased someone's palm," he muttered. "It's really something! They're more like sisters; you'd never tell they're mother and daughter. You should have seen what a ragamuffin she was when she came to me at the kolkhoz to ask for a job as an agronomist. Her Galka was only about six then. I don't know if she got knocked up or if her husband left her, but this very same Katerina was thin, dark, like a cracked board. . . . I told her, 'Join the kolkhoz, we don't hire workers.' And she said, 'Fine, no problem, I'll join, just take me!' And now she's raised a spoiled little looker, and she herself, I remember, told me how she got a higher education: she froze in a dorm, they heated the iron stove with straw and had an oil lamp for light, and in the morning the girls would wake up looking like Negroes, with soot even in their nostrils. In class they used to get a break every ten minutes, just so they could stamp their feet a bit. They'd sit in their sheepskin jackets and felt boots, but would still be dying. . . . She had her fill of running around barefoot and ragged; she went around half-starved. And now—you saw her!—she's sure spread out!"

The wind rushed to meet them from the fields—a dry wind, hot, rich, full of grain . . . The kolkhoz workers were finishing the stack. Two tractors pulled a plump pile of hay held by ropes sparkling in the sun, and swaying and bumping, it climbed up the slope of the stack to the top, where stackers with pitchforks were waiting to spread it out evenly and stamp it down more firmly. The stack rose high, like a radiant palace.

Shubalyi got out, and dragging his leg along the crunching stubble, he approached the women waiting with pitchforks at the foot of the stack for the tractors to pull the ropes away and to chug up to the new piles of freshly mown hay.

"How's it going, gals?" he asked in a high-pitched voice that endeavored to seem authoritatively cheerful but only sounded like the voice of an offended retiree.

"We're working," only one of the women responded vaguely, and she bent down, hiding her face, seemingly to put saliva on a scratch on her leg.

From a distance Tykhoniuk shyly examined the women dressed like workers, painfully trying to recognize at least one of them. Wasn't that Teklia Kravchuk? And wasn't that Leska Muravko, the mother of Stakh, the local militiaman? Wasn't that Budnyi's wife—the old one, her legs covered with thick blue veins? The women had already noticed him, possibly in response to his intense, vitally interested gaze, because usually no one pays much attention to the indifferent "representatives" who frequently roam around the farms, except for a cursory glance of impersonal curiosity at the stranger's face, and even then with mockery. But they gazed excitedly at Roman Iosifovich, and if they turned their backs to him quickly, it was just because they were embarrassed when they recognized him. . . . And suddenly they started running up to him en masse, streaming around the startled Shubalyi from both sides. While still a couple of paces away from Tykhoniuk, they crowded together and stared at him, smiling uncertainly.

"Hey," spoke up the old woman with the ropes of veins on her legs. "Is it you? Is your name Tykhoniuk? Roman Iosifovich? Our former boss?"

"Yes, it's me," replied Roman Iosifovich quietly. "It's me! And who're you—Maria Budnaia, right? Am I right?"

"Yes, Maria, Maria! You recognized me!"

"And you, you there, you!" He indicated with his chin the woman with the large faded eyes. "Are you Lesia? Lesia Muravko?" He recalled how she'd sobbed then, begging him not to take her Stakh to court, and kept humbly trying to catch his hand, attempting to kiss it.

"Yes, Leska, Leska!" "And do you remember me, Tykhoniuk?" asked the one whom he'd instantly taken for Teklia Kravchuk, the dairymaid. Because of the fodder shortage, during the winter she'd lost the three best cows: Kvitka, Ryzha, and . . . what was the third one called?

"I remember you, Teklia," said Tykhoniuk and felt shame and bitter pain like wormwood in his heart. He'd left, abandoning them all; he'd deserted them. And what could he have done—he'd have been taken to court, he couldn't have done anything, so why was he tormented by shame and pain beneath these women's gaze?

They continued to question him about this and that, and he replied at length; their sympathy only stirred acute pain in his heart.

"Okay, gals, that's enough gabbing!" yelled Shubalyi from the stack, and the women scattered back to work, their long skirts fluttering.

Tykhoniuk suddenly left the car and went into the golden mowed field stretching out evenly before him. He pretended in front of Shubalyi that he was fingering the dry pile of mowed hay, but actually he was recalling his hard work during the harvest long ago—when there had been no sun, and instead, as bad luck would have it, the rains had started and it had poured almost without respite.

6

At first, at the very beginning of summer, there was good weather. The harvest ripened in the sun, and Tykhoniuk rode around the fields on his Grey, which was so well trained that it would trot from one work team to the next on its own, stopping wherever necessary. One morning he was riding in the field where earlier there had been a Polish land-owner's estate; he was looking at the wheat and calculating how much a hectare would yield when suddenly an explosion resounded, and a huge black bush of burdock seemed to leap a short distance above the wheat; it hung in the air, debating whether to fall or not, and then descended, emitting a cloud of black smoke. Immediately soldiers, who he didn't know were in the village that day, ran to the place where the explosion had taken place. Lashing his horse, Tykhoniuk set off in their direction, puzzled as to what exercises were being conducted there without his knowledge and why the damned devils had chosen a field where the crop was most abundant. But as he rode up, he heard a woman's sobs and a man swearing crudely.

The field was in shambles, as though it had been turned inside out; scattered chunks of earth formed little islands sprouting roots of wheat that flattened the bright yellow grain, and in the crater made by the explosion and beside it lay something liquid red and some torn bloody rags. He jumped down from the trap and, pushing aside the soldiers who were in his way, ran closer. The first thing he saw on the ground in front of him was a mysterious arm in a field-shirt sleeve lying by itself on a bed of drooping wheat stalks.

He gave a cry of fear, and as he looked around for help, his gaze fell on the face of Orysia Lutskiv, the leader of the kolkhoz field team, who was scratching her cheeks with her nails, her mouth opened dreadfully. He became even more afraid of this gaping mouth, for he couldn't hear a shout, and when at last her shout reached his consciousness, he felt that he'd collapse on the ground that instant. Yet the thought that he might have to fall on that severed arm or, God forbid, into that red liquid that had splashed everywhere, made him get a hold of himself and come to his senses.

A soldier, who turned out to be in charge of the security men, came up to him and told him what had happened. Toward morning they had surrounded Orysia Lutskiv's cottage, knowing that the Bandera man whose remains now lay there amid the wheat was spending the night with her. When Lutskiv stepped out to answer nature's call, she sensed something was wrong and at once led her guest, who was her lover for sure, through the vegetable gardens along the back way to the kolkhoz field. But the bandit, realizing, of course, that he wouldn't be able to get away from ten armed men, decided to blow himself up with a hand grenade. . . . And here, if you please, was what remained of him, and it was essential to interrogate this bitch as soon as possible.

They drove some carts into the field, made the wailing Orysia collect the pieces of the decimated Bandera man, placed the severed arm on the pile, then left. At the interrogation Lutskiv implicated several other people in the village.

And when harvest time came, although the rains had washed away all traces of the bloody incident, the combines still gave the damned place a wide berth, and the little island of wheat that was partly flattened and weighed down by the earth and showed yellow, with a green crater overgrown with weeds in the center, stayed there until the fall.

They turned in only half of the grain delivery, and every day the phone in the office crackled feverishly—the district authorities were demanding the centners[3] that they hadn't delivered. Roman Iosifovich walked around gloomy, hoarse, unwashed, not eating for days, and looking like a scarecrow, in his opinion. One moment the rains came down hard, then the next, they lay in the clouds like the enemy in the trenches; as soon as the kolkhoz workers would spread out the haycocks for drying, if not in the sun, then at least in the wind, the sky would start trickling down some even, dirty, grey rain, as if the Lord God were squeezing a floor mop onto them.

Once, after a sleepless night, and after an argument with the long-suffering Khristina that was trivial and thus especially painful for him, Tykhoniuk made a desperate and unusual decision for that time: he wouldn't turn in another gram of grain to the state delivery, but instead would give the kolkhoz workers at least a small part of what was owed them. Otherwise people would soon start falling like the horses that had spent the entire winter hanging on straps as if they'd been strangled. Since he, as the unfortunate, accursed head of the "Red Star," had to answer in court anyway, one crime more or less made no difference. And as soon as he reached this decision, he suddenly felt that he was not a scarecrow in a torn cap, but a human being, and it became easy for him to overcome his pride, to be the first to approach his wife as soon as she returned from milking at the farm, and say:

"Listen, I'm going to distribute what we thresh today to the first work team. I think three hundred grams each should be enough for a working day. You understand what I mean, don't you?"

At the sound of his voice Khristina turned round, at first sullenly, as she recalled the unfair things he'd said the day before; but as he spoke, his human essence flowed into her, and it dissolved her sense of injury and smoothed out the features on her face. She looked at him with that sweet woman's gaze of hers with which she was so good at enveloping and embracing him, as though in a sad and tender embrace. And she didn't say to him, as some other vulgar wife might have done, that he'd get into trouble for it and that it was dangerous to do that without first taking care of the grain deliveries; she simply exclaimed:

"Ah, that'll make the people happy! The people will thank you for that!"

"And tomorrow," he continued enthusiastically, tousling the lock of hair that had tumbled over his forehead, "tomorrow, Khristie, we'll distribute what we thresh to the second team, you hear! And then, to the third and fourth! Every worker down to the smallest one will get a centner or a little less, I think, and I'll sow later! If they don't let us sow during the day, then we'll sow at night, and if there's still some left, God willing, and I hope there will be, I'll take it to the state delivery. You understand, don't you?"

It was clear that she understood what misfortunes and disasters threatened not only him but also her, yet she didn't hold her husband back, but continued to envelop and embrace him with her quiet gaze. And he did then what he planned, without even picking up the crackling telephone receiver, pretending that he didn't hear the nerve-racking ring. He tried to drop by the office less frequently, and when a messenger from the office came running breathlessly to the threshing floor, he would brush him aside and answer:

"Tell them that you didn't find me, that the boss went off without telling anyone where, or that he's off on a drinking binge; to hell with them!"

... And now he also recalled that crazy sowing at night, kept secret from the authorities, when the district committee representative went off home to sleep after berating him, his voice breaking in distress. The seeding machine leaped along the fallows, and the tractor shone in the night with its weak headlights as it puffed and emitted a smell of kerosene and oil over the entire plain; Roman Iosifovich plodded behind and from time to time would bend down to check how the seed was settling, to see that it wasn't obstructing the plowshare, that there were no gaps and flaws. They kept pressing him to go and rest; even the tractor driver swore by all that was holy that everything would be fine and that the boss should have a bit of rest, but he didn't know a second's rest until all the grain was laid in the springy soil for an area of five hundred hectares.

"Tykhoniuk, Tykhoniuk, you gone crazy or something?" Shubalyi called him from afar, at a loss as to why Roman Iosifovich had taken it into his head to measure the stubble with cranelike strides from one end of the field to the other.

"But, Iakov Nesterych," said Tykhoniuk when he returned to the car, "this is the same field, you know—really."

"What field?"

"The one I sowed at night. . . ." And, peering into the other man's puffy face, he asked: "Do you remember what the yield was like? My wheat? What was the harvest from it, can you tell me?"

"What harvest are you talking about!" snorted Shubalyi. "Any self-respecting farmer would be ashamed to recall those harvests. What kind of harvest could there have been? At the very most ten centners. But now the average yield is close to thirty all over the region! There are still limits on mineral fertilizers, but it can't be compared with those years; there's nearly a quota per hectare of various technologies, crop rotation, a proper sequence of crops, and the varieties are chosen by their suitability to a region. . . . Farming culture! And what did we have then? Remember!"

Tykhoniuk imperceptibly repressed a sigh.

7

After examining everything that Shubalyi wanted them to, even visiting the club that was being built with a seating capacity of six hundred, where they were just then installing a molded plafond about the size of a turbine wheel on the ceiling of the auditorium, at Shubalyi's insistence they dropped by a kolkhoz worker's place. Four members of his family had erected a huge brick house with their work's earnings; they had decorated the walls with fashionable transfers, and dreamed of buying a Lvov TV in addition to three bicycles, a motorcycle, a radio, and a wardrobe by the end of the farming year. Tykhoniuk dimly recalled that under his management the same family had lived in a dirty Polish hut covered with straw, the man of the house had supplemented their income at a sugar factory, and the poor wife had stayed home with the small children.

"You see how average kolkhoz workers live?" asked Shubalyi in a tone that suggested that he was personally contributing to these people's well-being out of his own pocket.

"How long has it been like this?" asked Tykhoniuk timidly. "Did it start a long time ago?"

"Huh, of course it's easy to keep up a reputation now," replied Shubalyi, making a face. "They've raised the purchase prices and switched to monetary payment. . . . And who laid the foundation for that? When people were vegetating in other kolkhozes and still getting kopeks on workdays, I had things arranged pretty decently in the Red Star. True, I had to dash about like a dervish, I can tell you; and to take risks, and to play the diplomat, and to twist some people around my finger. . . . If you must know, they were afraid of me. I didn't drink, I didn't chase skirts— you couldn't fault me on personal grounds. And because of whom did the region become known for its moral strength? Whom did it use as a trump card in its reports? I was its glory! So they didn't stop me from having my way! And I certainly didn't play the liberal with my people— if needed, I would threaten them with Siberia! They had to knuckle under; discipline in the kolkhoz was tight. I have a theory: the primary thing is community farming, whereas personal profits—they're way down on the list. You won't get me to budge from that position, no way! I'm against a kolkhoz worker getting overly rich; you have to stick to the golden mean, buddy. If a person doesn't get anything at all, you won't force him to participate in community affairs, but if he's got too much, I'm sorry, then the extent of his interest weakens again. And it's not him, the kolkhoz worker, but me, his boss, who's got to decide for him how much should be put in his pocket. That's my credo!" Shubalyi proudly finished his speech with the resonant word.

They had just returned to the threshing floor when they overheard a squabble between Katerina Panasovna and the women clustered around her, who'd grown red with anger.

"But, girls, it's a prize![4] That's why it *is* a prize, so that everyone in turn won't get it!" Osadchaia was trying to convince the women.

"But listen, boss, it should be run fairly!"

"I didn't set it up—the management did."

"Ah, there's no point in gabbing about it! The team leader's wife works in that team, that's why they got the prize! You scratch my back, I'll scratch yours!"

"That's not true! You were first in line for the prize, but you didn't want to make the effort to compensate for the sick in your group, and in two lots the beet wasn't cut."

"But we cut our beet really well, and that team always does it any old way!"

"But what are those fifteen rubles to you? Is that really money to you?"

"But listen, boss, it's not a question of rubles; we care more about fair play!"

At first Katerina Panasovna answered with a smile, but then she got angry, and it was evident that the women's reproaches offended her. She found it especially unpleasant that the guests had witnessed this scene. When Shubalyi and Tykhoniuk approached, she started explaining to them the main point of the conflict, but neither guest listened attentively to her excuses—each was preoccupied with his own thoughts.

Shubalyi was terribly, agonizingly jealous. He was jealous of everyone over everything: of Katerina Panasovna over the kolkhoz, of the kolkhoz over Katerina Panasovna; he was jealous of every single person in the village now living independently of him; he was jealous of life, which also was no longer subject to him, and this jealousy had become so violent that it seemed to him a sacred, elevated, and pure feeling. He recognized in himself the hero of a contemporary Soviet tragedy, a doer separated from his whole life's work. His work was the chance to control and be the boss of people's fates, of a mass of mechanisms and millions of funds; his work was the risky navigation along the low waters and shoals of various, often contradictory resolutions and decisions, a search for the best channels not so much for the ship, with its passengers and cargo, as for himself, incarnated in the work that had become second nature to him. And now he couldn't control his involuntary satisfaction upon seeing Katerina Panasovna's skirmish with the kolkhoz workers. That satisfaction actually filled him with complacency.

"Well, okay, girls, why all this shouting? You should work better, then the prize will be yours!" he said with what seemed to be paternal severity, but the fact that he hadn't bothered to grasp the fine points and shadings of the argument simultaneously offended both sides. The women seemed to choke, fell silent, and dispersed to the winnowing machines and conveyors, and Katerina Panasovna pursed her lips.

"And you're to come today and get the grain as payment on account. I need the supply shed, there's no place to store the kolkhoz barley!" she yelled vindictively at the women's backs.

The last exclamation affected Roman Iosifovich even more keenly than the unrestrained anger with which the female kolkhoz workers had attacked the chairwoman and which had so startled him. "Where did the former timidity go, the downtrodden passivity of the locals?" he thought. "And that's what we've lived to see—they don't bother to take the grain. Good God!"

"Who on earth is that?" Shubalyi suddenly asked Osadchaia cheerfully, indicating a tall old man who was just entering the gates of the threshing floor.

"Don't you know? That, as we say here, is the second chairman, a former local landowner, or rather, his son, Mr. Mikola Demkiwski. He spent some time in a psychiatric ward—he went crazy back in '39⁵—then, since he was quiet and harmless, they transferred him to an old folks' home, but he ran off and returned here two years ago."

Roman Iosifovich had also immediately noticed the figure of the crazy old Polish landowner in the colorful crowd at the threshing floor. Wearing a black winter coat draped over his shoulders, despite the August heat, with stooped shoulders, grey hair, and a neat grey beard, he resembled a noble Spaniard in a dark cloak from some theatrical performance. His clothes were absurd and threadbare, but tidy and mended, with everything in place: buttons, strap, laces, and even a tie; there was an aura of a somewhat pompous and haughty propriety about the clothes.

"But where does he sleep? What does he live on?" asked Tykhoniuk.

"People here like him," replied Katerina Panasovna. "He's never hurt a single person in his whole life. The Polish landowner himself, people say, was all right too, not overly cruel, and this son of his got his education in Belgium, I think, and whenever he'd come home for vacation, he'd teach the village kids to read and write in Ukrainian. Even now he remembers his foreign languages; our schoolboys run to him so he can translate for them. He receives a pension of twelve rubles. He has no home, so he either spends the night on the farm, in the recreation and reading room or in the dispensary, or at the kolkhoz workers'. People in the village take turns giving him food, and he always pays them—he's proud! Only he doesn't understand what's what, and when he gets his pension he'll spend two or three rubles, and later he'll leave something, even if only five kopeks, on the table. The dairymaids on the farm give him skim milk. He really loves skim milk!"

"Lack of order!" frowned Shubalyi. "Disgraceful goings-on! You should send him to the old folks' home. That's an ugly blot on our new life. A birthmark."

"People have sent him there—he runs away! . . . And we've gotten used to him, Iakov Nesterych—let him live. He takes me for his manager. He'll come to the office, demand to see the accounts: why is the stacking behind schedule, who this, why that—it's funny!"

"Nonsense!" snapped Shubalyi. "What you need this for, I can't understand."

"Let him live!" answered Osadchaia rebelliously. She had already forgotten the unpleasant skirmish with the female kolkhoz workers, and her eyes shone cheerfully again. "Look, let's go have dinner."

8

After dinner Shubalyi grew bored; he thanked his hostess coldly for her hospitality and got ready to leave. He was suddenly tired from the emotions he'd experienced that day, and he was fed up with everybody. He didn't particularly like Katerina Panasovna, and now she especially irritated him with her youth and health. Forgetting that he too had been healthy and young once, for some time now he'd equated these qualities with stupidity. He watched this woman move, laugh, and sip wine from her glass, a woman who was occupying his position, against all rights, and he saw her as a fat goose. The fact that the people in the region and the district were friendly with her—well, one had to have one or maybe two, three women as chairwomen and heroes. Even Shubalyi sadly acknowledged the need for that.

He was also angry at himself—for having got soft and emotional at the beginning in front of Tykhoniuk, for being so happy to see his visitor, to whom he could boast a bit, let himself go, get things off his chest. He couldn't forgive himself this weakness—before whom had he cast his pearls! If Tykhoniuk had been a real person, it would at least have been all right. But no, he arrived looking as nondescript as they come, and right away starts nosing about, he's interested! What especially bothered him was that those two—Tykhoniuk and Osadchaia—even before they'd had time to exchange a single word, had already come to terms and had joined forces against him, Shubalyi. He, the sucker, had introduced them to each other, and they smirked disrespectfully one moment and exchanged looks the next. . . . He started feeling offended and bitter. So when Roman Iosifovich, embarrassed, said that if their hostess permitted, he would like to stay on until the next day, Shubalyi cheered up.

"Stay," he said. "Have a good time!" And he rose.

"Is he putting the make on her, what is the idiot up to?" he muttered to himself. "He's buried his wife, so is he hoping to get something going here now? Well, well, go ahead. What's it to me!"

Katerina Panasovna accompanied him as far as the gates, and as they were saying their goodbyes—she was one of them, after all, under the wardship of the region, and had been his protégé—he said:

"Where he's concerned, don't . . . don't believe everything he tells you!"

"Why, what do you mean?" asked Katerina Panasovna in surprise.

"Well, he'll start telling you how the people saved him from being put on trial. Don't believe him! It's all nonsense, you get me?"

Katerina Panasovna returned to the house in a thoughtful frame of mind. Halting at the threshold and inclining her head, which was weighed down by her tall hairdo, toward her shoulder, she shot her guest a slanting glance. He, without turning around, also saw her with his lateral vision, and in her rust-colored dress she suddenly struck him as resembling a purebred cow. "What a wonderful woman," thought Tykhoniuk sadly. He wanted to ask her about a lot of things, but he felt shy.

Katerina Panasovna instantly sensed his embarrassment, and after an infinitesimal hesitation, she sat down beside Tykhoniuk on the couch. For a second they gazed at each other in a friendly and open way, then Katerina Panasovna broke into speech as if continuing a conversation they'd started a long time ago:

" . . . and that's the way he is as a rule. A difficult person, hard to get along with. He's always been a morose fellow, unsociable to the point that it's sick. He'd keep silent mostly, but as soon as he opened his mouth, he'd offend someone. Everyone was afraid of him. That's how he maintained his position."

"Do tell, Mom, how he—you remember, when the Old Mlynovtsy people got the idea of merging. . . . You remember, don't you? How proud he was then, strutted like a turkey, as if all of it was just *his* doing!"

"All right, dear, what's the point of rehashing nonsense to no purpose. . . ."

"What was it? What was it?" asked Tykhoniuk with interest. "Tell me, Galochka."

"Mom's being modest," said Galia, putting the plates that she'd been taking to the kitchen back onto the table. "Here's what happened. . . . My mother spent all her energy working at the kolkhoz, but he only yelled at her. I suffered on her account and his, too. His even more. You see, I—can you understand?—I quickly got a high opinion of him! I wanted him to be the most kind, the most just! All you heard around you was: Shubalyi, Shubalyi! . . . He was the boss, he was talented, he was—everything. Other chairmen choked on dust in their state-owned jeeps, whereas ours had his own Volga. He drove it himself! And when I heard his crude remarks, I'd cry. I'd think, what's with you, Iakov Nesterych? Why aren't you the way you should be? Why are you destroying my dream?"

"Hush, Galka, why are you going on like this?"

"No, I'm going to tell him. Once Mother was driving through the neighboring village, the very same Mlynovtsy, and she sees—right, Mom?—a tractor driver driving through a field with empty barrels. They were in the middle of feeding. The fertilization was over, so he was driving around without doing anything, just to chalk up the amount of distance he could report having covered."

"That's true," corroborated Katerina Panasovna, eyes lowered. "I simply couldn't believe my eyes! I leaped off the trap and made for the tractor. 'Have you been driving aimlessly like this with empty barrels over sown fields a long time?' I asked. And he says to me: 'It's none of your business!' 'Oh, really—not my business?' I reply. 'But I'm an agronomist, you so-and-so scoundrel!' It upsets me to see these blockheads scoffing at things that grow! Well, I wasn't too lazy to find their team and field leaders, and I created such a stir. . . . That's what Galka remembered, only I don't understand in what connection."

"What do you mean, in what connection? In this!" Galia clasped her hands. "In this, Roman Iosifovich, that the people immediately asked to be admitted to our kolkhoz. . . . 'Comrade Osadchaia,' they said, 'take us on! Your team leaders in the field live well, look at the excellent harvest they get, whereas we try no worse, but everything with us turns out cockeyed. . . .' Well, are you going to tell me what I'm saying isn't true?"

"Oh, no, it is," said Katerina Panasovna, and the dark blood rushed to her cheeks. "I told them I couldn't do anything about that, of course, that they had to see Shubalyi and raise the question at a meeting, and the meeting would decide. And they came directly from the lot, in their dirty boots, to our office. We calculated everything, estimating the pluses and minuses, of course, and we merged with Old Mlynovtsy."

"But he," Galia took up the narrative, her eyes flashing passionately, "whenever any talk started about this incident, he'd boast: 'They were in a bind,' he'd say. 'So to whom did they come to beg? Shubalyi, of course, who else?' And not a word about my mother. Well, am I telling the truth?"

"He can't overcome his own nature," said Katerina Panasovna. "He doesn't have what it takes to do it. He tries every now and then, makes an effort, but he just can't."

"Also, how about when the lowlands were flooded by rain in the spring . . . Remember how you worried? I haven't forgotten that, either, though I was in sixth grade then," said Galia. "You went around sunk in gloom, it was a nightmare! He'd gone off somewhere, and you, without his knowledge, sowed the beet in a different place. I remember how they hauled the manure day and night, scattered it, plowed, and sowed. But he turned up and started threatening Mother, that he'd take her last kopek if there was no harvest. You told him: 'But, Iakov Nesterych, we couldn't wait any longer, you know, the deadline for sowing is approaching, and the water is still standing in the lowlands!' He only snorted and swore. But when they harvested the crops and turned in five hundred centners each, with an additional savings at cost price of—how much? . . ."

"Twenty-four thousand," uttered Osadchaia quietly.

" . . . There! they got twenty-four thousand above the plan, and what did he do? Well, Mom? He also bragged at the annual meeting, claimed it was due to him; I heard him myself: courage, he said, overcomes all obstacles!"

Katerina Panasovna sighed and gave a laugh.

"Ah, 'our sea is lonely!'[6] I feel sorry for him. . . . He suffers a great deal."

"Truly suffers," confirmed Tykhoniuk.

The conversation ended. Galia carried the plates to the kitchen, and Katerina Panasovna got up.

"You rest, but I've got to go to the threshing floor. It makes no difference. I'm here, but my mind's there. They're harvesting the grain."

. . . That evening all three of them got in the car and drove to the stadium to watch the match between the kolkhozes. The stadium in Plebanovka was mediocre: an uneven clearing covered with turf, enclosed by a necklace of stretched wire. Thousands of people were gathered there: old men, children, young dandies, and fashion-conscious girls.

Roman Iosifovich didn't like soccer. The sport frightened and pained him—events on the soccer field accumulated too inevitably, mercilessly, and wildly: the hollow, dull sound of the ball, the collisions, the falls, the trauma, the blind rush of several desperate players toward a single deliberately dangerous spot, the sideways leaps of the goalkeepers, who raised the ball beneath their stomachs, the whistles of the umpires, the limping of the victims, the stupid violence of the fans. . . . It all seemed to him a cruel copy of the modern world, and if Tykhoniuk's weak will allowed his friends to drag him to a match, he would return home overwhelmed and grown thin, as if he'd lived through a lightning-quick serious illness.

And here, on this village field, everything was as usual, but because this was his kolkhoz, the kolkhoz where once the very idea of cheerful games for the massess would have seemed blasphemous, he stood and gazed without his customary sense of alienation, but with good will and sorrow. "Well, well," he thought. "Well, my friends, go ahead and play!"

With curiosity he looked around at his companions and saw Galia shifting her tanned legs with impatience, like a bay foal, and whispering mindlessly, "Oh, I've got a headache. Oh, Mom, it's simply splitting." "Oh, what's our Mishka up to? Mish-ka!!" she yelled loudly without hearing her own yell; Tykhoniuk saw children running from one group of spectators to another, doubled up, their heads poised like a bull's, ready to ram into the crowd; he saw a bunch of motorcycles, propped up against each other in the bushes—probably the men had rushed down from the harvesting after turning off the tractors and combines; and he saw the face of his neighbor Osadchaia, who'd hypnotized the Plebanovka players with her falcon's gaze: win! win!

There followed cheers, whistles, bouquets flying up in the air, the triumphant laughter of hundreds of Plebanovkites, embraces, congratulations, the presentation of the cup of honor, the departure of various makes of cars, the modern knights and cavalry on motorcycles, the slow, soothing procession of well-dressed old women along the highway to the village, and the whirlwind of the truck racing by with the workers from the threshing floor.

. . . They made up a bed for Roman Iosifovich on the couch in the dining room; he turned out the light and lay down, but sleep eluded him. For a long time he heard mother and daughter walking about, talking, clattering dishes in the kitchen, and he felt a little hurt that they had nothing at all to do with him. Then Katerina Panasovna told Galia to go to bed—"I'll wake you up tomorrow just as soon as it's light, else you'll be late!" and banged the door. "Mommy, sweetie, where are you off to—work?" Galia called after her mother, and the latter, opening the door a crack, replied, "Quiet, why are you yelling? The man's asleep!" Then everything quieted down.

9

But he couldn't get to sleep for a long time. Before him loomed the vision of the last day in the Plebanovka of long ago, the form of which was that year's annual meeting, and the essence of which was his being put on trial. The entire administration was assembled: the secretary of the district committee, the chairman of the district executive committee, the director of materials and technical supplies, the head of the political section, the public prosecutor, and he, Shubalyi. . . .

Roman Iosifovich remembered himself as having been shamefully fussy and dressed up; for some reason he'd kept giving orders left and right, largely useless ones and all for show: to change the red tablecloth, to pour fresh water into the carafes; and he found it especially unpleasant to recall how he'd pounced on the cleaning woman for no reason, blaming her for the fact that there were husks of seeds scattered in the office.

But they didn't try to restrain him; the heads observed his behavior in silence, walked about in a small group, and conferred in secret. Khristina came to the meeting in a smart jacket, sat down on the side of the third row, and in her whole pose—her neatly placed feet, straight back, and hands in her lap—he saw the courage of a meek woman.

The heads made presentations one after another. And the accusations that they leveled at him were really something! He'd squandered the kolkhoz on drink (and what was there to squander—surely not the rotten hay? and moreover he didn't drink), and he'd wasted funds and given bribes (he'd bought tires on the side, but how else could he get them if they'd not been officially allotted any rubber?), and he'd not made the state deliveries, and he'd violated regulations and earned himself a cheap popularity. He sat in the presidium, head bent, listened, and thought: "Why didn't you let me work at least a year longer, my dear comrades? I'd actually need three years to get the farm going at least a little. And why doesn't any one of you say what I came here for and whether it's my fault that during the winter we lost sixty-nine head from lack of fodder, for God's sake!"

The kolkhoz workers sat in rows and listened to the speakers in silence. Tykhoniuk, who presided over the meeting, would get up and in a toneless, unnatural voice would ask the people to speak up; according to regulations he appealed to their conscientiousness, and invited them to point out what other flaws there were. But not a single person stood up. Some of the heads ascended the rostrum a second time, their speeches now containing a hint of direct threats; they mentioned his serious political deviation, his complicity with the enemy. The meeting dragged on past midnight, but not a single kolkhoz worker had uttered a word yet.

And then Old Man Budnyi got up and said from where he stood:

"Folks, let our boss go in peace. He tried as best he could, folks. Why should he be prosecuted for our sakes? You can't do that!"

It was as if a dam had broken:

"Let him go! Let him go! We'll do it your way, we'll choose your candidate, Comrade Shubalyi the veterinarian, but let Tykhoniuk off! He's not to blame. He worked well, he did!"

They tried to argue with them, explaining that there was direct evidence of serious errors bordering on crime, but the meeting was in an uproar.

"No! No! Let him go! Else we won't elect a new head! We're satisfied. We're satisfied with everything, everything!"

They were satisfied, these penniless people! They were all satisfied, these naked, barefoot, dear people of integrity!

. . . Tykhoniuk lay on the couch and restrained his breathing, which had grown loud. It distressed him that he'd listened then to the voice of fear instead of the advice of his quiet wife, and that he hadn't stayed in Plebanovka even as a simple driver for the kolkhoz, but had left. Like Shubalyi, he elso envied everybody everything, but in a different way. Now he wished that along with the people from his Plebanovka, he'd been oppressed long and hard by Shubalyi, that he'd not received his earnings for many years, that along with all of them he'd kept his peace and endured, waiting for better times, but that during his stay the harvest had increased gradually in the fields, that he'd seen the cows give more and more milk, that he'd shared everyone's joy at each new machine, each new construction. . . . He regretted that the gradualness of the changes in Plebanovka didn't belong to him; the suddenness of the picture that he'd discovered in a single moment, as if with a knife, cut him off from this life, deprived him of the sacred connection with it. And he wanted to participate in the misfortunes and the joys of Plebanovka. In the misfortunes, perhaps, even more than in the joys.

Suddenly he heard women's voices speaking softly beneath the window. One was unfamiliar; the other belonged to Katerina Panasovna. At first only isolated exclamations and giggles reached him, then the women evidently perched on the porch steps, and their conversation flowed audibly without a break.

"Ay, Ania, Ania, I simply don't understand how you can live all alone."

"It's nothing, I've already got used to it. It's our age—forty years old! You know how many family men there are. Just take our Plebanov school—you can count them on the fingers of one hand. Go on, tell me what happened next?"

"Well, then. He came here, the last one I was with, and I thought I'd die of shame. The whole area started talking, people were already setting May as my wedding date, but I couldn't make up my mind. And my Galia was dead set against it! 'Mommy, Mumsie, we'll live together, I'll never leave you!' What an egoist. She even threw herself at my feet. I wouldn't have paid attention, Ania, if it had been love. . . . But I didn't love him. I would watch him as if through a double pane—there was glass upon glass between us!—he'd walk around—he wasn't one of us, do you know what I mean? And I told him no. What can you do? Better to be alone, and besides, there's no time, you know, Ania: first there's the sowing, then cutting the beet, or else the threshing, and then, on top of that, the kolkhoz cows ate too much young peas, the fool of a herdsman drove them in. You can imagine the yelling! And the panic! We pierced the cows' stomachs; one died, we saved the rest. . . . What kind of marriage can I have? There's no time! Can you believe, my friend, that I have no time to get married! Absolutely no time! . . . There was one fellow who wrote to me; he wrote after Truskavets[7]—we met there—wonderful letters, and like a fool I lived just for them, from letter to letter; I adore getting letters better than any gifts. But there was the harvest, Ania, and then the rains. There was no place to dry the grain! We closed off the highway, all five kilometers of it, built a dirt-road detour, and spread the grain on the asphalt, and every single night, like a madwoman, I'd drive in my Volga along the side of the road, back and forth. I was afraid it'd get stolen or the rain would start pouring again—if it washed the wheat off into the ditch, what then? I had no time to write a reply, and so it all ended. And it's a pity, Ania. He was a fine, good-looking man, an engineer! God, I have no luck!" she exclaimed, and Osadchaia's voice was filled with a powerful, deep sound.

"Look—it's raining!" said Ania after a silence.

"Ay, we had only a little bit left to harvest, all we needed was two more days or so. . . . Listen to it pound on the burdocks, the scoundrel!" said Katerina Panasovna. "Ay, Anechka, thank you, I've got it all off my chest and seem to feel better. . . . You know, I'd be happy to receive any letters—not love letters, but simply friendly ones. . . . But whom can I ask? I have one old acquaintance in Belaia Tserkov,[8] but I'm very shy about asking him."

"Nobody writes without something in mind," sighed Ania. "Guys won't start writing to you just as friends!"

They said their goodbyes. Katerina Panasovna entered the house, lay down on the other side of the wall, and gave a profound, heartfelt sigh, with a sweet, childlike half-sob.

The raindrops were now falling less frequently on the burdock, and Roman Iosifovich dozed off.

In the morning he awoke alone in the empty house. He walked about the rooms, looked through an old copy of *Ogoniok*,[9] and glanced out of the window—it was overcast, warm, and still. . . . Suddenly he saw a note on the table.

"Roman Iosifovich, don't leave without having breakfast: there are potatoes and tomatoes under the newspaper. If you decide to leave before I return, put the key under the step on a brick. Katerina."

He did as she'd told him to, put the key on a brick and set off for the bus. "Khristina," he thought, "what if I write to her as a friend, eh? Only as a friend! You believe me, don't you? Khristina, Khristina, my poor dear!"

NOTES

Introduction

1. Ruf' Zernova, *Zhenskie rasskazy* (Ann Arbor: Hermitage, 1981), p. 5.

2. For a critical review of Ioffe's book and five other autobiographical memoirs recently published in New York, see Laura Engelstein, "In a Female Voice," *Slavic Review*, Spring 1985, pp. 104–107.

3. Sandra M. Gilbert, "What Do Feminist Critics Want? A Postcard from the Volcano," in *The New Feminist Criticism*, ed. Elaine Showalter (New York: Pantheon Books, 1985), pp. 31, 35.

4. Judith Kegan Gardiner, "Gender, Values, and Lessing's Cats," in *Feminist Issues in Literary Scholarship*, ed. Shari Benstock (Bloomington and Indianapolis: Indiana University Press, 1987), p. 122.

5. Elaine Showalter, "Towards a Feminist Poetics," *Women Writing and Writing about Women*, ed. Mary Jacobs (New York: Barnes & Noble, 1979), p. 35.

6. "Feminine writings" here is not used synonymously with what French feminists such as Luce Irigaray and Hélène Cixous designate as *écriture féminine*, i.e., "a process or practice by which the female body, with its peculiar drives and rhythms, inscribes itself as text." See Nancy K. Miller, "Emphasis Added: Plots and Plausibilities in Women's Fiction," in *The New Feminist Criticism*, p. 341; and Elaine Marks, "Women and Literature in France," *Signs* 3 (Summer 1978): 832–42.

7. Gardiner, p. 115.

8. For a book-length elaboration of the same notion, see Barbara Heldt, *Terrible Perfection: Women and Russian Literature* (Bloomington and Indianapolis: Indiana University Press, 1987).

9. The roles of Pisarev and Mikhailov in the women's movement in Russia are assessed cogently in the excellent study by Richard Stites, *The Women's Liberation Movement in Russia* (Princeton: Princeton University Press, 1978).

10. For a more complete listing, see N. N. Golitsyn, *Bibliograficheskii slovar' russkikh pisatel'nits*, St. Petersburg, 1889, reprinted in Leipzig, 1974; S. I. Ponomarev, *Nashi pisatel'nitsy*, St. Petersburg, 1891, reprinted in Leipzig, 1974.

11. Temira Pachmuss, *Women Writers in Russian Modernism* (Urbana: University of Illinois Press, 1978), pp. xi and 12.

12. Silvia Bovenschein, "Is There a Feminine Aesthetics?" trans. Beth Weckmueller, in *Feminist Aesthetics*, ed. Gisela Ecker (Boston: Beacon Press, 1985/1986), p. 26.

13. *Women and Russia: Feminist Writings from the Soviet Union*, ed. Tatyana Mamonova (Boston: Beacon Press, 1984), p. xx.

14. Ibid., p. 3.

15. Leon Trotsky, *Literature and Revolution*, trans. Rose Strunsky (Ann Arbor: University of Michigan Press, 1968), p. 41.

16. For more on this question, see Lev Ozerov, *Moscow News*, 1987, no. 5 (February), p. 16.

17. Thick journals in Russia seem to have established the peculiar policy (unless chance accounts for the consistent pattern) of having no more than two women on their editorial boards, which consist of anywhere from twelve to eighteen members. Such is the case with *October* (Oktiabr'), the *Star* (Zvezda), and the paper *Literary Russia* (Literaturnaia Rossiia). *Friendship of Nations* (Druzhba narodov) has three women among its twenty-five editorial board members.

18. Ronald Hingley, *Russian Writers and Soviet Society, 1917–1978* (New York: Random House, 1979), p. 172.

19. Maggie McAndrew, "Soviet Women's Magazines," in *Soviet Sisterhood*, ed. Barbara Holland (Bloomington: Indiana University Press, 1985), p. 87, passim.

20. *Moscow News*, 1987, no. 10, p. 16.

21. On this, see the article by Fyodor Turovsky, former chairman of the legal committee of the Moscow Construction Workers' Union, who corroborates other commentators' claims regarding the widespread violation of Soviet women's right to and at work. See Fyodor Turovsky, "Society without a Present," in *The Soviet Worker from Lenin to Andropov*, ed. Leonard Shapiro and Joseph Godson (New York: St. Martin's Press, 1981/1984), pp. 184–86.

22. The oft-quoted phrase originated with Kuzma Prutkov, the pseudonym adopted by A. K. Tolstoy (1817–75) and his two cousins for their joint publications of humorous, satirical, and nonsensical verse.

23. I. Grekova, "Real Life in Real Terms," *Moscow News*, 1987, no. 24, p. 11.

24. "Galina Volchek with and without Makeup," *Moscow News*, 1987, no. 12, p. 16.

25. On the sociocultural origin of women's relationship to clothes and on the significance of various fashions, see Susan Brownmiller, *Femininity* (New York: Fawcett Columbine, 1984), pp. 79–102.

26. Mikhail Gorbachev, *Perestroika: New Thinking for Our Country and the World* (New York: Harper & Row Publishers, 1987), p. 117.

27. Judith Newman, "Making—and Remaking—History: Another Look at 'Patriarchy,' " in *Feminist Issues in Literary Scholarship*, p. 129.

28. A point of consensus among women who may disagree about practically everything else is the primacy of love. See, for example, the essay by Ekaterina Mironova in Mamonova's collection, which proclaims, "Love is life itself." Ekaterina Mironova, "About the New Americans," in *Women and Russia*, p. 132.

29. For a thorough examination of the social origins and psychological processes behind the cult of the Virgin Mary, see Michael P. Carroll, *The Cult of the Virgin Mary* (Princeton: Princeton University Press, 1986). For a feminist analysis of the same phenomenon, see Marina Warner, *Alone of All Her Sex: The Myth of the Virgin Mary* (New York: Alfred A. Knopf, 1976).

30. Natasha Maltsev, "The Other Side of the Coin," in *Women and Russia*, p. 111.

31. Ann Rosalind Jones, "Writing the Body: Towards an Understanding of *l'Ecriture féminine,*" in *The New Feminist Criticism,* pp. 368–69.

32. Elizabeth Berg, "Iconoclastic Moments: Reading the *Sonnets for Héléne,* Writing the *Portuguese Letters,*" in *The Poetics of Gender* (New York: Columbia University Press, 1986), p. 220, pp. 208–221 passim.

33. Probably the best-known icon of motherhood to appear in recent women's fiction is Anfisa Gromova in I. Grekova's *Ship of Widows,* rather woodenly translated into English by Cathy Porter (Topsfield, Mass.: Virago/Salem House, 1985).

34. The English version of the novel is Julia Voznesenskaya, *The Women's Decameron,* trans. W. B. Linton (London/New York: Quartet Books, 1985).

35. Russia is not unique in this respect, of course, as many studies have confirmed. See, for example, the balanced account contained in the eloquently subtitled volume by Sylvia Ann Hewlett, *A Lesser Life: The Myth of Women's Liberation in America* (New York: William Morrow & Co., 1986).

36. Grekova, p. 11.

37. Iurii Trifonov, "Net, ne o byte—o zhizni!" *Kak slovo nashe otzovetsia,* M. "Sovetskaia Rossiia," 1985, p. 102.

38. The feminist Ekaterina Alexandrovna has described the type of relationship that reigns in the average Soviet family as follows: "Dissatisfaction with another, mutual misunderstanding, difficult relations between the generations, and a deep-seated discontent with life all too frequently turn into open hostility and then into hatred. Strained relations in the family, constant arguments, and a lack of respect for one another that would surprise a 'civilized' person turn family life Soviet-style into a living hell." Ekaterina Alexandrovna, "Why Soviet Women Want to Get Married," in *Women and Russia,* p. 33.

39. If, as some traditionalist critics maintain, the touchstone of a superior piece of autobiography is the retrospective stance and the resulting temporal duality, then contemporary Russian female authors continuously produce autobiographical fiction, with one vital reservation: their bifocal perspective does not yield the serene aloofness that traditionalists seem to impute automatically to retrospection. See the essay by Norine Voss, " 'Saying the Unsayable': An Introduction to Women's Autobiography," in *Gender Studies: New Directions in Feminist Criticism,* ed. Judith Spector (Bowling Green: Bowling Green State University Popular Press, 1986), pp. 218–233, especially pp. 219–220. Feminist critics have drawn attention to the "quasi-autobiographical voice" adopted repeatedly in recent feminist novels. On this, see Rosalind Coward, "Are Women's Novels Feminist Novels?" in *The New Feminist Criticism,* especially pp. 228, 231.

40. Whether an identifiable gender-specific style exists or not, of course, is one of the major questions vexing contemporary feminist theory.

41. Elaine Showalter has argued that women's traditional piecework, quilting, and patchwork have consequences for the structures, genres, themes, and meanings of American women's writing in the nineteenth and twentieth centuries. She detects correspondences between the processes of "piecing" and "structuring" texts that carry suggestive implications for the format of *The Women's Decameron.* See Elaine Showalter, "Piecing and Writing," in *The Poetics of Gender,* pp. 222–247.

42. Interview taped with Nina Katerli in Leningrad, 1987, provided by John Fred Beebe, who has my gratitude.

43. Trifonov regularly employs the same tactic in his fiction in the service of moral epiphanies.

44. For an analysis of Tolstaia's treatment of gender stereotypes, see my forthcoming "Monsters Monomaniacal, Marriageable, and Medical: Tat'iana Tolstaia's Regenerative Use of Gender Stereotypes."

"The Kiss"

1. Natulia—diminutive form of Natalia, as is Natasha.

2. "Solvejg's Song"—part of the music composed by the Norwegian Edvard

Grieg (1843–1907) as accompaniment to Henrik Ibsen's fantasy play *Peer Gynt* (1874–75). Many consider "Solvejg's Song" the musical highlight of the suite.

"Peters"

1. Friedrich Schiller (1759–1805)—German dramatist and poet whom the Russians associate with freedom, uncompromising idealism, and noble aspirations. The strong conflicts and elevated sentiments in his dramas, such as *Kabale und Liebe* (1784) and *Don Carlos* (1787), have inspired many opera composers, among them Giuseppe Verdi.

2. Friedrich Hölderlin (1770–1843)—German poet who evolved from hymnic poems to the ideal values of humanity, harmony, friendship, and love in his early poetry, to the lyrics of alienation and skepticism, expressing his desire to merge with the absolute, that characterize his more mature years.

3. "dawn, dawn" (zaria, zaria)—the last two words of the twelve-line lyric poem by Afanasii A. Fet (1820–92) known by its first line, "Shopot, robkoe dykhan'e" (1850). The poem beautifully recreates the magic of a love tryst without the use of a single verb.

4. "Admire, Adele . . . " (Liubi, Adel',/Moiu svirel')—the last two lines of a poem in an Anacreontic key by A. Pushkin entitled "To Adele" (Adeli, 1822).

5. Ilia Repin (1844–1930)—painter of portraits and landscapes, associated with the group of Wanderers or Itinerants who advocated social commentary and a realistic style.

"Herbs from Odessa"

1. *Smertonosnaia* means "death-bearing" or "fatal," the first of many motifs used to create an atmosphere of ominous mystery. Others include the name Skazka (Fairytale), the bathhouse (in Russian folklore traditionally associated with the devil), the cat, metamorphosis, the "magic" potion, the Gothic story (of death and supernatural events) within the story, and throwing out the icon.

2. Ezhov purges—the ghastly purges of 1936–38, headed by Nikolai Ezhov, the chief of the NKVD (secret police, now KGB), which entailed a wholesale elimination of personnel in various walks of life (e.g., the army, navy, etc.).

3. The promise becomes a leitmotif that contributes to the aura of uneasy mystery permeating the story.

4. Liusik is the husband of Liusia, and the nearly identical names make for puzzling confusion.

5. Galina Ulanova (1909/1910)—renowned ballerina transformed by the Soviet government into a living icon for her contributions to the development of classical Russian ballet. At the Kirov Theater in Leningrad (1928–44) and the Bolshoi in Moscow (1944–60), she worked up an extensive repertoire of roles which she executed with lyricism and simplicity of means.

6. Oleg Popov—a circus performer who has entertained millions with his antics on the highwire and his routines as a clown. The "Sunny Clown," as he is called, has traveled abroad frequently with his act.

7. Carmen—the carefree protagonist of Prosper Mérimée's tale "Carmen" (1841), on which George Bizet based his famous opera by the same name. The latter, in turn, inspired Rodion Shchedrin's meretricious *Carmen Suite*, conceived explicitly to showcase the dancing skills of his wife, Maia Plisetskaia.

8. The verb contains a pun, for it means both "saw out" and "cheated."

9. Another instance of paronomasia, for the noun means both "potion" and "poison," an ambiguity that intensifies the menacing overtones of the story.

10. This story within the story combines elements of folklore with the Gothic, as does the girl's observation that at night black cats metamorphose into witches.

11. The capacity to alter appearance is a standard feature of the devil and of other spirits in Russian folklore.

12. Octobrates—Russian *oktobriata* are schoolboys in the first to third grades who belong to a politically based organization that prepares them to make the transition to the older group of similarly indoctrinated representatives of social consciousness, the Pioneers.

13. Beriozka—a foreign currency store, where the best Soviet and imported goods are reserved for sale both to the Soviet "privilegentsia" and to foreigners for foreign currency. The average Soviet citizen never gains access to these items.

"Nothing Special"

1. "Maiak"—since 1964, a twenty-four-hour nonstop radio program which broadcasts information and music. Also a brand of radio.

2. Korolkov—derived from *Korol'*, meaning "King," the name in its English equivalent would best be rendered as Kingly or Kingsley.

3. Nadezhda—literally, "hope."

4. Toropets—town in the Kalinin oblast.

5. Oksana—a formal version of the name Kseniya.

6. Moskvich—small Soviet car produced since 1946.

7. Baikonur—launching base in Kazakhstan from which the cosmonaut Iurii Gagarin (1934–68) took off for his historic space flight in 1961.

8. Nikolai Vavilov (1887–1943)—botanist and geneticist of enormous prestige until he opposed Lysenko's misguided theories about heredity. As a consequence, he was deposed as the head of the Academy of Agricultural Sciences (which he had founded) and arrested (1940); he perished in the Siberian concentration camps at Kolyma. His reputation was rehabilitated after Stalin's death. His brother Sergei Vavilov (1891–1951) was a physicist specializing in luminescence in condensed systems.

"Love"

1. Raisinville—in Russian, Iziumsk *(izium* means "raisin").

"The Wall"

1. The tenants in a communal apartment share kitchen and bathroom facilities. Since families of vastly different backgrounds may live together for most of their lives, these apartments often breed strong hostilities that become very unpleasant for the tenants. See, for example, I. Grekova's *The Ship of Widows.*

2. Novodevichye—dating from the nineteenth century, the most famous cemetery in Moscow, located beside the walls of the sixteenth-century Novodevichye Monastery. Many renowned representatives of Russian culture are buried there.

3. Vagankovskoe—cemetery situated in the northwest section of Moscow that dates from the plague epidemic of 1771. The prominent Russians interred there include the poet Sergei Esenin, the lexicographer Vladimir Dal, and the actor Pavel Mochalov.

4. Sergei Esenin (1895–1925)—a lyric poet who sang of a vanishing rural Russia and was associated with the Imagist movement in Russian literature. Esenin had a short, turbulent life. He gained notoriety abroad for his drinking sprees and his stormy, highly publicized marriage to Isadora Duncan, a pioneer of modern dance.

5. Iulian Semionov (1931–)—author of popular suspense novels dramatizing the activities of the Russian secret service.

6. In Maksim Gorky's play *The Lower Depths* (Na dne, 1902), the idea that

compassion is a degrading lie is articulated by Satin and stands in direct opposition to the philosophy of comforting kindness represented by the pilgrim Luka.

7. Shcherbakova or the publisher substituted the name Kostia here by mistake.

8. Satin—one of the "down-and-out" characters in Gorky's *Lower Depths* who does, indeed, emerge as a spokesman for clear-sighted, unflinching confrontation of facts, however unpalatable they may be.

9. The reference is to Nikolai Ostrovskii's insufferably optimistic novel entitled *How the Steel Was Tempered* (Kak zakalialas' stal', 1932–34), in which the preternaturally stoic hero, Pavel Korchagin, comes to the realization that life is humankind's most precious gift, to be lived as an active struggle for the sake of others' happiness, so that at death one need harbor no shame or regrets. The pertinent passage may be found in Nikolai Ostrovskii, *Sochineniia*, Moscow: Molodaia gvardiia, 1953, vol. 1, p. 196.

10. Elista—the capital of the Kalmykian Autonomous Republic, in Caucasia.

11. The candidate's degree corresponds more or less to the American Ph.D. In the Soviet Union, the doctor's degree and dissertation normally come after several years of successful work in the field of specialization.

12. Q.E.D.—*Quod erat demonstradum,* Latin for "which was to be shown," the phrase conventionally invoked in mathematic proofs.

13. *The Dancing Master*—a play by Lope de Vega (1562–1635), Spain's first great dramatist, who also authored verses and novels.

Vladimir Zeldin (1915–)—an actor best remembered for his role in the above-mentioned play.

The Queen of Spades (1890)—P. Tchaikovsky's opera based on A. Pushkin's superb tale of the same title.

Georgii Mikhailovich Nelepp (1904–1957)—celebrated tenor known principally as an exponent of Russian songs and Russian operatic roles.

14. Although officially Soviet authorities deplore the popular practice of acquiring residency in Moscow through marrying a Muscovite, they know it is a frequent ploy even nowadays.

15. In other words, he had spent time in the camps, or was Jewish or otherwise politically suspect.

16. Viacheslav Molotov (b. 1890)—Russian statesman who filled the post of commissar of foreign affairs 1939–49, 1953–56, after whom a crude form of incendiary grenade was labeled the Molotov cocktail.

17. Tuapse—a resort town on the Black Sea which attracts vacationers and tourists.

"Through Hard Times"

1. Pobeda—make of Soviet automobile.

2. Zhuchka—a generic name for dogs in Russian, like the American Rover.

3. New Volgograd—a port on the Volga River that was called Tsaritsyn until 1925 and Stalingrad until 1961. During World War II, heavy bombardment practically decimated the city, which had to undergo wholesale reconstruction.

4. Orenburg shawl—a "luxury" item, made from the fine goatskin for which the Orenburg oblast in the mineral-rich Ural industrial region is famous.

"The Farewell Light"

1. Sokolniki—a recreation park in the north-northeastern section of Moscow, with a rich history behind it.

2. Cheliabinsk—a city in the eastern Urals on the river Miass.

3. The Prague—a good restaurant located in the heart of Moscow that specializes in Czech cuisine.

4. Contemporary Theater—a Moscow theater founded in 1956 by a group of

young actors, graduates of the Moscow Art Theater. Today the theater is headed by one of its founders, the actress and director Galina Volchek.

5. Izmailovo Park—a huge recreation park in the northeastern part of Moscow, just within the Sadovoye Ring that encircles the city.

6. All the passages in verse, as well as the title of the story, are from the poem "Last Love" (Posledniaia liubov'), written in 1852–54 by Fiodor Tiutchev. The poignant lyric belongs to the Denisyeva cycle, inspired by Tiutchev's autumnal love for the young E. A. Denisyeva.

"Be Still, Torments of Passion"

1. *Little Dorrit* (1855–57)—a novel by Charles Dickens that offers his typical blend of social commentary and sentimentalism, adapted for the stage.

2. Florence, Mr. Dombey, Little Dorrit—protagonists of Dickens's novels *Bleak House* (1852–53), *Dombey and Son* (1846–48), and *Little Dorrit* respectively.

3. Leonid Vitalyevich Sobinov (1872–1934) was a renowned Russian tenor.

4. *Easy Money* (1859)—a play by Aleksandr Ostrovskii (1823–86), with his typical depiction of corruption among the new middle class.

5. Masha—the middle sister in Anton Chekhov's play *Three Sisters* (Tri sestry, 1900), psychologically the most complex of the three.

6. *Fruits of Enlightenment* (Plody prosveshcheniia, 1889)—Lev Tolstoi's four-act light comedy exposing the idle rich, in which Tania is the traditional clever servant who outwits her master.

7. "Fools" is a popular Russian card game.

"Stage Actress"

1. Shiva (also Siva)—the supreme god of many Indian sects. In Hinduism, Shiva is "the Destroyer," the third member of the Trimurti, along with Brahma the Creator and Vishnu the Preserver, these three being the principal deities.

2. Pushkin Museum—a museum in Moscow second in scope and importance only to the Hermitage Museum in Leningrad. It houses West European art as well as ancient Eastern and Egyptian masterpieces, and in September 1987 held the first major exhibit of Marc Chagall's works in the Soviet Union.

3. Kathakali—a spectacular lyric dance drama of southern India based on Hindu literature and performed with acrobatic energy and highly stylized pantomine.

Bharata natya—a traditional Indian dance formerly performed exclusively by devadavisis, who were dancing girls and courtesans of the Hindu temple.

4. tabla—a musical instrument popular in India, consisting of a set of double drums made of wood, clay, or copper resembling kettles in shape. The difference in pitch between the two is approximately an octave. Usually the right is called the tabla, the left, the dagga.

5. Palace of Culture—a building attached to most Soviet institutions and industries which is intended to provide employees with the chance to participate in cultural activities and find an outlet for creative talent.

6. Mossovet Theater—a theater established in Moscow in 1923 and associated with the pioneering efforts of Iurii Zavadskii (1894–1977), who took charge of productions in 1940 and strove for a lively repertoire of domestic and foreign plays.

7. The Hermitage in Moscow—a theater built by Ia. Shchukin in 1894 among the gardens in the center of Moscow where the Mossovet Theater held its performances 1923–48.

8. Nikolai Dmitrievich Mordvinov (1901–?)—a Soviet actor known for the tragic, dramatic, and comic roles he played in the Moscow Mossovet Theater from

1940 on, under the tutelage of Zavadskii. Much of his fame rests on his interpretation of Shakespearean roles, especially Othello (1944) and Lear (1958).

9. Olga Arturovna Viklandt (1911–)—an actress associated with Moscow's Mossovet Theater from 1938 to 1949, and subsequently with the Pushkin Theater. Pert comic roles were her forte.

10. *Vaniushkin's Children* (Deti Vaniushkina)—a four-act drama written in 1901 by Sergei Aleksandrovich Naidenov (né Alekseev). In this, his first and best work, he continued the tradition of the mid-nineteenth-century playwright Nikolai Ostrovskii by portraying the grasping, unenlightened nature of the merchant class.

11. Alma Ata—since 1929, the capital of Kazakhstan, in the Asian part of the Soviet Union.

12. Tashkent—since 1930 the capital of Uzbekistan, in the southwest part of the Soviet Union and in Asia.

13. Nikolai Pavlovich Akimov (1901–1968)—famous Soviet director born in Kharkov who first worked in a children's theater, then won a reputation for his *Hamlet* at the Vakhtangov Theater in 1932. From the mid-thirties he was the artistic director of the Leningrad Comic Theater, and from 1951 he headed the Lensovet Theater in Leningrad. He taught and published widely about the theater.

14. Polina Antipyevna Strepetova (1850–1903)—an actress renowned for acting in the Realist plays of Ostrovskii and A. Pisemskii, she was immortalized by the famous Realist (Itinerant) painters Ilia Repin and Nikolai Iaroshenko (1846–1898).

15. Krasavino—a river town famous for its lace, located in the northwest part of the Soviet Union.

16. Serenus Zeitblom—the narrator of Thomas Mann's immensely complex novel *Doktor Faustus* (1947), which traces the downfall of a demonic musician, but on a more profound level treats the problems of Nazi Germany.

"Between Spring and Summer"

1. Throughout the story, Katerli employs several variants of Ksenia's name—Kena, Kenka, Kenia, Ksana—which is standard practice in Russian usage.

2. The Russian patronymic is derived from one's father's name and is the obligatory second name of every Soviet citizen. The use of the first two names, i.e., the Christian name and the patronymic, is the most common form of respectful address.

3. The Khibins—the highest mountains in the Kola Peninsula, north of the Arctic Circle.

4. Karelia—an autonomous republic in the northwestern USSR having close geographical and linguistic ties with Finland. The Khibins are not located there, but they are close by.

5. Uchkeken—northeast of Elbrus and the highest mountains in Europe.

6. Novyi Afon—settlement in the Abkhazian Autonomous Republic, located eighteen kilometers northwest of Sukhumi, the capital, on the Black Sea coast. Known primarily as a health resort and tourist base, it also boasts the Novyi Afon monastery, a museum, and a number of karst caves.

7. Lezghinka—a lively, demanding Caucasian dance requiring skill and stamina.

8. On the side—not as part of his job, but done for private individuals. At this time it was technically illegal, but filled an important gap in the economy, so it did not have to be done secretly.

9. Mankurt—a zombielike human in the novel by Chingiz Aitmatov entitled *A Day Lasts Longer Than a Lifetime* (Dol'she veka dlitsia den', *Novyi mir,* 1980, no. 11). In 1981 it was published separately as *Burannyi polustanok* and translated into English as *The Day Lasts More Than a Hundred Years* (Indiana University Press, 1983). The novel contains the report of a legend in which the Zhuan-Zhuan people take

their prisoners and wrap their heads in saturated camel's udders, so that the udde. shrinks and compresses the head. Most of the prisoners die, but the survivors completely lose their memory and their humanity, so that in one instance a mankurt kills his mother when she tries to help him.

"The Road to Aktanysh"

1. Aktanysh—a town close to the northeast border of the Tatar Autonomous Republic in the Soviet Union.
2. Tuimazy—a regional center in the Bashkir Autonomous Republic with a flourishing oil industry.
3. *Grim River* (Ugrium reka)—Viacheslav Ivanov's panoramic novel (1933) about the mercantile development of Siberia at the turn of the century.

"Between Heaven and Earth"

1. Anna Magnani—Italian actress born in Egypt whose film career from 1934 coincided with the development of Italian Neo-Realism. Magnani's powerful portrayal of lower-class women made her name synonymous with passionate intensity in cinematic characterization.
2. *Field after Battle*—characteristic painting by Vasilii Vereshchagin (1842–1904), a painter connected with the Itinerants (Realists). The majority of his canvases depict battle scenes in a colorful, nationalistic vein.
3. At this stage they shift from the formal mode of address *(vy)* to the informal *(ty)*.

"A Threesome"

1. Stepan A. Bandera (1908–1959)—leader of Ukrainian nationalist partisan bands in the West Ukraine during the years 1943–47. The area suffered the trauma of one takeover after another, passing from Polish into Russian hands, then into German during the Second World War, and back into Russian.
2. As part of the process of extensive socialization, students in the Soviet Union must fulfill certain nonacademic duties useful to their society, such as participation in construction projects.
3. centner—a unit of weight equal to 220.46 lbs.
4. prize—it is standard practice for the administration of a kolkhoz or a factory in the Soviet Union to award incentives of this kind to encourage greater productivity.
5. Presumably as a result of the German invasion of Poland that precipitated World War II.
6. The phrase is the first line of the poem "Plovets" (The Swimmer) by Nikolai M. Iazykov (1803–1846).
7. Truskavets—a resort town in the Lvov oblast in the Ukraine close to the picturesque Carpathian Mountains.
8. Belaia Tserkov (lit. White Church)—a resort town and the regional center of the Kiev oblast in the Ukraine.
9. *Ogoniok*—an illustrated popular weekly filled with items covering social trends, political issues, the arts, etc., in a "popularizing" key that has changed radically in orientation and quality since Gorbachev's policy of *glasnost*. It has become a harbinger of "things to come" in the more serious, prestigious cultural magazines.

ADDENDUM

The publication history of the stories in this volume is as follows:

Baranskaia, N. "Potselui," in *Zhenshchina s zontikom*, Moscow, 1981, pp. 261–267.

Ganina, M. "Teatral'naia aktrisa," *Novyi mir*, 1971, no. 10, pp. 99–118. An earlier version of the story, almost identical to the journal edition, appeared as "Zolotoe odinochestvo" (1970) in Maiia Ganina, *Izbrannoe*, Moscow: Khudlit, 1983, pp. 269–301, and Maiia Ganina, *Sozvezdie bliznetsov*, Moscow: Sovetskii pisatel', 1984, pp. 387–411.

Katerli, N. "Proshchal'nyi svet," *Iunost'*, 1981, no. 9, pp. 53–61; "Mezhdu vesnoi i letom," *Neva*, 1983, no. 4, pp. 67–84. Both stories were reprinted in Katerli's collection entitled *Tsvetnye otkrytki*, Leningrad: Sovetskii pisatel', 1986, pp. 4–26 and 45–72 respectively.

Kazakova, R. "Eksperiment," *Fantastika*, 1965, vyp. 3, pp. 147–155.

Kozhevnikova, N. "Domoi," *Iunost'*, 1975, no. 2, pp. 60–62.

Makarova, E. "Travy iz Odessy," in *Perepolnennye dni*, Moscow, 1982, pp. 38–55.

Mass, A. "Doroga na Aktanysh," *Zvezda*, 1974, no. 3, pp. 57–65; "Komandirovka domoi," *Nash sovremennik*, 1979, no. 9, pp. 32–42.

Petrushevskaia, L. "Skripka," "Mania," *Druzhba narodov*, 1973, no. 10, pp. 151–153 and 154–157 respectively.

Shcherbakova, G. "Stena," *Znamia*, 1979, no. 6, pp. 163–186 reprinted in Galina Shcherbakova, *Vam i ne snilos'*, Moscow, 1983, pp. 84–119.

Tokareva, V. "Nichego osobennogo," *Novyi mir*, 1981, no. 4, pp. 113–133. Reprinted in V. Tokareva, *Nichego osobennogo*, Moscow: Sovetskii pisatel', 1983, pp. 276–310; "Mezhdu nebom i zemlei," *Novyi mir*, 1985, no. 3, pp. 60–68.

Tolstaia, T. "Peters," *Novyi mir*, 1986, pp. 123–131. Reprinted in T. Tolstaia, *Na zolotom kryl'tse sideli*, Moscow, 1987.

Uvarova, L. "Liubov'," in *Rasskazy*, Moscow: Moskovskii rabochii, 1978, pp. 52–63; "Uimites', volneniia strasti," *Zvezda*, 1986, no. 3, pp. 132–143.

Addendum

Varlamova, I. "Troe," *Nash sovremennik*, 1968, no. 6. Reprinted in I. Varlamova, *Tri liubvi*, Moscow, 1974, pp. 222–264.

Velembovskaia, I. "V trudnuiu minutu," *Znamia*, 1965, no. 3, pp. 85–97. Reprinted in I. Velembovskaia, *Zhenshchiny*, Moscow: Sovetskii pisatel', 1967, pp. 257–282.

AUTHORS

NATALIA VLADIMIROVNA BARANSKAIA, b. 31 December 1908 in Leningrad.

Baranskaia was born into a doctor's family in Leningrad when the northern city still bore its historical name of Petersburg. As a result of their clandestine revolutionary activity, her parents were imprisoned when she was only one and a half years old. Upon their release, they emigrated to Switzerland. Right after the outbreak of World War I, at the age of six, Baranskaia returned to Russia with her mother. She attended Moscow State University, graduating in 1930 with a degree in language and literature and an additional specialization in history and ethnography. That training led quite naturally to Baranskaia's professional work in museums, where she prepares and oversees exhibits. Apart from her experiences as an editor, for several decades she has devoted most of her energies to research, spending as long as eight years, for example, assiduously poring over Pushkiniana at the Pushkin estate-museum at Mikhailovskoe.

Baranskaia has managed to combine a professional life with a domestic one, though not without struggle. Her husband perished in World War II (1943), leaving her with two children, with whom she was evacuated to Altai. When she moved back home to Moscow, to a house with shattered windows and no heat, her mother helped her cope with household tasks and the arduous conditions in which she, like countless other war widows, raised her fatherless children.

Baranskaia suddenly started writing fiction as a grandmother nearing sixty. She gained almost instant recognition with the publication of her novella *A Week Like Any Other* (Nedelia kak nedelia), which appeared in the prestigious journal *New World* (Novyi mir, no. 11) in 1969. Translated into half a dozen languages, this chronicle of the daily vicissitudes of an urban working wife and mother sparked controversy chiefly because of its sociological, rather than literary, value. It dramatizes the frantic struggles of a Moscow wife beleaguered by what has been called the "double duty syndrome": a relentless barrage of domestic chores and professional demands for which the twenty-four-hour day never suffices. Widely interpreted in the the West as a feminist tract, the novella is characteristic of Baranskaia insofar as it focuses on a female protagonist in the context of a modern city, shows a sensitive grasp of human psychology, and reveals the author's penchant for irony. These traits likewise mark the stories Baranskaia has published in various magazines and her two collections. Baranskaia's first novel, *Den' pominoveniia* (Memorial Day), is scheduled for publication in 1989.

Works in English translation: "The Alarm Clock in the Cupboard" (usually rendered as "A Week Like Any Other"), trans. Beatrice Stillman, *Redbook*, March 1971, pp. 179–201; "The Retirement Party," trans. Anatole Forostenko, *Russian Literature Triquarterly*, Spring 1974, no. 9, pp. 136–144. "Woman with an Umbrella" is being translated for a British publisher.

Works in Russian: *Nedelia kak nedelia*, Copenhagen: Rosenkilde and Bagger, 1973; *Nedelia kak nedelia: Povest'*, Paris: Institut d'études slaves, 1976; *Otritsatel'naia Zhizel'*, Moscow: Molodaia gvardiia, 1977; *Zhenshchina s zontikom*, Moscow: "Sovremennik," 1981; *Portret, podarennyi drugu*, Leningrad: Lenizdat, 1982.

Works in non-English translation: *En ganske almindelig uge*, Kvindehusets Bogcafe: Abenra 26, 1972; *Une semaine comme une autre*, Paris: Editions l'Age d'homme, 1973; *Une semaine comme une autre et quelques recits*, Paris: Editions des Femmes, 1976; *Woche um Woche: Frauen in der Sowjetunion: Erzählungen*, Darmstadt: Luchterhand, 1979; *Sovremennye russkie pisateli: Moderne russische Schriftsteller*, Munich: Max Heuber Verlag, 1980; *Das Ende der Welt: Erzählungen von Frauen*, Darmstadt: Luchterhand, 1985.

MAIA ANATOLIEVNA GANINA, b. 23 September 1927 in Moscow.

Of all contemporary women authors published on a steady basis and accorded a measure of recognition in the Soviet Union, perhaps Ganina more than any of her colleagues deserves the label of feminist. Apart from focusing in her own fiction on working women endowed with independence, strong will, and professional skill, Ganina has involved herself in several publishing ventures undertaken specifically to educate the Russian reading public about women's status in the outlying regions of the Soviet state. Certain aspects of her biography indicate that her intense awareness of gender distinctions has roots in the early formative years of her life.

Ganina was an unwanted child resulting from a misalliance between twenty-year-old Lidia Ilinskaia and Anatolii Ganin, a Siberian eighteen years her senior. Both parents worked at the Supreme Court until public knowledge of their marital strife and their child's birth ruined Ganin's legal career. He eventually landed a job as an engineer at an auto plant, where he remained until his retirement. He died in 1974 at the venerable age of eighty-five. As Ganina herself acknowledges, he was the single greatest influence on his daughter.

Abandoned by her mother and neglected by her father, Ganina led an idiosyncratic and lonely childhood that centered on books and forced her to rely on her imagination. Although she started composing poetry and prose early, Ganina received her education during her late teens at a technical school in Moscow. Upon graduation she worked as a technician in a plant, simultaneously pursuing a training in literature through correspondence courses at the Gorky Literary Institute. In 1954 the institute awarded her a diploma and *New World* (Novyi mir) published her novella *First Trials* (Pervye ispytaniia), which offered a close look at working-class youth. Since then, Ganina's prose has appeared regularly in journals and collections.

Ganina's fiction explores subjects that have cropped up fairly frequently in recent prose by Russian women: the drive for personal and professional fulfillment; the difficulties of sustaining a career while also managing the role of wife and mother; the emotional hardships attaching to romantic and domestic love in a context of compromise, boredom, and habitual infidelity; the value and resilience of female friendship; the destructive seductiveness of material comfort; the dearth of strong, efficient, ethical men; and the heavy burden of responsibility carried by Soviet children in widowed, divorced, discordant, or illicit families. Many of her narratives evidence her attraction to Eastern culture and philosophy.

In addition to her stories, novellas, and novels, Ganina has written a sociological study of the working and domestic life of the women residing in an industrial town on the Kama River; translations from Tatar and Tuvinian; children's stories; travelogues; and musical commentaries. She has also given interviews and made public her opinions about contemporary trends in Russian literature. A member of the Writers' Union, at its last congress she rebuked the organization for not appointing women into influential positions within its structure.

Ganina cannot be called a brilliant stylist. Her strength as a writer lies in her understanding of human psychology and her ability to portray convincingly, often subtly, forceful characters torn by contradictory drives and allegiances.

Works in English translation: *The Road to Nirvana,* Moscow: Progress Publishers, 1971.

Works in Russian: Collections of fiction: *Matvei i Shurka: Rasskazy,* Moscow: Sovetskaia Rossiia, 1962; *Ia ishchu tebia, chelovek,* Moscow: Sovetskii pisatel', 1963; *Rasskazy,* Moscow: Sovetskaia Rossiia, 1966; *Zachem spilili kashtany?* Moscow: Sovetskii pisatel', 1967; *Povest' o zhenshchine: Povesti, rasskazy, ocherki,* Moscow: Sovremennik, 1973; *Dal'naia poezdka: Rasskazy,* Moscow: Sovetskaia Rossiia, 1975; *Sozvezdie bliznetsov: Povesti i rasskazy,* Moscow: Sovetskii pisatel', 1980, 1984; *Izbrannoe,* Moscow Khudlit, 1983; *Sto zhiznei moikh: Roman, povest',* Moscow: Sovremennik, 1983.

Novels: *Slovo o zerne gornichnom,* Moscow, 1965, Moscow: Sovremennaia Rossiia, 1971; *Esli budem zhit', Oktiabr',* 1983, no. 6, pp. 18–132; *Poka zhivu—nadeius', Oktiabr',* 1986, no. 10, and *Oktiabr',* 1987, no. 11, pp. 13–118.

Travelogues: *Zapiski o pogranichnikakh,* Moscow: Molodaia gvardiia, 1969; *K sebe vozvraschaius' izdaleka,* Moscow: Sovetskii pisatel', 1971; *Dorogi Rossii,* Moscow: Molodaia gvardiia, 1981.

Children's literature: *Tiapkin i Lesha: Povest',* Moscow: Detskaia literatura, 1977.

Essays: *Kamazonki na rabote i doma [Ocherki o zhenshchinakh Naberezhnykh Chelnov],* Moscow: Sovetskaia literatura.

Translations: A. Giliazov, *Devich'i pis'ma [Povesti],* from Tatar, Moscow: Sovremennik, 1973; *Povest' o svetlom mal'chike,* from Tuvinian, for children, Moscow: Sovetskaia Rossiia, 1977.

Musical commentary: *Russkaia muzykal'naia literatura,* vyp. 4, 1973, vyp. 4, 1977, vyp. 4, 1982.

Bibliography: Rena Sheiko, "Na semi vetrakh," *Literaturnaia gazeta,* 12 December 1984, p. 5; E. Starikova, "Portrety i razmyshleniia," *Novyi mir,* 1963.

NINA SEMIONOVNA KATERLI, b. 30 June 1934 in Leningrad.

A native and resident of Leningrad now in her fifties, Katerli decided to follow in her mother's footsteps when she turned to writing. A graduate of the Lensovet technical school with a degree in engineering, Katerli claims to have gradually realized that the only satisfaction she derived from her job as an engineer was writing reports and correspondence. Since her literary debut in 1973, she has published comparatively little, most of it contained in her two prose collections of 1981 and 1986.

At her most experimental, Katerli gives free rein to her imagination, incorporating pure fantasy, inexplicable shifts in locale and point of view, radical temporal jumps, unexpected juxtapositions, and modified stream of consciousness into her narrative. Her forays into fantasy represent only one side of her fictional manner, and the risks she takes in that mode sometimes yield uneven results. In a less venturesome but more consistent vein, Katerli also recreates in concrete detail modern urban settings, against the background of which she explores romantic ties, family problems, communal living, and the inconsistencies and irrational, destructive involutions of the human psyche. The point of departure for her fiction is human relations, people's failure to make meaningful contact and to understand each other. Whereas her early stories were rooted in autobiographical experiences, with time she branched out to encompass narratives structured around hypothetical situations and purely imagined personae. Her cast of characters covers the full spectrum of old, middle-aged, young, and adolescent of both sexes. Unlike the majority of Russian women prosaists, Katerli prefers to view events from a male center of consciousness. She favors parallel plot lines, and an elliptical style complicated by animal imagery and literary allusions, marked by jagged sentence fragments and rich in colloquialisms.

Works in English translation: "The Barsukov Triangle," trans. David Lapeza, in *The Barsukov Triangle, the Two-Toned Blond, and Other Stories,* ed. Carl and Ellendea Proffer, Ann Arbor: Ardis, 1984, pp. 3–71.

Works in Russian: Collections: *Okno,* Leningrad: Sovetskii pisatel', 1981; *Tsvetnye otkrytki,* Leningrad: Sovetskii pisatel', 1986.

Novellas: *Treugol'nik Barsukova, Glagol,* no. 3, Ann Arbor: Ardis, 1981, *Kurzap, Zvezda,* 1986, no. 11, pp. 88–115; *Zhara na severe. Povest', Zvezda,* 1988, no. 4, pp. 3–73.

RIMMA FIODOROVNA KAZAKOVA, b. 1932 in Sevastopol.

Kazakova's early childhood was spent in Belorussia, though she was born in the southern Ukraine. She obtained her advanced education at Leningrad University, where she majored in history, and supplemented her training a decade later with courses in literature. Since the 1960s she has resided in Moscow. Her extensive travels, however, keep her constantly on the move, for Kazakova belongs to the literary establishment as much as any woman can in the Soviet Union. As a result, she acts as a spokeswoman for orthodox views at such official events as literary and political conferences, national celebrations, commemorative ceremonies, and activities associated with women (e.g., International Women's Day, the All-Union Women's Conference).

Kazakova's dominant genre is poetry, which she has published without interruption since the mid-1950s in such collections as *We'll Meet in the East* (Vstretimsia na Vostoke) and *I Remember* (Pomniu, 1974). Her pointedly titled story "The Experiment" represents her first attempt at prose fiction that is not memoiristic in nature.

Love is Kazakova's principal theme, though quite a few of her lyrics deal with war and warm attachment to Russia. Her poetry appeals directly and simply to the emotions and tends to rely on quite unremarkable similes and metaphors drawn from the world of nature. It contains more sentiment than originality.

Works in English translation: *The Tender Muse: Collection of Verse,* Moscow: Progress Publishers, 1976; "And for Me the War Began," *Soviet Literature,* 1982, no. 6 (411), pp. 83–88.

Works in Russian: *Izbrannaia lirika,* Moscow: Molodaia gvardiia, 1964; *V taige ne plachut: Stikhi,* Khabarovsk, 1965; *Piatnitsy: Kniga novykh stikhov,* Moscow: Sovetskii pisatel', 1965; *Elki zelenye: Kniga stikhov,* Moscow: Molodaia gvardiia, 1969; *Snezhnaia baba,* Moscow: Sovetskii pisatel', 1972; *Pomniu: Stikhi raznykh let,* Moscow: Sovetskaia Rossiia, 1974; *Nabelo: Stikhi,* Moscow: Sovetskii pisatel', 1977; *Ruslo: Izbrannye stikhotvoreniia,* Moscow: Khudlit, 1979; *Strannaia liubov',* Moscow: Molodaia gvardiia, 1980; *Probnyi kamen': Novaia kniga stikhov,* Moscow: Sovetskii pisatel', 1982; *Puteshestvie slezy: Izbrannye stikhotvoreniia: Perevod s persidskogo,* Moscow: "Nauka," 1984; *Soidi s kholma: Novaia kniga stikhov,* Moscow: Sovetskii pisatel', 1984; *Izbrannye proizvedeniia* v dvukh tomakh, Moscow: Khudlit, 1985.

NADEZHDA VADIMOVNA KOZHEVNIKOVA, b. 7 April 1949 in Moscow. A graduate of the Gorky Literary Institute, Kozhevnikova is a native of Moscow and a member of the Writers' Union. From her literary debut in 1967, her fiction has examined the romantic and domestic lives of the urban intelligentsia. Time and again she returns to the themes of love, familial ties and pressures, generational differences, the obligations and complexities of parenthood, the uncertainties and misunderstandings, as well as lack of communication, that undermine marital relations, and the erosion of romantic illusions. Although several of her works have also analyzed betrayal ("Vera Perova"), loss ("A Toy Shop" [Magazin igrushek]), and the impossibility of complete mutual understanding ("Eurydice" [Evridiki]), the mere title of one of her novellas, "About Maternal, Filial, Elevated, and Earthly Love" (O liubvi materinskoi, dochernei, vozvyshennoi i zemnoi), accurately points to her chief concern as a writer. Her entire output, in fact, may be seen as a modern gloss of sorts on Tolstoi's "Family Happiness" and *Anna Karenina,* with a touch of Iurii Trifonov.

A firm believer in gender distinctions, Kozhevnikova is fascinated by the contrasting roles carved out for men and women by biology, society, and historical precedent and circumstance. Accordingly, she equates professionalism with male values and "domestic" worries with female psychology. Her narratives often present women striving to balance these two spheres or to make the transition from one to the other. Whatever their situations, Kozhevnikova's women are acutely aware of just how significantly their psychology and conduct contrast with the cultural male paradigm.

Like the majority of women writing in Russia today, Kozhevnikova presents the world of her fiction through the eyes of her female protagonists, whose voice invariably merges with the omniscient narrator's. That conflation creates a distance between the reader and Kozhevnikova's male characters that frequently makes the latter objects of dispassionate dissection rather than full-fledged humans on a par with their female counterparts. With a few exceptions, Kozhevnikova depicts male characters externally, while leaving the field wide open for her women to reveal their inner world in minute detail.

Kozhevnikova adheres faithfully to a conventional, low-key, realistic narrative. Retrospection accounts for the modified time shifts in her fiction, which follows a linear plot, avoids mystification and ambiguity, and favors a language almost wholly devoid of striking imagery and anything that smacks of modernism.

Works in English translation: "The Stone-Mason," *Soviet Literature,* 1981, no. 1 (394), pp. 100–104; "Rush Hour," trans. Valentina Jacque, *Soviet Literature,* 1984, no. 3 (432), pp. 107–110.

Works in Russian: Collections: *Chelovek, reka i most: povesti i rasskazy,* Moscow: Sovetskii pisatel', 1976; *Bremia molodosti (ocherki),* Moscow: Sovetskaia Rossiia, 1978; *Doma i liudi,* Moscow: Pravda, 1979; *O liubvi materinskoi, dochernei, vozvyshennoi i zemnoi: Povesti, rasskazy, ocherki,* Moscow: Sovetskii pisatel', 1979; *Elena prekrasnaia,* Moscow: Sovetskii pisatel', 1982; *Postoronnie v dome: Povesti,* Moscow: Sovremennik, 1983; *Vnutrennii dvor,* Moscow: Sovetskii pisatel', 1986; *Posle prazdnika,* Moscow: Sovremennik, 1988.

Collections for children: *Okna na dvor: Rasskazy i ocherki,* Moscow: Detskaia literatura, 1976; *Vorota i novyi gorod: Ocherki,* Moscow: Detskaia literatura, 1978.

ELENA GRIGORYEVNA MAKAROVA, b. 18 October 1951 in Baku. As the daughter of two poets (her mother is Inna Lisnianskaia), Makarova grew up in a literary household full of tensions stemming from her parents' incompatibility. After studying at but not graduating from the Surikov Art Institute, Makarova enrolled in the Gorky Literary Institute in Moscow. Subsequently she obtained a job in an experimental school teaching art and sculpture to children of kindergarten age. That experience is evoked in her volume of essays entitled *"Free the Elephant"* ("Osvobodite slona," 1985). Her two illustrated collections of stories and novellas, mainly from the 1970s, draw heavily on her own biography. They portray primarily Moscow intelligentsia, though some are set in Baku, and combine subtle psychological insights, originality of subject matter and perspective, and a vivid language in which slang and colloquialisms consort with philosophical aphorisms and numerous literary references.

The majority of Makarova's protagonists are adolescent girls trapped in a variety of problematic situations that test their maturity. Their vulnerabilities, sense of inadequacy, or naiveté provides the focal point of many Makarova stories (e.g., "Bonjour, Papa . . . and a Curtsey" [Bonzhur, Papa . . . i kniksen, 1977], "Fish-Needle" [Ryba-igla, 1978]). For the most part Makarova's adolescents are cast back upon themselves as they grope their way through a world ruled by shabby values, selfishness, and impotent regret. One of the most unsettling aspects of Makarova's fiction is the spiritual isolation of its adolescents and children, the dearth of reassuring warmth in general among the adults populating her fictional world. Mothers in particular seem incapable of fulfilling the hallowed maternal role of nurturers, mainly because of their own instability, self-absorption, or physical frailty. With rather dispiriting regularity, Makarova's adult characters bicker, harbor grudges, and cling to petty prejudices; couples marry, become disillusioned with each other, and divorce with questionable speed, paying scant attention to the impact of their actions on their children. Men drink to excess, resort to physical violence against women, and so forth. Makarova's fiction assumes that frustration, melancholy, and restlessness are the common lot of humanity, only sporadically interrupted by fleeting encounters with joy or satisfaction. Nevertheless, most of her youthful protagonists seek some form of permanence, and while their search inevitably dissolves in disappointment, in the process they acquire a "sentimental education."

Owing to the elliptical nature of Makarova's style, which often omits logical links and gives no preparation for, or explanation of, temporal leaps and shifts in locale, her narratives proceed in spurts and bounds. The terseness, uneven pacing, and highly introspective nature of these narratives lend a vitality to her prose. She never underestimates her readers' abilities, preferring to stimulate their curiosity with cryptic allusions rather than offer them protracted explanations. The texture of her predominantly first-person narratives is enriched by linguistic diversity, brimming with ethnic vocabulary and slang, jargon comprehensible only to a specific circle, foreign phrases, and songs and poems. Her publications thus far reveal a talent for psychological analysis, a narrative flair, and a secure command of language.

Works in Russian: *Katushka: Povesti,* Moscow: Sovetskii pisatel', 1978; *Perepolnennye dni: Rasskazy i povesti,* Moscow: Sovetskii pisatel', 1982; *"Osvobodite slona,"* Moscow: Znanie, 1985; *Leto na kryshe,* 1987; *Otkrytyi final,* Moscow: Sovetskii pisatel', 1989.

Bibliography: Nancy Condee, in *Newsletter* no. 9 to Institute of Current World Affairs, 29 July, 1985, pp. 3–11.

ANNA VLADIMIROVNA MASS, b. 6 April 1935 in Moscow.

Mass graduated from the Department of Languages and Literatures at Moscow State University. After marrying a geologist, she entered a geological techical school. Upon completing it, she spent a decade with her husband in geological expeditions that took them all over the Soviet Union. Now a member of the Writers' Union, Mass started publishing in the 1960s. Since then she has brought out more than five anthologies of stories, and has regularly worked for radio and published in journals. It is all the more surprising, then, that even among her colleagues in the Soviet Union she remains relatively unknown.

In much of Mass's fiction, one encounters women geologists at work in the field or returning home for a brief visit, frequently divided by the conflicting claims of personal obligations and professional advancement. At the heart of these narratives, which often unfold in the form of a familial or group gathering, lies the complex problem that lends weight and meaning to the plot line: the question of individual identity and how to realize that sense of self in decisions and actions, especially under powerful social pressures.

Mass's straightforward, unadorned style presents few complications for the reader beyond the occasional use of technical geological terms. Juxtaposition, which is a favorite device of hers, enables Mass to make her point and to create dramatic effects both eloquently and succinctly.

Works in English translation: "Lyuba's Wedding," trans. Anatole Forostenko, *Russian Literature Triquarterly*, Spring 1974, no. 9, pp. 145–159.

Works in Russian: *Zhestokoe solntse: Povest' v deviati novellakh*, Moscow: Molodaia gvardiia, 1967; *Raznotsvetnye cherepki: Povest' i rasskazy*, Moscow: Molodaia gvardiia, 1970; *Dereviannyi tiulen'*, Moscow: Molodaia gvardiia, 1972; *Beloe chudo: Rasskazy i povesti*, Moscow: Moskovskii rabochii, 1982; *Na Kolodozere: Rasskazy Iriny Konstantinovny Bogdanovoi*, Moscow: Sovetskii pisatel', 1982; *Mal'chik i sneg: Rasskazy i povest'*, Moscow: Molodaia gvardiia, 1984.

LIUDMILA STEFANOVNA PETRUSHEVSKAIA, b. 26 May 1938 in Moscow.

Petrushevskaia came to literature in 1963, but had to wait almost two decades before receiving grudging recognition for her innovative drama. Known principally as a playwright, Petrushevskaia worked as a radio reporter, studied journalism, and wrote fiction before becoming interested in the theater. A graduate of Moscow University with experience as an editor at a television studio, Petrushevskaia is a married mother of three who translates from Polish in her spare time. She first gained a reputation among fans who read her plays only in manuscript form, and among theater personnel who rehearsed them enthusiastically, only to undergo the frustration of having permission for a performance revoked at the last minute. The 1980s, however, have witnessed a happy reversal in her fortunes: her plays are appearing on the stage; they have gained a degree of official acceptance, and are even eliciting critical debate, excited commentary, and voluble praise. In fact, Petrushevskaia may be in danger of becoming a fashionable playwright.

Petrushevskaia's plays revolve around domestic incidents in the quietly depressing and lonely life of spiritually and financially dispossessed urbanites on the brink of psychological disintegration. The crushing emptiness of their existence unfolds gradually and unspectacularly in plays that on the surface seem devoid of significant, highly dramatic events. In an insistently understated tone, the dramas disclose the brutal, rarely acknowledged aspects of everyday familial and marital life. The eerily offhand manner in which Petrushevskaia's dramatis personae refer to multiple instances of cruelty, betrayal, compromise, and disaster offers a bleak picture of the moral indifference and psychological isolation that have pervaded Russian society, especially during the Brezhnev years. Convened in such mundane settings as poorly furnished apartments and decrepit housing, her personae matter-of-factly relate events in lives that are a string of dismal failures leading to a blind alley. Many of their revelations emerge through silence, for what is withheld or left glaringly unsaid tends to provide a key to the psychological makeup of Petrushevskaia's characters.

Petrushevskaia's fictional monologues have a somewhat narrower focus. Their unmistakable signature is the garrulous, almost obsessive narrator who disgorges a stream of gossipy information about the misadventures of painfully average individuals—usually young women. In virtually all cases, these tractable have-nots lead abortive or maimed lives, subjected to abusive treatment by selfish, pragmatic men or domineering relatives. The darkly ironic tone adopted by Petrushevskaia's dialogic narrator serves to emphasize the quiet desperation that is her heroine's customary state. And the chatty mode of narration intimates that repeated disheartening defeats and futile searches for significance or security are the common lot of the majority. Like her plays, Petrushevskaia's fiction blends the mundane with the insupportable in a steady flow of linguistically idiosyncratic patter that constitutes less a means of communication than a reflection of the solipsism in which her personae are immured and from which they seem incapable of escaping.

Works in English translation: *Four,* trans. Alma Law, New York: Institute for Contemporary East European Drama and Theatre, 1984.

Works in Russian: Plays: "Dva okoshka: P'esa-skazka," in 1 act, 6 scenes (for children), Moscow: VAAP, 1975; "Bystro khorosho ne byvaet, ili chemodan chepukhi (skazka v trekh kartinakh)," *Sbornik odnoaktnykh p'es,* Moscow: Sovetskaia Rossiia, 1978, pp. 97–111; "Prikhodite v kukhniu," *Odnoaktnye p'esy,* Moscow: Sovetskaia Rossiia, 1979; "Liubov'," *Teatr,* 1979, no. 3; *Uroki muzyki* and *Lestnichnaia kletka,* in V. Slavkin and L. Petrushevskaia, *P'esy,* Moscow: Sovetskaia Rossiia, 1983; *Tri devushki v golubom, Sovremennaia dramaturgiia,* 1983, no. 3. Unpublished plays: "Cinzano," *Teatral'naia zhizn',* 1988, no. 6, pp. 19–23; "Den' rozhdeniia Smirnovoi," "Pesnia dvadtsatogo veka," "Andante," "Komnata Kolumbiny," both in *Teatr,* 1988, no. 2, pp. 2–8, 8–12.

Stories: "Rasskazchitsa" and "Istoriia Klarissy," *Avrora,* 1972, no. 7, pp. 11–13, 13–15; "Skripka" and "Mania," *Druzhba narodov,* 1973, no. 10, pp. 151–153, 154–157; "Seti i lovushki," *Avrora,* 1974, no. 4, pp. 52–55; "Smotrovaia ploshchadka," *Druzhba narodov,* 1982, no. 1, pp. 56–70; "Cherez polia," *Avrora,* 1983, no. 5, pp. 113–114; "Tri rasskaza," *Avrora,* 1987, no. 2, pp. 87–94; "Tri rasskaza," *Neva,* 1987, no. 7, pp. 85–91; "Svoi krug," *Novyi mir,* 1988, no. 1, pp. 116–130.

Translation from Turkmen: *Moi chetyre kolesa: Na svoiu golovu,* comedy in 2 acts, Moscow: VAAP, 1975.

Bibliography: Melissa Smith, "*In Cinzano Veritas*: The Plays of Liudmila Petrushevskaya," *Slavic and East European Arts,* Special Issue: Recent Polish and Soviet Theatre and Drama, Winter/Spring 1985, vol. 3, no. 1, pp. 119–125; M. Turovskaia, "Trudnye p'esy," *Novyi mir,* 1985, no. 12, pp. 247–252; E. Nevzgliadova, "Siuzhet dlia nebol'shogo rasskaza," *Novyi mir,* 1988, no. 4, pp. 256–260.

GALINA NIKOLAEVNA SHCHERBAKOVA, pseudonym of Galina Nikolaevna Rezhabek, b. 10 May 1932 in Dzerzhinsk.

Born in Dzerzhinsk, Shcherbakova is a graduate of the languages and literatures department at Rostov University. She taught school before turning to journalism. That job required constant travel all over the Soviet Union. Married to a journalist, with a son in medicine and a daughter and grandchild, Shcherbakova now lives in Moscow. A member of the Writers' Union, she took up fiction in the 1970s. Her comparatively modest output of fiction, comprising two collections, plus a few individually published stories and novellas, deals with a generation indelibly marked by the events of World War II. Her narratives examine the psychology of love and the effects of time's passage on the postwar generation in a modern setting. One of her better-known novellas, *You Wouldn't Dream of It* (Vam i ne snilos'), adapted into a popular film by the same name and a play entitled *Roman and Julie* (Roman i Iul'ka), portrays the self-sacrificing life of two tenthgraders. Other pieces, such as "The Wall" (Stena) and "The Incident with Kuz-menko" (Sluchai s Kuz'menko), explore the dynamics of marriage, tracing the disillusionments, betrayals, and dissatisfactions that accumulate over the years and the price paid in human values by those self-deluded careerists motivated solely by utilitarian principles.

Like most contemporary women writers in Russia, Shcherbakova has the habit of retrospection, seeking clues to characters' current dilemmas in experiences and decisions of the past. As part of that movement backward, she allows her characters to reveal themselves in interior monologues and mental free associations that provide highly suggestive links and explanations.

Possibly because of her training as a journalist, Shcherbakova's writing has the concise, spare preciseness of reportage. It also reflects a keen eye for the eloquent gesture and an ear sensitive to individual speech patterns.

Works in Russian: Collections: *Sprava ostavalsia gorodok: Povesti,* Moscow: Sovetskii pisatel', 1979; *Vam i ne snilos',* Moscow: Sovetskii pisatel', 1983; *Otchaiannaia osen': Povesti,* Moscow, 1985; *Dver' v chuzhuiu zhizn',* Moscow, 1985; *Krushenie,* Moscow: Sovetskii pisatel', 1990; *Anatomiia razvoda,* Moscow: Molodaia gvardiia, 1990.

Play: *Roman i Iul'ka: P'esa-razmyshlenie,* Moscow, 1982.

VIKTORIA SAMOILOVNA TOKAREVA, b. 20 November 1937 in Leningrad.

Although she graduated as a pianist from the Leningrad Music School, Tokareva's early ambition was to become an actress. With that goal in mind, in 1963 she enrolled in the Moscow State Institute of Cinematography (VGIK); she published her first story a year later, while working on her institute diploma. Her daughter has followed Tokareva's example by also enrolling in the institute. After graduating from VGIK's scriptwriting department in 1967, Tokareva continued to write fiction and started authoring scripts for television and film, including *Ship of Widows* (Vdovii parokhod), based on I. Grekova's novella of the same name. A recipient of several film awards, among them the Golden Prize at the Tenth Moscow International film festival in 1977 for *Mimino,* Tokareva has also gained wide popularity in the last decade for her wryly witty fiction, some of which has appeared in the most respected literary journals and has been translated into a number of foreign languages.

Tokareva defines her talent in ironic stories that have affinities with the satirical sketches of earlier writers such as Nadezhda Teffi and Mikhail Zoshchenko. Lightness of touch, brevity, and inconclusiveness characterize her laconic narratives, which are peppered with pseudosyllogisms and mocking literary references. Their humor is underlaid with a profound seriousness that has surfaced increasingly in recent years. Tokareva's overriding concern is the quest for a meaningful and authentic existence, a quest undertaken in the teeth of human fallibility and discouraging external circumstances. Success and happiness for the most part recede in the inaccessible distance, for Tokareva's fictional world rests on the philosophical premise of discrepancy—between individuals, between aims and means, desires and actual possibilities, expectation and realization, intention and execution, style and essence, etc.

For her protagonists, Tokareva favors a young or youthful heroine from whose calculatedly guileless perspective the narrative unfolds. This protagonist's amorous pursuits or familial problems, which underpin her efforts to find her appropriate goal or niche in life, provide the plot material and narrative momentum. Plot, however, often plays a subordinate role, creating the impression that it exists solely to afford the distinctive voice of Tokareva's narrators opportunity for commentary. It is above all the highly individualized narrative voice, dispensing ostensibly casual generalizations about life in a breezy, ironic, self-deprecatory tone, that holds the key to Tokareva's art. The narrator's double-voiced, bifocal perception of situations and events distances Tokareva's reflective, ingenuous protagonists, as well as the reader, from experiences that otherwise would seem unbearably painful, for the events per se in Tokareva's fiction convey a gloomy picture of life. Tokareva's wittily skeptical treatment of human interaction, however, transforms melancholy insights into amusing scenarios that have won her a sizable audience.

Works in English Translation: "Oh, How the Mist Came Stealing," *Soviet Literature*, 1970, no. 6 (267), pp. 73–80; "On the Set," *Soviet Literature*, 1975, no. 3 (323), pp. 66–73; "That's How It Was," *Soviet Literature*, 1978, no. 3 (360), pp. 91–102; "Sidesteps," *Soviet Literature*, 1986, no. 6 (459), pp. 184–188.

Works in Russian: Collections: *O tom, chego ne bylo: Rasskazy*, Moscow: Molodaia gvardiia, 1969; *Kogda stalo nemnozhko teplee*, Moscow: Sovetskaia Rossiia, 1972; *Zanuda: Rasskazy*, Tallin: Periodika, 1977; *Letaiushchie kacheli: Rasskazy, povest'*, Moscow: Sovetskii pisatel', 1978, and Tallin, 1982; *Nichego osobennogo: Povesti i rasskazy*, Moscow: Sovetskii pisatel', 1983.

Film and television scripts: *Dzentel'meni udachi*, 1971; *Sovsem propashchii*, with Georgii Daneliia, 1972; *Mimino: Kinostsenarii*, with G. Daneliia and R. L. Gabriadze, Moscow: Iskusstvo, 1978; *Mezhdu nebom i zemlei*. Play: *Eksprompt-fantaziia*, 1982.

Bibliography: L. Lench, "Strannye, strannye liudi," *Literaturnaia gazeta*, 11 February 1970; I. Shtokman, "Mig povorota" (review of *O tom, chego ne bylo*), *Druzhba narodov*, 1970, no. 10, pp. 275–276; N. Zelenko, "Ne kantovat'—smekh!" *Sovremennaia kul'tura*, 18 January 1972; A. Marchenko, "Vremia iskat' sebia," *Novyi mir*, 1972, no. 10, pp. 221–242; Iuliia Marinova, "Fantaziia na temu liubvi: Eksprompt-fantaziia" (review of *Eksprompt-fantaziia*), *Sovetskii teatr*, 1983, no. 1–2, pp. 10–12.

TATIANA NIKITICHNA TOLSTAIA, b. 1951 in Leningrad.

A granddaughter of the poetess Natalia Vasilievna Krandievskaia and the prosaist Aleksei Nikolaevich Tolstoi, famous for his *Aelita, Peter the First*, and *The Road to Calvary*, Tolstaia has risen to prominence among the literati with unusual rapidity. She graduated in 1974 from the Department of Languages and Literatures at Leningrad State University and moved to Moscow. Although she whimsically claims to have dreamed since childhood of a nursing career, her attraction to literature as a profession manifested itself early in the several years she spent after graduation working at the publishing house Nauka in the Eastern Literatures division. Her literary debut in 1983 unaccountably attracted little attention, but the publication of her longer narrative "Peters" just three years later in *New World* (*Novyi mir*) sparked lively enthusiasm in both Moscow and Leningrad. It established her reputation as an original and exciting young talent. Translations of her prose have appeared or are scheduled for publication in Greece, the United States, Italy, Holland, England, Hungary, and Sweden.

Tolstaia's stories focus on the isolation of the individual personality, the universal inability to grasp the essence of other human beings, and the indifference on the part of the overwhelming majority to the psychological complexity of others. Especially children and the elderly, situated at the two extremes of the age spectrum, suffer from the incomprehension and callousness of those around them.

Convinced that the significance of a life becomes partially revealed only after the person dies, Tolstaia treats the experience of death as a moment of epiphany. Yet whatever insights death may vouchsafe, individual identity in Tolstaia's world eludes definition, being located somewhere in the interstices of seemingly irreconcilable contradictions.

Since Tolstaia entertains an unidealized, even bleak view of romantic love, her protagonists' amatory aspirations and involvements appear in a humorous or grotesque light. Myopic delusions, on the one hand, and brute physicality, on the other, erode elevated notions of love. In general Tolstaia's fictional universe is aggressively physical, populated by countless objects, bodies, and faces that she evokes vividly in striking metaphors and similes. Yet the relationship of Tolstaia's protagonists to this tangible reality is curiously unstable, and reality itself seems contingent, incessantly open to multiple interpretations.

Tolstaia's instantly identifiable signature is her exuberant, condensed style, and above all her eccentric, logorrheic narrator. Rife with contradictions and illogicalities, ellipses, erratic shifts from pathos to humor, flaunted lapses of memory side by side with perfect recall of apparently irrelevant and minute details, the brilliantly colorful, obtrusive narrative voice that marks almost all of Tolstaia's fiction sets Tolstaia stylistically apart from her more conventional fellow literati.

Works in Russian: Collection: *Na zolotom kryl'tse sideli,* Moscow: Molodaia gvardiia, 1987.

Individual stories: "Na zolotom kryl'tse sideli," *Avrora,* 1983, no. 8, pp. 94–101; "Svidanie s ptitsei," *Oktiabr',* 1983, no. 12, pp. 52–57; "Sonia," *Avrora,* 1984, no. 10, pp. 76–83, reprinted in *Rasskazy: 1984,* Moscow: Sovremennik, 1984, pp. 373–80; "Chistyi list," *Neva,* 1984, no. 12, pp. 116–125; "Reka Okkervil'," *Avrora,* 1985, no. 3, pp. 137–146; "Milaia Shura" and "Okhota na mamonta," *Oktiabr',* 1985, no. 12, pp. 113–117, 117–121; "Peters," *Novyi mir,* 1986, no. 1, pp. 123–131; "Spi spokoino, synok," *Avrora,* 1986, no. 4, pp. 94–101; "Ogon' i pyl'" and "Samaia liubimaia," *Avrora,* 1986, no. 10, pp. 82–91, 92–110; "Poet i muza," "Fakir," and "Serafim," *Novyi mir,* 1986, no. 12, pp. 113–119, 119–130, 130–133; "Krug: rasskazy," *Oktiabr',* 1987, no. 4, pp. 89–104; "Vyshel mesiats iz tumana," *Krest'ianka,* 1987, no. 4, pp. 32–35; "Plamen' nebesnyi," *Avrora,* 1987, no. 11, pp. 130–139. Parody: "Uta-monogatari," *Voprosy literatury,* 1984, no. 2, pp. 259–264.

Bibliography: Nancy Condee in *Newsletter* no. 17 to Institute of Current World Affairs, 1 June 1986, pp. 8–9 (also contains the English translation of "Sonia"); Helena Goscilo, "Tat'iana Tolstaia's 'Dome of Many-Coloured Glass': The World Refracted through Multiple Perspectives," *Slavic Review,* Summer 1988, pp. 280–290; Elena Nevzgliadova, "Eta prekrasnaia zhizn'," *Avrora,* 1986, no. 10, pp. 111–120.

Interviews: "Ten' na zakate," *Literaturnaia gazeta,* 23 July 1986, p. 7; "A Little Man Is a Normal Man," *Moscow News,* 1987, no. 8, p. 10; "Chetvertoe izmerenie," *Moskovskii komsomolets,* 1987, 29 November, p. 2; "Eto bylo tak legko-ne uchit'sia," *Nedelia,* 1988, no. 21, pp. 10–11.

LIUDMILA ZAKHAROVNA UVAROVA, née Liubov Zakharovna Mednikova, b. 21 November 1918 in Moscow.

One of the most prolific and established contemporary Russian women authors, Uvarova comes from an educated Muscovite family, of which the father was a professor of language and literature. Uvarova studied at the Maurice Torez Institute of Foreign Languages in Moscow, graduated in 1950, and taught German at the Frunze Military Academy before making a transition to literature. She subsequently worked as a correspondent for the papers *Moscow at Night* (Vecherniaia Moskva) and *Moscow Truth* (Moskovskaia pravda), as well as for the Soviet Information Bureau. She has some proficiency in English. Her first stories, published individually from 1947 on, appeared in an anthology under the title of *Olkhovka Is Listening* (Ol'khovka slushaet) in 1959. Since then she has produced over twenty volumes of stories and novellas, and, like her writer-husband, belongs to the Writers' Union.

Recurrent themes in Uvarova's fiction include integrity in personal and professional life, love and marriage, familial conflicts, the transformation of perceptions and human relations by time, and the importance of continuity, most often expressed in the form of generational ties. In her best narratives Uvarova authoritatively portrays credible characters faced with dilemmas that carry moral overtones. Without delving minutely into the psychology of the given individual, she nevertheless manages to suggest the complexity of her or his inner life. Conclusions, or the absence of them, tend to be Uvarova's major failing as a writer: her narratives sometimes do not conclude, but run down like an overwound clock, thus vitiating the overall impact of a text. Her most successful fiction, however, overcomes this weakness.

Works in English Translation: "The Veterans," *Soviet Literature*, 1984, no. 7 (436), pp. 128–132.

Works in Russian: *Ol'khovka slushaet*, Moscow, 1959; *Sirenevyi bul'var: Povesti i rasskazy*, Moscow: Sovetskii pisatel', 1966; *Mys Dobroi Nadezhdy: Rasskazy i povesti*, Moscow: Sovetskaia Rossiia, 1966; *Leto v razgare*, Moscow, 1967; *Moi sosed Mishka: Povest' i rasskazy*, Moscow: Moskovskii rabochii, 1968; *Gde zhivet goluboi lebed'?* Moscow: Sovetskaia Rossiia, 1970; *Prodolzhenie sleduet*, 1961; *Starshaia sestra*, 1962; *Nochnoi razgovor*, 1963; *Syn kapitana Aleksicha*, 1964; *Mytnaia ulitsa: Povesti i rasskazy*, Moscow: Sovetskii pisatel', 1971; *Sem'ia Maksima: Povesti i rasskazy*, Moscow: Moskovskii rabochii, 1973; *Poezdka k moriu*, Moscow, 1974; *Semeinoe skhodstvo*, Moscow: Sovetskaia Rossiia, 1974; *Peremennaia oblachnost'*, 1975; *Blizkie rodstvenniki* (for children), 1976; *Rasskazy*, Moscow: Moskovskii rabochii, 1978; *Zabot polon rot: Povesti, rasskazy*, Moscow: Sovetskii pisatel', 1978; *V kazhduiu subbotu vecherom: Povest' i rasskazy*, Moscow: Sovremennik, 1979; *Sosedi*, Moscow: Moskovskii rabochii, 1981; *Na dniakh ili ran'she*, 1981; *Poslednii passazhir*, 1980; *Oblachno, s proiasneniiami* (for children), 1981; *Sumerki posle poludnia*, Moscow: Sovetskii pisatel', 1982; *Rechnoi zhemchug*, 1983; *Doma steny pomogaiut: Povesti i rasskazy*, Moscow: Sovremennik, 1983; *Istorii ot pervogo litsa: Povesti, rasskazy*, Moscow: Sovetskaia Rossiia, 1984; *Kontsert po zaiavkam: Povesti i rasskazy*, Moscow: Moskovskii rabochii, 1987; *Ot mira sego: Roman, povesti, rasskazy*, Moscow: Sovetskii pisatel', 1987.

INNA GUSTAVOVNA VARLAMOVA, pseudonym of Klavdia Gustavovna Landau, b. 21 January 1922 in Novgorod.

Varlamova's teenage years were peripatetic. In 1934, for political reasons, her father was officially exiled from his native city of Leningrad, and thereafter the family moved from one area to another in search of a stable residence. World War II found Varlamova in the Urals, where as the daughter of an "enemy of the people" she encountered difficulties in obtaining regular employment. After the war she worked in a soil laboratory during the construction of the Kakhov Hydroelectric Station, an experience that lies at the foundation of the stories assembled in *A Live Spring* (Zhivoi rodnik, 1957) and *Window* (Okno, 1965).

After Stalin's death in 1953, Varlamova settled in Moscow, started a career as a journalist, and traveled about the country, partly to absorb impressions for the sketches and articles that she began publishing in 1955. In 1957 she turned to fiction, and produced several novels, including *A Counterfeit Life* (Mnimaia zhizn', 1978), a highly autobiographical work set mainly in a cancer hospital. The personal drama of the heroine, stricken with breast cancer, is projected against the background of the 1960s sociopolitical scene, which the novel captures in understated fashion. Varlamova's stories of the 1960s and 1970s, dealing with adjustment to change, divided loyalties, love, and integrity, appeared in the collections *Tertium non datur* (Tret'ego ne dano, 1969) and *Two Loves* (Dve liubvi, 1974).

Varlamova is not a very prolific writer. Moreover, stories and novellas provide a better vehicle for her talent than does the large-scale novel form, in which her besetting temptation is the inclusion of the inessential, which leads to a certain slackness. Her writing in general blends eloquent detail with compassion, gentle humor, and a faith in human perseverance. If Varlamova's concern with human emotions and relations between the sexes allies her with the majority of today's Russian women authors, she differs from them in at least one significant respect: she focuses not on the city, but on the northern and eastern outskirts of the Russian empire. In those works where the action is situated in these locales, she reproduces the regional dialects with accuracy and skill.

In addition to her own fiction, Varlamova, who is a member of the Writers' Union, has published a number of translations from French and from languages of the minority Soviet republics. Her many reviews have appeared in well-known Russian journals, such as *New World* (Novyi mir).

Works in English translation: *A Counterfeit Life,* trans. David Lowe, Ann Arbor: Ardis, 1988; "A Ladle for Pure Water," trans. Helena Goscilo, in *The Barsukov Triangle,* ed. Carl and Ellendea Proffer, Ann Arbor: Ardis, 1984, pp. 169–189, also in *Russian and Polish Women's Fiction,* ed. Helena Goscilo, Knoxville: University of Tennessee Press, 1985, pp. 181–198.

Works in Russian: Novels and Collections: *Zhivoi rodnik,* 1957; *Liubit' i verit',* 1959; *My iz Novoi Kakhovki,* 1961; *Ishchu tebia: Roman,* Moscow: Sovetskii pisatel', 1964; *Okno,* 1965; *Liubit' i verit': Roman; Ishchu tebia: Roman,* Moscow: Sovetskii pisatel', 1966; *Tret'ego ne dano: Roman i rasskazy,* Moscow: Sovetskii pisatel', 1969; *Dve liubvi: Povesti i rasskazy,* Moscow: Molodaia gvardiia, 1974; *Mnimaia zhizn',* Ann Arbor: Ardis, 1979.

Translations: L. Uri, *Proletarii: Roman,* Moscow: 1977 (French); A. B. Badmaev, *Reki nachinaiutsia s istokov: Roman,* Elista, 1971 (Kalmyk); A. Paityk, *Naslednik: Povest',* Moscow, 1971 (Turkmen).

Bibliography: T. Motyleva, "Chelovek poznaetsia v trude," *Oktiabr',* 1958, no. 5; V. Kantorovich, *Zametki pisatelia o sovremennom ocherke,* Moscow, 1962, pp. 207–216; F. Levin, "Nado by po azimutu . . . ," *Literaturnaia gazeta,* 25 September 1968.

IRINA ALEKSANDROVNA VELEMBOVSKAIA, b. 24 February 1922 in Moscow.

A native Muscovite whose real name is Shukhgal'ter, Velembovskaia during World War II was evacuated to the Urals, where she worked at a plant and held a series of physically demanding jobs. Upon her return to Moscow in 1949, she combined studies with factory work. In 1959 she enrolled in correspondence courses at the Gorky Literary Institute; her fiction began to appear in print in 1961, although she graduated from the institute only three years later. Since then, Velembovskaia has published comparatively little, perhaps because of personal circumstances: she has a daughter who is a professional historian with a daughter of school age.

From the outset Velembovskaia's prose concerned itself chiefly with women— the nature of their everyday existence, their interaction with men, the role they play in community life, and their self-perception. Velembovskaia typically portrays hard-working, unsophisticated women of strong moral fiber, with a natural goodness uncorrupted by "civilization." Their male counterparts represent a lesser order of humanity, inclined to violence, heavy drinking, and indecisiveness. They lack that center which enables her stoic, buoyant female protagonists to surmount all adversity, much of which seems caused by men.

Many of Velembovskaia's narratives—e.g., "Women" (Zhenshchiny, 1964), "Family Matters" (Dela semeinye, 1966), and "A Sweet Woman" (Sladkaia zhenshchina, 1973)—have been adapted into films. Unlike many contemporary Russian authors of her sex, until recently Velembovskaia regularly situated her narratives in the village or small town, which accounts to an extent for the rather old-fashioned flavor of her fiction that is further reinforced by her conservative style. By contrast, all the selections in her latest volume, *A View from the Balcony* (Vid s balkona, 1981), depict city-dwellers, principally Muscovites.

Works in Russian: *Lesnaia istoriia: Povesti i rasskazy,* Moscow: Sovetskii pisatel', 1965; *Dela semeinye: Povest', Znamiia,* 1966; *Zhenshchiny: Povesti i rasskazy,* Moscow: Sovetskii pisatel', 1967 and Moscow: Sovetskii pisatel', 1971; *Sladkaia zhenshchina: Povest',* Moscow, 1973; *Tretii semestr: Povesti,* Moscow: Sovetskii pisatel', 1973; *Vid s balkona: Povesti i rasskazy,* Moscow: Sovetskii pisatel', 1981.

Bibliography: V. Kardin, "Nado li prosit' izvineniia?" *Novyi mir,* 1966, no. 10, pp. 264–266; Feliks Kuznetsov, "Chelovek 'estestvennyi' i obshchestvennyi," *Literaturnoe obozrenie,* 1973, no. 6, pp. 28–37, esp. pp. 34–36; A. Marchenko, "Voprosov bol'she, chem otvetov" (review of *Sladkaia zhenshchina*), *Novyi mir,* 1973, no. 8, pp. 264–268.